THE BLOOD OF OTHERS

THE BLOOD OF OTHERS

CHARITY ELESON

There is no sure foundation set on blood,
No certain life by others' death.

The Life and Death of King John, William Shakespeare

ISBN: 979-8-9895749-1-9

For Steve
With love always

CHAPTER 1

SEPTEMBER 11, 1857

Malachi and his walking stick left three-pointed prints in their wake, muddying the tracks made by the dog that trotted in front of him. She stopped now and again, looking at him with her marble blue eyes, whining at his slow progress. Her belly nearly dragged the ground, marked by a set of baggy pointed teats that had nursed pups a season ago. He called her Two Bits. He thought her ugly, but she was good with the sheep.

Malachi limped down the narrow, rocky path that wound its way away from Jacob Hamblin's ranch toward Mountain Meadows. It was early morning. Cool fall air sliced through the residual warmth of late summer. The sun burnished the deep amber of his skin and warmed his straight black hair, cut blunt across a wide forehead. He was short for his 15 years, his body on a jagged pace from boy to man, with hands and feet that had outgrown the rest of him. His right leg was shorter than the left, a souvenir of a broken thighbone that had been carelessly set. He compensated by walking with a tilt, balancing himself with a walking stick nearly as tall as he was. At the top of his stick two hawk feathers twirled back and forth, their shafts clicking in the morning breeze.

The deerskin pouch that hung around his neck carried a pair of severed fingers. Two Bits, back from her evening wanderings the night before, had dropped them at his feet while he was eating supper. He'd stared at them as he chewed a chunk of venison and washed it down with water from his tin cup. Sometimes he thought tin smelled like blood. The stumps of fingers gave off the smell of dirt. He scooped them up off the ground and hid them in the pouch before laying out his bedroll under the stars, where he and the other boys slept so they could keep watch of the sheep. He drifted off, feeling the weight of the fingers on his chest as he listened to the Mormon men singing their hymns around the campfire near Jacob Hamblin's house.

That morning the dog nudged him awake before sun-up. She would not leave him alone until he crawled out of his bedroll and followed her lead toward Mountain Meadows. Now he walked behind her, cursing her in his low, guttural voice, looking behind him to make sure he wasn't being followed. He would be punished if they discovered he had left the sheep, but more if they found him near the meadows.

Albert, one of the boys who herded the sheep with him, had warned him off yesterday when Malachi asked about the shots he'd heard and the men gathering at the Hamblin ranch. Albert had grabbed him by the shirt, held his face close to his, warning him he'd pull out Malachi's fingernails if he left the sheep.

Malachi lightly curled the tips of his fingers toward his palms then released them. He was more inclined to follow his dog than do what Albert told him. He slid and tripped his way down the scree on the hillside that led away from the huddled sheep to the meadow below. The pouch thudded against his chest, and he smelled the tang of sweat and dirt and blood from the fingers. When he got to the bottom of the hill, he stepped into the shade of a small grove of cottonwoods.

He looked out over the meadow. To the south, the Magotsu Creek tore a careless gash across the meadow's lush feeding grounds. Just to the north of the creek, nearly three dozen wagons were circled tightly together. A thin stream of smoke rose from the center. The men at the Hamblin ranch said the wagons belonged to emigrants, what the Mormons called those passing through their territory. The people on this train had come from a state called Arkansas. They were known as the Fancher train, named after one of the emigrants, and had been camped on the floor of Mountain Meadows for nearly a week. Like others who had passed this way, they'd come to graze their stock and revive them before they made the last of their trek over the stark Mojave to California. Unlike the others, the Fancher train had stayed longer, and had more cattle and a herd of high-priced horses that the Mormon men envied.

His eyes flicked over to the eastern ridge of the meadow, searching for the band of Paiutes who had installed themselves along the meadow's rim, hemming in the train. They were there to harass the people on the train and prevent their departure. The men who gathered at the Hamblin ranch said that George Smith, a traveling preacher who was one of Brigham Young's most trusted emissaries and possessed a fearsome reputation that made the other men tremble, had encouraged the Paiutes to tag the train, follow it to Mountain Meadows. Malachi heard the men call the emigrants devils; say they tarried in the meadows out of spite. They complained the people on the wagon train were intent on letting their sleek animals grind down the lush grasses on the meadow floor, which would make it useless for the Mormon families to feed their own small herds in the fall. It seemed that Prophet Smith had sent the Mormon men who gathered at the Hamblin ranch a problem to solve.

Malachi leaned on his walking stick and peered out across the expanse of grass. He wanted to spot one of these devils, to see if they looked any different from the Mormon families he lived with. He wondered how much of what he'd heard about them was true and if the fingers hidden in his pouch belonged to one of the people from the train.

The grassy field below had been eaten to the nub. It would be weeks after the train left before the meadow grew back enough to let any of their own animals graze there; the men were right about that. But Malachi could not see cattle or horses outside the wagons' protective circle. The emigrants must have driven their animals into the ravine below where they were out of sight and protected from the Paiutes. They had also widened the circle of their camp and built a thick, protective bank of earth around it. The earth shielded them from the Paiutes' assaults but allowed them to keep watch on their animals below. They might be devils, Malachi thought, but they were clever.

The meager trails of campfire smoke buffered the smell of roasted meat. His mouth watered. Breakfast. The families in the train must be eating it. He regretted not having had his. The dog flared her nostrils, taking in the odors before huffing out her breath. She suddenly stood, ready to move on, then her head snapped toward the sound of a man's voice shouting from the circle of the train. Malachi grabbed the scruff of her neck, wrapping his hand around her muzzle to silence her.

"Come out you cowards!"

A child's shrill cry punctured the air. Two Bits growled, and Malachi felt her muzzle vibrate. He pulled her back into the camouflage of cottonwoods. Gunshots rang out from the wagons, followed by whoops from the rim of the basin near the train. A small volley of arrows arced through the air and skittered harmlessly along the ground outside the ring of wagons. It was the Paiutes. He hoped they hadn't seen him. If they had, they'd tell the men at the ranch, and that would only bring him trouble.

Malachi stood still as he watched for movement from the direction of the arrows. He wondered how much longer the emigrants would stay and whether the Paiutes would encroach on them further. Perhaps they'd strike a deal with the emigrants, demand some of their cattle in exchange for safe passage out of Mormon territory. The Paiutes were known for that, extorting what goods and stock they could from the trains that passed through these lands. He lightly touched the pouch on his chest. The dog whined at him and snuffled at his legs to urge him along.

"Okay," he said. "We'll go."

They started along the path that led west out of the meadows. The sounds of the train began to fade. He stumbled as he tried to keep up with Two Bits, who had picked up her pace. When they walked up and over the rise, the swampy smell of rotting flesh reached him before he saw the bodies. His gut clenched, and he swallowed back the vomit that surged into his throat. He steadied himself on his walking stick, pulling a faded blue rag from his pocket that he tied around his nose.

Two Bits had dropped behind him now, nipping at his heels like she did the sheep. He walked to the crest of the hill and stopped. Before him was a jumbled confusion of bare flesh, tangled limbs, and dried blood. The sun, now fully risen, cast a harsh light on the corpses of two men, one dumped over the other, their bodies forming a human cross. The left hand of the man on top rested almost tenderly on the upturned cheek of his companion. They'd been stripped of their clothes and their flesh was striped and raw with lacerations. Both men had been scalped.

As he drew closer, he saw three bullet wounds in the back of the man who lay on top. The morning sun had brought flies, and they fed lazily on the blackened, bloody crust that laced the men's flesh. Malachi's heart thudded against his chest, making the pouch tremble. He wondered who had killed these men. They'd been shot from behind. They had to have come from the emigrants' camp. Other than emigrants on their way west and the Paiutes who had always lived here, no one else had reason to linger in this region that the Mormons had claimed as their own.

He looked beyond the bodies to the path that led west and wondered if these men had left the train in hopes of finding help. Perhaps the people on the train felt more threatened by the Paiutes than he thought. He had heard they were armed to the teeth, yet they hadn't rid themselves of the scant band of Paiutes that rimmed the meadow's eastern border. Maybe it wasn't possible for the train to leave and these men had been sent to scout for help. If that was true, the people on the train were trapped, still waiting for these men who lay dead in the sun to return.

A hawk let out a high lonely whistle in the distance. Malachi breathed in deeply, then immediately regretted it as the rancid smell of the men's rotting flesh gullied down his throat. He leaned over and spat, trying to get the taste of death out of him. He looked up at the dog. She sat at his feet, suddenly patient, and turned to gaze at the men's bodies then glanced at Malachi, waiting.

"What d'you want me to do, mutt?" he asked her as he leaned over, resting his hands on his thighs. He scowled at her, thinking to spit again. He regretted following her. What kind of idiot followed a dog, he thought, shaking his head. Two Bits reached out and touched her wet nose to the back of his hand. The cool of her snout calmed him a little, and he stood upright and sighed.

Realizing he couldn't risk having someone discover the fingers in his pouch, he shook them out into his hand, cupping his palm as he examined them. The skin was dry, and black grit lined the fingernails. The nail on one finger had been partially ripped off. Pink, puckered skin had settled into place around the scrap of remaining nail. It brought back Albert's threat. Malachi winced before folding the pouch around the fingers. He dropped them on top of a nearby boulder. He stepped closer to the bodies. The dog glanced anxiously at the fingers but made no move to retrieve them.

The Paiutes hadn't scalped these men. The men's killers had tossed the bloody mops of hair and skin into the nearby grasses. The Paiutes would have taken the scalps with them to celebrate and honor the braves that carried out the kill. He walked around the matted grasses that cushioned the men's bodies. The dog followed him, her nose snuffling along bare patches of ground, blowing up small puffs of dust. He knelt slightly and poked at the men with his walking stick. He knew they were dead, but the inert sag of their flesh against his stick reassured him.

Their foreheads and cheeks were crusted with blood that had oozed from the raw wounds of their scalps and dried in the hot sun. The right eye of the man who was face up had been gouged out. But other than that, the faces of both men, though stained with blood, were still intact. Each of them was missing the pointer fingers of their right hands. He wondered at that. Had they pointed at those who had taken their lives, accusing them before being shot? Perhaps the fingers were offensive reminders to the killers of their own perfidy.

He stood and looked around him. Hillocks of matted grass occasionally gave way to sprays of purple asters and gold bursts of black-eyed Susan. The flowers and grass were spattered with dried flecks of the men's blood. He spotted a bare patch of dirt close to where the scalps lay. He walked over to it and knelt, pushing the anxious dog out of the way. She refused to leave his side now and growled as he leaned in low to examine the ground. There were footprints in the soft soil surrounding the scalps. He made out two sets of prints, both from the square-toed, square-heeled boots favored by the Mormon men.

Malachi leaned back on his heels in a squat. He slowly exhaled as he gazed at the men. Their narrow noses and pinkish white skin were like the faces of the men Malachi lived with. He thought about what had happened here, who would have killed them and why. He knew the men in the southern settlements resented the emigrants and wanted them out of Mountain Meadows, and that there had been an increasing drumbeat of animosity and suspicion directed toward all those who were not Mormons entering their sacred Deseret. But could they have shot these men in the back and ripped off their scalps? A small chill went through him and he twisted to look over his shoulder, worried someone might be watching. But he saw only grass and trees. He looked at the men's bodies and thought about telling someone. He considered Jonah

Blank, the man who had purchased him from Jacob Hamblin and called himself his father. Someone should know so the men who'd done it could be held responsible. But there would be questions about why he had left the sheep, why he hadn't done what he'd been told, and that would mean trouble for him, certain punishment. Even if he did tell someone what he had seen, it wouldn't help the men who had been murdered. No, he would tell no one.

He closed his eyes, trying to remember the death ritual of his own people, the Shoshone. It was so long ago. He was young, maybe five, not long before Jacob Hamblin had bought him and Albert. His father, his real father, had died of the pox. He watched as his mother wept and cut her arms and legs in mourning. His aunts, grandmother, and sisters joined her. The men in his tribe prepared his father by wrapping him in the dried skin of an elk. They sang over his body then carried him to a cave where his mother said his father would live on in the heart of the earth. Malachi had longed to go with him, to stay warm forever against his father's broad chest, safe in the earth's deep center. Loved, cared for.

He scrubbed away the tears that ran down his cheeks. He did not weep for the men who lay dead on the ground, and he would not bury them. He knew he could not leave a sign that he had been here and he could not reveal what he had seen to anyone. Still, it seemed wrong not to do something to put them to rest.

He removed the fingers from the boulder, held them up above his head and blew gently on them, blowing away the evil that had touched them. He looked around and wished he knew where the dog had found them. What if the killers returned? What if the fingers had been placed just so, in the dead men's mouths or beside their bodies and what if the killers came back to examine their handiwork and noticed they were missing? He decided, in the end, to bury the fingers. He used the sharp end of his walking stick to dig a deep hole in the earth near the men's scalps. He dropped the fingers in the hole and filled it with dirt. He found a large flat rock nearby and dragged it over to cover the bare ground, then erased his own tracks and took a last look at the men.

He turned, leaving them to the flies, the rising sun, and the animals that would soon pick their flesh clean. He snatched his leather pouch from where it lay on the boulder and tied it around his neck, feeling lighter without the weight of the fingers pressing against his chest. He gripped his stick and whistled to Two Bits. She fell in place at his heels and they walked back toward the Hamblin ranch and the familiar order of the herd.

CHAPTER 2

Malachi and the dog stayed on the trail that hugged the ridge along Mountain Meadows and would eventually take them back to the upper pasture where they grazed sheep. Grit and rock crunched lightly beneath his feet as he picked up his pace. He was anxious about being missed. As he followed the line of cedars that shouldered the trail and obscured it from the meadow below, he began to weave a story to tell in case anyone asked where he'd been.

A sudden movement on the hill at the end of the line of cedars brought him to an abrupt stop. It was a white man. Malachi stepped quietly behind a tree and motioned for Two Bits to come sit at his feet. She trotted over to him and planted her wide haunches on the ground. He reached down to grasp the meat of her neck as he peered through the trees at the slope below. More men, Mormon men, had joined the Paiutes and were stationed at intervals across the hill. Brush and trees hid them from view of the wagon train, but from where he stood, he saw many of them clearly. Some were stripped down to the waist and had daubs of war paint smeared on their bare chests and arms. Others were seated upright and waiting, facing Mountain Meadows. A few were stretched out on their sides, their heads propped up by their arms in order to watch the meadow floor. They all had sidearms and many had shotguns on the ground between them.

To their right were the Paiutes. He counted twelve of them and they were clustered together and farther away, armed only with their bows. He was surprised at how few of them there were. They looked relaxed, like they were waiting for a game to begin. One of them pointed to a clump of cottonwood trees at the base of the hill and mimed someone shooting, catching the attention of the others. All the men looked as though they were waiting for a word, a movement, something to call them to action.

Malachi looked up the hill behind him and back at the men. His scalp itched with sweat and worry. If he continued to the Hamblin ranch, he could be spotted by one of the men on the hillside when he walked into the open. He could not risk being caught, cursed himself for being here, seeing what he had seen. He looked at the dog and thought about sending her back to the herd, but rejected the plan as quickly as he thought of it. He would need her if anyone discovered him. He would say she'd run off and he'd come in search of her to take her back to the pasture.

He looked for a spot to hide and wait, thinking there would be an opportunity to slip back to the ranch unnoticed. He squatted and surveyed the slope below. There was a large sandstone boulder surrounded by scrub juniper. He dropped to his belly and crawled to it. He turned, hoping the dog would follow, and sighed with relief when he saw she was at his side and had flopped to the ground, her back legs stretched out and her head wedged between her front paws. He slid between the boulder and the brush, staying low enough to keep out of view. From this perch, he could keep an eye on the men below and the circle of wagons they all watched. He waited as sweat beaded and coated his forehead. An uncomfortable edge of anticipation crept into his chest as he wondered why the men had gathered here.

Without warning, a tiny dark-haired girl in a bright blue dress emerged from between two of the wagons. She carried a white flag that was tied to a slender branch and held it in front of her. She waded uncertainly into the tall grass and looked briefly behind her, as if listening to someone. She turned back toward the meadows and lifted the branch higher to wave the tatter of white cloth back and forth.

John Lee, a church bishop who'd come from Harmony, a settlement north of the Hamblin ranch, emerged from the copse of cottonwoods at the base of the hill. Lee walked toward the train. He too held up a white flag, bigger than the girl's and knotted to a thick branch. His other hand was raised in greeting. Once the girl saw him, she turned and fled back to the safety of the wagons, slipping out of sight. Her flag lay fallen on the ground in front of the wagons, an inert token of peace.

Lee called out in his deep, baritone voice, "I am Brother John Lee and am here to make your acquaintance and give you help!"

"We want you to lay down your arms, John Lee," a man's hoarse voice called out. "If you have none, we want you to show that to us. The girl shows our intent. We will not shoot."

Lee did not hesitate. He carefully laid his flag on the ground beside him and opened up his long black coat, holding it out, cape-like, as he turned around slowly. After a few minutes, the wagons creaked opened. Two men emerged and walked toward Lee. One man wore his arm in a dirty sling of cotton cloth and he limped as the men made their way out to meet Lee. Their stooped figures were stamped with fatigue and wariness.

Malachi was surprised at their appearance. These were the devils? Given all he'd heard about them, he wondered why they didn't show more swagger, reveal more confidence. He thought they'd need it against Lee. He was a force at the Hamblin ranch, prevailing in arguments between the men, soothing them, scolding them, advising them, directing them, and leading them in prayer and song in his rich, penetrating voice.

Lee talked to the men and motioned toward the woods, pointing to the north. The men with the train looked up into the woods and briefly scanned the hill where the other men were camouflaged. Malachi instinctively pulled back behind the boulder. The men from the train turned to each other, their heads nearly touching as they talked. The taller of the two pivoted toward Lee and nodded at him, then motioned to the emigrants' camp. Lee followed the two men toward the circle of wagons where the three were admitted through the gap. Unseen hands slowly closed the wagons behind them.

Malachi's eyes swept across the hill below, looking for movement. But the men waited. He recognized some of the men who had gathered at Hamblin's ranch over the last several days. John Higbee, major of the southern contingent of the Nauvoo Legion, the church's military. He also saw Philip Klingensmith and Oscar Hamblin, Jacob Hamblin's brother and Albert's adoptive uncle. They had all come to the Hamblin ranch. He saw other men from farms in the region and younger men, not too much older than he was. They must have been called here just for this, he thought, whatever this was. He spied Jonah Blank, his adoptive father. His heart beat faster at the sight of him and fear surged into his chest. He could not be discovered here. He'd have to find a way out.

Then he saw Albert, off alone, claimed by neither the Mormon men nor the Paiutes. He was splayed out behind a clump of tall grass that partially shielded him. The black hat that Jacob Hamblin had given Albert last year was pulled down over his eyes and he looked like he was asleep. Figures, Malachi thought. He spotted a knife and rifle at Albert's side and wondered what purpose the men had for his cousin here. Albert would do anything to please the Mormon men. He was always anxious to be of use, eager to prove his loyalty. An oily film of hatred coated Malachi's thoughts as he toted up the number of times Albert had turned on him, his own flesh, his own blood, in order to prove that loyalty. He took a last long look at his cousin and turned away to fix his eyes on the wagons below.

The afternoon sun was hot and beat down on the meadows. Malachi licked his parched lips. His throat was dry and he cursed himself for not bringing any water. Over an hour had passed since Lee disappeared into the emigrants' camp, and some of the men on the hillside had stretched out on the ground, using their hats to shield their eyes from the sun. Malachi began to wonder if the emigrants had killed Lee. Then the wagons below groaned and opened, and Lee emerged. His hat was tilted back on his head, and he waved and called to someone Malachi couldn't see. Two wagons rolled out from behind the clump of cottonwoods, their wheels creaking toward the emigrants' camp.

Malachi made out the faces of two other men who'd been at Hamblin's over the past week, Samuel Knight and Samuel McMurdy. Each of the men was driving a wagon. As they approached the camp, a handful of Mormon men left their posts on the side of the hill and walked swiftly down to the flats of the meadow to take up places alongside each wagon. All of the men carried rifles. Neither the Paiutes nor the men dressed to look like them descended to the meadows.

Malachi wondered briefly if the Mormon men were there to help the emigrants and if the emigrants would resist them once they saw the men were armed. He had heard the men from the train were excellent shots. But he watched in disbelief as unarmed men from the Fancher train transported wounded men and women from the camp and loaded them into one of the wagons. Then they loaded a second wagon with children, very young children. Many of them cried and called out for their mothers. One was a boy with golden blond hair that curled around his forehead and ears. The whole of his lower arm was bound up in a bandage and he was crying out to no one in particular. Malachi had never seen such a beautiful child. He had a sudden, wild urge to protect him.

Knight was carefully settling the children into the wagons, tucking blankets around them. He tried to gentle the boy with the golden curls out of his crying. But the boy was having none of it, and he pushed Knight away with his one good hand. He called out for his mother, tears clotting his high, keening voice.

Someone had given Lee a rifle. He cradled it in his arms as he watched the preparations and called to the wagon drivers to take their places and head away from the camp toward Hamblin's. Lee fell in between the wagons, and the procession made slow progress toward the northern edge of the meadows. The boy with the golden curls called again and again for his mother as the wagons pulled away from the train. Malachi's heart wound tight at the sound of the boy's voice.

Major Higbee appeared now too and was mounted on a horse that must have been waiting for him in the cluster of trees below. He kept his gaze fixed on Lee as the men scurried back and forth to organize the emigrants. A group of women emerged from the circle of wagons. Some of them peered anxiously at the wagon that carried the children. But not all the children had been placed in the second wagon. Some had remained with their mothers, and the women carried them or led them by the hand. Malachi thought the women looked confused, and he wondered what questions they were asking of the men Lee had sent to walk by their sides. Some smiled shyly as they spoke to the Mormon men. Relief and hope shone on their faces as though they hoped the men were rescuing them from days of being cooped up, surrounded, smelling their own stench.

The men frowned at the women, some jutting their chins forward, motioning them to follow the two wagons. Malachi watched as six more of the Mormon men from the slope below got up and walked out to the meadow, falling into step alongside the women. Each man had a rifle resting lightly on his shoulder. The men costumed in war paint were still hidden on the hill, and the Paiutes had all slid to their bellies to watch the procession below. An acid drip of worry ate at Malachi's stomach, and he swallowed a sour taste in his mouth as he waited and watched.

The children in the wagon twisted around to see their mothers straggling behind them and called out to them in sharp, sobbing voices. Some of them scrambled to the rear of the wagon, clutching to the gate, their small heads swaying back and forth as the wagon lumbered out of the meadow.

"Mother!" cried a girl in a checked dress with braids wound on top of her head. She leaned out and stretched her arms toward the women.

"You be good, Sarah," a woman in a rose-colored dress called out to her. "God will keep us safe. These good men mean to help us, dear one! God is watching over us!"

The other women joined her, pleading with their little ones to be calm, to be brave. They clustered together as their voices quavered and echoed throughout the meadow and engulfed Malachi in a watery swell of sound. The emigrant men followed their women. Their depleted state disappointed Malachi. He wanted them to look like the fierce, frightening devils the Mormon men had described. He wanted them to fight, to rise up and meet the expectations of all the stories he had heard. Instead, they had a bleak hunger on their faces and their bodies were bent with weariness. They are just men, he thought, men who hope to be saved. One of them attempted to draw a Mormon man into conversation, but the man shook his head and roughly shouldered him back into the line of men that inched along the floor of the meadow.

The men still hidden on the side of the hill began to move. The Paiutes squatted, notching their arrows into their bows, tense and ready. The Mormon men, their pale skin splotched with war paint and reddened from the sun, crouched, gripping knives and rifles. Albert was upright now too, one leg kneeling, his opposite foot planted on the ground, ready to push away from the hillside. His rifle was in his right hand and his knife in a sheath lashed to his left hip.

Malachi shifted uneasily and his dog raised her head from the dirt, waiting for his signal. His hiding space was tight and his bad leg had cramped. He moved so he could stretch it out in front of him. He wrapped his other leg around his butt as a cushion. The dog sighed, as if resigned to the fact they would remain where they were. She rested her chin on his knee and kept a watchful eye on him.

Suddenly Major Higbee raised his arm. His command rang across the meadow. "Halt! Do your duty!"

Lee and the men walking alongside the second wagon turned. They aimed their rifles at the wounded men and women and fired. The emigrants' weakened bodies convulsed and collapsed beneath the gunfire. Armed men turned toward the straggling line of men that brought up the rear of the procession and shot them at close range. The men from the train tried to back away, some put their hands in front of their faces, bracing for what was to come before they were shot and toppled to the ground. One, still struggling, reached out his hands to the man who had shot him, clasping them together in supplication. But the man put his rifle to the pleading man's forehead and pulled the trigger.

Amidst the noise of gunfire, the men on the hillside rushed down to the meadows, slashing their knives through the air and whooping and calling to the men below. The screams of the women and children filled the meadow now. Malachi covered his ears to mute the sound, but he could not take his eyes off the mayhem.

When the women realized they had been tricked, they broke out of their soft communal knot and splintered in several directions, some running after the wagon that held their children. Others, those carrying a child or grasping one by the hand, ran toward the protection of the trees. Their armed escorts tucked the butts of their rifles against their shoulders and one-by-one picked off the women closest to them. Their death moans filled the air. The women the men's rifles could not reach were stabbed and scalped by the men rushing down the hill. The children in the wagon stood along the wagon's sides, their bodies teetering uncertainly as the wagon rolled across the uneven road. They sobbed and screamed, clawing at the air with their hands, their shrill voices choked with tears, snot, and fear.

Malachi's breath came in quick, stifled gasps as he watched. His body went rigid with terror. Then he saw her, a woman running as fast as she could toward the hill where he was hidden. She carried a child, a boy, not more than three years old, bundled up close, his small blond head bumping against her chest as she ran. She held up her long skirts with one hand and hung tight to her boy with the other. A stack of lace from her petticoat fluttered as she struggled up the side of the hill. The child's arms and legs were wrapped tightly around her. She ran in fits and starts, frantically looking back and forth for an escape route and finally settling on the path that led toward Malachi's hiding spot.

Malachi had dropped his hands from his ears now and panicked as he heard her ragged breath drawing closer to him. He grabbed the dog, clamping his hand hard around her muzzle. The woman was close enough that he smelled the raw stench of her fear and saw the terror that contorted her face. He shrank back, pulling the dog with him. Then she spotted him. She was at least ten feet from him. She grasped her whimpering child tight to her chest with her right hand and held out her left toward Malachi.

"Help us!" she sobbed.

Malachi opened his mouth to call to her, but he spotted Higbee over her shoulder. The man had reined in his horse. He raised his rifle and shot her squarely in the back. The bullet tunneled through her and the fear on her face was replaced with a sweet look of surprise as she fell forward and pinned the child to the ground with her dead weight. The tiny boy bellowed.

Malachi opened his mouth again in a dry, silent cry. He'd pressed himself to the ground between the boulder and the juniper, hugging the dog close. He could smell the juniper's tangy scent. His face turned out toward the meadow. The boy's small hand, covered in blood, scrabbled across the rocky soil as if searching for something to hold onto. Malachi hated himself for not rescuing him, but he hoped Higbee would spare this child. He was so tiny, so harmless. Malachi stayed frozen in his hiding spot, his arm wrapped tightly around the dog, his hand muzzling her snout as he watched Higbee, bent low over his horse, galloping toward the woman.

Higbee's horse came to a stop just in front of her. The child cried and gasped for breath as he struggled under the weight of his mother's body. Higbee dismounted and walked over to the woman and child. Malachi kept his eyes on the Major's boots as he kicked the woman's flaccid body, flipping her over to expose the child beneath. He removed a pistol from the leather belt slung around his hips. The child sobbed and Higbee pointed the pistol at the boy. The child reached out to Higbee and let out an eerie cry. Malachi closed his eyes. Then he heard the shot. He opened his eyes just as the boy's small hand dropped.

Malachi lay very still. A flat metallic taste rolled across his tongue, as though he'd inhaled the blood of the boy. The dust by his nostrils eddied in and out with his breath. His heart thudded against his chest as fear and nausea seized him. He was certain Higbee would hear the din rising up from him. He trained his eyes on Higbee's boots and relief laced his chest as he watched Higbee turn and walk back toward his horse. The saddle groaned as the man settled back into his seat. His spurs sank into the flesh of the horse's dusty withers and the animal cantered back down the hill.

When Higbee had ridden to a safe distance, Malachi lifted up a few inches to survey the meadow, avoiding looking at the dead woman and child. He watched as the chaos below reached a frenzied pitch. The men smudged in war paint had taken possession of the meadow and were assaulting the women, bludgeoning those who still struggled with life, scalping some and tossing the long bloody tresses of the women up in the air with yells of triumph. Their victory whoops created an eerie, incongruous harmony with the women's screams.

Two girls in their teens with loosened streams of hair trailing down their backs raised their skirts and fled up the hill, holding hands as they ran to the northern side of the meadow. Albert had stationed himself at the edge of the meadow and Malachi saw him suddenly shoulder his rifle and scramble up the hill in pursuit. The girls fled toward a wooded area between the meadows and the path that led back to the Hamblin ranch and Albert followed them, alone. Malachi thought he should follow them, too. Maybe he could save the girls. But, then what? How would he protect them after? He had no weapons. Albert would kill them all, say Malachi had betrayed the men. He stayed in his hiding place wishing he had never followed the dog away from the safety of the sheep that morning, wishing, for once, he'd listened to Albert and had not seen any of this.

As suddenly as it had begun, the killing stopped. The screams of terror of the pursued and punished were silenced. Malachi watched as some of the men began stripping the bodies, removing rings from fingers of the corpses, ripping jeweled ear bobs from the delicate lobes of the women, and emptying men's pockets of whatever treasures they stowed there. The children still wailed in the distance as the wagon that carried them made its ponderous way through the trees and up the hill out of the meadow and north toward the Hamblin ranch. A few children who had not gone in the wagon but whose lives had been spared were wandering from body to body, dazed, their clothes and faces covered in blood and dust. They called out for their parents. Their faces were streaked with tears and disbelief. Malachi wondered what was in store for them. He thought of the exquisite boy with the curling blond hair.

The air was thick with the smell of blood and shit. One of the men scared up a killdeer as he moved toward a woman's body. The bird keened and ran crazily across the man's path, her wing held out akimbo as she tried to distract him from her nest. The man shot at the bird, but missed. Other than the sound of the bird and a child here and there sobbing out for his mother, the meadow had gone quiet. A sudden pall fell over the men as they applied themselves to the serious business of looting the dead.

Albert suddenly sauntered into view. His knife was sheathed and he carried his rifle across his chest. The tail of his shirt was untucked and the brim of his hat was pulled down low over his face. Phillip Klingensmith called him over to help turn over the body of a heavy-set man. Once they had flipped him over, Klingensmith yanked off the man's wedding ring and emptied his pockets. Albert removed a watch on a chain from the man's vest and secreted it away. When Klingensmith noticed, he yanked Albert's arm and shook it until Albert yielded the gold watch.

The Paiutes had gathered near Klingensmith and Albert, observing as the man and boy bickered over the watch. They called out. Klingensmith shoved Albert toward them, directing the boy to talk to them. Albert stumbled, then nodded and approached the Paiutes. He had learned their language several years ago, much to Jacob Hamblin's pleasure. Now he talked to the leader of their band, a tall, broad-chested man wearing a soft leather vest with silver buttons. Malachi could see the Paiute didn't like what Albert was telling him. Soon the band of Indians gathered in a tighter knot around Albert and began to gesture and yell at him. One of the Paiutes stepped toward Albert, his knife raised.

Just then, Lee rode over the hill, mounted on a horse that Malachi recognized as Jacob Hamblin's. The horse trotted easily toward Albert and the Paiutes, and Lee dismounted. The leader of the band turned toward Lee and jabbed his finger in the direction of the circle of wagons and then toward himself, making apparent his unhappiness at not benefiting from the plunder. Lee nodded calmly and led the Paiutes over to the wagons. He motioned to a couple of the other Mormon men to keep watch as the Paiutes entered the circle of wagons. The Paiutes emerged not long after, having taken their fill of what was left, holding stacks of blankets, clothes, and gunnysacks drooping with loot. Some wore women's hats and men's jackets over their buckskins. They laughed at each other, one of them mimicking a white man's swagger.

Malachi thought about leaving, thinking the men below were so focused on the task at hand they wouldn't see him. But just as he was about to stand, he saw a couple of the men from the council gather the four remaining children and start their way up the north bank of the meadows back to the Hamblin ranch. He stayed where he was.

A group of men followed Lee, who rode down into the gulch behind the wagons where the emigrants had kept their stock. Lee rode back into view leading a tall bay horse. Men gathered round the animal to admire him, stepping forward to run their hands down his legs, feel his wide chest. Lee dismounted and said something to Albert, who removed the saddle from the horse Lee was on and slung it over the bay's back. Impatiently, Lee elbowed Albert aside. He stepped forward to cinch up the horse himself, then mounted him, towering over the men.

"Those of you in the council," Lee called out. His rich, deep voice was loud enough to carry up to where Malachi was hidden. "You're to meet back at the Hamblin ranch as soon as you are able. Brothers Dame and Haight will join us there tonight. The rest of you, I want you to know that you've participated in a somber deed today." The men stopped their restless movements and gathered around him. They looked up at him as he talked, their eyes squinting against the bright sun.

"We have done the right thing," Lee said. "But we must treat this act as we would our most guarded secrets. These are acts that cannot be easily understood by those who were not here. I exhort you to keep these events to yourselves. When you return to your homes, do not talk of what happened here today, do not talk of it to your wives, not even to each other. Now go and know that together we have done the work of God."

The men began to break up. They kept their eyes to the ground as if fearful of what would happen if they acknowledged each other. The remaining men from the council took the valuables that had been collected and dropped them into the gunnysacks that someone had left in a heap. Another small group of men on horseback stayed behind to herd the stock from the Fancher train to Hamblin's property. There, Malachi guessed, the members of the council would decide how everything should be divided, who would be rewarded and recognized for this gruesome deed.

The remaining men, not part of the council, were left to their own devices to find their way back to their farms and families. They had served their purpose and their task was done. They had destroyed these people they had come to think of as enemies. They turned to walk out of the meadow, sometimes stumbling over but mostly trying to avoid the bodies of the men, women, and children from the Fancher train who were left stripped, bloody, and forlorn in the afternoon sun.

Two Bits rested her head on the ground. She made a low grunting sound followed by a light yip. It was her sign. Malachi knew she wanted to leave, get back to her work with the sheep. He sat still, his thoughts spinning as he played John Lee's last words to the men over in his head, warning the men not to speak of what they had done. He ran his tongue along the dry rim of his teeth. If the men had done the right thing, why wouldn't they speak of it?

For the past few nights Malachi had searched out the men gathered at the Hamblin ranch. Their arrival in sudden numbers had made him uneasy and curious. After the other boys in the pasture had fallen asleep, he left the safe warmth of his bedroll to hide at the edge of the darkness that surrounded the men as they stood around their campfire talking and singing hymns. He listened, unseen, as he strained to make out whatever truth lay behind their words and understand their reasons for coming here. They poked at the night air with their fingers to emphasize their anger. They linked their sinewy arms together and prayed to God to give them guidance. He thought of it now, pawing through their conversations and their prayers, looking for their intent. He'd heard them say they wanted to teach the emigrants a lesson. But this? He shook his head. Whether the emigrants' sins were real or imagined, this revenge was too huge, too brutal. Surely it would come at a cost.

He'd first heard stories about the Fancher train from Albert weeks before the emigrants arrived at the meadows. Albert, come back fresh from working in the barn with Jacob Hamblin, would strut around their small campfire, his chest puffed out like a rooster's, rattling off tales he'd picked up at the Hamblin house. But Malachi only half-listened. He knew Albert was full of lies and mischief.

Later, Jonah Blank and his wives started sharing their complaints about the approaching emigrants. They'd gather with their neighbors after church while Malachi waited in the wagon, as he'd been instructed. He watched their faces grow sour and angry as these tales ate at their good will and turned them against the people in the train. As far as Malachi knew, these were people they had never seen, never spoken to. In the past week, once the emigrants arrived and set up camp, the stories had gone even further. The men stewed about how the people on the train were harming them, threatening their families. Each day, the sins of the people living in the midst of the circled wagons on the meadow floor grew more heinous and despicable. The emigrants' women were whores. The men fornicated at night with each other's wives. The children were thieves and full of the pox, carrying the mark of the devil, just like those that born them.

Albert claimed that the train had sold a poisoned cow to a Mormon family and the poisoned beef was said to have killed the family's boy. He'd said it was intentional, that it was murder. Some of the Mormons also began spreading the rumor that some of the men in the Fancher train had taken part in killing Brother Parley Pratt, who had gained a folk hero's status amongst the Mormons. At the time of Pratt's murder, Malachi had heard it was a jealous husband from Missouri who had murdered him in revenge for Pratt taking the man's wife in plural marriage. But by the time the emigrants from the train were settled in Mountain Meadows, they'd been saddled with Pratt's murder and the Mormon boy's too.

Malachi twisted the frayed cuff of his pant leg and looked at the fresh corpses in the meadow below. Lee and the others had duped the people in the train in order to kill them. Was it because of these rumors? Even if some of the stories were true, why not find those who were responsible instead of slaughtering the whole lot? It made no sense. Had Lee somehow also tricked the men who had been summoned here to carry out the killing? Had they been told the people of the train had done something so horrible, so awful it could never be forgiven? Perhaps Lee had been duped too. Malachi knew Lee never acted alone. No man in the Mormon Church ever acted alone. He'd heard Lee say to the men that Dame and Haight, both prominent leaders in the church, were coming to the Hamblin ranch that night. They must have known. They must have ordered this, and if they had ordered it, Brigham Young must have known too.

As he waited now, still jammed into his hiding place, he looked at the woman and child Major Higbee had murdered. Their skin was papery white except for a delicate pink that smudged their cheeks and the tips of their noses. The woman had a spatter of freckles across her nose. The boy's hair bunched in blond peaks on his head. They looked to him just like the Mormons he lived with. Yet, they'd been killed. And for what?

Malachi lived on the edges of this community of Mormons that claimed southern Utah as their own. He lived with them, but was reminded every day he was not one of them. He tended their sheep, did their chores. He knew no one much cared for him. His silence and his unwillingness to adapt to their religious ways fueled their dislike of him, their mistrust of him. But, if he wanted to eat, he had to do their work for them. He liked tending the sheep, and he was good at it. None of the other boys had his skill. In exchange, the man who bought him—Jonah Blank, the one who called him his son—kept him fed, housed, and clothed. But Malachi knew Jonah Blank did not love him. He had known a father's love, and Blank had none of that for Malachi.

There was no one for him to tell what he had witnessed that day. He wondered if he could live amongst the men who had done this and keep his secret safe. As these thoughts flooded him, he felt his spirit hover high, an apparition looking down on this huddled heap of a boy, understanding how small he was compared to the enormity of what he had just witnessed. If it came to it, he could flee, but he didn't know where he would go, and he didn't know how, really. He owned nothing, didn't even own himself. He had lived in this southern scrap of Utah for most of his life and, while that time had taught him much about those he was forced to live with, he knew little of the outside world.

In the early days when they had first arrived, he and Albert had schemed to run away and return to their tribe. They'd dreamed of stealing horses and money, going north, trying to reunite with the surviving members of their tribe and living as free boys again. But it was just talk, the hopeful chatter of lonely, cowardly boys around the campfire as the shadows of night closed in. They knew they'd be punished if they tried to run. Although they did not admit as much to each other, each believed himself inadequate to the task. Then all that changed. Albert had changed. He had seen his opportunity and shifted his allegiance from Malachi to the Mormons and the family he lived with in hopes that life would be better for him. Now Malachi was utterly alone. He had no one to turn to, to share this terrible knowledge of what had happened, and no one to help him know what the right action would be.

Wearily, he pushed himself up and looked out over the meadow. The dog stood and leaned up against him, whimpering. Malachi looked down and touched her coarse hair for comfort. He took a final glance at the killing fields below, assuring himself that all the men had finally gone. What remained were the bloody corpses. His body was stiff with fatigue and fear, but he knew he needed to get back before someone discovered he was missing. For now, he would continue to live as though none of this had happened. He took a deep breath and whistled softly to the dog. They turned their backs to the meadow and headed up the trail to the Hamblin ranch.

CHAPTER 3

There was movement all around, men running back and forth, shouting, children crying. All was chaos. Malachi slipped into the barn unnoticed and the dog padded behind him. He climbed to the top of the haymow where he settled behind a bale to watch the men in the barnyard below. Some had formed a half circle around the wagon that Samuel Knight had driven up from Mountain Meadows. The wagon was just outside the barn, its horses still hitched to it. Someone had thought to attach feedbags to their heads.

Twelve children from the train clustered together in the wagon. They looked to be between the ages of 3 and 5. Four more—all slightly older—stood outside the wagon, with their backs to it, holding hands and facing the men as though to protect the others. They were all sobbing and carrying on, calling for their parents, and screaming out when the men got too close. The children's agony saturated the air. It was as though their raw pain awakened all who had taken part in the slaughter and revealed their own treachery. Men, who hours earlier had ruthlessly killed the people from the train, now jockeyed for position to soothe and touch and baby-talk the children whose lives they had spared.

The front door of the house suddenly flapped opened. Rachael, one of Jacob Hamblin's wives, emerged and walked purposefully toward the wagon. Her arms were piled high with blankets. Her face was pinched and faded, and her graying hair was pulled back into a bun that perched like a small fluffed-out bird sitting at the nape of her neck. She stopped at the wagon and eyed the tumult of wailing children. Then she set the blankets down and turned to face John Lee. Lee was leaning comfortably against the fence with his arms folded across his chest. He chewed a piece of wheatgrass and seemed to be the only man who hadn't fallen into a panic over the children.

"These young ones," she said. "They need to be tended to."

"Tend to them, then," Lee replied smoothly, nodding to the wagon. "We want no harm to come to them. You know that."

Rachael paused for a moment, her eyes searching Lee's face. He met her gaze and said nothing more. He seemed a man content with a job well done. Malachi reconsidered his earlier thoughts. Perhaps Lee had planned this. He was powerful in these parts and Malachi had seen his sway with the other men who had congregated at Hamblin's ranch. He was church bishop in Harmony and a favorite of Brigham Young's. But would Lee have set himself above William Dame and Isaac Haight? Would he have acted without Brigham Young's blessing? From everything Malachi had learned about the church and how Young ruled the people in it, that didn't seem likely. No Mormon acted independently if they wanted to stay in the church. But why would Young have ordered the men to butcher the people from the train?

Rachael pursed her thin lips then walked over to the wagon. She motioned to Philip Klingensmith to come help her. The tall, red-haired man lumbered over. His hands hung heavily at his sides as he meekly waited for Rachael to tell him what to do.

"Here, take these and bundle up the littlest ones nice and snug and take 'em into the house. I've put out beds for them on the floor in the parlor. Put them there, two to a bed," she said as she handed a blanket to him. Then she gazed at the children, shaking her head and added to no one in particular. "These poor lambs need to be fed."

Klingensmith rolled up the blanket and tucked it under one arm, then moved slowly toward the wagon to gather up the first child. His clothes were stained with blood and Malachi was sure the man reeked of it. He reached out and grasped the boy with the golden curls by the shoulder, but the boy twisted away from his grip and emitted a high-pitched wail. Klingensmith drew back as though he'd been scalded.

"He killed my mother!" The boy screamed and pointed at Klingensmith. "He killed my mother. Don't let him touch me!"

All movement around the wagon stopped. Rachael hugged a blanket to her chest. Circles of sweat bled through the underarms of her plain gray dress. She threw a quick look over her shoulder at Lee then walked over to Klingensmith, who stared stupidly at the boy. She took the blanket and whispered something to him, and the man turned to go stand by Lee.

"There, there you sweet boy," she said, turning to the sobbing child. "It was the Indians that killed your mother, you poor dear. You're suffering, deluded by what you've gone through. These men who stand here are good men of God and only mean to help you. They were trying to rescue you, don't you see, rescue you from the Indians."

The ease of her lie took Malachi's breath away. But the courage of the blond boy captivated him. In the midst of this chaos, surrounded by the men who had killed the children's kin, he had named his mother's murderer. Rachael put her hand on the side of the wagon near to where the boy sat. He scuttled back away from her. She dropped her hand into the pocket of her apron, searching for something, then pulled out a small rag doll and held it toward the boy.

"Look, look what I have for you," she said in a coaxing voice, wiggling the doll back and forth, the yellow yarn on its head flapping in a goofy arc. The boy's sobbing had died down to a whimper and the other children gathered around him, trying to comfort him. He peeked up at the doll and hesitated before reaching out with his good arm to snatch it. Rachael let it slip easily from her hand to his. He pulled the thing toward his chest then buried it inside the sling that held his injured arm.

"Let me wrap you and your poppet up in this lovely blanket. I'll bring you and your friends into the house. Only me," she assured him. "I'll bring each of you in and then we'll have some bread, just baked, warm with butter."

This promise of normalcy and food captured the attention of all the children. Their looks sharpened as they eyed Rachael and wiped away snot and tears with the cuffs of their sleeves as if they were trying to look more presentable for what awaited them inside. It reminded Malachi of when he and Albert first arrived in Salt Lake. They were so scared, so hungry. He remembered the plump woman who had tried to clean their dusty faces with her laced handkerchief, comb their knotted hair. She gave them pieces of bread smeared with lard. He had wolfed down his share immediately. Her kindness had given him hope that he might survive, a hope that had wiped away some of his fear.

Rachael gathered up the boy with the golden hair and wrapped the blanket around him, whispering soothing words to him as she did. Although he was still weeping and resisted a little, she was able to calm him, pull him into her arms and take him into to the house. When she re-emerged, she did the same with each child. One-by-one, she managed to gently coax all the children into allowing her to take them inside. After she brought the last one in, she returned to stand at the doorway of the house and nodded slightly in Lee's direction then closed the door.

Malachi spotted Albert hovering near the corner of the barn, closest to Lee. Once the children were inside, Lee motioned him over.

"Tomorrow we'll take the stock and provisions from the train back to my place." He reached out to grasp Albert's shoulder. "We'll leave the sheep to winter over here. I want the boys—Idget and the one you call

Mudface—to come with me, to Harmony. Go on up to the pasture now and let 'em know."

Lee's ranch was north and a one-day trek on horseback. Although Malachi knew that Idget—who belonged to Lee—would need to return north for the winter season, he was unnerved that Lee would want him to go to his ranch. He wondered if Lee suspected him of something.

"What if they ask me what happened?" Albert asked. "They might of heard the shooting."

"You tell 'em nothing," Lee started. Then he paused, looking toward the house. "No, you tell them what our Sister Rachael said. It was the Paiutes. No more, though. I don't want you yakkin' at those boys about any of this. You hear me? Just tell them what they need to know."

Albert nodded and blinked up at him. Uncertainty pocked his face. "What about me?"

"You'll stay here, wait for your father. Let him know all that happened, make sure he understands." Albert's shoulders sloped in disappointment, but he didn't argue.

Malachi had to beat Albert back to the pasture. He climbed down from the loft of the barn as quickly as he could and slipped away with the dog tight to his heels. Albert was the same age as Malachi, but long-limbed and taller and could easily reach the pasture before he did. He hoped Albert would be delayed talking to the men, but he picked up his pace just the same. The faster he walked the more his bad leg started to cramp until it seized up so fully that it collapsed from under him and sent him sprawling on the ground. Two Bits reached him and stuck her cold nose on the nape of his neck, licking his salty skin with her warm tongue. For the first time that day he smiled. He pushed himself up and as he did so, a foot landed on his rump and pushed him back to the ground.

"Going somewhere, Mudface?" Albert asked.

Malachi's cheek was sticky with sweat and pressed into the rocky path. Next to him, Albert's shadow stretched long and dark in the late afternoon sun. Malachi grunted as he tried to get up then muttered, "Dog ran. Just went to find her. What of it?" Albert let him get up this time.

"I told you not to leave Idget on his own with the sheep. Ever. What did you think? Did you think I wouldn't find out?"

"Nope, didn't think about it at all on account of needing to get that dog," Malachi said as he stood and brushed the dirt off his pants. He kept his gestures slow and deliberate, his gaze on the ground.

"Why are you trying to clean yourself up, Mudface?" The boy laughed. "It'll never work. You'll always be dirty."

Like Malachi, Albert was Shoshone. Their adoptive families didn't know how old they were when they bought them, so they decided both boys were six years old the year they had been purchased, which made them fifteen now. The Mormons were particular about the dates of births and deaths and weddings, and they carefully recorded important events in their journals. Seemed like everyone kept one. But Malachi had concluded some time ago that his birthday—even the made up one—wasn't recorded in anyone's journal.

Malachi's Shoshone name meant *rolls in mud*, but Albert used *Mudface* to remind him whenever he could how dark his skin was, of where he had come from. Albert took great pride in the lightness of his own skin. Lately, he had started wearing a wide-brimmed hat. It was a hand-me-down from Jacob Hamblin and it protected his face from the darkening rays of the sun. He also only wore long sleeves, even when the summer sun was at its hottest.

Albert's Shoshone name meant *hungry*. He had the look of a hungry wolf now as he gazed at Malachi. Malachi knew he was trying to piece out whether he was telling him the truth. Albert ran his tongue along the front of his teeth, leaving behind a sheen of spit.

"It'll come hard on you if you're lying," Albert said, giving him a shove that nearly knocked him to the ground again. "You shouldn't of left Idget with the sheep. That boy's not right in his head."

Idget was the third boy, a Paiute, bought and adopted like Malachi and Albert. He belonged to John Lee. His given name was Lemuel, but everyone called him Idget because the tip of his tongue had been cut off, causing him to speak in rounded, clumsy syllables that few but Malachi were able to fully understand. For the past two summers, Idget had come from Harmony to help the boys with the sheep. Albert believed Idget was daft and would have little to do with him. But Malachi had taught Idget how to care for the sheep, and he felt responsible for him, protective of him. He stood still, considering how to draw out Albert.

"Have you been with the men?" he asked.

"What's it to you?" Albert replied.

"Just wondered."

"You're not to be trusted," Albert said, folding his arms across his chest. "You haven't been sealed to your family. You don't pray. You don't worship. My father says that makes you a heathen. So, why should I tell you anything?"

Malachi listened as Albert ticked off his favorite taunts. He hesitated. He knew he had to choose his words carefully. "I heard shots again, toward the meadows," he said. "Then I saw the men go there and later, just now, I heard children screaming, up near the house."

Albert looked at him, evaluating. Malachi knew it made him feel important to be the one who knew things the other boys didn't, to be the only one of the Indian boys the men trusted.

"It was a massacre," Albert said at last.

"How was it?" Malachi asked, startled by Albert's revelation. For a brief moment, he wondered if Albert would tell him the truth.

"What do you mean?" Albert scowled.

"I mean how did it happen? Where were you and the other men when it happened?" he asked.

"It was the Paiutes that done it," Albert said, stepping closer to him, as if to take him into his confidence. "There was nothing but blood.

We seen that it was the Paiutes when we got there, men had their scalps scraped off, their cocks lopped off. Women with their hearts cut out, hands gone. Their babes wandering, crying, nothing but a bloody mess."

"There were children?"

"Yep, sixteen in all, those that survived at least." He flicked the brim of his hat with his finger, tipping it back off his face. "I counted 'em. We had to round them all up. They were scared, and they scattered like sheep running this way and that all over the meadows trying to get away from us. Couldn't tell the difference between their saviors and those Paiute devils that kilt their kin."

"Where will they go?"

Albert looked sharply at him.

"Go? They won't *go* anywhere. They'll stay with us. Become ours." He scuffed the toe of his boot in the dirt.

"But don't they have their own kin? I mean back from where they come from?"

This raised a memory of the earlier life both boys had shared. Their lost kin, their lost lives. He and Albert hadn't been much older than the children from the train when they'd been bought. He still remembered that day when Jacob Hamblin rode into their camp, a serious man in his dusty black coat, sitting stiff and tall on a mangy brown horse. Both boys were curled up on either side of their grandmother, snuggling against her like pups, leaching whatever warmth they could from her frail body. All three were starving. The boys' eyes and noses were rheumy with infection, their hair matted and filthy with lice. They were all that remained of their band. Everyone else had either died of the pox or been killed by the Utes or gone off in search of food. In the end, their grandmother had sold them to Jacob Hamblin for two sacks of beans, a bag of flour, and some bacon. She said she couldn't take care of them, but that Jacob Hamblin would. Malachi remembered how he had wailed as she shook his hands free of her dress, telling him to be brave. She was crying too, but she told the boys she had to let them go with Hamblin so they could survive.

"Who would want to go back to that?" Albert sneered. "They come to our way of thinking, our way of life. It will be like they've had no other and won't want it neither."

Malachi was silent. "It don't matter." He shrugged. "Won't happen anyhow. We're not going anywhere and neither are they."

"You're going somewhere, you and Idget at least," Albert said, hitching up his pants.

"Me?" Malachi asked. "Where?" He looked at the knife sheathed and hanging from Albert's hip. He thought of the girls, their skirts lifted high as they fled the meadow, and he wondered what role the men had told Albert to play in the massacre.

"To Harmony, to the Lees. You're going to winter over there."

"Why not you? Why aren't you going?"

"I have important work to do here with my father. You, you're not but a hired hand. You will always tend to the animals and do what you're told. 'Sides, Jonah Blank wants you out of the way. One less mouth to feed."

"I like the animals."

"'Course you do. You're like them, stupid and slow. It's who you're meant to be with, and that idiot Idget, too." Albert adjusted his hat and ran a hand around the front of its rim. "It's time you got him ready. Make him understand what's to happen." Albert turned on his heel and walked back to the Hamblin house.

Malachi watched him go. He was relieved. Albert seemed to believe he had not seen the killings. Albert had been sealed to the Hamblins two years previous. The sealing was a point of on-going pride and bragging rights for Albert. He would be a part of the Hamblin family now, have a real family to himself throughout this life and into the next. He didn't need Malachi. The belonging that Albert talked about was something

Malachi longed for too, but he knew it came at a cost. He saw what Albert had to do, how he had to act, the parts of himself he had to give up and forget. He also knew that even if he learned the Book of Mormon forwards and backwards and put all that was in it into practice, Jonah Blank wasn't about to seal him and accept him as one of his own.

Around the time Albert was sealed, he'd overheard Jonah Blank discussing Jacob Hamblin's decision. "Folly this is," Jonah Blank had said to his wives one night after supper as the women sat on either side of him mending his shirts. Malachi sat by the fireplace polishing the man's boots. It was winter and although Malachi slept in the barn, he took his evening meal in the house. After everyone had eaten, he was always told to stay to do some small chore, make himself useful before turning in.

"It's enough that the church makes us adopt them, these dark young devils and act like they're part of our families," he said looking at Malachi. "But to seal them to our own blood for eternity, it's like sealing tar to gold. It's not right, not right at all."

It was one of the few times Malachi had heard the man grumble about the church's teachings. It was Brigham Young who required the Mormon families to adopt the Indian children they bought, part of some holy plan that would turn the Indians—at least the children—to the ways of God. But it was rare that families thought of them as their true children. However, Jacob Hamblin seemed to, and his decision to seal Albert to his family was a confirmation of that. It was that acceptance that Malachi envied. But even though he longed for even a meager dose of it, he steeled himself against the yearning. Why long for something he would never receive? It was the reason he rejected the repeated attempts by Jonah Blank's wives to become a Mormon. What was the point? He yearned for love from other people, not some distant God he couldn't see, couldn't touch.

He consoled himself with memories of his true mother, his father, his grandmother, and the aunts and uncles from his tribe. But his memories of them became hazier with each year that passed. Soon even their ghosts would abandon him. It used to be, when they first lived in the Mormon settlements, that Albert talked to Malachi about how he missed them too and how one day they would find them again, their true kin, or what was left of them. But those days were over.

Malachi turned to face the pasture. He could see Idget standing on a small hill looking at him. Idget waved and gestured to the dogs to stay. The boys made their way toward each other.

"What's happened?" Idget asked.

"Better you don't know, don't ask questions," Malachi warned. He reached down to scratch Two Bits' ears.

"I heard the gunfire. Then, after, they brought children by here on their way to the house," Idget said, gesturing toward the house with his chin. "I heard 'em as they passed. They were raising a racket. Lots of crying and screaming." Saliva dripped down his chin from the effort of shaping his words.

Malachi was silent. He wanted to unburden himself, but telling Idget the truth would put them both in danger. He worried the other boy might let it slip and word of what Malachi knew would get passed on to Lee.

"They rescued them from the Paiutes," Malachi said. The lie came to him quickly and easily, and it shamed him that it did. "The Paiutes killed the rest of the train, and the men got there only in time to drive them away and rescue the children."

He watched the sheep, not looking at Idget as he said this, hoping the boy believed him. Idget sidled closer to him.

"And Albert? Did he help?" He reached out his hand to touch Malachi's arm. Malachi startled at his touch and looked up at him. "Did he help rescue the children?"

Idget's straight black hair was cut in a jagged line across his forehead as though he cut it himself. Maybe he had. It gleamed nearly purple in the afternoon sun. His nose was long and gently hooked. His face was flattened slightly, so that it spanned out from his nose in a wide smooth plane. It was a face that did not convey much feeling. Malachi had seen how frightened the Mormon children were of Idget, not only because of the way he talked, but because they could not read his face. Malachi looked into the boy's eyes. His eyes held all his expression. They were lively and warm, the color of the stones at the bottom of the Magotsu. He realized with a pang that Idget might know he was lying.

"Yes," he said. "Albert was there. He's with the men now. They had to bring the emigrants' stock back and find a place for the children."

Idget let his hand rest lightly on Malachi for a moment longer. He swallowed and squeezed Malachi's arm slightly before letting it go. He wiped the spit from his chin and turned toward the sheep.

"The dogs were good. They helped me while you were gone."

Guilt shot through Malachi's chest. He knew he was the best with the dogs. Leaving Idget with them for so long put both the sheep and the boy at risk. The Mormon families kept careful count of their sheep, and if any had gone missing both boys would suffer for it.

"Did you have to follow strays?" Malachi asked.

"Just one. I missed her, but the white dog saw her and brought her back right away. No others after that."

Malachi reached down and gave Two Bits a rough rub on either side of her rib cage. She licked his cheek and looked back at the sheep. She was done with distractions for the day.

"We leave tomorrow," Malachi said. "I'm to go with you back to Harmony."

"You are?" Idget asked and gave him a cockeyed smile. "I hoped John Lee would have you come with us this year. It's good. We'll live like brothers there."

Although Malachi was relieved to be leaving Albert behind, Lee worried him. He was a swaggering presence at the Hamblin ranch. He could hear the man now barking out orders to the other men, probably organizing everyone to leave tomorrow with the emigrants' stock and belongings.

It was Lee who came to the pasture that night to talk to them about preparations for their departure the next day. He walked into their small camp at dusk. A flat-topped, felt pork pie hat was clamped onto his head, and he was wearing the black wool coat that came to his knees. He was medium height and his face was ruddy and slightly baggy around his eyes and chin. His body was stout, but bristled with the energy of a much younger man. His eyes were remarkably blue, and Malachi was unnerved by the calculation, the intelligence he saw in them.

"You boys need to be ready to go at day-break," Lee announced.

The command and depth of his voice reminded Malachi of the earlier speech he'd given to the men at Mountain Meadows. It was a voice few would dare to contest. According to Albert, his Sunday sermons were the favorites of the people in Harmony, and he was known for moving women and girls to tears. Idget looked up and nodded but said nothing. Idget had told Malachi that Lee thought his thinking was stunted because he couldn't talk right, which made him impatient and angry with the boy. So Idget rarely spoke around Lee, only said what was essential.

"You boys hear me?" Lee raised his voice, his eyes fixed on Malachi.

"We heard you, sir. We'll have everything ready," Malachi said, inching away from him.

"You boys might of heard," Lee said. "We got ourselves a passel of children."

Neither boy responded.

"It's on account of the Paiutes," Lee said, shoving his hands into the pockets of his coat. Malachi slid his eyes over to him, and he could see him fiddling with something in his right pocket. Malachi imagined a bauble filched from one of the emigrants and a ripple of fear traveled up his chest.

"They're a people like your own," Lee said, clearing his throat. "Without a care for the sanctity of life. It's why we're trying to help you boys, change you, bring you up in the ways of our Lord, our good church."

Idget chewed the inside of his left cheek. Malachi glanced at him then fastened his gaze to the ground.

"It's a sad day when emigrants can't move through this territory without being assaulted by the tribes. It's a sad day."

The dogs looked at Lee and got up from where they had been sitting, snuffling the ground, moving away from Lee and closer to the boys.

"You best be ready early. We'll leave come dawn, get a full day's ride in tomorrow. I don't want any delays. Idget, you and Mudface can ride the pinto pony together. Come up to the house later, but don't you be lingering. Don't want you bothering none of the men, nor Sister Hamblin either. They got enough on their hands. Rachael's taking care of those young ones, but I'll tell her to put out some food for you, leave it in the bin by the tack shed. I want you to pack it up, nice and neat in your saddlebags. Should be enough to get you through the trip to Harmony. Bring your bedrolls in case we need to camp for the night."

He stopped talking and gazed out over the sheep. Then, he turned and walked back to the house, passing Malachi without looking at him. As he walked past, Malachi thought he caught a whiff of blood.

Idget waited until Lee was out of earshot before he said anything.

"I'm thinkin' you don't like him."

"Nope," Malachi said quietly. "Not that."

"Wouldn't know it by the look on your face," Idget said, his face inching into a grin.

"I just want to be left alone, left to the sheep." The urgency in Malachi's voice drew a sharp look from the other boy. A small silence pressed into the space between them, and Malachi was visited by the certainty that this life he'd known and grown used to was getting ready to change.

✳ ✳ ✳

Just after sundown, Malachi went to the Hamblin house. He feared running into Albert, but he wanted to get the supplies he and Idget would need for the trip and be ready to go in the morning. No point starting out on the wrong side of Lee by being late. Rachael Hamblin had left two packets of food, wrapped up in squares of cotton cloth. He stuffed it into a saddlebag and scrabbled through the bin looking for additional hard tack for the road. He stopped when he heard a man's voice in front of the bunkhouse, slowly lifting his head and silently easing down the lid of the bin. He pulled close to the side of the building, hidden in its shadow.

"It's a grievous thing, I tell you."

Malachi recognized William Dame and Isaac Haight. The two men stood facing each other in the rapidly falling light. Although he'd seen both men at the Hamblin house earlier in the week, he hadn't seen either in the last couple of days. Their horses were hitched to a snubbing post, still saddled.

"Too late to have second thoughts," said Haight. "The deed is done." Haight was the head of the military in the southern region. The men in the Nauvoo Legion took their orders from him. Major Higbee, who had given the command in Mountain Meadows that day, was Haight's second in command.

"Should not have been," Dame muttered, shaking his head. "Should not have been."

"What is this?" Haight's voice cracked. "You gave the orders your own self. This came from you."

Malachi's ears sharpened. Dame was the stake president, Brigham

Young's religious lieutenant in the region. Malachi knew from Jonah Blank that the order of things in the church was strict. "We all obey the higher ups," he'd told him. "They make the big decisions, keeping watch over us and we do what we're told. It's how it is. They keep us safe."

"No, no," Dame muttered. "I didn't understand the truth of it, how far it would go. It weren't represented to me in an honest way."

"You can wear your high hat if you want to, Brother Dame," said Haight. "But we all know the truth here, and we knew it weeks ago when these emigrant fools first set their feet on our soil."

"Klingensmith said there were so many women, so many children," Dame countered. Malachi heard the pleading in his voice. "Surely that's not God's work."

"Oh, it is God's work and God's will, Brother Dame," said Haight. His voice was slight, nasally as though it was forced out through a tube. "And your will, too, when it comes to that. This was what you said would need to be done. The men only did what they was told."

"But it was you who told me wrong." Dame's voice was threaded with a slight whine, and Malachi wondered why this man in charge felt like he had to plead with Haight. "You told me it was just the men who'd be killed."

Haight said nothing and looked steadily at the man. Haight had an elongated forehead and wide-set eyes that gave him a placid, sheep-like look. Albert had said Haight was one of the ones responsible for carrying out punishments when men in the southern settlements erred, following up with them when they stole, lied, cheated, or left the church. Albert said Haight was known for concocting punishments that uniquely fit the transgression. The man sent a chill through Malachi.

"You listen to me, Brother Dame," Haight said, bringing his face close to Dame's. "I will not be saddled with this. You and I know full well that your name is on those orders and that you are Brigham Young's appointed leader in this region, you're the one responsible for carrying out what he says. You're the one who tells the settlements how to live and you're the one who tells me how to direct the military. You're the man that gave that order for what happened today, and you best not try to hang this on me because you're shitting your pants like a half-grown boy and can't take the heat of what you yourself brought about."

Malachi heard heavy footsteps coming down the steps of the bunkhouse, and he melted farther back into the shadows. A man's voice called the men's names.

"Brother Lee," Dame replied. "I'm glad to see you. We were told you'd turned in. Did we wake you?"

"Brothers." Lee's voice sounded husky with sleep.

"We've heard a report from Klingensmith," Dame said. "Come join us."

Lee walked over to the men and set down the kerosene lantern he was carrying on a tree stump between them. The light illuminated their faces from below and sharpened their features.

"It's been a bear of a day." Lee rubbed his hands across his face. "This thing we did in the meadow was hard, even though I know we've got right on our side. Even my dreams are full of it."

"Bad business," Dame said, shaking his head.

"It's God's business," Lee said sharply. "Your arguing is what woke me. It's not a time for conflict between us. You issued the orders, we did the deed, and now it's time for resolve."

There was an extended silence as Haight glared at Dame. Dame removed a silky kerchief from his pocket and mopped his forehead. He was a large man, and the rigors of the long trek on horseback he'd just taken must have exacted a toll. He looked like a man meant for a snug hearth at home, tended by his wives.

"Hot here still," he said lightly, as if to change the subject.

"It is," Lee agreed. "Though not so hot as where we've sent the Fancher train. Sent them to where they belong. They were a poisoned, cowardly lot. Sent a child out with a flag to gentle me. Imagine that: a child." He shook his head and kicked the square toe of his boot into the tree stump.

"We have not heard from Brother Young on this yet," Dame said after a pause. "He'll want to know the full extent of it, how we did it, that is if it hasn't already reached his ears." He spoke slowly, seeming to pick his words carefully.

"Brother Young will bless this act," Haight declared. "It's in keeping with what he himself set in motion, all we've done to purify ourselves, strengthen the settlements, and help protect this land God has given us."

"'Tis true, Brother Haight," Lee said, pulling at his chin. "We have been about the business of cleansing ourselves, readying our people for some time. You and I have been part of that holy work. We've steeled and honed ourselves for the work of God and readied ourselves to defend this land against those who would take it from us, and we showed ourselves capable in that task today." Malachi thought Lee's words sounded forced and wondered if he had crafted them for his current audience's benefit. He imagined Lee testing them out earlier when he was alone.

"But women, Brother Lee, children!" Dame's voice cracked again. He turned away from the other two and began to pace in a small circle. "It's not like we thought, like we planned."

Lee and Haight exchanged looks and Haight shook his head. Lee moved to stand in front of Dame, stopped his pacing and placed both hands on his shoulders.

"Brother Dame, you listen to me now," Lee said forcefully. "We must accept the fact that the work God asks us to do is not always easy, not always well understood, and we cannot, we will not lose our resolve on this."

"And what is our resolve? Was that our resolve? To do that deed?" Dame blurted out, his breath catching in his throat.

"It is to save the souls of these pitiful children God has seen fit to bestow on us. It is to use the bounty of the stock and the other goods that our blessed Lord gave to us to enrich our own people—good, God-fearing people, mind you, who've experienced want and deprivation because of their commitment, their love of God, and love of their church. And it is to carry on with our work to make this land safe from all those who would harm us!"

Dame was breathing hard now, covering his eyes with his hand. Lee slid his arm around Dame's shoulders, shaking him slightly as he held him in the crook of his arm.

"Brother Dame, remember why we did this! Remember our brother in the Lord, Parley Pratt! Remember how he was killed as he carried out God's will. Think on it, he was likely killed by the kin of the very same people as we sought vengeance on today! Remember the innocent boy who was so violently poisoned by these white heathens in that wagon train. Those poor women, as you call them, these poor souls were the sluts who slept with the men who kilt that boy, may have had a hand in killing Brother Pratt. For God's sake, get hold of yourself, man. Remember Nauvoo and all we have sacrificed!"

Dame shrugged off Lee's grasp and turned his back on both men. "But we don't know for sure if that boy was poisoned by intent or mere accident." He was breathing hard and his words were halting. As Dame tried to collect himself, he brought out his kerchief again, wiped his eyes and blew his nose.

At that moment the saddlebags Malachi had left on top off the storage bin slid off and landed with a dull thud. Malachi scrambled under the legs of the storage bin, pulling the saddlebags after him. Lee strode to the side of the tack house. Blood roared through Malachi's ears as he watched Lee walk by the bin, his boots moving slowly along the side of the building as he looked for the source of the sound.

"See anything?" Dame called.

"Nope. Can't see a thing. Must have been a coon or a coyote. Albert says the boys taking care of the sheep claim the coyotes have been fierce lately."

He walked back to join the men.

"Those boys," Haight said, clearing his throat. "One of them is yours, but who does the other belong to?"

"He's Jonah Blank's boy. Hamblin bought him at the same time as Albert, and Jonah bought him off Hamblin. Different as night and day, those two boys."

"Do they know about this business?" Haight asked.

"Albert was there, of course," Lee said. "He likes to be in the middle of ever little thing, and Hamblin has encouraged him in that direction and made him one of his own. I'd say, he's useful, that boy. Smart, wily."

"What about the other two?" Haight pressed. "What do they know?"

"They know what I want them to know and will never be the wiser," Lee said. "My boy ain't nothing but an idiot. Can't talk, can barely feed hisself. Can't imagine him understanding what happened, much less talking of it, and even if he did, no one would know what to make of it and decide he was talking nonsense. Albert says the other one is none too bright either. He calls him Mudface. Albert's kept a good eye on both of 'em for me. He'll tell me if he sees anything that's off."

"Can't have them telling tales," Dame said. He seemed to have regained his composure.

"We leave soon to go back to Harmony," Lee replied. "Albert will stay here, but I'll take the other two boys with me and keep a close watch on them there."

"Good man," Dame said. "If they cause any difficulty, you'll need to take care of it."

"What about the innocents from the train?" Haight asked.

"Rachael Hamblin's got them in hand. You know young ones," Lee said. "Their memories are just as easy to be the stuff of make-believe.

Rachael knows what to do. Simple woman, but she's got our cause at heart and will make sure the children begin to doubt their own eyes."

"We'll have to farm them out," Haight said. "Best to separate them. Does no good to have even young ones together. They talk to each other, reinforce each other. Can't countenance that."

"Intend to take care of it once we're back to Harmony," Lee said grudgingly. "We'll give 'em a day, maybe two of rest here. Then I'll decide who they go to. I'll tend to them."

"But they are to live," Dame said sharply. "Will do us no good if word gets out that we harmed these little ones that are left."

"Best we go take a look at them now," Haight said. "Perhaps Rachael can rustle up something for us to eat while we're there. It's been a long night."

Lee picked up the lantern, and the three men turned toward the faint lights of the house. Malachi waited until the sound of their voices had died away then eased out of his cramped hiding place and hurried back to the pasture.

CHAPTER 4

SEPTEMBER 12

Malachi stood with John Lee in the back room of the church in Santa Clara. He was dressed in a white robe. Isaac Haight was with them, leaning over a tall oak pedestal writing something in a large book. As Malachi watched him, he realized Haight was preparing to seal him to Lee. The robe Malachi had on was floor length and damp around his ankles. When he looked down, he saw that the hem of his robe was soaked with blood. Lee wore his long black coat and pants. He reached into his pocket and pulled out a gold necklace with a cross pendant. A cold trickle of fear spiraled down Malachi's spine. It was the necklace he'd seen around the neck of the woman Higbee had killed in Mountain Meadows. Lee held up the necklace to the light at the window and examined the dangling cross. He turned and walked over to Malachi and fastened the necklace around his neck. He said, "With this cross of the holy spirit, I seal you to me." Malachi felt the tiny cold cross pierce the soft hollow of his neck. "You are my son in the eyes of God," Lee continued. "With this act, we are bound forever, even into the realms of the ever-after."

As Lee's hands settled heavily on the boy's shoulders and forced him to his knees, Malachi woke with a start. The wool blanket that covered him was soaked with morning dew and lay in a sodden weight on his body. The small fire from the night before had burned down to fine ash. The sheep were beginning to stir, and the dogs were stretching and scratching their ears. Malachi rubbed the sleep from his eyes and tried to shake off the dream. Two Bits sat at his side. At his first movement, she leaned down and gave him a short lick. She was ready for food and the other dogs were nearby waiting expectantly. He pushed off the wet blanket and left it piled by the fire. Idget was still asleep and snored lightly. He was always the last to get up.

Malachi fed Two Bits first and then the others. He'd tried once to feed the other dogs before her, but his bitch had gone on the attack, fearlessly tearing at them until they surrendered their portions. Malachi knew that for her, it was about keeping the pecking order. The dogs ate quickly, making low snuffling noises as they wolfed down the scraps of food. He thought again about the conversation he'd overheard between the men last night. There must have been forty men in the meadows. What would happen if any of them told the truth? It was going to be up to Lee, Dame, and Haight to keep them in line, make sure they maintained their silence.

Idget began to stir. He stuck his arms out of his blankets, first one and then the other. He yawned loudly as he stretched. "Is it time to go?" he asked sleepily.

"Nearly."

"Dogs fed?"

"Yep. Got some food here for us too."

"Did you get it from up at the house last night?" Idget asked, sitting up now. His hair stood up in dark spikes all around his head. He fished for his pants from under his blanket and stood, pulling them on over his thick, muscular legs.

"Yes," Malachi answered. "I got us some supplies for the trip, too."

"What was happening there?" the boy asked as he pulled on his jacket. The morning was cold, but Malachi hadn't made a fire because they'd soon be leaving for Harmony.

"Not much. Pretty quiet." Malachi paused. "Haight and Dame were there."

Idget looked up. "Oh, they came," he said matter-of-factly.

"You knew they were coming?" Malachi asked. It amazed him how Idget found things out. He thought it was because no one really saw him or, if they did, they didn't guard their tongues around him.

"They were waiting for a letter from Governor Young," Idget said.

Malachi broke a loaf of bread in two and handed Idget half. He bit off a bit of his bread and chewed slowly, savoring it. Best to enjoy it. No telling when they'd be able to eat again. Malachi swallowed his first bite.

"A letter?"

Idget shrugged. He tugged two chunks of soft bread from the innards of his portion of the loaf. Slowly and deliberately, he rolled each into round smooth balls that he set on a blue kerchief he had draped across his lap and popped one ball after the next into his mouth. Malachi watched him. He always did this. It made the bread last longer.

"Father Lee told the men who'd come here earlier this week that they were waiting for a letter from Salt Lake," the boy said. "It was to tell them what to do about the Paiutes in the meadows."

Malachi mulled over this piece of information. It helped explain the conversation the men had the night before and why Dame was so worried. Maybe Young hadn't made up his mind what he wanted the men to do. Maybe his orders had only gone so far, and he'd told them to kill the men, but not the women, not the children, or maybe he'd said let the Paiutes do the work. If Young hadn't blessed what they'd done, or how far they'd gone, the men involved would have to seek his approval for what they'd done after-the-fact. That wouldn't be easy. Jonah Blank said Young was fair, but harsh when his orders had not been followed.

A twig snapped and they both jumped. They turned to see John Lee approaching their camp. Albert was swaggering behind him. Malachi guessed he had stayed at the Hamblin's last night, probably on the floor of the bunkhouse with Lee and the other men.

"What could they want?" Malachi muttered.

"Probably come to give us breakfast in bed," Idget said.

"You lazy sons 'a guns are up!" Albert called out to them.

Lee walked over to the fire pit and stood without saying anything, surveying the boys' breakfast and jumbled blankets. Malachi's heart beat faster when he saw Lee's gaze rest on the saddlebags Malachi had retrieved last night.

"See you got your provisions for the trip," Lee said, nodding slightly at the saddlebags.

"Yep, got up at sun-up and got what we needed," Malachi said, looking down. He felt Idget's eyes on him.

Lee said nothing and turned his back on the boys to gaze out over the herd of sheep. Malachi watched Idget out of the corner of his eye. His head was down and he was carefully gathering the remaining balls of bread, secreting them away into his pants pocket.

"What's the count of the herd you got here these days?" Lee asked, turning back to the boys.

"Nearly one hundred," Albert replied quickly.

"It's sixty-seven, sir," Malachi said, looking evenly at Albert. "Lambing wasn't as good as usual last spring and we lost some of the ewes last winter."

Lee looked at Malachi. Albert scowled at him over Lee's shoulder.

"Who taught you to count?" Lee asked Malachi.

"It were Rachael Hamblin, sir," he replied. "She taught me to read some, too. I'm not expert, but I can piece out words, read a page of a book if I have to."

The boys were silent and watched Lee as he contemplated this bit of news. Malachi's father, Jonah Blank, had not cottoned to Rachael Hamblin's desire to educate the boys. He'd relented only when Jacob Hamblin had intervened and overruled him, telling him it was God's will. Malachi had joined Albert and the other children from the settlements during the winter months for classes that Rachael and some of the other wives taught. Their primary reading material came from the tattered books of Rachael Hamblin's childhood. She'd also read aloud to them from the Book of Mormon.

"Can you write your name?" Lee asked.

"Yes, sir," he said. "But not much else."

"Hear that, Idget?" Lee said to the other boy, who had slipped another ball of bread into his mouth. "That's what you could do yourself if you had something in that head of yours besides corn mush."

Idget swallowed then hiccupped loudly.

"You want we should be ready soon?" Malachi asked.

"Nope," Lee said. "Turns out we're going to tarry here for another day. Got some decisions to make about those young ones we saved."

Albert drew himself up and shot the boys a smug look. Lee turned his back on the boys to leave, then stopped. He walked over to where the three boys stood and looked at Malachi.

"You're to come with me today," he said.

The three boys looked at each other.

"You mean me, Brother Lee?" Albert said, stepping in front of Malachi.

"No, you're going to stay here with Idget, help him tend the sheep. I want this one," he said as he reached around Albert and clapped his big hand on Malachi's shoulder. Malachi recoiled inside as the weight of Lee's heavy hand brought back the memory of the dream.

"Where we going?" Malachi asked. His voice caught in his throat. He was afraid he knew the answer.

"To the meadows," Lee said. "Got to show Dame and Haight the damages." He paused before adding, "Good for you to see what your kind can do when they don't follow the word of God."

"Now?" Malachi was embarrassed at the squeak in his voice. Albert glared at him. Malachi knew there'd be hell to pay later for this sudden attention from Lee.

"Now," Lee said and turned abruptly.

He guessed Lee expected him to follow him back to the Hamblin house. Malachi grabbed his bread and stuffed it into his leather satchel. He threw the satchel's strap around his shoulders. He searched frantically for his walking stick and was relieved when Idget handed it to him.

"I'll be back as soon as I can," he reassured him. Idget would likely suffer from Albert's foul mood, but it couldn't be helped.

Lee's stride was long and fast and Malachi couldn't keep pace with him. Lee easily arrived at the Hamblin's house before him and was waiting at the corral when he limped in. Lee was talking to Dame, and Haight was giving orders to Philip Klingensmith to saddle their horses. The big bay from the Fancher train was the first one Klingensmith saddled. He handed the horse's reins to Lee, who ran his hands appreciatively over the beast's neck and withers. The horse trembled at the man's touch. Malachi had never seen such a magnificent horse. Lee gathered the reins at the pommel of the saddle. He grasped the horn and swung easily onto the horse. Malachi watched the men as they mounted their horses and wondered how he was to keep up with them.

"Boy!" Lee called out to him. "Bring yourself over here and climb on up behind me."

Malachi walked tentatively over to the horse.

"What are you going to do with that stick?" Lee asked.

"Need it, sir," Malachi explained. "Holds me up."

"Okay, then," Lee said, shifting in the saddle. He leaned down and held out his hand. "Give it to me."

Malachi stood uneasily by Lee's left stirrup as the man tied the walking stick to the saddle. His stomach gathered in apprehension as he watched the horse's muscles quiver at the feel of the stick by its side.

"Now you," said Lee, turning back to Malachi and opening his hand.

Malachi had no feel for how he was to mount this tall creature. He grasped Lee's outstretched hand and felt the calluses on it and the heat of his skin as he pulled him up.

"Grab hold of my waist," Lee grunted.

Malachi's hands scrabbled across the back of the saddle's seat, searching for something to secure himself.

"Grab hold and swing your leg around."

He did as Lee instructed him, and suddenly he was on. He settled tentatively behind the saddle, balancing on the horse's generous rump. His arms hung awkwardly at his sides. He looked down and thought about grabbing onto the lariat straps on the back of the saddle.

"Wrap your arms about me," Lee said to him. "We're going to move."

Malachi wrapped his arms around Lee's waist. The girth of the man beneath his rough wool coat was as powerful as the horse's body beneath him. Lee's movement matched the animal's smooth, confident gait. Malachi had been on other horses before, but they were hard-packed, low-slung things given to rubbing him off at the nearest tree. He tended to stay clear of them, suspecting them of harboring malevolent thoughts. But this animal seemed to come alive under Lee's hand, as though a human's touch caused the beast to become an even more perfect version of itself. Malachi felt transported as the horse lifted his head and widened his stride.

"That's a beautiful horse," Haight said as he rode up along-side Lee.

"So he is," Lee said. Lee settled himself deeper into the saddle. Dame rode a ways behind the two men, and Malachi could hear him talking with Philip Klingensmith about farming.

Haight leaned over to Lee.

"Got to keep Dame in hand," he said in a low voice.

Lee looked at Haight, then ahead again.

"Won't get this worked out now," he said noncommittally. "Let's see what kind of damage lies ahead."

Haight looked so briefly at Malachi that he wondered if he had imagined it.

"Your intent is the same as mine, Brother Lee," he said tightly.

As they approached the killing fields, the smell of human excrement and the stench of sour bodies grew stronger. Their party interrupted two turkey vultures pulling at the flesh of a woman who'd been stripped bare. The birds danced awkwardly away from the woman's body when the men rode near them, but they hovered nearby, greedily eyeing the woman's corpse. Bodies of women and children littered the western side of the meadow. Haight and Lee pulled up their horses in the midst of the dead, waiting for Dame and Klingensmith to arrive. Malachi could hear Dame laughing at something Klingensmith had said, but his laughter stopped abruptly as the field came into view.

"Oh, dear God," Dame said hoarsely. Haight and Lee exchanged looks. Both men touched their horses' flanks and continued moving through the meadows.

"They were picked clean," Haight said as his horse daintily walked around the bodies half-submerged in the grass.

"What did you expect?" Lee said. "The Paiutes weren't going to leave any valuables. No point in that."

Malachi knew Lee's words, this painting of the story and hanging the killings on the Paiutes, was for his own benefit. This was the story now. It would be repeated and reinforced at every opportunity. It would be the accepted version of what had happened and there would be a cost if anyone questioned it. He tried not to look at the maimed and wounded bodies. He felt an odd humming in his head, and the distance between his head and feet spread out precariously. He clung more tightly to Lee and breathed in hard, tasting the caked blood and stench of the dead. Nausea unfolded in his gut, but he fought it. He didn't want to be sick in front of Lee. He felt this was just the first of a long set of tests that he had to pass in order to survive.

Dame groaned. Malachi glanced back and saw him bent over the side of his horse's neck, retching. His vomit spattered on the corpse of a woman. He cleaned off his mouth and dropped the soiled kerchief to the ground. It fluttered down and fell on top of the woman's face, half covering it.

"These bodies need burying," Haight said. He'd tied a red scarf around his face. As he breathed in, it made a deep pocket of shadow over his mouth.

"Something for Hamblin to take care of when he gets back," Lee said. "We'll leave some of the men here to help him."

Dame was sobbing openly now. Philip Klingensmith rode alongside him still, his gaze to the ground as if embarrassed. Lee slowed his horse so that he fell into step with Dame's.

"Brother Dame, there's no tears that can bring 'em back. What's done is done."

Dame blew his nose and wiped his bulging eyes with a fresh kerchief. He seemed to have an endless supply in his saddlebags.

"It'll never be said that I had anything to do with this," he said. The trembling in his voice matched the vibration in the thick fold of fat beneath his chin.

"Course not," Lee said smoothly. "It's all the Paiutes doing. Nothing to do with you." In spite of Lee's calm, Malachi felt his thick-set body tense under the wool of his coat.

Dame suddenly pulled up his horse's reins bringing his animal to an abrupt stop.

"You're the one here who has to convey the word of this and how it happened to Brother Young," Dame said, turning to face Lee. Spit had formed at the corners of the man's mouth and he dabbed at it with his wadded kerchief. "He'll want to hear it from you."

"Not sure I'm the best one to tell this story," Lee said, slowly. He'd also brought his horse to a stop, and Malachi felt him shifting in the saddle. "Could be said it is Brother George Smith who should do the telling. He's the one, after all, who sent the Paiutes here to keep the train in place. Or even you. You're the one in charge in these parts, best it comes from you."

"No, no, who better than you!" Dame insisted, nodding his head and looking down at his horse's neck as though he were in some argument with the animal's neck and not with Lee. "You were at the Hamblin ranch, saw the aftermath, rescued the little ones. You are the one who can explain it best."

"But the telling has got to take place in Salt Lake, in person," Lee said. "I'm not so sure I'll be able to take the time to go there. I've got my family to get back to and I need to settle some business at my farm, take care of the livestock from the train. Better that you and Haight should make the journey to Salt Lake and set things right."

"No, Haight and I are not the ones," Dame said firmly and met Lee's gaze. "You are his undisputed favorite, Brother Lee, his adopted son. You were sealed to him, after all. He has always favored you. He'll understand this coming from you."

Lee was quiet as Dame watched him. Malachi sat as still as possible. He did not know why Lee had insisted he come with them this morning. He felt the men were choosing their words carefully in his presence, but still he thought that this disagreement between them would be something they would want to keep to themselves. Dame seemed determined to push the issue, settle it.

"You think on this, Brother Lee," Dame said. "Brother Haight and I have talked it through, and we think there is no other answer for it." With that, he turned his horse sharply and went to join Haight and Klingensmith.

Lee sat without moving. Dame's horse trotted away and the beefy man bounced sharply up and down in the saddle. Lee suddenly twisted around to look at Malachi. He felt the horse's muscles gather at Lee's movement.

"Get off," Lee said.

Malachi stayed put, puzzled about how he was to accomplish this feat of leaping from the horse's back to the ground. "Give me your hand and I'll swing you down," Lee told him. This made no more sense than saying sheep could fly, it was such a long way to the ground and once he got there, he didn't know what he would do amidst the corpses. But he did as Lee told him and miraculously landed on the ground at the horse's feet. A few feet away, a mass of women's bodies had been heaped into a pile. Malachi desperately wished he were not so close to them. Lee handed him his walking stick. A canteen full of water dangled from the stick on a strap. Malachi took the stick and the canteen.

"Got a job for you to do, boy," Lee said.

"What's that, sir?" Malachi asked apprehensively. Blood rushed through his head muffling the sounds around him. The smell of the dead curdled the scant contents of his stomach.

"Want you should walk through this meadow and check the bodies for anything worthwhile," he said, looking out over the meadow strewn with corpses. He sat up straighter in his saddle. "Then, you bring anything you find to me. You hear?"

Malachi's stomach went watery. He was afraid he'd lose control of his bowels. "You'll wait while I do this thing?" he asked uncertainly.

Lee laughed shortly and looked up at the other men clustered together out of earshot.

"Nope, this is for you to do alone." He paused. "You should be good at it, picking up after the dead."

His mouth went dry. Perhaps Lee knew more about Malachi's whereabouts the day before than he had let on.

"You hear me, boy?" Lee said.

"I did, sir," Malachi stammered. "I do."

"Good. Now get a move on. Meet me back at the Hamblin place when you've finished it. Don't tell no one else if you find something. Come straight to me with it."

Lee lightly touched the horse's flanks with his heels and went to join the other men. When he got there, he said something to them and they looked back briefly then all turned away and rode out of the meadows, leaving Malachi alone with the corpses. He stood still as the men rode away, and he felt the heat of the morning sun beat down on his head. A thrum of desperation and nausea took hold of him. He thought about fleeing, but where would he go, after all, on foot with a half a hunk of bread and a canteen of water?

He tried to calm his mind and force himself to consider the task at hand. He was not confident he could find anything of value. The men must have plundered it all the day before. But, if he proved himself a worthy scavenger, Lee might treat him more favorably. Surely if the man thought Malachi had seen the murders in the meadows, he would not have brought him here. Perhaps the fact that Lee had assigned him this task was hopeful. He had heard him say Albert was useful, as though that was a good thing. Perhaps he could be useful too and prove his worth to Lee. A clutch of shame gripped him but he put the feeling aside. He knew he couldn't afford it.

He assessed the carnage in front of him and decided to skip over the pile of women's corpses nearest him. They'd been stripped bare and he could see no jewelry glinting in their earlobes or at the base of their necks. He left them in favor of a small knot of four children, one boy and three girls. The boy's head had been bludgeoned and the girls' throats had been slit. Unlike most of the adults, the children had been left fully clothed. He walked carefully around the bodies, considering how best to search them. He opted for the boy first. He guessed the boy was about his age. His brown curly hair was tangled and had matted into dried bloody clumps on his skull. His features were a pulpy mass of blood, skin, and bone. A lone tooth protruded out of what had been his mouth, and his ear had been partially torn off. Blood had coagulated and dried at his neck, leaving a crusty, blackish necklace of gore on the collar of his dust-brown jacket. He wondered which of the men had killed him and why. What had this boy done to deserve this?

Malachi forced himself to concentrate, to mute the questions inside his head, to not think of the ghoulish faces of the children. The fear he felt for his own life sharpened his senses and cleared his head. He reached into the pockets of the boy's jacket then searched through the pockets of his pants. Empty. He turned his attention to the girls. The head of one, who looked to be about eleven or twelve, tilted back as though she was laughing. The bones and muscles of her neck were exposed, partially severed from her delicate shoulders. Malachi turned away from her face, willing himself not to be sick as he searched the pockets of the apron that covered her dress. Nothing.

He searched the other two next. One had the edge of a shawl that covered her shoulders clasped tightly in one hand, as though she was hanging on to some remnant of comfort. Malachi slipped his hand into the wide pocket of her apron and found a small leather-bound book with *Holy Bible* printed in gold leaf across the front. He laid it aside and searched her other pocket. He pulled out a small packet of letters tied together with a faded crimson ribbon, their edges stained with blood. Then he dipped his hand back in her pocket and pulled out a delicate, knotted hanky. He untied it and found two ear bobs, each inset with a tiny ruby and pearl, along with a gold locket on a delicate chain. His heart beat faster. Just a few more finds like this and he might be safe. He was ashamed at his excitement over this minor success, but he continued his search.

There weren't many children, but he found that most of them had been entrusted with some small treasure. The Mormon men must have overlooked them—or avoided them—in their plundering. He wondered if the adults from the wagon train hadn't believed Lee was there to rescue them, but they had hoped their children would be spared. He imagined the last-minute whispers of mother to daughter, the urgent messages of, "Be safe! Take grandmother's earrings, my necklace. I've written this letter to your uncle, give it to him when you see him! Do not forget us."

By the time he'd finished, he had gathered fifteen earrings, five necklaces, two silver money clips, some loose coin, a ruby brooch, one Bible, and a packet of letters. He knew Lee would be pleased with the jewelry and silver money clips. He thought briefly about leaving the Bible and letters behind. He looked at the letters. They had no value and he doubted Lee would want them. He rubbed his thumb along the letters' sharp edges. There must be nearly twenty of them. He wondered about the loved ones they were written to, waiting for a word from the people on the train. Maybe there would be a way to send them, make sure they got them. He could try to do that much for the dead. Even though he knew he shouldn't, something called out to him to keep them, to somehow preserve the memory of the people who'd been killed. He stuffed the packet of letters and the Bible into the bottom of his satchel and placed the other things he found on top. He did a final walk around the meadows, both for good measure and so he could tell Lee he'd checked everyone.

The dead stirred less emotion in him now. The terror on their rigid faces, their pulpy flesh, severed necks, and bared genitals and breasts had become more familiar and left him numb. He reminded himself there was no help for them now. If he wanted to live, he had to keep silent as to what he had seen and do the bidding of Lee and others who had been a part of this horror, at least for the time being. Silence and observation would be his constant companions, keeping him safe, keeping him alive until he knew what to do.

CHAPTER 5

SEPTEMBER 13

The small band of Paiutes waited just off the road that led to the Hamblin ranch. All young braves, they sat idly on their horses, legs slung easily over their animals' necks, laughing and talking together in their square, blunt language. Malachi and Idget waited with them, but off to the side and ignored. The boys were perched on a fat pinto pony that kept his head to the ground. The beast grazed as though this was the last of the grass left on earth.

It was early and a chill had snapped into the autumn air. The boys had been up before dawn to get ready so they could meet at the end of the road like John Lee had told them to. The plan was for them to arrive in Harmony by the end of the day. Malachi had carefully packed the packet of letters and Bible he'd taken from the bodies the day before. He'd given all of the other treasure to Lee. He had hoped for some recognition of a job well done, but Lee had taken the booty from him and dismissed him without a word.

Malachi tried to pull up the horse's head, but the plump beast was strong and stubborn and ignored his tugs. Idget sat behind him on the pony's fat rump. One of the braves noticed Malachi's attempts to rein up the horse and pointed it out, laughing and mimicking his effort.

"No use," Idget said. "Anyhow, it don't matter, when everyone else moves, he will too. Horses are like that. They move when they have to and follow the others."

"You should be the one in the saddle, not me," Malachi muttered. "You're much better with horses."

"I think it's important you learn about them," Idget said. "No telling when you'll need a horse's help."

They'd been waiting for nearly an hour and Lee still hadn't shown up. They'd been surprised by the Paiutes. Lee hadn't mentioned they'd be riding to Harmony with them. One wore a tall stovepipe hat that must have belonged to one of the men in the Fancher train. He kept sweeping it off and saying a clumsy, "How-dee-do!" and making the others laugh. Another, the man with the soft leather vest who Malachi recognized as their band's leader from the day before, fingered his silver buttons as he watched his friend. He was quieter than the others, but it was clear they respected him. Malachi envied their leisure and friendship.

As he watched them, he wondered at the Paiutes. They were tolerant of the Mormons who had taken over their land but they hated the emigrants who were just passing through. They called the emigrants the *Mericats*. Albert had said the Paiutes had accused the Fancher train of poisoning the stream they drank from, killing some of their own. Malachi thought back to the scene in the meadow two days earlier, the chaos, the killing, the blood, and the Paiutes' demands for loot from the train afterward. He wondered if these men knew they'd been blamed for the killings. Maybe they'd agreed to it in exchange for animals and riches from the train, which might explain why they were here now, ready to make good on what more would come their way.

Lee and two other men appeared on horseback. They cantered down the road and were followed by two wagons loaded with the goods taken from the train. And following the wagons, at least ten men spanned out on either side of the herd of cattle and horses, also from the train. There must have been at least two-hundred head of cattle, maybe more. Lee called out a Paiute greeting to the brave in the leather vest. Lee's voice was energetic, buoyant. The brave said nothing in return, only nodded sullenly. Lee looked at the man with an edge of a smile then shrugged and turned toward the boys.

"You settled on that plug of a horse?" He seemed in a good mood.

"Yessir," they said in unison. As Lee and the other two men rode by, the pony miraculously lifted his head and gathered his thick muscles to walk out. Lee was riding a palomino, a fine horse but nothing compared to the bay from the train. Haight had left the Hamblin ranch the evening before, and Idget had said Haight was riding the bay when he left. It meant some reckoning had occurred between Haight and Lee, with Haight gaining the upper hand.

"Okay, we're heading out," Lee called to everyone assembled. "We aim to be at Harmony by suppertime."

Malachi wrapped his legs around the pony's belly and Idget braided his fingers around Malachi's middle. He was embarrassed that he was a little afraid of the horse, but Idget seemed confident and Malachi took courage from that. His heart felt lighter with every mile between him and Mountain Meadows. The distance let him push away what he'd seen. Maybe he could forget about it, bury it, and move on. He didn't know the people who'd been killed. Maybe there was a good reason the men had done away with them, some reason he did not yet know. Not likely, countered an insistent voice inside his head. Not likely.

It was the first time he had left the region since he and Albert had moved there, nearly seven years earlier. The boys had come with their adoptive families who'd been sent from Salt Lake to settle the south. That started with Fort Harmony. Nearly two-hundred people had settled there. Later the Hamblins, Blanks, and other families moved further south, built the fort at Santa Clara, and established farms and ranches along the Magotsu Creek and Santa Clara River.

Although the families who had first settled the south had come from Salt Lake, many of those who lived there now had arrived in the last few years. They had come from far-flung places across an ocean, places Malachi could not imagine with names like Sussex, Blackmore, and Galway. Idget told Malachi that the two men who rode on either side of Lee now had come to Utah by handcart the year previous. They had walked with their families from the ocean to the east all the way to the Utah Territory, pushing a handcart holding all they possessed. When they arrived, they were greeted as the newest members of the Mormon church. They were welcomed, but they also had much to prove.

The men who flanked Lee discussed the people on the Fancher train, careful to keep their comments within the lines of the story that held the Paiutes responsible. The boys' pinto pony trundled easily now behind the men's horses, stopping now and again to snag a mouthful of grass, but never letting the men's horses get too far ahead. Malachi had knotted the reins at the pony's neck and let him do as he wished. Idget was right: the pony took his lead from his fellow beasts.

Malachi eyed the men riding next to Lee. He had heard that hundreds of people had died with the effort of rolling handcarts loaded with all their earthly belongings across the vast plains to Utah. But in spite of that, more continued to come. Brother Young thought it was a test of the commitment and strength of the newly converted to have them walk thousands of miles to their promised land. If that was true, Malachi thought as he watched the two men who had Lee's ear, it must mean that they were amongst the strongest people on earth, to make it all that way by foot. All manner of people had come—bookbinders, file hardeners, bakers, butchers, forgers, rope makers, doll makers, and wheelwrights.

Jonah Blank said the church needed them and their skills to help build and grow the southern settlements.

"Hussies they were, ever last one." A pale man with freckled skin and a shock of red hair talked to Lee as they rode. "Did you see the pox they had? After we rescued the children, I was afeard to touch their rotted bodies once they was stripped." His eyes slid over to Lee, appraising him briefly, then he shook his head and gathered a ball of spit that shot out of his mouth.

"These are facts and sightings we must always keep close to our hearts," Lee said calmly. "They were a wicked and pestilent people, intent on hurting us and all we hold dear. No telling, Brother Haslett, what evil they would have done if their lives had been spared by the Paiutes."

"Brother Lee, you took the words clean out of my mouth," Haslett replied. "I'm just glad the Paiutes took it on themselves to do away with 'em. Surely it was God's will. No telling what kind of mischief those devils from the wagon train would have gotten up to when Buchanan's troops invade."

"Yes," Lee said as he gathered his reins and clucked softly to his horse encouraging him into a smooth trot. "This event will be marked in history as one that turned the tide. It's what the church has readied us for. Perhaps that devil Buchanan in our nation's capital who wishes to snuff us out will leave us alone now that he and his minions see how God intervenes to take care of us, to preserve the Saints as his one true people."

Malachi wondered how the emigrants' sins had become so intertwined with the fear that the Mormons had of an invasion by the U.S. Army. Before the talk in the settlements had turned to the Fancher train, the invasion of Buchanan's army was all anybody talked about. There'd been a steady drumbeat of warnings from Salt Lake telling them to get ready to fight.

But there had also been another fear. Malachi had seen it in Jonah Blank, his wives, and their neighbors. They had come to live in terror of the leaders of their own church. Brigham Young was sending men to purify the settlements. They first showed up in Santa Clara some six months back, arriving on Sunday during the Sabbath service. Malachi had been waiting with Jonah Blank's wagon in front of the church, using his whip to flick off flies from the horses' backs. He was waiting for the service to end so he could drive Blank and his two wives back to their farm. Men in dark coats and hats thundered through the gates of the fort, their horses wet with heat and rimed with dust. Malachi watched people scurry out of the church doors, anxious to see what the commotion was. When they saw who had come, they grasped their children's hands and spoke to each other in raw whispers. He overheard them wring promises from their neighbors not to slurry each other. They made pacts to point fingers at those they did not care for as they hurried to their wagons, hoping to be overlooked.

Lee's two companions had fallen silent. Malachi wondered if they shared Lee's confidence or were simply afraid to offer a different opinion.

Albert claimed to have seen what the men sent by Salt Lake did to the people in the settlements. He told Malachi they rousted the sinners out of bed at night and took them to the meeting house to stand trial. He said they castrated a man for sleeping with his neighbor's wife and singed the tip of a woman's tongue for gossiping. One man had the palms of his hands branded for envying the property of another. Malachi had seen for himself boys publicly whipped for stealing a chicken and girls confined to a cellar for kissing a boy against her father's wishes.

Jonah Blank told his wives that Young's aim was to bring both discipline and redemption to his people, to destroy those who would try to destroy them, and preserve the Saints' way of life. Blank told his wives not to worry because they were all upright in righteousness. Still, the women fretted. Malachi wondered how this pain and this terror of punishment would lead the Saints to the God they said was so good. But he never uttered these thoughts aloud. Nor did anyone else.

Many of the settlers were recent converts. Malachi could see by their ragged and mended clothes that nearly all of them were poor. He saw their anxious smiles, the fear in their faces, and their desperation for everlasting life, but even more visible was their yearning for a plot of land they could call their own. It was what Brigham Young had promised. After Sunday service when the congregants gathered outside, Malachi watched the newcomers' faces screw up tight as they struggled to keep track of what they should say, what they should eat and drink, the company they should keep, and how they should act. There were so many rules. Malachi didn't bother with trying to follow them anymore. He had decided after Albert was sealed that the God who spoke to the Mormons had nothing to say to him. But the people newly arrived listened carefully as if to a distant voice, and they tried hard to obey.

As the men rode toward Harmony, Malachi wondered if that was the reason the Mormons had killed the people on the Fancher train: to show Young how much they wished to please him and how prepared they were to do whatever it took to defend this land they had come to call home.

Their party arrived at Fort Harmony late in the afternoon. The wide doors of the fort were flung open and the people of the town were taking their ease on Sunday after the morning service and mid-day meal. Lee and a handful of men on horseback led the way through the huge gate. They were followed by the two wagons filled to bursting with clothing, dishes, tools, guns, and dried goods all on display, all things that had been taken from the Fancher train. Some of the women craned their necks to see what was in the wagons then looked uncertainly at the Paiutes who brought up the rear. Others protectively gathered their children toward them, whispering softly into their ears. A few women, oblivious to the band of Paiute braves, waved gayly and smiled at the Mormon men.

"The Lord has preserved you and brought you back to us, Brother Lee!" one of the women called out. Lee tipped his hat at her as the parade of men, horses, and wagons circled the full perimeter of the fort. The braves whooped and hollered. Malachi kept his eye on Lee as he gallantly swept off his black hat and called out to the townspeople by name. Lee's riding companions and the other two men driving the wagons did the same, and the people greeted them like heroes, come home from a victorious battle.

Malachi and Idget bumped along on their pony who seemed to warm to the welcome they received and held his head a little higher. Malachi felt in this moment what it must be like to be adored. The women and children smiled and clapped as the boys rode by, following the men as they took two full circles around the fort. Some of the women fluttered their lace handkerchiefs at the men. The sound of loosely packed dishes, tools, and tin cups jostling back and forth in the wagons added to the feeling of celebration and gaiety. When they stopped, people gathered around the wagons to get a closer look at what treasures lay inside.

Haslett, Lee's red-haired companion, called out for silence. "Brother Lee wishes to speak!"

Lee dismounted. A raven-haired boy scurried up to Lee carrying a squat wide stool for him. Lee stepped onto it. He handed his hat to the waiting boy and smoothed back his hair.

"My dear people of Harmony!" Lee began. His voice was deep and sure. "My fellow Saints." His hands gripped the lapels of his long black coat and he began to sway slightly. "We went to aid our enemy in Mountain Meadows. As you know, these were the very same infidels as had killed the boy in one of our northern settlements. These were the same devils as had poisoned our streams and, on account of that, killed many of our Lamanite brethren, those that are the beloved family members of the Paiutes that you see with us today. These were the same evil-doers who came into our midst, asking for our help, our grain, our chickens, our tools, and at the same time the very ones who blasphemed our leaders, our dear Joseph Smith!"

"Amen!" the crowd cried out.

"Who had a hand in the murder of and spoke ill of our beloved deceased saint, Parley Pratt!" Lee shouted.

"Amen!" the crowd shouted again.

"And who denigrated and dirtied the name of our own dear living leader, Brigham Young!"

"Praise be to God, praise be to Brother Brigham!" Some men covered their hearts with their hats and a few of the women had tears streaming down their faces.

"We found a sorry state of affairs in Mountain Meadows when we arrived, and found we were too late to save our enemies, too late to show mercy to the very ones who had wronged us." The crowed quieted and pressed toward him.

"The Paiutes, savages that they are, had gone ahead and slaughtered the lot of those that had done them wrong, but keep in mind, those that had done *us* wrong too, dear brothers and sisters."

Malachi glanced at the braves. They were still mounted on their horses and most were slumped over their ponies' necks, oblivious to what Lee was saying. But the tall one with the broad chest wearing the leather vest with silver buttons watched Lee and listened intently.

"There weren't no saving them, the evil doers who we were prepared to help in spite of all the harm they had done to us," Lee said. He paused, gazing out over the crowd. Tears coursed down his face and created pinkish lines on his dust-covered skin. "All was gone and done with by the time we had arrived." He paused and brought out a large kerchief to wipe his forehead and eyes. Many of the women pulled out hankies from their dress sleeves and delicately dabbed at trickles of tears that ran down their faces. Lee looked at them and smiled.

"But we did what we could to save the innocents. Sixteen children, too young to know the wicked ways of their elders, will be adopted out to goodly Saint homes."

At this, Malachi heard a swell of whispered exchanges between the people that surrounded him. Two women standing nearby leaned toward each other.

"Such good fortune!" One woman said as she took her companion's hand. "The little ones were saved. Praise be to God and God bless Brother Lee!"

Idget nudged Malachi in the side. "See? Told you they love him here," he whispered. Malachi turned to look at him and smiled. Idget was right. Lee was clearly adored by the people who had gathered around him. He could see it in their faces as they looked up at him, some of them holding their small children aloft so they could see Lee standing on the stool that raised him just over the crowd.

"Some of these young ones will be arriving here in Harmony in the next few days," Lee continued. "I know there are those of you who are pining to care for a child of your own and to raise him in the righteous ways of our Lord and our church.

"I want to be both fair and wise in placing these young souls with you," Lee said. "So those who wish to be considered should petition me in the next day and prove your worthiness, your commitment to tenderly care for these young babes."

The women standing next to Malachi and Idget began to talk to each other again.

"Rebecca, you and William could make your plea to Brother Lee! It could be God's answer to your prayers."

The woman called Rebecca smoothed her skirts and she replied, "I will consult my husband in all things."

"Of course, you must," her friend agreed. "But truly, this is a sign from God."

CHAPTER 6

SEPTEMBER 14

The day after the boys arrived at Lee's farm, Isaac Haight and several men rode into the sprawling compound. Malachi and Idget were outside cleaning and sorting tack. Lee was with them, attentively working on a finely tooled bridle that made up his extensive collection of bridles and saddles, occasionally barking out some instruction to the boys. As Malachi rubbed the silver fitting of the bridle, he thought about how much the Lee family had. Their house was huge and looked as though it had recently been made bigger. It was banked with a spacious garden lined with fruit trees. There was a large barn surrounded by several other outbuildings, including a couple of bunkhouses that Lee's oldest sons slept in. Sleek cattle dotted the extensive fenced pastures. The emigrants' stock had been added to Lee's own. Lee had said the stock would be divided amongst the families in Harmony, but the day before, he'd told the men driving the cattle and horses to take them to his farm, bypassing the pastures at Fort Harmony.

Lee and the boys sat on squat logs that circled a fire pit, sheltered from the sun by a huge cottonwood. The autumn days had turned warm again, and the shade of the tree was soothing and welcome. Haslett, the red-haired man who had ridden by Lee's side on the way to Harmony, was with Haight. Idget had told Malachi that Rebecca, the woman who had stood next to the boys at the fort and talked to her friend about adopting one of the children from the train, was married to Haslett. There were two other men Malachi didn't recognize.

Surprise registered on Lee's face when he saw Haslett, but the look quickly faded as he rose and strode over to greet the men. On the way, he dropped the bridle he'd been working on into Idget's lap without a glance.

"How do, Brother Lee," Haight said.

"What brings you back to us so soon?" Lee asked. He was smiling, but his voice was tight. "Thought you'd bring the little ones with you here to us."

"Brought the children, of course, like we'd planned," Haight said as he tossed the reins lightly over his horse's neck and dismounted. Lee motioned for Idget, and the boy scurried over to take the reins of Haight's animal. He led the horse to the nearby corral. The others corralled their own horses and returned after their animals were situated. Lee and Haight walked over to the fire circle. Lee waved Malachi away from his seat to make room for the men. Malachi gathered the tack he'd been working on, but since Lee hadn't told him to leave, he moved to sit at the base of the cottonwood within earshot of the men. After stabling Haight's horse, Idget joined Malachi, and the boys resumed cleaning the bridles.

"I'd reckoned for the children to come here, to me," Lee said. "I've told the families to wait for my decision, and they're looking for me to parcel 'em out."

"I've saved you the trouble," Haight said, leaning back and hitching his thumbs over his vest pockets. "No need to agitate yourself about matters such as these."

"I am in no agitated state of mind," Lee said. His lips pulled back into a smile that didn't reach the rest of his face. "I simply want to receive what is mine to rightfully mete out. I had planned to divide these children amongst families in my community."

Haslett, who stood near Lee, shifted and kept his eyes on the ground.

"I've already seen to the children," Haight said in his odd, fluting voice.

Malachi wondered if Haight had a heartbeat. He looked so calm he could be dead.

"What's that?" Lee asked, frowning. "What's that you've seen to?"

"Two of the children are with William Haslett here," Haight said. "They're in safe-keeping with him and his wife, Rebecca. As you know our Father has not blessed them with any young ones. The others are in good homes too." Haight's voice carried through his nose like the bellows of a weak-lunged organ.

"You know how much we've prayed for children of our own, Brother Lee," Haslett said. His pale freckled skin had gone whiter and his mouth bunched with worry. He twisted the corner of his jacket as he looked at Lee. "Brother Haight here was sent to us on a mission of mercy, real mercy when he decided to bestow these little ones on us to raise as our own."

There was a long silence between the men. The jingling of the bridles filled the air as Malachi and Idget worked. Malachi glanced up. Lee had leveled his gaze on Haslett, who seemed to have shrunk back into himself.

"There's another thing," Haight said, breaking the silence. The men who had come with him all shifted in their stances and let out a collective breath.

"There's more?" Lee asked, turning to look at him.

"We've made a decision that it's you who needs to go to Governor Young and tell him what happened in Mountain Meadows."

Malachi's ears sharpened and he stopped working on the bridle. He could feel Idget's gaze on him, but he ignored it.

"And how did you come to this?" Lee asked. His voice sounded bland, unconcerned, but Malachi sensed deception in it. "I already told Dame I was not the best one for that task. Too much to attend to here."

"Salt Lake sent a letter," Haight said. "It arrived by messenger yesterday."

Lee leaned forward, folding his hands in front of him.

"What did it say?" Lee asked. "Something unexpected?"

"You know how Brother Young can be…" Haight paused. "He can run up one side and down the other and can be so fast and dexterous in his thinking that it's sometimes puzzling to divine his meaning."

"To those not familiar with his ways," Lee said, raising his eyebrows.

Haight shook his head and shrugged. "How ever that may be, *this* letter calls for us to mind the doings at the meadows," he said patting his pocket.

"Which we well did," Lee declared.

Haight glanced briefly at Malachi and Idget then dipped his hand into his breast pocket.

"Here, it's best for you to read it your own self," he said as he handed the letter to Lee. It was written on a piece of dirty beige paper that had been folded and refolded, like it had been read many times over.

Lee scanned the letter then calmly refolded it and slipped it into his pants pocket. He looked at Haight. "You think this letter bears evidence of some shift in his thinking, from where he was?"

"I do, Brother Lee," Haight said. "And it needs be remedied by you. You have to gain by it yourself, and he will listen to you and understand that we acted in good faith on what he'd asked of us earlier, even though now it seems some change has overcome him."

Malachi listened intently, wishing Lee would hint at what the letter said. What had Young asked of them earlier? Had he asked the men to kill the people on the Fancher train? The stirring up of the Mormon settlements over the past year had been so steady, so complete, it was hard to imagine Young had asked the men from the southern settlements to help the Fancher train in any way. But perhaps he had not instructed them to go as far as they had, or perhaps he had simply shifted his thinking. Jonah Blank had declared time and time again that Brigham Young was a man of surprises, with an agile mind that was both intelligent and changeable. Because of that, he was simultaneously admired and feared.

"And what if I was to say no?" Lee said, calmly eyeing Haight. "What if I was to say it was up to you and Dame to tell Brother Young what happened?"

Haight locked eyes with Lee. His mouth quirked up into a lop-sided grin.

"I would say there's little I could do to prevent Brother Dame and Governor Young from discovering a piece of business that you and I had long ago agreed to forget."

Lee's features sharpened, like a dog assessing a rival. A minute passed as the two men fixed their eyes on each other.

"Then it is decided," Lee said finally.

"It is decided," Haight said.

"I am Brother Young's dear son," Lee said. A note of buoyancy sprang into his voice.

"You are," Haight agreed. "It is known how much he loves you and cares for you."

Lee vigorously rubbed his hands back and forth. He suddenly leaned back and laughed. "Yes, and the beloved son is likely to have some gifts bestowed on him," he said, winking broadly at the other men who stood still, their shoulders sloped in anxious expectation.

✳ ✳ ✳

That night, the boys slept side-by-side in twin cots. The small room they had been given was just off the kitchen of the main house. Idget dropped off to sleep almost immediately, but Malachi stirred restlessly, the rough wool blanket twisting around his legs. He never much liked sleeping inside and could not get an anchor in sleep. An hour or so after they had gone to bed, he heard the thud of footsteps on the floor overhead. His heart beat anxiously as he listened to doors open and close, followed by the lurch of bedsprings and groans of ecstasy that dissolved into quiet before the sequence all began anew. He realized Lee was making the rounds to the rooms of his wives.

The house teemed with lust and agitation, keeping Malachi even further from sleep as the sounds reverberated through the floor above. He tried at first to bury his head beneath his blankets to muffle the din, then slowly withdrew, his attention locking on the sounds of Lee perambulating from bed to bed, saturating Malachi's imagination. He felt himself grow hard and found release again and again with his own hand as he absorbed the creaks and moans overhead; he imagined burying himself between the soft, pliant legs of woman after woman, as if he and Lee were one. The echoes of lovemaking engulfed him as Lee continued to move relentlessly from room to room, settling into stillness only when dawn began to creep above the steep hills that surrounded the farm.

CHAPTER 7

SEPTEMBER 15

Lee presided over the huge dining room table like a lord. This morning he was happy and expansive. Malachi, who sat at the table's far end with Idget, thought that whatever demons the man had gone to bed with had fled during the night. Lee was smiling and joking with those who seemed to love him most, his many wives and dozens of children. It was a huge lot, so large that they had to eat their meals in shifts. According to Idget, this wasn't even the whole family. Another set of wives and children resided at Fort Harmony.

Because they had work to do, Idget and Malachi were in the earliest group and surrounded mostly by younger children. Wives scurried around the tables serving food. As the children ate, the women scolded them, took gentle swipes at their heads, and cleaned up the small messes the youngest ones made, all in a seamless, flowing stream of movement. Agatha, the oldest of the wives and the one who Idget had said had been with Lee the longest, sat at her husband's side and presided over the women, directing their activity and dominating the care of the house. She was a tidy, well-ordered presence in the midst of the chaotic mass of activity.

Malachi and Idget were in the middle of a row of children, spanning in age from toddlers to a couple who were in their early teens. As he ate his oatmeal, Malachi wondered what they'd made of the sounds of Lee and his wives coupling last night. Maybe they were used to it. Idget and Malachi said nothing as they kept their mouths close to their bowls and shoveled in as much food as the wives would serve them.

It was a new experience for him to be among such a large family. Jonah Blank's offspring were confined to a few girls, and when Malachi had eaten at the Blank's house, Blank had ordered him to be fed separately. "Family meals is for family," Blank said to his wives.

He'd also only ever slept with the sheep during the warm season and in the barn when winter settled in. But Lee drew no such distinctions. He clearly considered both boys lesser creatures than his own children and didn't let them forget their place, but he also showed an easy generosity and openness toward them in other ways. They slept in Lee's rambling house and Lee seemed to consider it natural that they should be under his roof.

"Malachi!" Lee called from the far end of the table.

All chatter stopped and heads swiveled toward the two boys. Malachi had never had so many people looking at him at once. Blue eyes, brown eyes, hazel eyes stared at him, and it made him so nervous he dropped his spoon on the floor. He leaned down to grab it from under the table, but a girl who sat across from him placed her foot on the spoon and slid it out of his reach. He tried to rise up but bumped his head. His fumbling generated a fine titter of laughter from the children at the boys' end of the table. The girl who'd captured his spoon was near his own age and smiled at him. He thought of last night, and a whip-chord of desire moved through him. He blushed in spite of himself.

"Boy!" Lee called to him again.

Idget jostled his arm and whispered, "Answer him!"

"Sir?" Malachi bleated.

"You having some trouble?" Lee said, leaning back in his chair.

"No, sir," Malachi stammered. He glanced at the girl. Her gaze was bent toward the table, but he could tell she was smiling.

"Just dropped my spoon is all."

The girl looked up and graced him with a crooked grin.

"It's time you got to work this morning," Lee said as he shoved himself away from the table. "I want you should finish cleaning the rest of that tack you worked on yesterday, then we'll have you muck out the stables. Get them ready for winter."

"Yes, sir," Malachi said, not realizing that this was their cue to leave. Idget tapped him on his arm and motioned toward the door. Malachi stood to follow but took a last furtive look at the girl who'd taken his spoon. Her hair was the color of dark honey and plaited around her head. Her eyes were a deep blue and she had a light scatter of freckles across her nose. Both cheeks were tinged with pink. She glanced at him then turned away.

Idget saw the exchange between them and tugged at his coat. "Time to go," he said.

As the boys turned to leave the table, a din of chatter rose behind them.

"They're having one of their family meetings," Idget explained once they'd got outside.

"What's that?" Malachi asked, craning his neck to look through the dining room window.

"Dunno exactly," he said scratching his nose. "Mostly, I think Father Lee talks about what needs to get done and they finish with a prayer."

"Do you ever get to stay?"

"No," he said. "I'm not part of it."

They walked out to the barn in silence and gathered the remaining halters and bridles that needed to be soaped and polished.

"Do you ever want to be part of it?" Malachi asked when they reached the barn. "The family I mean?"

Since it was a fine day, they brought the tack behind the barn and sat, their backs up against the sun-warmed wood of the barn's weathered exterior. By the time they'd settled into work, Idget still hadn't answered him. The other boy focused on cleaning the silver grommets of the bridle he held. Then he looked up, his gaze arcing out over the field. "Maybe, sometime. I wanted to at first, but not so much now."

"Why not now?" Malachi asked.

Idget shrugged then blew on the silver, polishing it again. "I don't know." He looked at Malachi. "Sometimes I wished for someone to care for me, but who would? I know I'm not like everyone else, even you. I can't talk so good and people think I'm not right here," he said. His thick finger tapped the side of his head.

Malachi thought about protesting this last bit, but stayed silent. He felt for Idget. He could still remember what it was like to belong, the sweetness of being part of a family, a tribe. Had he been with them now and seen the kind of trouble he had seen, he would have known where to go, where to seek solace and protection. He wondered if Idget had ever had anyone who had loved him.

Idget pulled his knees toward his chest and let the bridle rest on top of them. "I know something," he said, looking at Malachi. A sly and mischievous look crept into his face and hovered there.

Malachi glanced up and grinned. "I know you do," he said. "You've got all sorts of stuff inside that head of yours."

"Not that way." He shook his head and let the bridle slide off his legs to the ground. Impatiently, he rubbed the slow drip of saliva that dangled from his chin and held Malachi's eyes.

"What do you mean?" Malachi asked. His chest tightened. "What is it you know?"

"I know who it was that really kilt those emigrants," Idget said slowly.

He looked down and fiddled with the leather strap of the bridle. Black rinds of dirt edged each of his fingernails.

Malachi caught his breath. Fear, which had receded only slightly in the last few days of work and routine at the Lee farm, made a fierce comeback. It filled his chest with pressure, his mind with memories of hair flying as the woman ran toward him, her pleas for help, her little boy's gaping, bloody chest.

"It was the Paiute," Malachi insisted. "I told you that."

"Weren't," Idget said, shaking his head as he picked up the bridle again and examined it, scowling. He opened his mouth wide and blew a puff of breath on the silver grommet, rubbing off the cloudy residue.

"So, who was it?" Malachi asked. He watched Idget nervously. He knew how the boy got when someone doubted him, agitated and sometimes explosive. Besides, he thought, might as well know what he knows.

"Don't know ever-one, but Albert was with them," Idget said.

Malachi hesitated.

"Did Albert tell you this?" he asked. He could hear Albert, see him, bored from watching the sheep, edgy and out of control, compelled to entertain himself and spill what he knew in order to brag up his role in the killings, trying to impress Idget.

"Didn't have to," he said. "I heard it directly. That's how I know it's true."

"When?" Malachi asked.

"The day Father Lee took you with him to the meadows," he replied. "After you left, Oscar Hamblin come to the pasture looking for Albert."

"What did he want of him?" Malachi asked.

"Dunno exactly," Idget shrugged. "Just seemed to need to talk to him. I was down in the swale, keeping the sheep out of the wind. They couldn't see me, didn't know I was so close by."

Malachi thought again of what Lee had said about Albert to Haight and Dame. Maybe they'd sent Jacob Hamblin's brother, Oscar, to make sure of Albert: test him and size him up to the task of keeping his mouth shut. After all was said and done, even if Jacob Hamblin had sealed Albert to the family, Albert was still an Indian, not one of them.

He glanced at the circle of wet that darkened Idget's collar and waited for him to talk.

"Albert was talking up what he done to two girls from the train."

Malachi remembered the girls, their long tendrils of hair flowing behind them as they fled the meadow, seeking safety. He should have tried to protect them, he thought as he rubbed the waxy soap into the bridle's rusty-colored leather, wishing he could erase the memory.

"But Oscar Hamblin didn't want to talk about that, told Albert to stop," Idget said, shifting a little. "He started crying."

"What do you mean? Albert?" He was trying to imagine Albert crying. He'd never seen it.

"No, it was Oscar Hamblin doing the crying," he said and ducked his head. "He said they shouldn't a done it."

"Done what?" His tongue was dry, hardtack at the roof of his mouth. He tried to swallow but couldn't.

"He said they killed those people," Idget said. "He was sobbing and carrying on 'til Albert finally told him to shut it. But he didn't, he kept at it. Said those children would know and that they might say something. Then Albert said if the children said anything, they'd get rid of 'em. But then Oscar whacked him hard, I heard it because Albert yelped like one of the dogs and Oscar told Albert he wasn't to hurt those kids, wasn't to touch a hair on them."

"Did he say why they did it?" Malachi asked. His words felt strangled, like his throat was packed with sawdust.

"No, only told Albert that Brother Young needed to make damn sure the Paiutes took the blame and that he and Albert had to work on Jacob Hamblin, make sure he understood so that he'd help mount the story of the Paiutes."

Malachi looked at him. Now they both knew the truth.

"I wonder if anyone will ask us what happened," Idget said. His round black eyes locked on Malachi's.

"Why would they?" Malachi replied. The boy's gaze unnerved him. It was like Idget could see into his mind. "We're nobody. We're just the Indian boys that tend the sheep, do the chores."

"But, if someone does," Idget insisted. "If someone does ask, should we say? Should we say what we know?"

"You listen to me." Malachi reached over and grasped Idget's muscular arm. He felt the boy's warm flesh tense beneath his fingers. Idget didn't like being touched, but Malachi didn't care. He had to make him understand. "You can't tell anyone what you know, ever. We talk only to each other of it, but no one else. You promise me?"

Idget pulled away from his grip. "But what if they ask me, what if Father Lee asks me what I know?"

"I heard him," Malachi said. "I heard him talking to Haight and Dame at the bunkhouse, the night it happened. They'll kill us, do away with us if they find out we know what really happened. You got to promise me you won't say anything."

"Why didn't you tell me?" Idget searched his face. Then he pulled his chin back a little, like he was trying to bring Malachi into focus. "You saw it, didn't you?"

Malachi held his gaze. He nodded slightly and opened his mouth to speak, but only a dry sound came out as he pulled in his breath. He pressed his lips together and swallowed.

Idget's eyes rested gently on his face.

Malachi looked at him.

"I can't," he said. It was all he could say. He couldn't speak about it, not now, not yet while the blood and the screams and the agony of those who had died were so fresh in him still.

"Never mind," Idget said. "I promise."

CHAPTER 8

SEPTEMBER 20

The days following Haight's visit were consumed with preparations for John Lee's journey to Salt Lake City to see Brigham Young. The entire household was devoted to helping him get ready. Even the smallest children were put to work polishing his boots and folding his white handkerchiefs so that Agatha could neatly pack them in his saddlebags. The morning Lee was to leave, as Malachi and Idget were washing up at the outdoor pump before the mid-day meal, the girl with the honey-colored hair who had taken Malachi's spoon from him, emerged from the back door of the house and walked toward them.

Malachi watched her as she approached. He guessed she was about his age, maybe a year older. She was tall and moved with confidence. As she walked, her eyes scanned the horizon and her chin tilted up a little as though she wanted to see before being seen. Her hair shone in the morning sun. Pieces of it had escaped the braid she wore and she pushed the strands back behind her ears as she approached.

"If you boys are all done washing up here, I'm supposed to tell you you're wanted in the house," she said. She'd folded her arms lightly in front of her, and she had that smile again, hovering on her lips as though she was about to laugh but was still thinking on it. Both boys quickly dried their hands on a rough towel that hung by the water bucket, and Malachi slicked back his thick bangs that wanted to fall down his forehead. He hoped the girl would talk to him, but she ignored him and kept up a steady chatter with Idget as the three walked alongside each other to the house. As they walked, Malachi wondered why they were being summoned. They hadn't seen Lee for the past two days. He didn't know why the man was so keen to see them now, just as he was getting ready to leave. The girl left them for the kitchen and motioned the boys toward the dining room. Malachi worried as she walked away from them. Somehow having her near made him feel all would be well.

When the boys arrived, Lee was sitting with two of his wives. Agatha, who sat in her usual spot at Lee's right, dismissed the handful of women and girls who were busy setting the table to get ready for dinner. She ordered them to go into the kitchen and close the door. The aroma of food and comforting sounds of women's voices did little to ease the clench in Malachi's gut.

Lee looked up when the boys entered the room. Impatiently, he motioned them to come to the far end of the room where he sat with Agatha and another woman, who Malachi had learned was Rachel, Agatha's younger sister and another of Lee's many wives. One of Rachel's roles, it seemed, was to keep the family journal. She sat with paper and a pot of ink nearby, her head bent slightly over the table as she dipped the nib of her pen in the ink and carefully wrote something on the paper in front of her. As the boys made their way toward them, she put down the pen and laid her hands in her lap.

Malachi wondered if Lee had told the women the truth of what had occurred at Mountain Meadows, and whether Rachel Lee had entered all that had occurred into the journal splayed out in front of her. Did Lee's warning to the men the day of the massacre not apply to him? Perhaps even Lee would have to unburden himself to someone. Lee and the two women stopped talking as the boys approached. Malachi's walking stick thudded along the wood floor.

"You boys know this is my household," Lee said when they reached him. "And you know that I am to know all that goes on in it."

Malachi trembled inwardly and wondered if the girl who'd taken his spoon had overheard their conversation about Mountain Meadows two days earlier. Even though they hadn't spoken of it since, perhaps she had heard them and told Lee.

"Yes, sir," they said in unison. They looked at the floor. The floorboards were wide-plank pine, honey-stained and polished clean.

"And in my household," Lee continued. "I see all that is going on."

Malachi was certain now that someone had overheard them. He raised his head slightly and met Agatha's eyes. They were a dry shade of blue and revealed nothing. Rachel was still and kept her gaze on the paper in front of her.

"I see everything that comes into this house and everything that goes out," Lee said. "For it all belongs to me."

The boys were silent. Malachi was uncertain if he should agree with a point so evidently obvious. Then Lee nodded at Rachel, and she reached over to the chair on her right and brought up the Bible and the packet of letters that Malachi had secreted away in his satchel. Air rushed through his ears and he gripped his walking stick, hoping his knees wouldn't buckle out from under him. He cursed himself for the stupidity of hanging on to these things, these insignificant objects.

"Those," he stammered. "Those belong to me."

"Nothing belongs to you," Lee said. "I thought I made that clear."

"I mean, those were in my satchel," he said, pointing to the Bible and the letters. His finger felt limp and out of place. He dropped his hand to his side. "I took them that day you had me searching the bodies. That day…" His voice trailed off.

Idget's head was bowed and Malachi watched him jump as Lee slapped his big hand on the table in front of him.

"You betrayed me, boy!" he roared.

Malachi looked up and realized Lee's gaze was directed at Idget. He stepped in front of Idget and locked eyes with Lee.

"Idget didn't know nothing about those things," he said. "He had nothing to do with them."

"What are you playing at?" Lee asked, his eyes leveling on Malachi, his voice suddenly quiet, dangerous.

"Nothing, sir," Malachi said. His heart hammered against his chest. He was certain Lee could see the pulse of fear fluttering underneath his shirt. "These were just things that I put away and didn't think you'd want. Please, Idget didn't know anything about them."

"Look at him," Lee said, smiling widely. "He's pissed himself."

A look of disgust flitted across Agatha's face and she pursed her lips and let out a pouf of air. The crotch of Idget's pants was soaked, and urine spattered and puddled on the immaculate pine floor. Rachel stared steadily at the table in front of her, as though she did not trust herself to look at the boys.

"I'll help get him cleaned up, sir," Malachi said, thinking this was the end of it.

"You'll not," Lee replied. "He's to wear those soiled pants the day long as a reminder of the traitor he is."

Rachel shifted in her chair and cleared her throat as if to say something. Lee flashed her a quick look, challenging her to defy him. She shook her head slightly but kept quiet.

"And what of him?" Agatha asked, jutting her chin toward Malachi.

"I will think on it," Lee said.

Jonah Blank would have beat him and it would have come quickly, brutally. Waiting for it, imagining what it would be was more terrifying in its way. But he met Lee's gaze.

"If you're done with us, sir, we'll just go back and finish our chores," he said, glad his voice held steady.

That ignited Lee. He leapt out of his chair, tipping it over. Agatha crouched toward the table as Lee flew past her and grabbed Malachi by the shoulders. He threw him to the floor and Malachi's head made a sharp smack as he landed. The impact made him bite his tongue and he tasted blood inside his mouth. When Lee reached him again, he picked him up and slammed his dangling body against the wall, pinning him there. Malachi's face was parallel to Lee's. The man's breath was hot and smelled of the sausage he'd eaten for breakfast. Sleep crusted at the corner of his right eye.

"I will tell you, boy, when I am done with you, and I tell you now if I ever find you sneaking around like this again, hiding things from me, hiding what you know or what you have, I will make you wish you'd never lived. You follow me?"

Malachi's words were swallowed by the effort of catching his breath. He felt a slow drip of spit or blood dribbling out the side of his mouth.

"Yes, sir," he gasped. Lee slapped him hard against his face then dropped him to the floor where he lay in a crumpled heap while Lee took out a large white kerchief from his pocket and wiped Malachi's blood from his hands. Once done, he handed the soiled handkerchief to Agatha who delicately set it to one side.

"You boys stink of fear and piss," Lee said. His back was to them. "You'll not eat with this household today or the next, and you'll sleep in the barn until I say you can come back to the house. Now take your stench and yourselves out of my sight."

Idget had picked up Malachi's walking stick and made his way over to him. He reached around his chest and pulled him up. Idget handed him his stick then positioned himself on the other side, offering Malachi his arm as they made their way out of the room. As they were leaving, Malachi heard Lee say, "I want you to watch that boy careful while I'm in Salt Lake. He's not to be allowed back in the house until I return. I'll sort out what to do with him then."

Idget led Malachi outside.

"You okay?" Idget asked, tentatively letting go of his arm.

Malachi staggered to the side. His head ached and was spinning.

"Let's get you to the barn," Idget said. He reached out to grab Malachi's arm before guiding him to the barn and up the stairs to the loft. In a corner, someone had arranged straw bales to form a small, pleasant alcove. A couple of wool blankets were folded neatly on the floor and beside them a kerosene lamp and the Book of Mormon sat on top of a wooden crate. Malachi wondered who'd done it, or if it was always like this, always ready for whomever Lee decided to ban from the house. Idget carefully spread out the blankets on the floor and told Malachi to lie down.

"I'll go get you some water and something for your face to help with the swelling," he said. Then he disappeared down the stairs.

Malachi stared up at the rafters in the barn. His face throbbed with pain, and when he reached around to feel the back of his head, he felt a knot where it had hit the floor. It wasn't the worst beating he'd ever taken, but he hoped it would be the last from Lee. He remembered Idget's face as he'd watched Lee fulminating. He had been terrified. Malachi wondered how little it would take for Idget to reveal everything he knew. He shifted, trying to find a position that didn't hurt.

Sounds of John Lee making his departure to Salt Lake filtered up from the yard to the hayloft. He would be gone for at least a week. He knew Lee had not trusted him, but the welcome he'd received here, eating with the family, sleeping under the same roof, being part of their daily routine had lulled him into thinking he might be able to bury and forget the horrific events at Mountain Meadows. He'd even thought briefly about the possibility that Lee would buy him from Blank. It had happened before. Then he and Idget could live as brothers. They would have each other. But now all that seemed like a piece of foolishness. He should have known better than to keep the Bible and the letters. What possible use had he hoped for them? He could barely even read, and the idea of mailing the letters now seemed foolish. He had given Lee a reason to watch his every move.

He listened as Lee's children and wives called out their goodbyes. The sound of his horse's gallop mounted and faded in the distance. Then one of the wives called the children in for dinner. Their voices littered the air as they entered the house for their mid-day meal. Although he fought it, tears began to seep down Malachi's cheeks and wet his swollen, bloodied lips. He scrubbed his tears away with the back of his hand. He wondered where Idget was. It wouldn't do for Idget to see him crying.

He wished he were back in the pasture with the sheep, sleeping under the stars with the warm comfort of the dogs beside him. At least when he cared for the sheep, he would have been left mostly alone. Here, under the watchful eyes of Lee and his endless family, Malachi worried what others would overhear or what Idget might reveal about the dreadful secret they now shared. He closed his eyes and drifted into a half-sleep as images from the day at Mountain Meadows flooded him. He came to with a start when he heard footsteps.

"Malachi?" A girl's voice called to him. "Malachi, that's your name, right?"

He rolled over and tried to push himself up. His head throbbed with pain and he dropped back to the blanket, sick with dizziness. It was the girl.

"What are you doing here?" he asked, his voice sharper than he intended. He immediately wished he could take it back.

But she didn't seem fazed by him. She stood over him, looking at him with an equal measure of curiosity and friendliness.

"Mother told me to bring you some hot soup," she said holding out a large covered bowl for him to see.

He glanced at it. He was hungry, and the aroma of the soup made him forget his pain.

"Where's Idget?" he asked.

She waved a hand. "Oh, he's getting himself cleaned up and fed is all," she said. Her voice was light, warm. She moved toward him, with the covered bowl of soup in both hands. Her cheeks were slightly flushed and the scant dusting of freckles sprinkled across her face and nose stood out.

"I thought we was not to eat," he mumbled. He was confused. John Lee's orders were clearly not being followed.

"Father Lee's gone a lot." She shrugged. "Lots of business and doings in Salt Lake. Mostly the mothers manage things around here."

She unrolled a heavy napkin to reveal a large silver spoon and set down both napkin and spoon by the soup bowl on the wooden crate. Then she brought out a thick slice of buttered bread from her apron pocket.

"Here," she said handing him the bread. "You eat."

He managed to prop himself up against a bale and ate slowly, gently sucking the rich broth through his swollen lips. He tore off small bits of bread to soak up the broth and ate them as well. Every once in a while, he looked up at the girl who watched him steadily while he ate. He could smell her scent, clean like morning air. He felt he might be dreaming.

"My name is Priscilla," she said.

He looked briefly at her and smiled as best he could through his stiff, sore lips.

"How do," he said, wiping his hand along the length of his thigh before holding it out to her.

She smiled and gently took the end of his fingers to shake his hand. Her fingers were warm and smooth. He noticed one of her front teeth overlapped the other when she smiled.

"Mother Rachel says you're smart," she said.

This revelation surprised him. Why should her mother be saying such a thing? He'd never thought of himself as smart or stupid, for that matter.

"She says on account of that, you're to be watched," she continued, smiling. "Closely."

He looked at her, and he chewed his bread slowly, uncertain what to make of her.

"So, I told Mother I would make it my task to be your minder while Father is in Salt Lake." She stood and smoothed out the folds from her apron.

He swallowed one of his soggy lumps of bread and felt a warm tumble in his stomach. Her revelation should have worried him; instead, it pleased him.

"What does that mean?" he asked. His heart hammered with anticipation.

"Oh, just that I'll bring you soup and such until those nasty bruises Father gave you are nearly healed," she said smiling.

"Are Idget and me to come back to sleep in the house?" he asked.

She leaned down to retrieve the empty soup bowl, spoon, and napkin from the crate. He stole a glance at the bare white skin of her neck as she gathered up the spoon and empty bowl.

"No," she said firmly. She stood up straight and her smile faded. "It's not like we can do anything we want." She stopped, looking at him, evaluating him. "Life here is good. We have more than most families on account of Father's position in the church. Plus, he's a favorite of Brother Young and that helps us all."

He waited, saying nothing. Was she telling him to go along, to try to please Lee because things would be good for him if he did?

"But you best watch yourself. A few of the wives are tattlers, so others have to work around them. It was them, the tattlers, that found your satchel and what was in it," she said. "Take care what you say and what you do."

"Who do I watch out for, then?"

She was silent for a minute, considering. She took a few steps toward him.

"It's mostly Polly and Lavinia," she said. "They're not the favorites, so they're always looking for ways to curry favor, better their standing, give Father Lee little bits of this and that to please him. They've got ambitions for themselves, their children, hoping for their own house one day, which would please us all just fine. Get 'em out of our hair."

He wanted to ask more questions, but the sound of a horse galloping into the yard pulled her over to the loft door where she looked out. She frowned and shook her head before turning back to him.

"I've got to go. You get some rest. Sleep'll do you good."

"Who's come?"

She paused and looked back out the loft door and frowned.

"It's William Haslett," she said. "I best get down to the house. I'll come back with your supper later."

Malachi raised himself up, craning to see out the loft door. His head felt like it would split open.

"What do you think he wants?" he asked, suddenly worried that Lee had told Haslett to come fetch him.

"Wants?" She looked at him and smiled stiffly. "It's me he wants. He's asked Father to marry me when I turn sixteen."

"When's that?" Malachi croaked, embarrassed at the crack in his voice.

"Best go," she said.

She disappeared and in the next instant he heard Haslett calling out to her. Malachi crawled over to the loft door to peer out. Priscilla was standing in front of Haslett, her head bowed, looking at the ground. He was talking to her, stroking her cheek. Then he put his finger and thumb underneath her chin and lifted it so that she had to gaze at him. Haslett leaned down to kiss her full on the lips. Jealousy unfurled inside Malachi. He hated Haslett.

"You feeling better?"

He turned. Idget stood at the top of the loft stairs. He had on fresh clothes and his thick hair was wet and slicked back. He walked over to Malachi and looked briefly out into the yard then back at the boy.

"You best stay in your bed," he said. "Let yourself rest some."

He did feel like the barn was still spinning out from under him. He leaned hard on Idget's arm and they made their way back to the cell of bales.

"She said she'd bring me my supper," Malachi said as Idget helped him down to his makeshift bed.

"You mean Priscilla?" Idget asked. He eased Malachi onto the blankets and covered him up.

Malachi nodded.

"If she said so, she will," he said and stood up. "But Haslett is staying for supper, so she might be late. I wouldn't worry. She's true to her word."

Malachi felt heat move from his stomach to his chest. Something in the way Idget talked of her made him realize Priscilla was just being kind to him. It was in her nature to be. He was nothing to her. He fell far outside the circle of light she seemed to inhabit. How could he have thought that his dark, crippled self would call to her?

"What you thinking?" Idget asked him. The boy was watching him closely.

"I don't know," Malachi said, shrugging and turning away from Idget. "Wish we was back with the sheep and the dogs is all." He tried to push away the thicket of feelings inside.

Idget smiled.

"Yep, I bet Albert has his hands full about now."

Malachi was quiet, then blurted out, "Do you think she really cares about Haslett? He's so old."

"Priscilla?" Idget asked. He squatted then sat cross-legged in front of him. "Not up to her to care about him, is it?" He reached toward Malachi and patted his arm clumsily. "What I say is that it's good you're all worried about her and not thinking on what Father Lee done to you."

His stomach coiled at the memory of how Lee had hurt him, but he turned and smiled at Idget. "Better to think about her," Malachi said, smiling weakly and pushing the other thoughts away. "She's a sight prettier."

Idget smiled back then turned serious. "Thank you for standing up for me. Nobody's ever done that before."

"It was my own fault," Malachi said. "I was the one who kept those things and shouldn't of."

"Probably not," Idget agreed. "But you could have let me take the blame for not telling on you and you didn't."

"That's what he wants you to do?"

"Course it is, you heard him," he said, shrugging. "It's how the family works, how the settlements work."

Malachi knew he was right. Neighbor told on neighbor; friend told on friend. Wives watched their husbands, and when there was something to tell, they'd tell the higher ups on them too.

"Do you think that's going to happen after John Lee tells Young about Mountain Meadows?" Malachi asked. "Do you think those men that done it are going to get punished?"

Idget looked away for a moment. "I'm thinking that's different. There were all those stories about those people and what they'd done."

"But what if the people on the train hadn't done those things? What if they was just a bunch of people passing through, minding their own business?"

"Then I'm guessing how the story is told will have to change," Idget said. He gazed at the floor.

"How do you figure?" Malachi asked skeptically. "You figure John Lee has some magic in his pocket that will make that happen? You think he can make those children disappear, make their memories disappear, make all those bodies in the meadows disappear?"

But in his heart, he knew Idget was right. What was black would become white and what was bad would become good.

"Father Lee will work all that out with Brother Young," Idget said certainly, looking up at him. "It's what they do, it's what is always done."

CHAPTER 9

OCTOBER 15

John Lee returned home in a cloud of dust and glory. It was mid-October but summer still lingered and the day was warm. The wives had sent most of the Lee children outside to work, preparing the farm for winter. Some of the youngest ones played games of tag and hide-and-seek in the yard, and their cries and laughter surrounded the big house with a feeling of happiness. Malachi and Idget were scraping and whitewashing the western wall of the house when Lee rode into the yard. His children cheered his homecoming and rushed to greet him. Malachi stopped scraping and watched.

"How does he seem?" Idget asked.

"Happy," Malachi said.

Indeed, Lee looked jubilant, greeting his children as they danced around him, all talking at once. He scooped up one of the younger boys, laughing and hugging him as the boy took off his father's pork-pie hat and slipped it on to his own small head. His tiny face peeped out from under the brim and he squealed as Lee bent his face toward the boy's and gently whiskered him.

"That tickles!" The boy screeched as he grabbed the hat that was slipping off his head.

"Looks fine on you, young sir," Lee said.

He set the boy down on the ground in front of him, straightening the hat. The boy took it off and returned it to Lee before running off to join the others who had already raced back to the yard to resume their games. Once the boy had gone, Lee walked to the front door where Agatha and Rachel stood, waiting to greet their husband. Lee asked how things had gone in his absence.

"With all the usual hubbub," Agatha said. "The older boys have spent much of their time in Fort Harmony gathering the supplies we need for the winter, and they've finished preparing the fields as well. The girls have been put to good use, helping us finally put up the last of the winter apples and vegetables."

"And you, dear Rachel," Lee said. "How does your work go?"

"I've finished making inventory of all you asked me to go through, including having the older boys do an accounting for me of the animals in the herd," she replied. Her voice dropped. Malachi stopped his scraping and strained to hear her last words. "I must say it's a sad task."

"Well, it's good you done it," Lee said. "Come now, into the house with me. I've got news."

The door slammed. Malachi and Idget exchanged looks. Malachi glanced toward the dining room window that had been left open to welcome in the fall air. He wanted to hear the news Lee was going to share with Agatha and Rachel. Perhaps they'd go to the dining room where they held their family meetings. His gaze swept across the gardens and yard. The younger children were absorbed in their game, and some of the older boys had gone back to the barn to finish their work. A few of the older girls were bent over in the garden, digging up the last of the fall tubers. He looked at Idget and placed his index finger over his lips before moving down to the end of the wall toward the window, crouching low. His heart beat steadily and he glanced out behind him to the garden. Reassured no one was watching, he picked up his scraping tool and leaned toward the wall. He heard movement inside. Chairs scraped against the wood floor and creaked as weight settled on them. Agatha told someone they were to be left alone, then a door closed and the sharp clip of footsteps moved toward the window. He pressed his body flat against the wall of the house.

"Leave it open," Rachel's voice called out. "It's so warm in here."

"As you like," Agatha replied. More footsteps, then someone pulled a chair across the floor.

"The Governor wants an accounting of all we gathered in Mountain Meadows." It was Lee. Malachi leaned in to listen, his cheek pressed against the house's splintered siding. Dry flecks of white paint floated down to his pant leg.

"We'll work with it to bill the federal agent. He and I agreed there's no return in us paying for the care and upkeep of the children and animals and, of course, he wants it to include a thorough explanation of how the deed was carried out."

"Then it was as you thought." This was Rachel.

"Yes, and he and I have agreed on the necessity of this thing and on how we tell of it," Lee said.

"You mean he wasn't angry?" Rachel asked.

"Far from it," Lee said. "He allowed that Prophet Smith himself set the thing in motion, and we men were carrying out the right thing in the eyes of God, the eyes of the church."

Lee paused, and Malachi heard the voice of a woman—one of the other wives—call in to ask if Lee wanted anything to drink. Agatha's sharp voice told her to leave and keep the door closed. Malachi glanced over his shoulder. The youngest children had moved their game of tag out to the orchard. The girls continued to stoop over their garden rows, stopping now and again to throw their harvest into a nearby basket and stretch their backs. He raised his scraping knife to the wall, moving it slowly up and down without touching the house, listening to the voices inside.

"I'll admit that the tell of it was hard," Lee continued. "But we got through it and I answered all his questions truthfully and thoroughly, just like he likes, and the next morning when we met for breakfast, do you know what he said to me?"

"Do tell us." It was Agatha's scratchy voice.

"He said, 'John, I feel first rate. I asked the Lord if it was all right for the deed to be done, and asked him to take away the vision of the deed from my mind, and the Lord did so, and I feel first rate.'"

"Oh, my!" Agatha exclaimed. "That is a good result."

"Did he say anything else?" Rachel asked. "Did he have any lingering worries about how this might be for us, especially for those of us here in the south?"

Malachi heard a chair squawk and imagined Lee's dense body settling back in it.

"Well, you're right to ask," Lee said. "He did share with me that he wants us to start looking for mountain hideaways, not only for us in the southern settlements, but also for our brothers and sisters in Salt Lake."

"Our boys have brought back word from their errands at Fort Harmony that more U.S. troops are coming," Agatha said. "This thing that was done in the meadows might speed it along, might make us a special target here in the south. I'm afraid of it. Is it a worry for him?"

"He's got a plan, as he always does, to protect us and we'll fight if we have to. We've done it before, and we'll do it again. But he's not worried about that so much as he is about those of our own who would betray us over the deed in the meadows, those who would somehow twist the story to that of their own making for their own ends."

Malachi strained to hear above the scattered cries and laughter of the children in the orchard. As he listened, it dawned on him that the women knew. Lee must have told them what had really happened in Mountain Meadows. He wondered if anyone else in the Lee family knew. He thought of Priscilla. Would she have learned of it?

"He's afraid one of our own will betray us? He said that?" Agatha's voice cracked.

"Indeed," Lee replied. "He said, 'The only fear I have is from the traitors.'"

"So, does Brother Young have a plan for this too, and does he have our best interests in his heart?" Agatha pressed. "You are sure of this?"

"Not only am I sure, I made a record of our conversation shortly after we had it," Lee insisted. "I have it in my journal because I didn't want to trust such an important conversation to memory later, in case I should have to recall it for one reason or another."

"What now?" Rachel asked.

"Father Young has asked me to make a full written accounting to him in a letter and describe all the particulars of what transpired, and that is to be our public story. We expect word of it to seep out soon, and he wants to be ready for it."

"And what of the particulars you shared with him in Salt Lake, the other parts?" Rachel asked. Her voice had dropped and Malachi thought he heard her ask, "Where does the accounting of that go?"

"Rachel, you are my dearest wife because you are so thoughtful, so careful in your thinking."

"But does he think it's *you* who are best positioned to be the one to put out a certain story?" she asked. "Why you? Why not Brother Haight or Brother Dame, or even Brother Smith for that matter?" There was a catch of uncertainty in her voice.

"Of course, he does," Lee said. "I was there. He sees it makes sense and he knows he can trust me. He knows the federal devils will do all they can to defeat us, to sully and destroy our lives here, and it's no different than what they done to us in Nauvoo. This piece of business at the meadows, as justified as he believes it was, would not be well understood, and he knows I am the best one to help him present the public story."

There was silence from inside the house then. Malachi wondered why Lee hadn't answered Rachel's question, at least not all of it. Why Lee? And still, he wondered, why had they done it? Why was it justified? The children had scattered away from the orchard back to the small meadow and the sound of their play receded into the distance.

"So, in the end." Agatha's voice sounded dry and brittle. "You made the right choice to tell him everything."

"You know there was no other choice to make," Lee said. "Even if I'd wanted to conceal it, which I never did, he would have known as he knows everything that happens in this land. Chances are he knew it all already, before I'd come, but just wanted to hear it travel from my lips to his ears."

"So, you think Brother Haight and the others were right to have you be the one to explain all this to him?" Rachel asked. "I worry that it leaves the responsibility for it at your feet, John."

"There could of been no other," he said. "I am his son in the eyes of God, and while many may betray Brother Young and God in the process, I will not and he knows the truth of that."

"But—" Rachel started. She was interrupted by a woman calling Agatha's name. A chair squeaked as it was pulled across the floor.

"Sakes alive, that woman cannot do a thing without instruction!" Agatha's voice was etched with impatience.

Lee's laugh was followed by the receding sound of sharp footsteps.

"I've got one more task to do today, then I am in need of a bath," Lee said. "I reek from my journey."

"Will you stay here tonight?" Rachel asked him. "With us? I've missed you." There was a thread of longing in her voice.

"Yes," he said. "And it will be in your bed and your bed alone, my dearest."

Malachi heard the rustle of cloth and the sound of bodies coming together. His face grew hot as he heard Rachel giggle and Lee let out a low groan. He looked at Idget, who had remained at the corner of the house where he continued to work. He glanced at Malachi, and Malachi nodded. He dropped to all fours to crawl clear of the window then stood and motioned for Idget to follow. The other boy lay down his tools and walked with Malachi away from the house as he filled him in on the conversation between Lee and his wives.

"What do you make of it?" Malachi asked.

"Good news for Father Lee and the others who did the deed," Idget said. "That's sure."

The boys were silent. They leaned against the pasture gate; their arms slung over it.

"It does make me think," Idget said finally.

"What's that?"

"Well." Idget hesitated while he rubbed off the spit on his chin. "You ain't going to like it."

"What you thinking?" Malachi turned to him.

"Maybe we should fess up to Father Lee what we both know."

Malachi let out an exasperated sigh. He looked at Idget and shook his head.

"You listen," Malachi said, his voice low. "There ain't nothin' in the four walls of that house that cares for us. We tell them what we know, and Lee or somebody else will snuff us out, no questions, no worries."

"I just was thinking," Idget said, shoving his hands inside his pants pockets.

"No," Malachi interrupted him, yanking at Idget's arm. "No, you heard me tell you what he said. It's the traitors they're worried about and they'll see us as traitors way before they see it in any of their own."

"But maybe it'd be like when Father Lee told President Young what happened," Idget said. He shook off Malachi's hand. "He'd see we were on his side and he'd reward us."

"That's all different," Malachi said. "That's them, not us. You know there's different rules for us."

He looked over at the house. They needed to go clean up their tools before someone discovered they'd left them there.

"Maybe we should tell the wives," Idget said. "They could help us decide."

Malachi sighed and looked up at the sky. He turned to face Idget. "What is it you promised me?"

Idget looked at him. "I know what I promised," he said impatiently. "I just think maybe he'd treat you better if he knew what you know, like you was one of them, like Albert."

"But that's just not the same," Malachi countered. "It's not thinking right."

"What's not thinking right?" Priscilla was approaching. Malachi looked at her and felt heat unspooling along the length of his spine. How much had she heard?

"He's just telling me I don't scrape the house right, that it's not the same as him," Idget said, flashing a grin. "Ain't that right?"

The boy was a born liar, Malachi thought admiringly.

Priscilla turned to face the house and put both hands on her hips and cocked her head.

"I believe that it's Mr. Malachi who has some brushing up to do," she said.

Idget smiled at her then looked at Malachi.

"See," he said. "Told you."

"But right now," Priscilla said. "Father wants to see you both."

She caught the look that passed between them.

"Sillies, no need to worry," she said. The left side of her mouth tilted up in a grin. "It's not a bad thing, I promise. There's just something he wants your help with, something he says he needs to fetch at another farm. The older boys are working on getting that new bunkhouse built and the animals settled for the winter, so they can't help. So, it's you two who has to."

Malachi wanted to believe her as she stood before them with that open smile on her face. When she turned, they had no choice but to follow her into the house. She jutted her chin in the direction of the dining room where Lee sat with Rachel reviewing some papers. The smell of roast beef filled the room. Lee was tackling a plate piled high with food as he leaned toward Rachel who was explaining something to him and pointing to a paper. Malachi's stomach clenched when he saw him, remembering the feel of the man's fist on his face. When the boys entered the room, Lee looked up. They waited at the entrance for him to call to them. Lee motioned them over.

"I want you boys to saddle up the horses," Lee said, when they neared where he sat with Rachel. He stopped and shoveled a forkful of beef into his mouth. As he chewed, he watched the boys. Malachi breathed in, trying to keep his thoughts steady.

"My own horse is too worn from the journey back from Salt Lake, so get the buckskin saddled for me," Lee said, swallowing and wiping his mouth with the back of his hand. "Idget, you ride the little bay mare, and Mudface here can ride the pinto pony."

"Where are we going?" Idget's hands gripped the back of the chair in front of him, his knuckles formed a tense white ridge along the back of his hand.

"To the Haslett place," Lee said. "Got something there that belongs to me and I aim to retrieve it." He looked briefly at Malachi then turned to Rachel.

"Where's Priscilla?"

"She's in the kitchen," Rachel said. "Helping with supper."

"Priscilla!" Lee called out. He stabbed a piece of potato, put it in his mouth and swallowed.

The girl stuck her head out of the kitchen door.

"Yes? I'm here." She had a smudge of flour on the tip of her nose and a streak of flour down the front bodice of her blue dress. Malachi thought the dress was the exact color of her eyes, cornflower blue.

"You get ready, too. You're coming with us to Haslett's."

"Me? Why?" she asked, a hint of defiance in her voice. "I'm helping Polly make an apple pie. We're nearly done." She stepped fully into the dining room now.

"It's time we reckoned with this thing," Lee said. "I know Haslett visited you when I was gone, so it's time to do what's needed. Go get ready now."

The color drained out of Priscilla's face. She looked at Rachel as she wiped her hands slowly on her apron. Rachel glanced at her then trained her eyes on the paper set in front of her. Malachi wondered if this would be the last he'd see of Priscilla. Disappointment filled his chest. Maybe she'd be taken to Haslett and given to him right then and there, a reward to the man for what he had done in Mountain Meadows.

"Am I to bring anything with me?" Priscilla asked.

"Nope, just yourself will do," Lee said, not looking up at her. Then he leaned over and murmured something to Rachel who had stood, her back bent down and her head close to his. It was as though they'd forgotten the others were in the room. The boys and Priscilla didn't move. Suddenly, Lee looked up and frowned at them.

"Come on now, all of you, get a move on and out of here. I want to get this business with Haslett taken care of and be back for supper with my family."

The boys made their way out of the dining room. Priscilla stood still with her eyes on Lee. She seemed unaware of the boys as they passed, and her mouth had drooped into a frown. Malachi wished he could comfort her, but he knew that was impossible. It made him feel awkward and, in his distraction, he tripped and bumped into her.

"Sorry," he mumbled, reaching out to the wall to regain his balance so he wouldn't further humiliate himself by falling. She looked up at him. Her lips inched into a wan smile and she waved away his apology. He waited for her to walk in front of him, and the boys followed her down the hall. He thought back to the scene in the yard, Haslett tipping her face up toward his. The kiss. Did she welcome it? He was so lost in his meandering thoughts about Priscilla that he hadn't heard Idget talking to him. The other boy jostled his arm.

"You listening to me?" Idget asked, peering into his face.

"No, sorry," he mumbled. "What's that?"

"I said, I'll saddle the buckskin and the bay. Can you take care of the pinto and the black horse over there with the blaze on his face? That's for Priscilla."

He nodded and followed Idget to the barn to get the horses' bridles. The animals were loose in the small corral adjacent to the barn. Malachi caught Priscilla's horse first and saddled it. He tied Priscilla's mare to the rail near the house and went to retrieve the pony. Just as he and Idget finished, Lee and Priscilla emerged from the house.

Priscilla had changed out of the blue dress and had put on a grey linen jumper with pants underneath. She had tucked her hair up under a wide-brimmed, brown hat that she wore tipped down over her eyes. Malachi felt a small surge of satisfaction when he saw she'd done nothing to pretty herself up for Haslett. Malachi retrieved her horse and handed her the reins. A thrill charged through him as his fingers brushed against hers. She swung up on the horse easily. Once she'd settled into the saddle, she reached down and stroked the horse's neck, whispering something to him that Malachi couldn't hear. When she looked up, she met his gaze and smiled. "I talk to him," she said. "He'll do whatever I ask him as long as we start out with a good understanding."

Malachi tried desperately to think of a reply. "Does he talk back?" His voice croaked, and his face flushed. He was furious at himself for not thinking of something better. But to his surprise, she laughed.

"Sometimes, just a little murmur here and there." When she laughed, the corners of her mouth went up like two small wings. He wanted to make her laugh again just to see her mouth lift up like a bird.

"Do you say anything to your horse?" she asked him. Her face was serious but he knew she was teasing him.

He looked at the pinto as the little beast waited patiently for Malachi to climb atop his back. "I say, please fat sir, do not bite me when I get on, and try not to scrape me off at the nearest tree."

His heart buoyed when she smiled at him again. Then Lee called out for them to get themselves ready. Malachi quickly secured his walking stick to the right side of the saddle. He limped over to the other side of the horse and put his foot in the stirrup and threw his leg over the pony's back. Lee had already begun to ride away from the house. Idget followed him, and Priscilla's horse stepped out. Malachi's pony fell into a hard trot as he tried to keep up with the others.

CHAPTER 10

The ride to the Haslett farm took nearly half an hour. Their property appeared abruptly on the rise in front of them, doing little to announce itself. Unlike the graceful, tree-lined entrance to the Lee's property, the Haslett farm was exposed, vulnerable. It was a barren sight and spoke of struggle. The single-story log cabin looked as if it had been built in a hurry. Its chimney tilted off to the left, and the roof hadn't been plumbed straight. The yard surrounding it was hard-packed and bare, with a lone pine tree standing sentinel just to the west of the house. A clothes-washing basin and scrub board leaned up against the tree, but looked as if it hadn't been used in some time. Nearby, an abandoned handcart weathered by the sun had one wheel that had split open. A squat building that served as the barn had a small corral attached. Malachi recognized the roan horse that belonged to Haslett. The animal wandered listlessly around the fence's perimeter. It appeared to be their only horse and lone head of livestock. The only other animals were a few cats afflicted with mange that sprawled out in the sun along the side of the house's southern flank.

When they neared the house, the horses pricked their ears forward and turned toward the sound of a child's wail coming from inside. The door opened and Rebecca Haslett staggered out, holding a boy in her arms. Malachi recognized the golden-haired boy from the train. He was crying and pushing away from Rebecca with all his might. His arm had been taken out of his sling, but was still bandaged. The woman tried to comfort him, but he was doing everything he could to escape from her embrace. He was surprisingly strong and with only one good arm managed to wiggle out of her grasp and land on the ground in front of her. Once he realized he was free, he ran from her then stopped short when he saw Lee, Priscilla, and the boys watching him from atop their horses.

Haslett emerged from the house next, and Rebecca looked back at him. "Help me," she pleaded. "I'm fearful he'll run away again." Haslett quickly strode over to the little boy, who had begun running in the direction of the barn. He easily overtook him and grabbed the boy's arm, reaching down with his other hand to pull him up toward his chest. The boy threw back his head and screeched, emitting a high-pitched wail that gave Malachi a chill. Haslett wrapped his arms around him and pinned his small body against his chest in an effort to calm him.

Lee had dismounted and stood watching the scene. His face held no expression. Malachi was reminded of the look Lee had worn the day of the massacre when the children from the train had been brought back to the Hamblin's house. Idget had gotten off his horse as well and Lee had handed him his reins. Malachi and Priscilla remained in their saddles. Malachi was uncertain what they were there for and felt apprehensive about what was to come. Haslett looked flustered and called out a greeting to Lee from around the boy's head, to which Lee put his finger to his hat and nodded slightly. Rebecca wiped her hands on the sides of her dress and walked over to Lee to greet him.

"Brother Lee," she said. "To what do we owe the pleasure?" Her voice was breathless and her pale skin was splotchy from her exertion with the boy. Her mousy brown hair was pulled tightly away from her face into a bun, revealing a high forehead that glistened with a patina of sweat. She smoothed the fabric of her brown dress, which had worn thin in places and had been mended over with thread that didn't match the cloth. Her leather shoes were cracked and worn.

"How do, Sister Rebecca," said Lee, tipping his hat again and holding out his hand to take her offered one. "Just here on some business on behalf of Brother Young."

Haslett had calmed the boy somewhat and the two of them walked over to Lee. The boy's curly hair was matted with sweat. Hiccups punctuated his sobbing, sending tremors through his tiny body.

"Got your hands full with that one, I'd say," Lee said drily.

Haslett looked down at the boy who was now staring at Lee with a scowl. Malachi wondered if the boy recognized Lee.

"Oh, he'll come round, I 'spect one of these days," Haslett said, sighing. "But I will tell you Brother Lee, these children are poor behaved. They swear like pirates and they seem full of the devil."

Lee looked speculatively down at the boy who stared back at him defiantly. Malachi watched the boy puff out his narrow chest challenging Lee and felt a flash of admiration for him. He was a mere leaf of a boy, probably not more than four or five, but without hesitation defied all the adults present, showing a ferocity that Malachi recognized. It reminded him of Albert in the early days, when they'd first been bought, his fierceness, his hatred of those who bought them.

"Are you full of the devil, boy?" Lee asked the child.

The boy pulled his mouth into a frown and grabbed onto the back of Haslett's pants, glaring at Lee. He pointed at Lee and spat out, "You are, that's who!" The dressing that was wrapped around his wounded arm was dirty and starting to unravel revealing spots where blood had seeped through and dried.

Haslett shrugged helplessly and reached down to gently jostle the boy's shoulder.

"Don't pay him no never mind, Brother Lee." Then Haslett looked at his wife. "The other one sleeping?"

"Yes," she said. "Finally, I done walked her and rocked her 'til I thought she would drop, but she just now fell to sleep, which is why I brought this young lad outdoors so as not to wake her with all his carrying on."

"Seems these two are a handful for you," Lee said.

"Oh, no, not so as you know it," Rebecca replied quickly, running her hands nervously across her hair, tucking stray tendrils back into her bun. Then she paused. Her hands dropped to her skirt and she smoothed it, as she seemed to consider what to say next. "They've been through a lot, as you know, Brother Lee. I 'spect it will just take them a spell to get over it, take 'em a while to get to know me as their own mother."

"You are not my mother!" The boy had emerged from behind Haslett's legs now. His body quaked. "You are not my mother and I want—I want my own mother!" With that he collapsed in a sobbing, heaving heap on the ground at Haslett's feet. Neither Haslett nor his wife seemed to know what to do. Neither made a move to comfort him. Malachi looked at Priscilla whose mouth had parted, as though she wanted to say something. Then the girl muttered under her breath and swung off her horse. She handed her reins to Malachi and walked swiftly over to the child where she dropped down beside him.

Priscilla was careful not to touch him, but brought her face close to his and whispered to him until the sobs that shook his body gradually subsided. He raised himself up and looked at her. He balled up his good hand into a fist and rubbed the grime and the tears off his face then asked, "Who are you?"

"I'm Priscilla," she said, smiling and straightening up. She placed her hands on her thighs and looked at him.

He gazed back at her blinking and rubbing his nose. "Do you have anything to eat?" he asked boldly.

"I have a half a ginger cookie here, in my pocket. I was going to save it for later, but you can have it." She fished in the pocket of her jumper and brought out a portion of thick cookie. She broke off a piece and offered it to the boy, who snatched it from her and ate it greedily.

Rebecca looked sheepishly at Haslett. "When I tried feeding him earlier, he wouldn't eat a thing."

Haslett ignored his wife and gazed longingly at Priscilla as she fed her cookie piece-by-piece to the little boy. They all watched in silence as the boy shoved the pieces of cookie into his mouth, barely chewing it.

"We've come to take the children," Lee said.

Rebecca spun on her heel and faced Lee.

"No!" she said, her lips quivering. "No!" She rushed at Lee and threw herself at him, dropping to her knees.

"Please, please, Brother Lee." She sobbed and wrapped her arms around his knees. "Please leave them with us. You cannot know what it is like not to have children of your own. You have so many and are so blessed, but not us. God has not seen his way to give us a child to share with this world until these young orphans were bestowed on us. It was God's will. You know it was God's will. All that happened that brought these children to us. You said so yourself! You cannot take them from us."

"What's this?" Haslett said, walking quickly over to face Lee. His hand absently found his wife's narrow shoulders and rested there as if to try to calm her but she was swaying back and forth so violently that his hand was left dangling in the air. "Haight said we was to have them, we was to become their parents. You know that. It was settled."

"Nope." Lee shook his head looking calmly at Haslett. "We're to take 'em back with us. That's on orders from Brigham Young himself!"

"But did you set this up, Brother Lee?" Haslett asked, his eyes squinting. "Did you put Brother Young up to this?"

Rebecca was now crying full bore. She looked up at Lee and grasped his pant leg. "Please," she pled with him, pulling at the fabric of his pants and jacket. "Please don't take these young ones from us. Even with all their crying and carrying on, it's a joy, a blessing to have them." She struggled to stand on her knees and, failing that, leaned in toward Lee, pressing her head awkwardly against his thigh, her shoulders and back heaving with sobs. Lee recoiled from her then clumsily patted the top of her head before gently prying her hands off his leg. He turned toward Haslett as the woman sank back into a heap on the ground.

"You take my meaning well from this," Lee said, looking at Haslett, his voice measured and cold. "I will not be crossed. This was not a decision you should have taken from Brother Haight, and you know it, and yet you did. You did it in direct defiance of me, and I will not tolerate it, what's more neither will Governor Young."

"But Haight's over you," Haslett whined, a slight tremor in his voice. "It was not a matter of me making the decision. He made it, not me."

Lee held up his hand for silence.

"And Governor Young is over all of us, and this is his word at work."

Rebecca still sat at his feet sobbing. She had wrapped her arms about herself as she rocked back and forth, her face a mess of tears and despair.

"Besides, I'm thinking that Brother Haight's decision wasn't made quite that way," Lee said. "You knew full well that the decision about who was to have these children from the train was mine and mine alone to make. I suspect you traded something to Brother Haight, but now I will set it right. We will take this child and the other that's in the house there. Priscilla, you go with Sister Rebecca and help her retrieve the other one. I'm taking both of them with me."

The boy had climbed into Priscilla's lap as she made an effort to distract him from the argument by playing finger games. Priscilla looked up at Lee now, a fleeting look of confusion on her face.

"But it's not—I don't—" Priscilla stumbled over her words then her voice cut off when Lee shot her a look. She turned to the boy and said something to him, at which point he began to cry again. She calmed him by holding out her hand to him. He took it and walked closely by her side. He whimpered, tightly gripping her hand as the two of them walked over to Rebecca.

Rebecca had fallen over her knees, her arms wrapped around her torso. Priscilla stopped in front of her and looked down helplessly. She leaned down to whisper something in the woman's ear. Rebecca looked up, as if seeing her for the first time. An unmistakable flash of hatred marked her face. She must have known her husband had been wooing Priscilla. Rebecca turned away from Priscilla and reached out her hand to Lee. Lee pulled his hand just out of her reach and shook his head at her, and she began to sob again.

"It's time to collect yourself," Lee said, moving away from her. "There's no turning back here. What's done is done."

She brushed away the hand Priscilla had offered to her, pulled in a long breath and pushed up to stand. She started toward the house, but stopped and turned to face Lee, her face drained of emotion.

"There's little a woman has to call her own but her ability to bear and care for children. If she cannot bear them, she can care for them, and that is the last of the gifts God has given her." Her eyes were red-rimmed and watery, but her features had hardened as she leveled her gaze on Lee. "You take that, and what's left? And what will a woman do when she has nothing left to her?"

If she expected a response from Lee, he did not satisfy her. Her chest heaved one last time before she turned and walked slowly past Priscilla toward the crooked house. Priscilla looked uncertainly at Lee, who jutted his chin toward the door. Then she turned with the boy still attached to her hand and followed Rebecca Haslett inside.

Once they disappeared, Lee faced Haslett. "Another thing," he said. "There's to be no marriage between you and the girl."

Relief unfolded inside Malachi's chest, but his face betrayed no emotion.

"She was promised me," Haslett objected, his voice hitched up an octave. "You yourself promised her to me after the doings in the meadows."

"And it's a promise I'm breaking right here, right now," Lee said. "You turned away from me. All who know me know that I'm faithful to the end to those that keep their word with me, but I will not abide those who turn their backs on me."

"This will haunt you," Haslett said. "This deed with these children, this decision with her, this will come to bear you nothing but bad news."

Haslett's face snapped closed with hatred, but Lee was unaffected by it. He shook his head as though he'd just heard a story that amused him and began to laugh softly.

"If it's left to you to be the bringer of that dark fate, then I think I'm up to the task of turning you back. You are a newcomer. You are here to populate and work this land, and we welcomed you for that. But you do not understand the workings of this church and this community. You best figure out how to keep in the good graces of those who matter."

"I am just saying, John Lee, you should watch your back. It's not everyone in these parts who sees you with as much esteem as you see yourself," Haslett warned. His skin had paled and the freckles on his face stood out like spattered blood.

Lee looked up briefly at the house then turned his gaze back to Haslett.

"We are done here," he said. "The children will come with us, and we'll give them a good home where they'll be well-cared for. As for you, I tried to help you, but you betrayed me."

The coldness in Lee's voice seemed to unnerve Haslett. He staggered backward, then he turned on his heel and walked toward his house, head bowed, his hands knotted into fists. As he approached the door of the house, Priscilla emerged. The small boy held her right hand and the other child, a girl with tousled brown hair and a heart-shaped face, held her left. Priscilla had a knotted cloth bag tucked under one arm. Haslett reached out to stop her and said something to her that Malachi could not hear. She glanced at Lee then shook her head briefly at Haslett, turning her body away from him. She grasped the children's hands more tightly and walked past Haslett with her chin up. He stepped back and let her pass. Rebecca stood in the door and watched as her husband gazed at the girl flanked by the two children. When he moved toward the house, Rebecca turned her back on him and retreated.

CHAPTER 11

NOVEMBER 2

Cold gripped the southern settlements with an unrelenting fierceness in the weeks that followed their return from the Haslett farm. Malachi and Idget worked outside, caught up in the family's frenzy to get the farm tucked in for the winter. They spent most of their time trying to finish white-washing the western wall of the house. Agatha was determined it would be newly finished before the first snow came. But one morning in early November they woke to nearly six inches of snow blanketing the ground, and Agatha finally relented, allowing them to give up the job for the season. After breakfast, she sent them outside to dig out their tools from the cold cuff of snow that had banked up against the house. The boys were in a stall in the barn storing their tools when they heard the commotion outside of riders approaching. Malachi looked up as Idget ran over to poke his head out of the barn door. He turned back to face Malachi, his eyes filled with worry.

"It's Jacob Hamblin and Haslett," he said. "Albert's with them."

Malachi flinched and sucked in cold air through his teeth. He finished cleaning his knife and gathered the other tools the boys had used, wrapped them in a stained cotton rag and placed them carefully in the wooden bin Agatha had instructed him to use. Then he walked out of the storage stall to join Idget.

"Why do you think they're here?" Idget asked.

"Dunno." Malachi shrugged. "Can't be anything good to have Haslett here with Jacob Hamblin, especially after that dust up he had with Lee over those children." But, in spite of his words, he was more worried about what Jacob and Albert Hamblin's appearance at Lee's farm meant for him.

One of Lee's older sons had come out of the house to greet the men. They had dismounted, and Hamblin said something to Albert. He took the reins of the three horses and led them to the hitching post nearest the house, fixing feedbags on each of their heads. Agatha had told Malachi and Idget to come to the house as soon as they were done putting away the tools. She planned to put them to work peeling potatoes and carrots needed for dinner that day. But Malachi wanted to avoid Albert if possible. He gently tugged at Idget's arm, pulling him back into shadows of the barn where they watched Albert tie up the horses and rummage through the saddlebags of the horse he had ridden. They watched as Albert turned and walked quickly to the house and went inside. When the door slammed, Malachi stuck out his head and scanned the yard. The horses' noses were stuffed into their feedbags, and steam rose slowly off their damp hides.

"You think we should go in?" Malachi asked.

"Better," Idget replied. "She gets owly if we don't do things just like she wants."

Malachi wondered if he'd have to return south with Hamblin and Albert. Jonah Blank may have changed his mind about lending him to Lee for the season. Given winter's sudden onset, Blank may have decided he needed some help around his own farm.

Returning to Blank's farm would mean leaving Priscilla behind. In the weeks following the incident at the Haslett's, Malachi and Idget had spent more time with her. Leah and Charlie, the two children they'd brought back with them, followed Priscilla around like tiny anxious shadows, and it seemed that he and Idget were the only other people at the Lee farm that the children were at ease with. Although left unspoken, Malachi thought what he, Priscilla, and Idget had experienced at the Haslett house brought them closer, fostering a friendship between them.

Jacob and Albert Hamblin's appearance could mean he'd have to return south. He didn't want to leave Priscilla, but he also worried about Idget. What would his friend do if Malachi weren't there to remind him to hold his tongue, to guard their dangerous secret? Idget had not given up on his notion that they should tell John Lee what they knew. A few days after they had returned from the Haslett farm, Idget had overheard something at the house that made him even more certain they should speak up.

Idget had been in the kitchen alone, finishing mopping the kitchen floor after dinner. The wives had taken the youngest children up to their rooms for an afternoon nap, but Lee and Rachel had lingered in the dining room. They were working on a letter addressed to Brigham Young. They were speaking freely, thinking they were alone. Idget used a chair to block the entrance to the kitchen from the hallway door, and wedged himself between the cupboard and larder close to the dining room door so he could hear their conversation. The letter recounted the story of the Paiutes' responsibility for the killing in Mountain Meadows, fulfilling the promise Lee had made to Young during his stay in Salt Lake.

"He said Governor Young told him to use the letter to lay out the expenses for caring for the animals that they'd say had been given to the Indians. And here's another thing, he told Rachel that Governor Young had told him to keep all that was left from the train for himself—the animals, the money, everything," Idget said later when he recounted to

Malachi what he had overheard.

"Well, it's helped him line his pockets, that's sure," Malachi said. "But I don't see why you think this means we should tell him what we know."

"No, it's for something else," Idget said. His eyes were gleaming. "Rachel was all worried over sending the letter, saying it would bring bad luck back to the family. And she was also saying they should share what they got from the train with some of the other families in Harmony. She was pressing him real hard on this point. So finally, he got mad and started stompin' around, you know like he does.

"He told her to finish the letter because Governor Young had told him to write it and to lay it out exactly as he said, and that he wasn't going to give up the property from the train because the Governor had told him to keep that too. He was yelling at her and said if word did leak out that some of the Mormon men was involved, he'd say he tried to stop them, but by the time he got there, it was too late and only the children could be saved. He'd say he eventually had to give up some of the animals to the Indians to keep the peace with them, but wouldn't let the other men take any of the rest of it and brought it back to his farm for safekeeping in case the children's next of kin were found. Then he could say he was making sure the train's belongings went back with the children and their rightful kin."

Malachi had looked at him, astonished.

"You swear you heard this?"

Idget's face puckered into a bright grin and nodded as he crisscrossed his heart with two fingers.

"It explains something," Malachi said slowly. "And that's why Lee wanted to get those kids back here. I mean, it's not like he needs another couple mouths to feed."

"It gives the smell of truth to what he might need to say," Idget agreed.

Malachi sighed. His head ached from these tangled possibilities. And he didn't know how they could use any of it to protect themselves if they told Lee what they knew.

"I don't know," he said shaking his head. "I still don't think we should say anything to him."

"But don't you see?" Idget said excitedly. "We can be the ones to tell others who might look into this thing that we know what the other men did."

"Do you mean we'd blame the others, and say John Lee had nothing to do with it?"

Idget nodded. "If need be," he said. "And we can give that promise to Father Lee. It would mean something for us, wouldn't it?"

Malachi remembered Haslett's threats to Lee several weeks earlier. Was what Haslett said true? Were others in the settlements unhappy with Lee? With the exception of a few bundles of clothing and tools that Lee had given to the small band of Paiutes at Mountain Meadows, Lee had taken nearly all of the rest of the property from the train. Malachi hadn't thought much of it at the time, but now he wondered if the other men resented it because they had hoped to benefit themselves from the horrible deed they carried out.

But if the boys did what Idget wanted them to do, it would be as good as if the two of them joined the ranks of the men who slaughtered the emigrants, and for what? It seemed far-fetched that John Lee would be thankful and protect them for it. Besides, if Lee knew the boys could name the men who did the killing, he would know Malachi and Idget knew about the blood on his hands too. Lee didn't seem like a man accustomed to leaving that kind of bargaining chip on the table, particularly not with the likes of them.

Idget had looked at him that day with a heady expectation. His eyes were glistening and he had that goofy half-cocked grin on his face, the kind he got when he thought he had a great idea and he desperately wanted Malachi to agree with him. Malachi had once again made him promise to keep mum, but he wasn't convinced Idget would.

The boys walked slowly from the barn to the house, their breath mingling in a plume of vapor that hung in the frigid air in front of them. Malachi felt a raw knot in the pit of his stomach. He opened the door for Idget and waited as he passed through. They wiped off their snow-caked boots on a small braided rug just inside the door. As they walked down the hallway that led to the kitchen, they could hear men's voices coming from the dining room.

Priscilla was in the kitchen rolling out a thick piecrust on the huge pine table that sat at the center of the kitchen. She looked up when the boys came in and gave them a quick smile then turned back to her work. She was assembling apple pies with apples that had been stored in the winter cellar. A huge crockery bowl piled high with apple slices that had been tossed in cinnamon and sugar sat on the table in front of her. Leah leaned against Priscilla's skirts, gnawing an apple wedge. Flecks of pulp dotted her lips and chin. Priscilla reached into the bowl in front of her and handed a piece of apple to Charlie, who sat on the floor at her feet. He cupped it carefully in his small palm, but made no move to eat it.

"We're to do some work for Sister Agatha," Idget said to Polly, one of Lee's younger wives. She had a pretty round face and wore a blue kerchief over her black curls. She looked up from kneading bread at the table opposite Priscilla. Polly jerked her head in the direction of the closed door between the kitchen and dining room.

"Her majesty is in there holdin' court," she said as she punched down the elastic hump of dough in front of her.

Idget started to go toward the closed dining room door when Priscilla called him back.

"No, don't go in there." Her voice was sharp, urgent.

Idget stopped and turned toward her. "Why?"

"They're talking just now, and it's not any of us who can hear."

Malachi shot a glance at Idget and waved him over. He had spied two buckets on the sideboard, one brimming with carrots and the other potatoes and guessed those were the ones that needed peeling. He asked Priscilla where he could find a couple of knives and she directed him over to a drawer in the sideboard. Idget sidled over to help him, and they pulled two stools up to the table.

The sound of John Lee's deep energetic voice was unmistakable. Even though they were on the other side of the kitchen and the dining room door was closed, Malachi could make out words now and again. Lee's talk was mostly followed by a second man's voice that had a steady, calm cadence. It was Hamblin. Malachi heard Hamblin say "children" several times and Lee say "no" in equal number. Then he heard Agatha say something, but she was curtly cut off by Hamblin. Not long after that exchange, she appeared in the kitchen, her neck a mottled red. She looked perturbed. When she saw Malachi and Idget, she smoothed her hair and walked over to them.

"You boys helped yourself to this chore," she said, eyeing the vegetables they'd peeled.

Malachi wiped his forehead with the back of his hand and ducked his head with an uncertain glance at her. "Yes, ma'am. We got the other stuff done that you asked, so we just decided to get started here, seeing as you was busy."

She didn't reply, but watched them work with a slight frown on her face. After several minutes she seemed to conclude they could handle peeling the vegetables without her supervision and went over to consult with Polly about seating for the noon meal. When Agatha's back was to them, Priscilla glanced at Malachi and aped Agatha's face exactly, then gave him a grin. He grinned back.

Hamblin's voice was followed by the scrape of a chair across the floor. Footsteps neared the kitchen and the door was drawn open. It was Albert. He filled the doorframe. It had only been two months since Malachi had seen his cousin, but he seemed to have grown taller, leaner. His high cheekbones made his face distinctive. He had begun to wear his hair longer—like Jacob Hamblin's—and he brushed it back off his face. It curled slightly at the collar of his shirt. Malachi grudgingly observed that Albert was good-looking. Albert sneered at the boys and his eyes settled on Priscilla whose attention was focused on the crust for her pies.

"Got to get some water for my father," he announced. His gaze swept Priscilla up and down.

Malachi hated how Albert looked at her and vowed to make him stop. Just as he was about to say something, Agatha abruptly left Polly's side and inserted her small, wiry body in front of Albert's. Her face had a sour look, and she blocked his view of Priscilla.

"Go on back in with the men," she said curtly. "I'll bring out a glass of water for your father."

Albert was nearly six inches taller than she was, and he smiled down at her. Malachi knew that look. He was unfazed by her.

"Just wanted to be helpful to you if I could, ma'am," he said politely and turned, but not before taking one last look at Priscilla.

Malachi watched him and remembered the girls Albert had followed out of Mountain Meadows on the day of the massacre. He knew Albert took what he wanted. He hoped that whatever happened, Hamblin and Albert's stay here would be short.

As if to answer his thoughts, Agatha announced that Brother Hamblin and his boy would be staying for dinner. "But Brother Haslett will be returning home," she said to Polly. "Let's get the youngest fed early, then have the girls set the table for an extra two for the main meal. Brother Hamblin will sit next to Father Lee, and his boy can sit with these boys at the other end." She nodded in Idget and Malachi's direction.

As the boys finished peeling their buckets of vegetables, snow began to fall again, at first lightly, then more heavily until it was nearly impossible to see the trees closest to the house from the kitchen windows. Malachi heard the sounds of movement in the dining room and someone leaving. He thought he heard Lee tell Albert to go put their horses in the stables, and he heard more steps. He looked out at the snow. He knew Albert and Jacob Hamblin would have no choice but to stay the night.

He reached into the bucket of potatoes and pulled out the last one. His fingers were pruny and white with potato starch. He wiped them lightly on his pants before he began to peel off the brown skin from the last potato. Idget had accumulated a big pile of carrots in front of him. While he worked, Idget softly hummed a tune that looped with the same five notes. Malachi peeled the potato slowly. The room was awash in the aroma of Polly's baking bread and snug from the stove's fire. He wished this moment could last. Agatha came over to examine the potatoes he had peeled and selected a handful that she wanted him to go over again to gouge out the dark eyes. Then she stood with her arms folded in front of her as she watched both boys work. Malachi glanced up at her and found her staring at him.

"Ma'am?" he asked. "Is there something else you want me to do?"

She stretched her lips across her teeth in what looked like a smile. Her lips were dry, and the delicate skin of them clung here and there to her teeth. She hitched up her mouth and rolled her lips together before she spoke.

"I've told Father Lee what good work you have been doing since you've arrived. I have been pleased with what you've done and how well you've done it."

Malachi looked briefly at Idget, who was smiling down at the bucket of carrots. "Thank you, ma'am," Malachi said. "That's real nice of you to say."

He watched the woman, waiting. Her face was broad and plain, and her skin had the elastic sheen of bread dough. Her dark hair was heavily threaded with silver and she wore a small cameo brooch in the center of the high collar of her dress. Her eyes, green and assessing, were intelligent and looked steadily at Malachi.

"Each thing I asked you to do," she continued. "You did, and I could see you tried your best at it."

He set his knife on the table and rested his hands lightly on his thighs. He thought about standing up because something in the woman's formal manner seemed to call for it, but he didn't. He had received few compliments in his life and felt uncertain as to how he should respond.

"Brother Hamblin thinks it would be a good time for you to return with him to the south, to Fort Santa Clara," she continued.

Malachi could hear Idget shift on the stool next to his, but he didn't trust himself to look at him.

"I have expressed myself in this matter to Brother Hamblin," Agatha said, straightening her back and jutting out her chin slightly. "And I cannot say that my opinion has been appreciated to the extent I would have liked."

"But what is that, ma'am?" Malachi asked.

"It is that you should tarry with us here a while longer," she said.

"I would like that," Malachi said, worried about the hurry in his voice. If he showed too much eagerness, he feared she might change her mind.

"I've pointed out to Father Lee that you've had a very good influence on our boy, Idget, here," she said, nodding her head in Idget's direction. Idget kept his head down and concentrated on peeling slender orange ribbons off the last of his carrots.

"But am I to go back to Fort Santa Clara, ma'am?" Malachi asked.

She looked at him for a few minutes without answering and Malachi found he could not hold her gaze.

"We have had but that one unfortunate incident with the Bible and letters," she said. Her voice seemed to have gotten both quieter and more sharp-edged. "It puts a question in our minds as to whether we can trust you."

He glanced around the room. Priscilla had finished her pies and had left with Charlie and Leah. The pies sat on the table waiting for space in the oven once Polly's bread was baked. Polly had disappeared too. Malachi could still hear the low boom of John Lee's voice exchange with the more moderate even keel of Hamblin's in the dining room. He met Agatha's eyes and she looked back at him with a neutral expression on her face.

"It was a mistake for me to keep those things," Malachi said quietly. He felt it was the truth. He'd had no reason to keep them, really. He'd just wanted them, something left for him to hold on to from the people who'd been killed.

"Of course, it was," she said. "But it's now that we're wondering how we can be sure you have our best interests at heart."

"Your interests, ma'am?" Malachi asked. "I think I do... well I know I do." He was stumbling over his words and his thoughts.

"It seems that this boy, Albert, Jacob Hamblin's boy," she began. "It seems he was near the scene of the killing in Mountain Meadows. Father Lee thinks he could have been there when it happened, seen it happen."

Malachi slid a look at Idget whose hands had grown still.

"Maybe," Malachi said numbly.

"Well, we want you to find out what he knows about this thing, to learn the story he tells," she said, smoothing back a wisp of hair that had fallen across her face.

"He did tell me that day," Malachi blurted out.

Agatha stepped toward him. She leaned forward until he could smell the sour tang of her breath and a slight whiff of soap rising off her skin.

"He told you what?" she asked sharply.

"He told me what happened," Malachi said lamely. "That it was the Paiutes who'd killed those people. Albert said he'd gone to the meadows with the other men after it had happened, and it was then that they found the children and rescued them."

Blood rushed through his ears as the words tumbled out. He thought he might lose his balance where he sat perched on a stool in front of Agatha. She peered at him as if she could see right through his skin and flesh and bones to the blood that pulsed through his heart.

"And you believed him?" she asked. Her words bit the air.

"'Course I did," Malachi said as forcefully as he could. "It made sense to me on account of hearing the gun shots all down toward the meadows, and then the children crying and carrying on up at the Hamblin house after."

He listened to the sharp scrape of Idget's utensil as he ran it down the length of a carrot and the intake of Agatha's breath as it whistled through her thin nose.

She spoke again. "The snow is such that I believe they'll be staying here the night, Brother Hamblin and his boy. Albert will stay with you and Idget in the bunkhouse, and we want you to query him about that day, find out how his story is now and whether it may have changed."

"You want *me* to do this?" Malachi asked, and immediately regretted it when he saw a veil of irritation cloud her face.

"Do you have some problem with it?" she asked, her voice tense.

"No, ma'am, no ma'am," Idget blurted out and stood. "We can get this story from him, we can do this thing."

She looked first at Idget and then at Malachi. "You'll bring it back to me once you've done it. You'll have to take care of it before dinner. Brother Hamblin thinks this snow will stop and is anxious to get back to Fort Santa Clara tonight." She looked out the window at the snow that blocked any visibility more than a foot from the house and shook her head. "Though for the life of me, I don't see how."

Agatha dismissed the boys and told them to be back at the house for dinner when the bell rang, which was only about an hour away. They walked out of the kitchen and to the entryway of the house and retrieved the coats they'd hung on pegs in the mudroom. Neither had gloves or a hat, so they flipped up the collars to their wool coats, shoved their hands deep in their pockets, and shouldered their way through the thick snow that whirled outside. It had snowed nearly four inches while they were in the house and it took them some time to trudge to their bunkhouse.

Not long after the boys had been banished to the barn loft to sleep, Rachel had told them they would be moving into one of the bunkhouses. There were three in all, and the other two—the larger ones—were shared by the Lee's oldest sons, so Idget and Malachi had had the third one to themselves all fall. Although a little rougher than the others, their bunkhouse was sound and comfortable. It had a cast iron stove and the boys had tried to keep a steady fire going in it now the days had turned cold.

When they arrived at the bunkhouse, Malachi used his walking stick to brush off a ledge of snow that had accumulated on the step leading up to the door. Idget hopped up to shove it open, and they both entered. The fire they'd built in the stove that morning had burned down to a few coals that glowed faintly. Malachi opened the stove and took the poker that stood against the wall to stir up the coals, generating a few sparks. He carefully laid on more kindling from their store at the side of the stove. When the flame ignited, he placed a couple small logs on the fire.

"Need me to get more wood?" Idget asked.

Malachi glanced at the wood bin. "Nope. Think we have what we need until tonight, and we can bring in more from the barn when we come back from the house after dinner."

Idget took a wool blanket off his bed and wrapped up in it, then came over to the stove and knelt next to Malachi, taking in the warmth that bled slowly into the room. Both boys were silent as the wood popped and sizzled and the fire sprang to life. Malachi continued to feed it until it settled into a strong, steady flame.

"Why do you think Agatha wants us to get Albert to tell us the story of what happened?" Idget asked.

"I can't figure it exactly," Malachi said as he reached out for a couple of small logs to shove into the belly of the stove. "Seems like she and John Lee don't trust Hamblin, or maybe it's just they don't trust Albert. Maybe they think he's a loose end, like us."

"You think we can get him to talk?" Idget asked.

Malachi looked at him. Idget's face was bronzed with the light from the fire. "I guess we'll try. Albert always has been one to talk more than is good for him so I doubt we'll have much trouble." He placed the poker back against the wall and closed the door to the stove. The room had heated up a little, but he kept his coat on. They both turned when they heard a loud banging against the front of the bunkhouse.

"It's Albert," Malachi said.

Idget pulled a chair over to the stove where he sat, using the blanket to wrap himself more tightly against the cold. He jumped a little when the door of the bunkhouse flung open. Albert stood in the doorway, leaving the door ajar while he took in the boys and their surroundings.

"Close the door," Malachi said. "We just stoked the fire and want this place to warm some."

The door had flapped back against the outside wall of the bunkhouse. Albert reached for it and slammed it shut. Then he took off his hat and coat and shook them off. He threw them on one of the beds.

Malachi looked up. "That would be my bed. Put your stuff on the one there," he said pointing to the bed closest to the door. "That'll be yours for the night. There's also pegs by the door you can use."

Albert first looked at him and then at Idget who sat hunched into his blanket. With a half-smile on his face, he picked up his coat and hat and tossed them onto the other bed.

"You found yourself a spine here," Albert said to Malachi. He dragged a chair over to the fire, spun it around and straddled it, facing the stove.

"Not really," Malachi retorted. "Just want to be warm is all and don't want your wet things messing up my bed."

Albert smiled broadly. "If I remember right, you mess up your own bed with all that jacking off you do. Don't think I haven't heard you."

"Can't say that was me," Malachi replied. "Must have been your own self you was thinking of. You're always talking of girls, but never have anyone real."

Albert snorted. "I got me plenty of live girls to put my own in."

Malachi raised his eyebrows and shook his head. "I s'pose." He could see Albert was excited and wanted to keep up the banter.

"There's a nice piece of girl up at the house," Albert continued. "That blue-eyed one."

"What of it?" Malachi shrugged, looking back at the fire. Boredom usually worked to extinguish Albert's moods.

"No, I know you see her too," he said. "But she don't want you, and you know it."

"Well, I'm not here to find me a wife, that's clear." Malachi reached for the poker and opened up the stove's door to stir the fire. He tried to tamp down his agitation with Albert.

"Who said anything about a wife?" Albert laughed. "I'd just like to poke that one is all. What's her name? Priscilla?"

Malachi and Idget were silent. Malachi felt a slow heat rising from his stomach up through his chest and into his head. He jammed the poker into the flames, stabbing the prong into one of the burning logs.

"Yep, she looks tasty." Albert licked his lips with an exaggerated flourish.

Malachi breathed in and watched the poker glow with heat.

"They say that these girls in Harmony are just so ripe that all you have to do is snap your fingers and their legs pop open for you," Albert said, clearly enjoying himself.

Malachi yanked the poker from the flames and shoved it under Albert's chin, knocking him to the floor. Albert jerked his head back and tried to get away from the glowing tip of the poker, scuttling backwards on his elbows and feet, but Malachi lunged at him, jabbing him with the poker until it was just inches from his left eye.

"You better not burn me with that thing," Albert said.

"You think I won't, but I will." Malachi shoved the poker closer to his eye. "I will gouge out this eye of yours unless you take back all the words you just said."

Albert looked at him. "You don't have it in ya'."

Although Albert was sneering, Malachi saw a flicker of fear in his cousin's eyes. Malachi nodded at Idget, who moved to stand over Albert. He squatted down and pinned Albert's shoulders to the floor. Albert was taller than Idget, but Idget was the stronger of the two, and Albert couldn't twist free from his grip.

Just then, they heard someone coming up the stairs to the bunkhouse, and the door swung open. It was John Lee.

"What's this?" Lee asked, as he stepped in and pulled the door shut behind him. His black hat and coat were covered with snow, and his boots were crusted with it.

When Idget looked at Lee, Albert twisted out of his grasp and backed out of the poker's range. Before Albert could speak, Malachi said, "He's telling stories, sir, stories about that day in the meadow when the Paiutes killed all those emigrants. I was making him take it back."

Malachi locked eyes with Albert. Albert's face turned ashen. Spit crusted in the corners of his dry lips. He opened his mouth, but no sound came out and his eyes darted over to Lee.

"That's not true, Brother Lee," Albert bleated. "These boys were gonna burn me, just 'cause I'd said a thing for fun. It weren't nothing but a jape and they were going to burn me for real. I said nothing about the meadows. I swear."

Lee walked to the middle of the room. He stood beside Malachi and looked down at Albert who still lay sprawled on the floor.

"What was the jape, boy?" Lee asked.

Albert looked at Lee uncertainly.

"It weren't nothing, sir," he said. "Just some fun about a girl we know is all."

"That so?" Lee said, looking around for a chair. He pulled over the chair Albert had been using and sat with his knees spread wide, resting his hands on his thighs. He looked down at Albert.

"And what about this girl you know, what did you say?" Lee asked.

The boys were silent.

"I want to hear what it was you said, goddammit!" Lee slapped the palm of his hand on his knee and the boys all jumped.

"I just said I'd like to kiss her," Albert said quickly.

Lee rubbed his chin and looked calmly at Albert then stood.

"You get yourself up," he said. "Come back to the house with me and we'll finish this talk with your father."

Albert began to protest, but Lee held up his hand and said, "Now." Albert scrambled to stand and went to find his hat and coat.

Lee watched him, then turned to Malachi. "I'll want to talk to you later."

Malachi said nothing and only nodded.

When the door slammed and Malachi and Idget were alone, they both let out a sigh. Idget laughed nervously. "What got into you?"

Malachi looked at him and smiled. He held up his hand. It was trembling. "Not sure. For once I didn't feel afraid of Albert. I felt like I could take him on if I had to."

"Yeah, funny, me too," Idget said. "What now, do you think?"

Malachi took a deep breath. "Well, it's sure that Albert won't admit to what he said about Priscilla to Lee. I wonder, though." He paused.

"What's that?"

"I wonder if he could have been standing outside the door and heard us," Malachi finished.

"I couldn't believe what you said about the meadows," Idget said.

"What were you thinking?"

"It just come to me. Lee must of told Agatha to get Albert to talk about that day, so it just seemed to fit." He shrugged. "It's what they all must be afraid of, that someone is going to let it out, start talking, start telling the truth about what happened."

Idget nodded. "I heard Lee's boys talking about some of the gossip they picked up at the fort. People are starting to say some of their own might have been there when it happened. But it don't sound like nobody knows for sure. It sounds like it's all just people talking in the wind."

"I've been thinking, Idget," he said after a pause. "Maybe you and I can make a plan together. A plan to leave." This notion of leaving had begun to take shape in Malachi's mind, lingering, getting built on each day, seeming possible. Perhaps he and Idget could hire on to one of the wagon trains on their way to California or maybe they could make their way to Salt Lake and get work with some trappers or miners who were going north from there.

"Leave?" Idget asked, wrapping the blanket around his shoulders again. "Not sure as I want to leave. Where would we go?"

"I don't know," he said. "Just know that as folks get more scared about the truth coming out, things will start to fray for bystanders like you and me, and we'd best be ready with what we're going to do." Irritation flared in his chest. Why did he need to keep explaining the danger they were in? Why couldn't Idget see it?

"But the only place I ever knew was here and Santa Clara with the sheep," Idget said. His voice was forlorn. "I was only two when they bought me. Don't know nothing else. Don't even remember my own people, like you do. I can't quite see myself living a life outside of here."

Malachi looked at the fire wondering if Idget was right. Where would they go? They had no money, no belongings to call their own. But, if they stayed, he wondered, what then?

CHAPTER 12

Albert was sullen and quiet throughout dinner. He wouldn't meet Malachi's eye, meaning Lee had probably given him a dressing down. Malachi watched Hamblin and Lee talking at the other end of the long dining table. Hamblin was a cipher compared to Lee. He was thin and wiry and wore his dark hair long and parted on the side. It reached down to the top of the white collar of his shirt. He wore a deep green silk scarf tied in an elaborate knot around his neck. Malachi had always known him to wear a scarf. It was an odd flourish of vanity on an otherwise modest man.

The men who had gathered at the Hamblin ranch before the massacre had said it was George Smith who had sent the Paiutes after the Fancher train, but they'd also said Hamblin had encouraged the people on the Fancher train to go to Mountain Meadows. The day of the massacre, Hamblin—who Young had recently appointed Indian agent—was in Salt Lake, marrying a third wife, so he hadn't been part of it. Malachi wondered if Hamblin thought himself lucky because it set him apart in case the truth of these murders should come to light.

Hamblin rarely smiled. When he spoke, which was only to Lee, he kept his eyes down and fiddled with his cup, tipping it first this way then that, as if looking in it for inspiration. When he listened to Lee talk—which seemed like much of the meal—he looked out at the people around the table, observing each one with a serious gaze. Albert, who'd been with Hamblin on his Indian expeditions and watched him cajole and bargain with the local tribes, had bragged that Hamblin could get a man to do anything he wanted. As Malachi watched Hamblin listening to Lee, Malachi wondered which of the men wielded more power.

Lee was in the depth of telling an animated story that Malachi could only hear snippets of, something about a lame horse that he'd sold to one of the newer families who'd come by handcart and had settled in the area. Malachi glanced up at the men, and Hamblin caught his eye. Malachi nodded at him and went back to his dinner. When he looked up again, Hamblin had leaned over to whisper something in Lee's ear, and Lee looked briefly at Malachi and shook his head. Idget, who was sitting beside Malachi, jabbed him with his elbow and said in a low voice, "They're talking about you."

"Yep," he answered shortly and stuffed a piece of bread into his mouth.

The women started to clear. Priscilla, who was sitting on the other side of Malachi, leaned over and told him to stay and have some of the pie she'd baked. "You won't be sorry," she said, smiling at him. Then she got up to go help the wives serve dessert. When she returned, she set down thick wedges of apple pie in front of both boys. Malachi and Idget dug in with relish. Albert was using his fork to shove his piece around on the plate. He was interrupted when Hamblin called him over. Malachi looked up to see Hamblin's arm resting on Albert's shoulders as he leaned in to talk to the boy. Lee had tipped his chair back, as though he wanted to listen to Hamblin's conversation with Albert, but he was also talking to Agatha, whose face had stretched again into that odd grimace of a smile. She looked out over the table and met Malachi's gaze. He wondered what was in store.

"I'm thinkin' we're going to get a talking to," Idget said quietly.

"Hopefully it's only that," Malachi murmured.

Both boys finished with their desserts and sat with their hands twitching nervously on the table, waiting to be dismissed. Malachi thought it should have happened by now, but Lee and Agatha were still absorbed in conversation and no one else paid them much attention. Priscilla had disappeared and just a handful of older children remained. A few of the wives were still clearing dishes. Albert had gone back to his seat and was shoveling the last of his pie into his mouth.

Lee got up and came toward Malachi and Idget. When he reached the boys, he pulled an intricately carved watch—a souvenir he brought back from his most recent trip to Salt Lake—out of his vest pocket and lightly pressed the release. The delicate lid of the watch flipped up. He looked at it and said, "Want to talk to you boys and Albert for a spell." Malachi and Idget twisted around in their chairs to look up at him, but Lee kept his gaze on his pocket watch, tapping the face of it lightly with his index finger.

"Where, sir?" Malachi asked. "Here?"

Lee looked over at Hamblin who had sat down by Albert and was talking to him as the boy gazed down at his empty plate. Lee closed up the watch and slipped it back into his pocket. "Nope, not here. Get on out to the bunkhouse and stoke up the fire. We'll be there shortly."

Both boys scooted back their chairs and went to find their coats. They pressed their bodies into the thick wall of falling snow. At least two more inches had accumulated during dinner. Malachi wondered if Hamblin and Albert would be able to leave the next day. They stopped at the barn to gather more firewood from the storage bin. When they got to the bunkhouse, they made quick work of building up the fire, saying little to each other.

Malachi tasted worry. He knew he should remind Idget to hold firm, say nothing. Idget had squatted down to pile the firewood that had cascaded out of both boys' arms when they'd come in earlier. Malachi went over to help him.

"What do you think?" Idget asked. "You think they're going to ask us about the killings?"

Malachi nodded and shoved a piece of wood on top of the pile. "I think they are."

"Have you changed your mind?" Idget stood now, a piece of firewood still grasped in one hand.

As the room warmed, the wood they were stacking let off a light sweet smell. "I haven't changed my mind. We shouldn't tell them what we know. That's sure," Malachi said with more certainty than he felt.

It had been at least an hour since they'd left the house, and still the others had not come. The longer they waited, the more agitated Malachi felt. Idget seemed content sitting by the fire and staring into the heat of it, but Malachi had to distract himself and tried to read a tattered book Priscilla had lent to him. He'd only made it through the third page, and had pieced together a story about a brave boy who'd left his family behind in England to come to America. He was struggling with the reading, but wanted to finish the book so he could tell Priscilla he had. She'd been delighted when he told her he knew how to read, and he didn't want to disappoint her.

Both boys looked up when they heard the sound of men's voices outside. The door opened and Lee stepped in, followed by Albert and Hamblin. Malachi and Idget stood and watched them remove their hats, coats, and gloves. Hamblin and Lee handed theirs to Albert. He glanced at Malachi then dumped the snowy, wet coats on Malachi's bed. Albert looked at his cousin with a gloating look of satisfaction on his face.

There were three pine chairs in the bunkhouse. Lee and Hamblin each pulled one closer to the stove and sat. Idget stood awkwardly by the stove, hands shoved into his pockets. Albert pulled a chair off to the side and sat, watching Hamblin closely. Malachi moved over to Idget's bed, closest to the stove, and sat on the edge of it. He and Idget locked eyes briefly. Lee examined the fingernails on his right hand and picked at a cuticle, his mouth drawn into a frown.

"It's time we talk about what happened in the meadows in September," he said, not looking up. His voice was quiet and showed no emotion. "There's bound to be others looking into what happened. Salt Lake tells us that the U.S. Army is coming, and there's sure to be an investigation. You boys were at the Hamblin ranch that day, so we figure we got to settle on what you know and feel confident that the particulars of the story are understood."

Hamblin watched Malachi steadily as Lee talked.

"I happen to know from Albert here that you boys know more about this thing than what you've let on," Lee said, glancing at Albert. "So, I want to hear now what it is you know and how you've come to know it."

No one spoke. An ember popped and sent sparks out the opening of the stove. A log on the fire let out a steady hiss of moisture. Malachi looked down at his boots. They were leather and laced up over the top of his ankles. The leather was cracked. He'd tried to soften it with the bear grease Priscilla had given him, and it had stained the leather so that it was dark now, almost black.

"You boys gonna talk or are we going to have to make you?" Lee looked at Malachi.

Malachi swallowed. "It's not like there's much to say."

"Well, how about if you start with where you were that day," Lee replied.

"As usual, we was caring for the sheep. That day was windy and the sheep were bolting. We lost one of the dogs when she took chase."

Malachi realized they should have prepared the story he was about to tell; they should have gone over it together and agreed on the particulars. But it was too late now.

"I left Idget with the sheep and went to find her." He clenched the mattress underneath him and leaned forward slightly. He was trying to remember that day, remember which path the Paiutes had taken out of the meadow. Had it been to the north? The image of them as they walked out of the circle of wagons, cavorting in the clothes they'd been given from the train came back to him, but he was struggling to remember which way they had gone. Would Lee and Albert remember if he didn't get this detail right? The Paiutes must have camped nearby so they could join them for the trip to Harmony two days later.

"Which way did you head?" Lee asked.

"North of the pasture, following the dog," Malachi said, willing his voice to stay calm.

"He told me he heard shots," Albert said to Lee. Hamblin looked at Albert and shook his head slightly. Albert stiffened, his gaze teetering uncertainly between Hamblin and Lee.

"I did," Malachi said. "I did hear shots, but earlier, when we were in the pasture with the sheep, before I went to look for the dog."

"What did you make of that?" Lee asked.

Malachi looked at him, puzzled. "Sir?"

Lee shifted and a look of irritation flitted across his face. "Make of it, who did you think was firing those shots?"

"Didn't know, didn't know until Albert told me later that it was the Paiutes, killing off those people on the train."

Lee looked at Albert then back at Malachi. "Did you ever think it was the men staying at Hamblin's?"

"Like I said, sir, I didn't rightly know who was firing those shots or who was getting fired at until Albert said what had happened. For all I knew, it could of been the people on the train firing at the Paiutes who'd been hiding in the hills watching them."

Lee looked at him sharply. "Had you been down to the meadows while the train was camped there?"

"No, sir," Malachi said quickly. "We'd been told not to go near and that if we did, we might get shot by the emigrants."

"Then how was you to know the Paiutes were in the hills by the meadows?"

How *was* he to know? Malachi cursed inwardly. He was so eager to bring the Paiutes into his story he hadn't foreseen the trap he had set for himself.

"I was the one who said it to him," Idget interrupted. Lee turned to him.

"And you, boy, how was you to know?" Lee asked.

"I was up at the house, getting some supplies and heard the men talking about the goings on down in the meadows," Idget said.

"Who was it you heard?" Lee asked.

"It were Phillip Klingensmith, sir," Idget replied. Malachi noticed Idget's pulse beating hard on the thick muscle of his neck. "He was talking to another man whose name I don't right now remember."

"When was it?" Lee barked at him, making Idget jump.

"Must have been just the day before all the commotion," Idget said. Malachi heard the tremor in Idget's voice, but he let out a quiet sigh of relief. Idget must have been telling the truth. Klingensmith had arrived at the Hamblin ranch a few days later than the other men, something Lee would have known too.

Hamblin had stayed silent, his eyes trained on Malachi. Then he finally spoke.

"So, finish up your story, boy," he said quietly.

Malachi sat back a little on the bed. His hands were trembling and sweat trickled down his underarms. He continued. "I found the dog, and on my way back to the sheep, I could hear there weren't no more shooting coming from the meadows. Then I saw a small party of Paiutes making their way up out of the northern rim of the meadow."

"How many?" Hamblin's voice came like a shot.

Malachi shrugged. "Not exactly sure, maybe a dozen." He knew he couldn't lie on this point.

"Did you find that odd?" Hamblin asked.

"How so, sir?"

"That it was such a small band of men that had done this thing to so many people?"

Malachi hesitated.

"Not at the time because I didn't know what had happened, but I did think about it later," he said slowly. "After, when I'd found out the truth, I thought I must of just seen a portion of them. Maybe the rest of their band had stayed on in the meadows. Maybe they were taking things from the bodies of those they killed while the men who'd been staying at the Hamblin's made it their business to rescue the children." The memory came to him of the pulpy face of the boy in the brown jacket and the dusty feel of the boy's empty pockets.

Malachi thought his answer had hit a note of truth with Hamblin because he didn't ask him any more questions after that. He wasn't as sure of Lee, whose chin had sunk into his chest as he stared at the floor. He seemed tired, like he'd grown weary with the task of conjuring up memories from that day. Only Albert, who knew Malachi the best of anyone in the room, had doubt stamped on his face, but Hamblin signaled him to stay silent every time he tried to talk.

Lee stirred and said to Hamblin. "Anything else you want to ask these boys?" His voice was raspy, as though he'd just come out of a long sleep.

Hamblin looked at Lee, tilting his head slightly. "Are *you* satisfied with what we've heard, Brother Lee? It seems something troubles you."

Malachi watched the two men. A look of distaste crossed Hamblin's face as he stared at Lee. He was certain that Albert had told Hamblin every detail about what had actually happened that day, including Lee's role in convincing the emigrants to surrender. Maybe Hamblin had an objection to blaming the murders on the Paiutes. Everyone knew Hamblin had a special closeness with the tribes. Perhaps he worried about what would happen to the Paiutes as a result of saddling them with these murders. Lee rubbed his hands across his face then back and forth on top of his thighs, seeming to revive himself. He looked at Malachi but answered Hamblin.

"It's not what we've heard, Brother Hamblin, that troubles me, it's what we've not heard."

Malachi's heart thudded against his chest. He willed himself to stay calm but he felt a quiver of nerves dancing around his left eye and he was sure Lee saw it. He resisted looking at Idget, for fear of raising Lee's suspicions further. But, to his surprise, Lee turned to Albert.

"Where were you that day, before we descended into the meadows?" Lee asked him. Albert's face twitched in surprise. He looked at Hamblin as if for permission to answer and when Hamblin nodded, Albert turned to Lee.

"I'd slept at the house the night before," he said. Malachi knew this was the truth. He'd been bragging the day previous that Rachael Hamblin had made up a bed for him at the house and told him to stay there that night, leaving Idget and Malachi to tend to the sheep themselves.

"The next day, Mother had me working on mucking out a stall in the barn and along about mid-morning, I heard a fierce racket coming up from the meadows and run out into the barnyard to see what I could. The other men who'd been staying with us were gathered round a fire, some of 'em playing at quoits. I asked them if they knew what was up, and they all said no, but it was probably just the Paiutes raising dust in Mountain Meadows, trying to scare the emigrants by shooting off their guns."

"No one thought to go down to see what was happening?" Hamblin asked.

"Well," Albert said. "Brother Lee asked me to go to see and come back and tell him as soon as I could. I ran fast to the meadows to see what I could find out. When I got there, I hid quick behind some trees because I could see the Paiutes spread across the floor of the meadows killing and shooting the whole lot of people from the train.

"When I seen what was happening, I high-tailed it back to the house to warn the men, who gathered their arms to go protect the emigrants. I went back with them, but by that time, it was too late. Everyone, but the smallest children, was slaughtered by the Paiutes. Every single one."

The fire hissed. Hamblin was sitting very still, but Lee seemed animated again, taking in Albert's story with relish, nodding while he told it and even smiling at certain points. Malachi wondered at the rehearsal of it.

"The Paiutes had it in their minds they were going to sell the children, but our men weren't having none of that, and Brother Lee you were especially strong in telling them that we would not let them have those children but would take them back to the house with us, where they'd be cared for. I was sent back to get a couple of the men who'd stayed at the house playing quoits. I was to tell 'em to bring a wagon down to the meadows to take back the children we had rescued."

Lee looked solemn now, but said nothing.

"So, we brought back the lot of them and Mother took 'em in right away and tended to them. They were so afraid that they screamed and carried on as though they'd never stop, but Mother gentled them and cleaned them up and fed them so that they slept like babes through the night."

Idget had been standing since Lee and Hamblin had first come in. He shifted back and forth while Albert talked. When Albert finished, Idget sat down with Malachi on the bed. The bed creaked loudly as his dense, muscular body settled in.

Lee looked at both boys. "You boys know this story to be any different than what Albert here has told?"

"No, sir," they replied in unison. Malachi could feel Idget moving restlessly as he sat on the bed.

"You have no reason to talk about that day," Lee said. "But if you do, this is the only story you know."

"What if someone were to ask me if the Paiutes did it, can I say?" Idget blurted out. He was leaning forward on the bed. Spit that had dripped down his chin left a wet spot on his pants.

"And who would ask you?" Hamblin interjected. "Has someone?"

Idget shrugged. "No, no one asked me," he said lamely. "I jus' heard some of the older boys talkin' up the army coming here and Father Lee just said that was true. Maybe they—I thought…" He trailed off.

Lee startled them by breaking out into hoarse snorts of laughter. It overcame him and tears trickled down the sides of his face. Hamblin watched him now with a quizzical look and an odd half smile. Lee's laughter punctured the tension that had seized the room.

"You are a prize, boy," Lee finally said, wiping the tears off his cheeks with the back of his hand. "No one will pay you no never-mind. Don't you hear yourself? I could barely make out what you said just now, and I'm used to your gibberish. No one would even think to ask you what you have to say because they wouldn't be able to understand a thing! If it comes to someone wanting to talk to you, it'll be Agatha who'll speak for you. You hear?"

Idget looked to the floor. His face had hardened and his hands gripped his knees, his brown knuckles bled into white. Idget's temper was slow to rise, but he exploded when it reached the boiling point. Malachi had seen him tear into those who tormented him like an enraged bear. Even though he couldn't imagine Idget going after Lee, Malachi still angled his knee over to Idget's, hoping his touch would calm him.

"But you." Lee's eyes wheeled over to Malachi. "*You* they will ask."

Malachi's heart thudded deeply against his chest.

"And what will you say?" Lee asked his blue eyes looked unblinking at Malachi. "What will you say if the army brings forward an investigation of this thing?"

"What was just said," Malachi said. His throat was dry. "I'll say where I was and what I just said."

"But that doesn't tell the thing the way it happened," Lee said. "It leaves out parts and leaves in gaps for people to guess and put their own mischief in it."

"You want me to tell what Albert said? That I was there, too?"

"Were you?" Lee asked.

Malachi felt the rest of the room drop away as though he and Lee were there alone.

"No," he replied. His scalp prickled with sweat. "I wasn't there, but if that's what you want me to say, I will say it."

Hamblin cleared his throat. "We don't want you to lie, boy. No need for that. We want the truth from you. That'll serve us best when it comes to it."

This is when Malachi realized they really didn't know. They didn't know if he had witnessed the killings or not. The army was coming and they knew there was sure to be an investigation. They were toting up the loyalty of those who were part of the massacre or who were at the Hamblin's that day, trying to suss out who could be trusted, who could not, and who else might know just enough to make them a danger.

There was another thing that nudged at Malachi's mind. Albert's loyalties had shifted, and he had decided it was Hamblin, not Lee, whose lead he was going to follow. There was good reason for Agatha and Lee to want to know what story Albert was telling when Lee wasn't around. Were loyalties shifting in general as Haslett had indicated? Were the men who were at the meadows starting to turn their backs on Lee, considering how to shield themselves from blame? Albert was still clearly terrified of Lee. He'd never seen him so scared as when he had accused him in front of Lee of talking to them about the killings. Malachi realized now; it may have been reckless on his part because it revealed he knew what was at stake. If he hadn't done it, he might have been put in the same column as Idget and simply dismissed.

"I can tell the truth of what I heard and what I seen," Malachi said.

Lee suddenly strode over to where the boys sat on the bed. He stood in front of Malachi and reached over above his head and thumped him hard on his skull with his fingers. Malachi jumped and drew back, looking at Lee.

"What is it you want, sir? What's it you want me to do?"

Lee grabbed Malachi around his neck and pushed him so that Malachi had to prop himself up on the bed with his elbows to keep from falling back. He was forced to look up as the man's eyes bored into him. "This is not something we're playing at, boy. You said to me what you did earlier about Albert's tale, but it weren't true, was it? He hadn't said anything to you boys about that day, did he now?"

"I said it so you wouldn't know what he really said." Malachi gasped for air as Lee's hands tightened around his neck. Idget was trying to pull Lee off of Malachi, but Lee pushed the boy out of the way and sent him sprawling.

"It's enough now." Hamblin was standing by Lee and thrust his arm between the man and Malachi, pushing Lee's chest back from the boy. "It's enough."

Lee released his hands and stood back, breathing hard. Hamblin's arm still rested on Lee's chest. Lee pushed it away and glared at Malachi. "What'd he really say then, boy? You're gonna tell the truth of it now."

Malachi was panting. His lungs felt like they had collapsed and he couldn't get enough air. He rubbed his neck and looked at Albert. Albert's face had turned ashen and he glared at Malachi. Malachi thought of all the times Albert had pummeled him, made fun of him, stole his food, and told him he was going to burn in hell. He thought of their old dreams of escape and how Albert had betrayed him, turned his back on him. He thought of all those things and how much he had come to despise his cousin. He knew it was in part that Albert had forsaken him, but he also hated Albert for his swagger, his bragging, his sucking up to the Mormon men, and his success. Albert had succeeded in becoming one of them, or at least seeming to.

"It was just about a girl we know," Malachi said, looking at Albert.

"What girl?" Lee barked.

"Your daughter," Malachi said. "Priscilla."

CHAPTER 13

The air in the bunkhouse had turned stale with nerves and mistrust by the time Hamblin and Albert finally left. Albert wouldn't admit to the worst of what he'd said about Priscilla, but he'd opened the door on the truth enough so that Lee could see that he had insulted her. Lee was angry, but not in the explosive way Malachi had expected. What followed seemed to drive a wedge between Lee and Hamblin. Lee wanted Hamblin to punish Albert, right then and there, without mercy.

"You own the boy," Lee said. "Do what's needed before it gets out of hand."

But Hamblin refused, saying he'd get to it in his own time, his own way. Albert stood between them, looking at the floor. By the time the men had finished talking, the snow had stopped and weak sunlight had begun to filter through the clouds in the west. Hamblin's face had turned grim and he looked out the window of the bunkhouse.

"Weather's cleared," Hamblin said, looking at Albert. "We'll find other lodging for the night. One of the families back at Fort Harmony should be able to put us up. Best get going now while we have some daylight left."

He got up and motioned to Albert, who flinched as though he'd been hit. He walked over to the bed and sorted through the coats to find his and Hamblin's. They pulled on their coats, gloves, and hats. Albert had his hand on the door, ready to open it and leave when Hamblin rested his hand on the boy's arm, stopping him. He turned back to face Lee.

"Malachi can tarry with you for the winter season," he said, nodding briefly at Malachi. "My boys will help out Jonah for the winter, but when spring comes, we need him back south to help with lambing and the sheep for the season. Idget too, if you can spare him."

Lee nodded. "I'll bring both boys down when the time comes." He rose and walked over to Hamblin. He held out his hand. "This thing has put a strain on all of us, but we've got to see it through together. The Governor is counting on us."

Hamblin hesitated before he took Lee's hand. He shook it briefly and said, "Of course we do, and we will get through this as we have everything else, God willing." He glanced at Malachi before turning and walking out the door that Albert held opened. After they left Lee stood staring at the door then turned to face the boys.

"I won't have no nonsense about what happened here today coming from either of you," he said. "You boys get my meaning. Don't want to hear that you've been talking of it."

"Yes, sir," they both said.

He walked over and got his coat off the bed and pulled it on. He adjusted the hat on his head and pulled his gloves out of his pockets, looking at the floor.

"You boys know, don't you, that Priscilla is not my blood daughter," he said, looking up at them.

Both boys looked at each other, stunned.

"No, sir," Malachi mumbled.

Lee looked at Malachi.

"We fostered her from the time she was a tiny baby, and she's grown up with us as one of my own. Her own parents lost their lives to cholera back when Priscilla was just a tot, so we took her in. She had nobody else." He looked down as he pulled on his gloves. "She knows, and she's grateful to me," he said, looking at Malachi. "She would do anything for me." He turned to open the door and step out into the half-light of the late afternoon.

After Lee closed the door of the bunkhouse behind him, Malachi stayed slumped on the bed, his hands gripped the edge of the thin mattress. His mind curled around the news about Priscilla like a baby's fist, hanging on. He turned to Idget. "Did you know?"

Idget bent down to retrieve another log and fed the stove. He looked at Malachi. "About Priscilla?"

"Yes, about her." His voice was rough.

"No." Idget shook his head. "Always thought she was Rachel's daughter. But I never knew. She's never let on."

They were both silent.

"You know we haven't heard the last of this," Malachi said.

He knew Lee wasn't done with him, but he realized that Lee was willing to draw a line when it came to another man's property. When it came down to it, the boys were all a piece of property, bought and put to work. He'd left it up to Hamblin to punish Albert in the way he wanted, in his own time, so perhaps Lee drew the same line with him, and it would be left to Jonah Blank to deal with him, silence him. The fire popped. Idget shoved his thick hands into the pockets of his pants and walked over to look out the small window of the bunkhouse. The afternoon light was quickly fading. He turned to face Malachi and took a deep breath.

"I know."

"If we can lay low 'til the spring, stay outta Lee's way, we may be able to find a way out when we get back south." He thought of Jonah Blank and wondered if he could find out where the man stored his money. He'd never stolen anything, but they'd need money to escape.

Idget looked at him warily. "I just don't know if we could."

"I don't know either," Malachi said. "But it's only a matter of time before Lee or somebody else shakes the truth out of us, and when that happens it's bound to be harsh." He could not bring himself to say he thought they'd be snuffed out, as if saying it aloud would make it so. He looked at Idget.

"I can't figure why it is you're so scared to leave."

Idget met Malachi's gaze and shook his head slowly. "It's just something I keep thinking about."

Malachi watched him and waited.

"I ever tell you about what happened to them boys belonging to the family a couple farms over that decided to up and leave?"

Malachi shook his head. He'd never heard of any of the Indian children trying to leave the families that had bought them. Even though he and Albert had talked about leaving, they had never tried. Mostly he figured they had nowhere to go and nothing to go with. Plus, they were so young. At least now, he might be able to pass for being older, find work somewhere.

"There were two of them living on the Barker place two farms over," Idget said. "Last year they both got punished by the church elders, something to do with fancying a girl at a church picnic and trying to kiss her. She told her father, and he complained about the boys to Brother Barker who brought it to the elders on account of not wanting to get on the left side of them if somebody should find out. The elders left them in a cellar for two days to teach 'em a lesson, and when they got out, they decided to run. Stole a couple of horses and got as far as Washington before Barker and his sons caught up with them. Brought both boys back and whipped 'em within an inch of their lives."

Idget stopped and shook his head. "One of them got sick after, infection or something bad. He died. And the other, he don't talk no more. Can't do a thing no more. Just sits and wets himself."

Malachi swallowed hard. He hadn't thought they'd be brought back. He was thinking their biggest problem would be to find a way to go, find money, horses, and a destination where two Indian boys dressed in cast-off white men's clothing wouldn't attract too much attention. But he hadn't thought that anybody would actually go to the trouble of bringing them back. He knew what they did to apostates. If you left the church, you were treated as a traitor. But them—he and Idget—both bought boys were their property. What would they do to them?

"But here, if we stay here, what do you think will happen to us?" Malachi asked.

The last burst of afternoon sun slanted through the bunkhouse window and illuminated the fear and agony in Idget's face.

"I figure," Idget said slowly. "If we can make it to the spring, get back south to Santa Clara with the sheep, we'll be good. They need us to take care of the sheep. It's what they have us for. We get back to our work, and they'll forget about us, go on to other things. Then we can decide, go from there if we need to."

Getting to the spring, Malachi thought. They just needed to get through until then.

CHAPTER 14

APRIL 15, 1858

April unfurled with an urgent beauty. The pear and apple trees that surrounded Lee's house were in full bloom and bees danced in eager, purposeful patterns around their branches. The soft scent of the trees' flowers and the richly tilled soil from the kitchen gardens filled the air. The farmhouse was alive with movement and spring-cleaning. Polly and Lavinia were getting ready to move, and the wives were helping them pack. Their new house had finally been built. Along with preparations for the move, Agatha had set in motion a tireless schedule of cleaning and repair. She'd marshaled all the members of the Lee household in her determined march to suss out the winter doldrums of dirt and cobwebs from every corner of the house.

No one was spared. Malachi's and Idget's pockets were festooned with rags and feather dusters, and they were thrust into the hum and buzz of it. They polished silver, finished whitewashing the house, moved furniture so the women could sweep and mop behind it, repainted walls, and climbed up ladders to wash windows and pull down the cobwebs Agatha had been eyeing and complaining about all winter.

That morning, Agatha had told Malachi and Idget to go help Priscilla clear and clean the root cellar. They walked down the narrow musty steps to find her standing on top of a short wooden stool, reaching back into shelves laced with cobwebs. She had pulled out dusty jars full of beets, pickles, green beans, and tomatoes, and she had lined them up on the floor to be cleaned. When Malachi and Idget arrived, she told them to wipe them off so they could be brought back to the house and used.

The weak strains of sunlight that filtered through the cellar door opening weren't enough for them to see what they were doing, and Priscilla had lit a lamp and attached it to one of the posts in the cellar. It cast a ghostly light on their activities. The three of them worked diligently, conscious of Agatha's warning that she'd be down later in the morning to check their work.

The large wooden bins that stored apples, potatoes, and carrots were nearly empty, with just a few forlorn carrots and shrunken apples still scattered here and there. The potatoes that remained at the end of the winter had already been cut up and planted in the garden. As soon as the soil could be worked, the wives tilled the huge vegetable garden to get it ready for spring planting. Rachel orchestrated the outdoor work. She had overseen the seed harvesting from the year before and added new seeds from Landreth's Seed Catalogue. She'd spent the winter months coaxing seedlings to grow in the flat beds of soil she had Idget and Malachi put on shelves facing the southern windows of the house. When the weather warmed and the soil was tilled, she fussed and plotted over the placement of every plant and seed. Now, lettuce was peeping up in rows of bright bibs of green, and carrot and radish seedlings formed neat grids, enjoying the cool spring soil.

Malachi had thought he would have to work hard to avoid John Lee during the winter, but Lee was occupied by other things and barely took notice of the boys. Late in the fall, he started construction on the new house for Polly and Lavinia in the town of Washington, about ten miles from Harmony. Whenever the weather cleared, Lee took some of his older boys and rode to the new place so that they could work on finishing the house. He'd announced to his family that his hope was to have Polly and Lavinia and their children living there by spring. As the move got closer, Polly and Lavinia had become increasingly cheeky, defying Agatha's authority and relishing their status as wives who would soon be the head of their own house.

Lee's responsibilities as a representative to the Utah Legislature also took him to Salt Lake City, where he spent the entire month of January in meetings with Brigham Young and other representatives from regions all around the territory. Rachel read his letters aloud when everyone was gathered around the dinner table, and the wives all offered opinions on their content. Agatha said there was hope that Young would succeed in his efforts to establish Utah as an independent state, giving the Mormons greater freedom. Since the boys weren't ordered away, Malachi and Idget would linger and listen to the wives' chatter. The women were full of speculation about the possible outcomes of these meetings Lee attended and what it would mean for them, for their family, and for the church. They were eager for Lee to return home with more news.

Lee surprised them in February by returning from Salt Lake with another wife. Her name was Emma Batchelor. She was an immigrant from England and had come cross-country with one of the handcart groups. Lee brought her to the farm, but she stayed so briefly that Malachi and Idget hadn't even seen her. Priscilla told them later that the other wives didn't take to her, and shortly after she had arrived, Lee moved her to Fort Harmony.

After Emma was installed at the fort, Lee rarely stayed at the farm. Gossip percolated through the house that Lee couldn't get his fill of this new Emma. Gossip turned to suspicion about which of the wives was most beloved by Lee, and arguments began to spill into every corner of the house, wrapping it in a braid of jealousy and tension.

The boys sought out Priscilla whenever they could, offering to help her with chores and help occupy Charlie and Leah. Lee's revelation about Priscilla filled Malachi's thoughts. He felt it bound the three of them—Priscilla, Idget, and him—even more tightly together, given they had all been orphaned and were without true family. He desperately wanted to talk to Priscilla about it but held his tongue, worried it would get back to Lee. He and Idget also talked sparingly to each other about the events at Mountain Meadows for fear someone would overhear them. Both boys felt a relief at Lee's prolonged absences, but they knew they were being watched.

The lamp bathed the root cellar in an eerie light, and Malachi looked up at Priscilla as she handed him dust-coated jars of vegetables to wipe clean. White cotton gloves protected her hands, and she wore a print gingham dress covered by a pinafore apron. A bright green scarf the color of pea shoots shielded her hair from the grime of the cellar. It was knotted underneath the thick hair that spilled down her back. Malachi and Idget flanked her as each of them took turns taking jars from her.

"Make sure you look for sealing wax or glass that's cracked. The ruined ones, we'll empty out, but save the jars if they're sound. We can use them again."

Priscilla talked less than usual that morning, confining most of her conversation to the precise directions she issued as they helped her clean and order the shelves to get ready for another growing and harvesting season. Malachi wondered what clouded her mood. He looked for her smile and waited for her to share some wicked piece of gossip she'd picked up from one of the wives.

Malachi reached up to take a jar filled with tomatoes and saw the tears seeping out of the corners of Priscilla's eyes. His glance flicked over to Idget. He'd seen it too. Both boys finished wiping off the jars, and Malachi set his on the shelf in front of him. He shifted to better support his bad leg and reached out to touch Priscilla's arm.

"What's wrong?" he asked.

She tilted her chin toward her chest and shook her head.

"Nothing that can be helped," she said, wiping the tears from her face. "I didn't care much for him and I didn't really want to marry him, but I didn't want him to die."

Malachi and Idget exchanged looks.

"Who?" Malachi asked.

"Brother William," she said. "William Haslett."

She stepped down from her stool. "I thought you knew."

Both boys shook their heads.

"What happened?" Malachi asked.

Priscilla wiped her gloves on the front of her apron, leaving dark grey smudges on the white cotton bib. She sat on the stool and looked at the floor as she peeled off her gloves. "I'm not sure, exactly," she said. "Rachel said his wife found him on the floor of their barn. Must have been terrible for her, all alone like that."

"Did he fall?" Idget asked.

Or had he been pushed? Malachi wondered. It might be that this was the first of the killings, guaranteeing silence about what had been done in Mountain Meadows and eliminating a threat to Lee.

Priscilla looked bleakly at the floor of the cellar and shrugged. "I think that's what Rebecca thought. It just happened last week. He'd gone into Harmony to get supplies and came back without telling her. She went out to the barn because she thought she heard horses arriving, but it was just him she found there, sprawled out on the floor. His neck was broke like he'd taken a fall from the loft. After, she took their horse and rode into Harmony. She's got a friend there, Eugenia. She's someone who'd come cross-country with the Hasletts, and Rebecca's staying there with her now. Some of the men from Harmony went out to take care of his body. I guess they had a quick funeral, with his wife and just a few folks who live at the fort or nearby, mostly the handcart folks, I suspect. They never had too much truck with any of the other families, except for us." She sighed and got up, wiping her eyes with the back of her hand.

"It's so sad." Her tears welled up again. "First she lost those children and now this."

Idget reached out his meaty hand and clumsily patted her shoulders. Malachi wanted to comfort her too, but he stood woodenly at her side, still gripping the shelf, worried his feelings for her would overwhelm him and cause him to do something that would embarrass them both.

"I imagine you think I'm silly," she said, smiling weakly at both boys. "Crying this way for a man I didn't want to marry, didn't even like that much, if the truth be known. It's just that I feel so bad for Rebecca. She's so alone. I think of her crying that day when Father Lee took the children from her. Nearly broke my heart to see her cry that way. And now she's lost William too. I think that if I had married him, at least she would have me now to help her."

"Do you think Father Lee will find another husband for her?" Idget asked.

"I doubt it. He's not the bishop of the church any more, and after what happened with Leah and Charlie, we'd heard that William and Rebecca had nothing but sharp things to say about Father, spreading nonsense about him, accusing him of things that nobody believes. Makes me think it's unlikely he'd want to offer to help her. He's stubborn that way."

She stopped and looked at the floor then shrugged.

"Maybe she'll marry into Eugenia's family. Makes most sense since they're already close and she would only be Eugenia's husband's second wife. When we go to the spring celebration at the fort this weekend, we may pick up some gossip of what her plans are."

To Malachi's relief, she had stopped crying and was eyeing the cellar.

"We should finish this. Agatha will be down soon." She stood and smiled. "It looks so much better down here. Nothing she can find to criticize. I'd like to see the look on her face when she sees it."

Malachi was glad to see her spirits lift, but the pall of William Haslett's death had fallen over all of them. The night before, Lee had made a rare appearance at the farm for supper. When they'd finished eating and the wives were clearing the table, Lee announced he was riding to Hamblin's ranch the following week and told Idget and Malachi they would be coming with him. When Priscilla climbed back on to the stool, Malachi felt Idget staring at him. He returned his look. He thought about the trip ahead. He wondered if Lee had some accident planned for them too.

Saturday arrived and the warm breeze and preparations to go to Fort Harmony for the celebration buoyed Malachi's mood. The Lees had been planning the event for several weeks. Lee had returned to Harmony, so Agatha was left in charge of marshaling the caravan that was to transport all thirty-five of them to the fort. According to Priscilla, there was to be a picnic, music, dancing, games, and contests. Everyone joined in. She'd told Malachi that Lee and his wives had organized the first one several years ago, and the families in the region had found it such a welcome end to the long, hard winters that blew through southern Utah that the Lees had decided to continue the tradition.

Agatha was in her glory as she organized the multitude of the Lee family and their picnic provisions for the day. She packed a side of beef, a whole pig that had been roasted and split, fifteen roasted chickens, dozens of baskets holding custard pies, loaves of bread, biscuits, pickled vegetables, and drink. They took dishes and silverware, and stacks of blankets for people to sit on. Agatha commandeered everyone, requiring them all to be up before the sun and apply themselves to their assigned tasks. Even the youngest children had been given something to do. Malachi and Idget got the horses and wagons ready and helped load the food. They hitched teams of horses to three different wagons. The wagons carried most of the wives, all the daughters, and the youngest children. Agatha and Rachel were distinguished in a smart black buggy Lee had recently purchased. Rachel drove their two-horse team, while Agatha sat beside her giving directions. Lee's older sons, Malachi, and Idget all rode on horseback.

The Lee caravan arrived mid-morning. Malachi had not been to the fort since the day they had arrived after the massacre. It was a massive, hulking structure, built of adobe and wood, meant to protect the families who lived there. But, when they arrived on the day of the picnic, the huge wooden gates were flung open and clusters of people moved around both inside and out, setting up for the celebration.

Men were hauling tables out for food and women were laying out blankets, chasing children, and setting up games. A handful of women rushed over to greet Lee's wives. Rachel pulled the team up short when the women hurried out to greet them. Malachi slipped off his horse and limped over to the buggy to hold the horses as Rachel and Agatha reached down to grasp their friends' hands and say hello. Agatha was reciting an inventory of all the work they'd done over the last several days to prepare for the celebration.

"Such a bother," she said as she gathered up the small baskets and cloth bags that surrounded her feet on the floor of the buggy and made her way to the ground. "Such a wonderful, wonderful bother. It is so good to see all of you. The winter has been long and I for one am so glad this day has come."

"Yes," said a plump woman in a bright blue dress with red hair that spiraled out of her hairpins in reckless curls that she kept trying to smooth. "We're so pleased to see you dear ladies. It's you we've missed. We've had

Brother Lee here, of course, but he's been otherwise occupied."

The red-haired woman raised her eyebrows then kissed both Agatha and Rachel on their cheeks and relieved Agatha of two of her bags. The woman slid her arm through Agatha's and the two women leaned their heads toward one another, whispering and smiling. Several other women clustered around them, saying things Malachi couldn't hear. He saw Agatha's gaze briefly rest on a knot of people greeting the children and wives in one of the other wagons. John Lee was there, his hand resting protectively on the shoulder of a tall, younger woman with dark brown hair and a serene face who stood by his side. It must have been Emma Batchelor.

Rachel motioned Malachi and Idget over and told them where to stable the horses. She reminded them they were to be on hand to help with set up. Then she went to join Agatha and the others as the women moved together chatting and laughing, making their way toward John Lee. Lee welcomed both his wives as Emma hovered silently nearby. Rachel and Agatha greeted her, then the group of friends they were with strolled away with their arms linked with Rachel's and Agatha's, leaving Lee and Emma standing alone. Another group of horses and wagons arrived, and Lee waved at the newcomers before putting his hand on the small of Emma's back and piloting her over to greet them.

The stables in the fort were full of boys and men, settling in their horses and feeding them. Malachi and Idget found two stalls with John Lee's name on them and stabled the buggy's horses. Then they brought back their own ponies and removed their saddles, leaving them to graze in the paddock next to the stable. Idget had gone ahead, and as Malachi was latching the gate to the paddock, he heard a man's voice say, "There's been some restlessness here." Malachi looked up to see a heavy-set man with a bulbous nose and large drooping eyes talking to Isaac Haight.

"Lee's done his best with it," Haight replied. "He's been spending more time here at the fort to silence the worst of it, but still people are talking, raising questions about what happened in the meadows. And this thing with Haslett hasn't helped. It's got folks stirred up."

He wanted to linger and listen, but knew he couldn't risk being seen. He quickly finished securing the gate and grabbed his walking stick to go in search of Idget who'd gone ahead to find out what Rachel wanted the boys to do next. He walked toward the fort, passing a group of musicians tuning their instruments and getting ready to serenade the gathering crowd. As they started to play, a few stray couples held hands and began to dance, wheeling around in front of the musicians. Further on, he spied Priscilla in the midst of a group of younger children. Charlie and Leah stood on either side of her, holding on to her dress, as she instructed the other children on the rules of a game. She saw him and waved him over.

"See if you can distract Charlie for me," she said, smiling at Malachi and settling Leah on the ground next to some other children. She peeled Charlie's hand from her skirt and gently steered him toward Malachi. Over the winter, the small boy had begun to spread his sparse reserve of trust to include Malachi and Idget.

"You stand with me," Malachi reached down to him, looking into the boy's liquid blue eyes. "She'll be right back."

Priscilla walked about twenty feet away and dropped a red kerchief then did the same on the opposite side where she dropped a blue one. When she returned, she called out to the children who gathered around her and explained the rules of *Capture the Flag*. Malachi felt the heat and damp of Charlie's small hand as it rested lightly in his. Suddenly, the boy gripped his hand and huddled closer to his legs. Malachi looked up to see Rebecca Haslett and another woman walking over to them. Malachi glanced at Priscilla and saw that she'd seen them too. She called over another girl and talked to her, then left her to finish getting the children started in the game.

When Priscilla reached them, she leaned down and said to Charlie, "Do you want me to hold you?" The little boy nodded vigorously and dropped Malachi's hand. She pulled him up and he wrapped his arms and legs around her, burying his face in her shoulder.

Leah trotted over just as Rebecca Haslett and her companion reached them. Rebecca's friend was a tiny creature with muddy brown eyes drilled into a foxlike face. Her hair was black and wispy. As she walked toward them, she swiped at thin strands that the spring breeze lifted into her eyes. She had one arm wound tightly through Rebecca's. Rebecca gazed at Charlie and Leah. She looked at the children as if she wanted to absorb them, use them as a salve for a heart sickened by sorrow and pain.

"Sister Rebecca, I want you to know…" Priscilla hesitated, searching Rebecca's face as the woman kept her eyes on the children. "I wanted to say how sorry I am about William, about Brother Haslett."

Rebecca's eyes swiveled to Priscilla's face. "So sorry, are you?" Her face had the fierce look of a downed blue jay. Her friend held her arm a little more tightly and Rebecca reached up to grab hold of her friend's hand. "My William was a good man. Never caused a problem. Did what he was told, faithful to the church. He shoulda' been rewarded." Her voice was raised. "You Lees, you say you want to help, you say you're sorry for the worry and the want and the pain the rest of us have, but you're altogether so high and mighty, thinkin' you have something over on the rest of us. But it's built on nothing but a passel of lies, lies that'll topple you all."

Charlie had begun to whimper, and his tiny rear end was starting to sag and slip out of Priscilla's arms. She hitched him up and he wrapped his arms more tightly around her. Malachi watched as a blush of red seeped up from beneath Priscilla's collar to her neck. "I know you've had such pain and sadness," Priscilla said. She kept her gaze steadily on Rebecca and lightly pressed the back of Charlie's head guiding it to lean against her shoulder, trying to calm him. "I'm sorry for it, and sorry for anything my family has done to contribute to it."

"But it's not over, is it?" Rebecca stepped toward Priscilla. Her friend pulled at her arm, trying to hold her back. "It's not over until everyone knows the truth about why these children are here."

She reached out toward Leah who shrank away from her. Rebecca's friend pulled more forcefully at her arm now and leaned forward to whisper urgently into her ear. Rebecca pulled away from her and crossed her arms in front of her chest as she faced Priscilla.

"I'm not sure what you mean," Priscilla said. A quaver of uncertainty crept into her voice. She looked briefly at Malachi. Charlie had started to cry in earnest now, and Leah was clamoring to have Priscilla hold her too.

"Everyone's afraid to talk about it, but I know the truth of it," Rebecca said, tilting her chin upward. Her eyes gleamed. Malachi thought she looked unsteady, like she might lash out with more than words at any time. "My William, he told me the truth of it before he died."

"Rebecca!" her friend warned, reaching out for her arm again.

Rebecca shook her off. "I'm going to speak my mind, Eugenia, I am."

"Speak your mind on what, Sister Rebecca?" Isaac Haight had come over. He stood behind Malachi, addressing Rebecca, then stepped in front of him as though he weren't even there. He placed himself between Rebecca and Priscilla, and Rebecca seemed to draw herself in a little as he faced her. A tremor of fear flashed in her eyes, then her face crumpled and she began to cry.

Haight reached out to her and lightly gripped both her shoulders, turning her to face him. His hands were long and slender, almost effeminate. "You've had a world of sorrow, Sister Rebecca. I know you have. I know how difficult these last few weeks have been for you, but God has a plan for you and we will make sure you're cared for."

Eugenia handed Rebecca a lace-edged hanky she'd had tucked up her sleeve, and Rebecca wiped her eyes and cheeks. The skin around her nose was raw and flaky. She dabbed at it lightly as if it hurt.

"I can't say I feel his plan for me, Brother Isaac. Can't say as I feel he has much to say to me at all. I thought his plan for me was those children yonder." She jutted her chin in Charlie and Leah's direction. "But

I guess Brother Lee knew better, knew better than what God may have had planned for me."

Haight was silent as he took in the woman in with his wide-set, unblinking eyes. Malachi felt a chill settle in his gut.

"Will you do me the honor of walking with me a spell? The food is nearly laid out and I 'spect it's a good sight to see." Haight offered Rebecca his arm. She pursed her lips then smiled shyly at him. She glanced at Eugenia.

"You go on," Eugenia said, waving her away. "I'll find you later."

They walked away, their heads tending toward each other in conversation. When they were gone, Eugenia scraped her hair off her forehead then turned to Priscilla. "You mustn't mind what she said to you. She's half out of her wits with grief and worry and doesn't track on her words most of the time. No need to repeat any of it. It's just a grieving woman talking."

"I understand." Priscilla nodded. "I can't imagine how she must feel, to have lost her husband, lost so much."

Eugenia looked over her shoulder. "My husband will be wanting me now that the food is out." She smiled stiffly at Priscilla and gave Malachi a brief, curious look before she turned to walk away.

Priscilla let Charlie slide down her body. He landed on the ground and immediately reached for her hand. "What do you think Rebecca meant?" She asked Malachi. "We know the truth of why Leah and Charlie are here, it's not like we don't."

Malachi looked at her and her expression shifted.

"Is there something you know?" she asked him.

He tried to say something, but the words lodged in his throat. Lying to her about what he knew seemed to violate something deep within him, but he knew he couldn't tell her the truth.

"Malachi, what is it?" she said, reaching out to lightly touch his arm. "I can see there's something that bothers you. Is there something you know?"

"I do," he said and looked at the ground. "But I can't tell you. I cannot tell anyone." He had said too much.

"But why?" she asked. "You're worried, I can see it. You could tell Father Lee. He knows how to take care of things."

"Not him," he blurted out before he could check himself. "I can't tell him. Don't ask me any more questions. Just don't ask me."

He walked away from her before she could say anything else. He hated turning away from her, but he could no longer face her. For a brief dangerous instant, he had thought if he told her what he knew it would bind them somehow, keep them together even after he had gone. How he longed for that, to find refuge in her. But refuge in what? He knew sharing this dark piece of truth would put them both at risk. And, worse, what if she did not believe him? She thought she knew the truth, the story of the slaughter by the Paiutes, the merciful rescue of the children, their protection. And what would she do if he told her differently? Lee's words came back to him: *She's grateful to me, would do anything for me.* He walked away, turning one last time to see her still watching him, flanked on either side by Leah and Charlie, who clung to her as though she were their rescue raft.

The musicians had left their instruments resting on stools and were clustered together at the back of the line for food. Malachi spied Idget in front of them. He'd been joined by some of the other Indian boys who lived with families around Harmony and Washington. Idget waved him over.

"I seen Rebecca Haslett there with you, talking to you," Idget said in a low voice. "How does she seem?"

Malachi shrugged and looked back to where Priscilla still stood, surrounded now by all the children who'd planned on playing *Capture the Flag.* She was motioning them over to the table and the group let out a few cheers when they saw the food was ready. A couple of boys charged toward the food tables, racing to beat the others.

"Rebecca's got a score to settle with the Lees, that's sure," Malachi said quietly so the other boys couldn't hear.

He spotted John Lee sitting on a chair talking to the large man he'd seen with Isaac Haight earlier. He sat on a chair next to Lee, his plump form spilling over the chair. Both men had plates piled high with food and balanced them on their knees while they ate. Lee tore off the meat of a chicken leg he held. He wiped off the grease that smeared his face with the back of his hand. As they ate, they watched Priscilla and the small sea of children that surrounded her progress toward the loaded tables. The large man eyed her and leaned over to Lee to say something. Malachi hated the way the man looked at her.

Priscilla walked by Malachi and Idget and smiled, and Idget motioned to her and the children to take their places in front of them in the line. When they gathered, the musicians behind them grumbled good-naturedly about losing their places. Priscilla still held Charlie's hand, but Leah had been spirited away by a couple of younger girls who had her between them, each holding one of her hands as they sidled up to the table and pointed out their favorite foods to her.

"This is probably the best meal some of these children have had in months," Priscilla said to Malachi and Idget as she watched the children in line ahead of them. "It's why I love this day. We can share some of what we have with others, plus it's so wonderful to see everyone after we've all been cooped up all winter."

Although her words were generous, her voice was stiff and colorless. Even Charlie glanced up at her, seeming to sense something was wrong.

Idget stepped away from Malachi and stood at her side. "You alright, Priscilla?"

She turned to him and smiled slightly. "All of life feels topsy-turvy, as though what I thought I knew isn't what I know at all."

"Don't take too much of what Rebecca Haslett says to heart," Malachi blurted out.

"Shouldn't I?" She turned to him and held his gaze, then looked away. "I don't know. I feel that somehow I am responsible for all that woman's sorrow."

"But you can't," Malachi croaked hoarsely. "You're not."

She faced him again.

"What is it I'm not meant to know, Malachi? Why won't you tell me?"

A small heated silence ignited between them. He feared that denying her meant splintering the heart of the friendship they had found in each other. There was something else, too, although he hated letting himself think it. But there it was, floating on their friendship, like oil on water: he wasn't sure he could trust her.

Idget caught Malachi's eye and he shook his head in warning. Malachi leaned heavily on his walking stick and turned to look at Priscilla, taking in the openness and warmth in her gaze. He sighed.

"This isn't something I can tell you." His voice was low, and she had to lean in to hear him. Her face was so close he could feel her soft breath on his cheek. "Not now, maybe not ever."

"Okay, move along now, or we'll never get anything to eat!" A man's voice boomed behind them.

Malachi glanced back and saw the fiddle player and the other musicians smiling at them, waving them forward. A gap had grown between them and the crowd of children who had clustered in line in front of them. Priscilla moved further up the line, putting distance between herself and Idget and Malachi.

Haight approached Lee and his companion. Rebecca had disappeared. Haight stepped back as the large man who sat next to Lee rose and set his plate down on the stool. He conferred briefly with the men then turned. Lee's eyes settled on Priscilla as the beefy man walked toward her. Several people moved to make way for him. He reminded Malachi of a large humped snail, moving steadily over the ground, leaving a trail in his wake.

"Who's that?" Malachi asked Idget.

"It's George Smith," Idget said.

"Wonder what he wants with her?" Malachi asked, but Idget said nothing.

Smith stayed at Priscilla's side as she filled a plate, then he pointed to where Lee and Haight sat. She cast a quick glance behind her toward the boys and gave them a stiff smile. She followed Smith over to Lee and Haight. Lee rose to kiss her on the cheek and offered her his chair. She sat, her plate balanced on her knees as she ate while the three men stood talking to each other over her head and occasionally looking down at her.

Malachi stared at them.

"C'mon." Idget nudged his elbow. "Let's go find some shade. It's getting hot."

The boys found a spot sheltered by the shade of the east wall of the fort. They sat in silence, consuming their heaping plates of food. Malachi's heart was roiling and thick with emotion. This could not be the last of his conversations with Priscilla. He shoved a biscuit around in the chicken grease that lined his plate. He must find a way to get some private time with her, make her understand. His gaze spanned out over the picnic grounds. The musicians had finished eating and had begun to play a reel, tempting a few couples and a smattering of children to dance. Leah had lured Charlie to the ground in front of the band and they were dancing awkwardly, looking like two small wrens, wings spread and pecking at the air. Priscilla was still surrounded by Lee, Smith, and Haight. He wondered about this sudden attention they were paying her. He asked Idget if he thought it was odd George Smith singled her out to join the three men. The boy shrugged.

"It's a compliment to her. George Smith is an important man, even more powerful than Father Lee. And he's got a fearsome reputation. I think even Father Lee is afraid of him. They say he's Young's right hand, carries out his orders for him, makes sure the settlements stay in good order. Just make sure you don't draw his attention to you. Nobody wants to get on the bad side of George Smith." He wiped a smear of grease off his face. "Anyhow, maybe Father Lee thinks she's seen too much in our company. I'm guessing he's still on the look-out for a husband for her and he just don't want her being seen with us all the time while she's here. I mean, lookit who we are."

A husband for Priscilla. The thought curdled in Malachi's chest.

"I wonder if it's one of them," he nodded toward the men gathered round Priscilla. "If it's Smith or Haight he's hoping to marry her to."

Idget followed his gaze and said, "If it is, she'll have a say in it. It's not like she has to agree to just anyone."

Suddenly, Lee threw back his head and laughed at something Priscilla had said. Smith had sat down next to her and leaned in to say something. She nodded at him but Malachi was certain he saw her pull back from the man's wide tilting body. Lee looked over at Smith, then rose and offered Priscilla his hand. She set her plate on the ground, took Lee's hand. Together they made their way over to where the musicians played. Lee placed his hand lightly on her waist and she took his other hand in hers as he guided her easily in a dance.

Malachi watched the two of them spin and turn. "Do you think it would be Lee?" he asked Idget. "Do you think Lee would marry her? She's not his daughter, his real daughter."

Idget looked up from his plate at the dancers. He shook his head as he chewed and swallowed.

"I don't think Rachel and Agatha would allow it."

"But it's done, isn't it? She's adopted, so he could marry her, add her to his wives if she accepted."

"I guess it is." Idget shrugged and set his plate on the ground. "I just don't think the other wives would stand for it. I think it'll be someone else."

Although the boys joined in the games and general celebration after that, Malachi continued to chew on the possibility that Lee was looking for a husband for Priscilla. He watched from afar as she danced first with Lee, then Smith, then others. Several younger men clustered around her too, talking and laughing. Later she disappeared with Charlie and Leah in tow, and Malachi did not catch sight of her again until the Lee family gathered at the end of the day. She rode in the back of one of the wagons, with Charlie on her lap and Leah dozing against her side. Malachi tried without success to catch her eye. Even though he desperately wanted to ride alongside to exchange a few words with her, Lee's older sons flanked the wagon. He promised himself he would seek her out the following day. He knew he had to talk to her one last time before he and Idget left with Lee for Santa Clara.

CHAPTER 15

APRIL 18

On Sunday Malachi lay in his narrow bed, watching the light of early spring angle through the bunkhouse window and listening to Idget's light snore. He woke up thinking of Priscilla. He knew she was upset with him for not telling her what she had wanted to know. He couldn't stand the thought that she would be unhappy with him, but he didn't know how to navigate these waters to repair the misunderstanding between them. And the stubborn question of trust still lodged in his head. It was a root he kept tripping over. He sighed and sat up, throwing off the blanket and swinging his bare feet to the floor to push himself out of bed.

He limped over to the chair at the foot of his bed and picked up his pants, standing unsteadily on one leg then the next to pull them on. Idget's snores had turned into a high rhythmic whistle, causing Malachi to stand for a moment, watching his friend stir and twitch with the last vestiges of sleep. Idget jerked and snorted when a sudden, sharp rap came at the bunkhouse door. Malachi opened it. Agatha stood at the bottom of the short flight of steps. She was wrapped in a light brown shawl.

"Come out," she said as she squinted up at him. "Got to talk to you."

She turned away, her back to the door, waiting for him to descend the steps and join her. Her appearance surprised him. Neither Agatha nor any of the other wives had set foot in the bunkhouse since he had been there and had always sent children to summon them when they needed the boys. He grabbed his coat from a hook inside the door and pulled it on. He stepped out and closed the door.

He walked up beside her. "Good morning, ma'am."

She didn't return his greeting, but turned to him, examining his face so closely that he wondered whether he had some crust on his mouth or eyes from the night before. Self-consciously, he wiped the back of his hand across his mouth.

"I am not one to beat around the bush," she said. "I know you care for our girl, Priscilla, and have found a friendship with her."

His heart picked up a beat. He was surprised Agatha had noticed, but it was her job to see everything that went on at the Lee's farm.

"Father Lee's made the decision that she's to go south with you to-morrow." She held up her hand when Malachi opened his mouth to talk. "She'll stay at the Hamblin place. Jacob Hamblin has sent word through George Smith that his wives could use some spare hands in caring for those children they kept from the train. Leah and Charlie will go too. As sure as I stand here before you, that boy Charlie would raise a racket night and day if she weren't around to soothe him. I know he's been through a lot, but I've got too much on my hands as it is, so it's easier that the children should go with Priscilla." She rubbed her arms from the chill in the air and pulled her shawl more tightly around her, then gazed out over the garden and the fields beyond.

The suddenness of the news should have warned him, but all he could think of was his good fortune at having more time with Priscilla. Knowing he would continue to be near her made the pain that plagued him earlier fly off on the morning breeze.

Agatha turned to him. "I don't much care for Jacob Hamblin's boy, Albert." She sniffed. "He's taken too many airs for himself, and I think Brother Hamblin's spoiled him a bit for honesty and hard work."

Malachi said nothing, but she didn't seem to expect him to.

"I know that Brother Hamblin is gone a fair amount, off on those Indian expeditions he's become so fond of," she continued, not looking at Malachi. "And I worry that while he's gone Albert will think he's king of the roost, take advantage." She paused. "He's a sizable boy, and I'm not convinced that Rachael Hamblin has the strength or the will to control him, nor Brother Hamblin's newest wife, for that matter. She's just a young slip of a thing and I hear she's sickly and in bed-rest much of the time."

"I won't let anything happen to Priscilla, ma'am, if that's what's worrying you," Malachi said, scuffing the toe of his boot in the gravelly dirt. "Idget and I, we'll watch out for her."

She turned to look at him, her lips folded into a thin line that he thought was a smile. "I hate to see her go, but it's not for me to say, I—" She stopped, looking as though she thought she had said too much. Then she turned away from him and looked out over the garden and the fields. "There are some days that I wish change just wouldn't keep coming because when it does, we have to find ways to make things work all over again."

"Ma'am?"

She looked at him, squinting slightly as though she found something objectionable in him but she wasn't sure what. Then her expression shifted and became more distant. "You boys, you Indian boys, you just don't know what we've sacrificed, what we've been through, what we've built and seen destroyed over the years by people who hate us just because of what we believe and how God has guided us to live our lives."

He shifted uncomfortably, not knowing what to say. He'd seen his own share of hatred, was familiar with its rough contours, and had felt its harshness directed at him just because of what he looked like, who he was. But his own experience didn't seem to figure into her thoughts.

"Others have despised us, despised our faith, how we practice. It's what forced us out here. What we'd built in the east—in Nauvoo—was so beautiful it would take your breath away if you saw it."

Her face, usually so closed and controlled, had cracked open with emotion and the rims of her eyes glistened with tears. "Our houses were the finest in the region and our temple was a sight to behold. We had the fattest cattle of all the farms around. The land was so easy there, we could grow anything." Her voice and face had grown wistful. She looked out at the fields again.

"But we lost it all, were driven out by those that hated us, hated our faith. The Lord brought us here, led Brother Young here and we followed him." She stopped and gazed across the fields. "Here you have to work and work and work to have just a little to show for it."

She'd stopped talking and Malachi could hear her breath lightly whistling in and out of her narrow, pinched nostrils.

"I shouldn't complain, though. God has given us much, another chance, and we have to be thankful for that." Her words suddenly sounded empty and tired. Malachi wondered how many times she had recited them to herself, to the other wives. She fell silent again, and the sounds of the farm waking up peppered the air. Slowly she drew herself up, seeming to take possession of herself once again.

"There's chores for you and Idget to do today while we're at service," she said. Her brusqueness returned. "I want you to muck out the stalls in the barn. Now the weather has warmed, we need to get those cleaned. Spread the manure on the half of the garden that hasn't been planted. After, there are two beds that need to be brought out of the house and put in the bunkhouse. We'll have more men here soon, and we need a place to put them. I'll want you to put them in this one here where you and Idget have been staying. Roust out Idget. It's time he's up. Come on up to the house and we'll feed you breakfast. After I'll show you the beds you're to move. We'll be back at one to prepare for Sunday dinner. I want it done by the time we return."

She looked at him briefly and her thin lips inched into a tight smile, then she turned to walk back to the house. As he watched her retreat his heart lifted and expanded in his chest, like a kite in a jagged movement toward the sky. Priscilla would come south with them. Even though his body was giddy and light with the news, Agatha's request to keep Priscilla safe tethered him, gave him purpose. He climbed the steps to go back into the bunkhouse. Idget was awake, but still in bed.

"I heard voices. Who was here?"

Malachi walked over to his bed and sat at the end of it. "Agatha came to tell us what chores she wants us to do while they're at service."

Idget rubbed his chest and propped himself up on his elbows. "What does she want us to do?"

"Muck the stalls, move some furniture. Nothing much."

"Anything else?" Idget looked at him. "Looks like you got something else to tell."

"Priscilla is coming south with us, with Charlie and Leah. Hamblin's wife needs some help during lambing."

Idget digested the news, saying nothing. He pushed his blanket away from his body and slid his feet to the floor.

"I wonder why," he said as he pulled on his pants and stood.

"Why is she coming?" Malachi asked. "Agatha said George Smith brought the news that the Hamblins needed the extra help, so they're sending her."

Idget turned to him. He nodded and his face was serious. "Seems off, somehow." He shrugged. "Dunno." He lifted his shirt off the bedpost. "Maybe Father Lee's got someone in mind for her to marry down there." He pulled his shirt on and buttoned it.

Malachi had considered that possibility too. But she was coming, and that's all that mattered to him at that moment. He didn't need to say goodbye to her just then. Even if she were coming south to be court-ed by someone, he would deal with that when the time came. Like he would deal with everything else. That morning, for the first time since the killing in Mountain Meadows, his heart was full of hope. Although it buoyed him, he shared none of it with Idget. As yet, he had no plan for how they were to deal with the truth that trapped them. Nothing in his life had taught him to speak of a future that would somehow be better than what faced him today.

After breakfast, Agatha showed the boys the beds she wanted moved. They followed her up two flights of stairs to the third floor. Malachi had never been beyond the first floor and as they walked down a long hall past multiple bedrooms, he looked curiously into those that had their doors ajar. These were the children's bedrooms and each had several beds and wardrobes. All the beds were neatly made and clothes were put away. He wondered which one belonged to Priscilla. He thought about the discipline the wives exerted over the house, marshaling their small troupe every day to do what was needed to keep life running in its rigorous, simple order. Agatha and Idget stopped at a bedroom at the end of the hall, waiting for Malachi to catch up.

Agatha eyed him skeptically. "Didn't think of your leg. Sure you'll be able to move these beds?"

"I can, ma'am. It's not like I have to have my stick to walk all the time. I'm slower without it, but Idget's strong as a horse, so he'll probably do most of the lifting."

Agatha glanced at Idget. He grinned shyly at her. She ran her tongue along the roof of her mouth, as if she had eaten something distasteful, then turned to lead the boys into the room. There were two single beds that had been stripped of their bedding. The beds had been pulled into the middle of the room and drop cloths had been placed around the baseboards.

"This room belonged to Polly's children," Agatha said. "They'll double up down the hall until they move, so we can get this painted and ready for a couple of the older girls."

Malachi hadn't thought Polly and Lavinia's move was to happen for several more months. He wondered briefly how the two wives viewed Agatha's eagerness to rid the house of their presence. As if she had read the tenor of his thoughts, she added, "They're glad to be gone, those two." She slapped her hands together as if flapping dust off them. "Can't speak of nothing else. And their house will be the nicest yet that Father Lee has built. He's taking great care with it." Agatha looked a last time at the room and without further comment walked out and down the hall.

Malachi and Idget glanced at each other and shrugged. They had no choice but to file out after her. When they reached the end of the hall, they followed her down a wide flight of stairs to the second floor, where she stopped. Malachi looked down the hallway. All the doors were closed and the sun poured in through the long window at the end of the hall, illuminating the pine floor and white washed walls. Malachi knew this was the floor where the wives slept.

"I want you in and out," Agatha said. "No wandering anywhere else. You boys understand?"

They both nodded. Malachi glanced down the hallway one last time before he turned to follow Agatha and Idget down the stairs. The memories from his first night in the house and the sounds of Lee's visits to his wives' beds flooded his mind. He wondered what it must be like to move from the softness of one willing woman to the next. He doused his imaginings, tugging his shirt out to hide the swelling in his groin. Wouldn't do to have Agatha noticing that.

Idget paused on the stairs and looked back at him, curiosity in his face. "You okay?" he asked.

Malachi nodded. He grasped the railing and made his way down the last flight of stairs. At the bottom, Agatha waited. She eyed both of them and said, "You can join us for Sunday dinner. Say your goodbyes." Abruptly she turned away from them and walked toward the kitchen.

The boys went out to the barn and into the storage area. They pulled out tools to clean the stalls, finding rakes, pitchforks, and a broad shovel. Idget got the wheelbarrow from where it leaned against the shed and piled the tools into it, wheeling it over to the first stall. They raked out old straw and manure from the floors. Its sweet, rotting smell filled Malachi's nostrils as he scraped it off the floor and scooped it into a wheelbarrow. Idget ferried each load to the vegetable garden and dumped it in a heap to be worked into the soil. Malachi enjoyed the labor and the morning went quickly. By the time they'd finished three of the four stalls, they heard the family leaving for Sunday service. When they finished the fourth stall, Malachi walked outside and leaned on his pitchfork as Idget careened the wheelbarrow with the last of the muck toward the garden. Sweat darkened Malachi's shirt at his chest and armpits and had beaded up on his forehead and face. He mopped it off with a rag from his pocket. Idget was running toward him now, a loopy grin illuminating his face as he yelled and whooped, zigzagging the wheelbarrow back toward the barn.

"Let's get some water," Idget said, after they'd put away their tools and walked into the house. Idget pulled out two cups from the kitchen cupboard and filled them from a jug on the table. He handed one to Malachi and they drained them. Idget rinsed them out and carefully dried them before placing them back in the cupboard.

"Shall we get to it?" Malachi asked.

Idget nodded and they made their way to the third-floor bedroom. They stood by the beds, considering how they would make their way out of the house with them. "Looks like it'd be easiest to pull 'em apart at the head and foot," Malachi said. "We can put them back together in the bunk house. See here, looks like it's been built to come apart that way." He bent over the bed and grabbed the frame, lifting it up and out of the headboard a little way to show what he meant.

Idget nodded and both boys set to work pulling off the feather mattresses, rolling them up, and carefully dismantling the bed frames. Idget carried the mattresses down first, while Malachi finished stacking the disassembled frames to get them ready to move. When he came back, Idget piled a headboard and the feet of both beds together and hefted them up to take them down. Malachi tested the weight of the sideboards and decided he could haul them. When he got to the bunkhouse, Malachi leaned the boards against the outside wall and slid one of them through the door. Inside, Idget was already rearranging the other beds so they could set up the ones they'd moved.

"Looks like we've got all the pieces here for one of the beds. Do you think you can start putting it together on your own?" Malachi asked.

Idget looked uncertainly at the frame and shrugged. "I could give it a try." He looked at him. "Almost time for them to come back?"

Malachi nodded. "Soon. I'll go get the rest." He stopped at the door and turned. "If you get stuck, don't worry. I'm not moving very fast. Just do your best. When I come back, we can work on the other one together."

Idget flashed him a grin and waved him away. Malachi limped toward the house. He'd left his stick at the bunkhouse. His leg was bothering him, but if he moved slowly, he could get through it. He walked into the house and gradually made his way up the first flight of stairs, where he stopped to rest. His leg started to cramp. He sat on the first step that went up to the third floor and looked down the hallway of closed doors on the second floor. Curiosity about what was behind those doors tapped his chest. The clock in the dining room downstairs had just struck noon. He stretched his bad leg out in front of him, working his foot back and forth to get the cramp to ease. He pulled himself up and gazed down the hallway, considering what he might find. When he took the first few steps down the hall, a floorboard squeaked loudly, as though the house was issuing a warning. The sound sent a shot of fear through him and he paused. But he tamped it down and continued to make his way to the end of the hall. At the last room on the right, his hand rested on the porcelain doorknob. He turned it and went in.

The room was handsome and spacious, occupying one corner of the house with its tall windows looking out to the west and south. Bookshelves lined the southern wall, and a hefty oak desk sat in front of them. A large oak rocking chair was to the left of the desk, and adjacent to the desk on the right stood two upholstered leather chairs flanking a small, delicate settee. The settee looked hopelessly feminine in the midst of the other bulky furniture. Malachi realized with a small surge of apprehension that it must be Lee's private room, a room which one could enter only by invitation from Lee himself. He knew what he was doing was a violation and that he should turn and close the door; but he stepped into the room, eager to examine it further. Other than the flimsy settee, there was no hint of a woman here. He imagined he could smell the tang of Lee in the air. His heart pulsed with fear as he wiped the sweat on his palm across his pants. He limped over to the oak desk. Its broad, polished surface held a letter opener with a horn handle that was precisely aligned with one side of the desk. There was also a pot of ink, a blotter, and a sheaf of paper. He turned and looked at the bookshelves, running his forefinger along the spines that neatly lined the shelves, proud that he could make out a word or two in their titles. He returned to the desk and walked to the back of it. He wasn't sure what he was hoping to find. Answers, perhaps. Answers as to whether John Lee suspected he and Idget knew more than they'd let on, answers to what Lee might have in store for them. He frowned as he wondered whether their lives would figure into Lee's thinking. Would he and Idget matter so much to Lee that he would take time in this solitary room to think of them, to make a record of his thoughts about them?

He pulled out the chair and sat in it, feeling a sort of thrill move through his groin and stomach. There were two drawers on either side of the desk and a wide narrow one in the middle, which he pulled out. He skimmed its contents: a small pile of coins, a curl of blonde hair that looked like a child's tied with a maroon ribbon, and another sheaf of blank paper, also wrapped in ribbon. He closed the drawer and pulled open the others, discovering a small hymnal, a book of house accounts, and an envelope fat with paper money. He looked at the envelope and his heart beat faster, thinking what it could mean for him and Idget, how it could help them. But he hesitated, remembering an overheard snatch of conversation between the wives: "He counts it careful. Always knows what we have so he can take care of us, all of us." He wondered if he could afford to steal it. What if Lee discovered it between now and the time they left tomorrow? He looked at the envelope, touched it lightly but left it where it was.

He continued his search, pulling out drawers, examining their contents, looking for more clues to Lee, to the killings, to his own fate. Perhaps he could find Lee's own diary. When he tried to pull out the bottom right-hand drawer, it stuck. He bent down on the floor and jimmied the drawer, but couldn't get it to move. He crouched down further and peered inside to find out what was jamming it. In the far back of the drawer, pushed behind books that appeared to be more house accounts, a book was tilted up, preventing the drawer from opening. He reached in and pulled the book flat, then opened the drawer. There, in the back, was a Bible. He pulled it out. The edges of its pages were mottled dark with blood. A shot of recognition went through him. It was the same one he had taken from the girl's bloodied apron that day in the meadows, the one Lee had claimed as his own after he'd discovered Malachi had hidden it. The one he'd been punished for keeping.

He looked at its hide-bound cover and lifted it open. Between the time he'd taken it off the girl's body and his arrival at the Lee farm, he hadn't had time to properly examine it. Slowly he read the words on the flyleaf, *to my dearest Magpie, with love in Christ, Mother*. He ran his thumb along the edge of the pages, ruffling their stiff edges. When he did, he felt a page out of place and opened the Bible to it. There, stuck between the pages of column-lined verses, he found a folded paper with handwriting on it, a letter. How had he missed this? His heart beat faster and he pulled the chair toward the desk then unfolded the letter, smoothing it out on the surface of the desk.

The top and bottom edges of the letter were stained with blood too, but the writing, fluid and uniform, was legible. The date at the top read 11 September, 1857. He thought for a moment. It was the day of the killings in the meadows. His mouth felt dry and tacky. The letter began, "Dearest Antonia, I write this knowing it may be my last word to you." His reading was painfully slow, his finger pressed on each word as his mind struggled to assemble the beautifully scripted letters into sounds, he could recognize. He stopped and ran the palm of his hand across the letter, wishing he could absorb its meaning. He wondered what had happened to the other letters and why Lee had kept this one. Had he read it? Perhaps it was Lee who had placed it in the Bible, which is why Malachi hadn't noticed it before. Or perhaps Lee had missed it just as Malachi had. Perhaps he hadn't even looked at the Bible, just carelessly threw it in the bottom drawer of his desk the same day he had discovered Malachi's betrayal, fury at the boy's insolence blinding him to all else. Yet, the letters he had taken from Malachi were missing. He checked the drawer, reaching to its back. Nothing. Only this one remained. He bent over it again.

"Malachi!"

Idget's voice startled him. The sound of his voice was urgent, frightened. It sounded as if Idget was at the bottom of the stairs, at least he hoped so.

"Malachi!" Idget called out again. "You here?"

Malachi hastily folded the letter. He unbuttoned his shirt and slipped it between the buttons, where it rested, an angled reminder against his undershirt. He buttoned up his shirt and placed the Bible back in the drawer. He closed it and looked one last time at the envelope full of cash, then reached for it, removing a sheaf of bills that he folded and jammed into the inside of his boot. He placed the envelope back in the place he'd found it, looking at the desk, making sure he hadn't disturbed anything. He rose, pushing the chair back under the desk and moved as quickly as he could toward the door, closing it softly behind him.

"Coming! Just give me a few minutes."

"You need help?" Idget yelled.

He limped quickly down the hall and stood at the top of the stairs. "I'm okay," he called down. "I can do it myself. I'll be there in a few minutes. Just meet me at the bunkhouse."

There was a brief silence. "Okay, just wanted to make sure you were all right."

Malachi heard Idget's footsteps. The front door squeaked open then closed. Malachi pulled himself up the stairs to the third floor and walked as quickly as he could to the bedroom. He piled the remaining side slats of the bed together and balanced them carefully as he moved steadily down the hallway, down the two flights of stairs and out the door.

Idget was sitting on the steps that led into the bunkhouse. He watched Malachi steadily as he made his way toward him with the last of the bed boards.

"Thought you was lost in there," he said.

Malachi limped over and leaned the boards up against the side of the building. "Nope. Everything just takes me a little longer. You know that," he said, keeping his voice neutral and his eyes trained on the pieces of the bed as he arranged the boards in the order they would need them.

He wouldn't tell Idget what he'd done, what he'd taken, at least until he had finished making his way through the letter and figured out what to make of it. Maybe it didn't mean anything at all. But it had been written on the day the killings had happened. Someone had penned it as other members of the train had discussed what they would do. Perhaps it had been written even as John Lee was standing inside the circle of wagons, convincing the people on the Fancher train that he and the other men were there to save them. The person who wrote it may have given it to the girl who owned the Bible, to Magpie. Maybe it was the girl's mother who gave it to her daughter because she hoped her daughter—*her dearest Magpie*—would survive her and deliver the letter to the person to whom it was addressed. Antonia.

Idget stood and looked down at Malachi. "We best get going on this last bed. They'll be home soon." He motioned for Malachi to hand him the sideboards. He slid them under his arm and turned to take them inside. Malachi climbed the stairs to follow him, the letter resting softly against his chest.

CHAPTER 16

APRIL 19

The door of the bunkhouse swung open at dawn on Monday morning. Lee stood in the doorway, a dark silhouette against the weak morning light. "You boys get up." His voice was loud, gruff. "Get yourself some breakfast at the house. We'll leave within the hour." He turned, stepping heavily down the set of three stairs, leaving the door wide open.

Lee had jarred Malachi out of a deep sleep, and he wallowed in his bed as he listened to Lee's boots squelch across the rocky path that led away from the bunkhouse up to the main house. Malachi balled his hands into fists. They were wet with sweat.

Idget groaned. "If I was rich, the first thing I'd do is sleep in for one week straight, with nobody waking me up and bossin' me to do stuff."

Malachi smiled and slid his damp palms across his belly. He reached down to the floor where he'd left his clothes folded in a neat pile the night before. He yanked his pants inside the bed cover and lifted his hips up off the bed as he pulled them on, trying to shake the foreboding that flooded his chest. He sat up and reached under his bed to pull out his leather satchel.

Last night, after Idget had begun to snore, he had rolled up the money and wedged it deep inside the leather sheath that held his knife. After wrapping his blade in a piece of paper he'd torn from a book, he carefully slid it down between the folds of money. He opened the seam of cloth that lined one side of the satchel, and slipped the letter between the cloth and the leather, pulling the tail of thread tight to smooth the cloth over it. He still hadn't found time alone to read the letter. Now, he slid his hand inside the satchel, running his fingers lightly over the cloth, feeling the letter's thin plane, satisfied it was safely concealed.

"Got something at the bottom of that?" Malachi looked up. Idget was propped up on his elbow watching him.

"Nope," Malachi said. "Just thought there was something in it, but there ain't." He slid the strap of his satchel over his shoulders. "You best get up."

Idget sighed. "I know. Least I've got all my stuff ready. Glad we got everything in the saddlebags last night." He swung his bare feet out of bed and sat with his elbows resting on his knees, rummaging his fingers through his thick, straight hair.

While Idget dressed, Malachi fastened the sheath of his knife to his belt and found the saddlebags, checking their contents one last time. They held his other pair of pants, a shirt, and a pair of thick wool socks Priscilla had knitted for him. He pulled his coat off its peg and grabbed his walking stick. He was ready.

"I'll wait for you outside," he said to Idget, who nodded at him as he buttoned up his shirt.

Malachi picked up the saddlebags, took a last look around the bunkhouse, and stepped through the door. Thoughts turned through his head. It would be the first time he and Idget would be in close company with Lee since that day in the bunkhouse with Albert and Hamblin. Idget had started worrying aloud about it several days ago. He was terrified of Lee and was convinced the man could read his thoughts, anticipate his every action. It was one of the reasons Malachi hadn't let Idget know about the letter and the cash, for fear he might telegraph it to Lee. Malachi was afraid of Lee too, but he had discovered he could deceive him. He carried that knowledge like a talisman.

As he stood waiting for Idget to come out, he saw a man on horseback cantering down the road toward the house. Lee emerged from the house and walked out into the yard. His back was toward Malachi, with his arms akimbo on his hips and his stance wide as he waited to greet the visitor. Idget walked down the steps of the bunkhouse to join Malachi. Malachi looked at him and nodded in Lee's direction. Both boys watched as the man reined his horse to a stop and dismounted. Lee shook his hands and clapped him on his back. It was Isaac Haight.

"What's he doing here?" Idget asked. "I thought he'd have gone back south already."

Malachi's mouth had turned chalky. He swallowed. "Idget," he said. "We got to agree on something."

"I won't say nothin'," Idget assured him, keeping a nervous eye on the men. "I won't. I know it won't help us. I know we're on our own."

"Okay, you got to stick with that, no matter what," Malachi said. "There's something else." He looked at the men who were huddled together talking. "Don't let them separate us."

Idget cleared his throat. "You think they might do away with us?"

Idget's words seemed sticky, like they didn't want to come out. Malachi watched the almost fragile, rhythmic pulse on his friend's wide neck. Doubt scraped at his thoughts, revealing other possibilities. He thought of Priscilla. Would they try to kill the boys with Priscilla, Charlie, and Leah there with them? Surely not. After all, they didn't know what or how much he and Idget knew. But something had shifted at the fort on the day of the spring celebration. What it was, he could not be sure.

"We should go eat," Idget said at last.

"Yep," Malachi agreed. "Let's get our horses saddled first. I have a feeling Lee will be in a rush to go today and I don't want to give him any reason to be impatient with us." Idget nodded and the boys walked to the paddock. They said little as they saddled their animals. Malachi's pinto pony blew out hard as he tightened the cinch.

"Saddle my horse for me, too." Priscilla had appeared. She was dressed in the grey shift she wore for riding. It covered pants underneath. He smiled at her, but she eyed him uncertainly before turning to walk quickly back to the house. His heart fell as he watched her retreating figure.

"What's wrong with her?" Idget's puzzled face was just visible over the back of his horse.

Malachi shrugged. "She knows we're not telling her what she wants to know."

"But this is different," Idget said. His hand rested on his horse's rump as he watched Priscilla's retreating back. "She seems mad at us, or maybe just you. Hope she gets over it."

"Yep." Malachi looked up. "No solving it now."

He handed Idget the reins to his horse. "Can you tie up my horse? I'm going to catch hers and saddle her up." Idget took both horses over to the hitching rail where they'd left their saddlebags. Malachi saddled Priscilla's mare, and by the time he led her horse to the hitching rail, Idget had tied on their saddlebags. They were ready for the ride south.

The boys walked toward the house. Malachi's stomach was rumbling. Seemed he couldn't get his fill of food lately. He wondered whether this was what he'd heard called a growth spurt. He guessed that's what he was doing. Explained the hollow hunger. Maybe it explained, too, how a new purpose had collected inside him, how it had settled out in him like sand at the bottom of a well and gave him clearer sight on what he needed to do. He thought of the letter, the money, Priscilla.

"You comin'?" Idget had walked ahead and was waiting for him at the door of the house.

Malachi dug his stick into the soft ground and sped up. The smells of coffee and baking biscuits engulfed him when he stepped through the door of the house. Dishes clattered in the kitchen. The wives' voices volleyed back and forth as they prepared breakfast, and the chatter of the younger children was steady in the background. The boys removed their hats and hung them on the pegs that lined the entry hall. In the kitchen, Priscilla stood at the big worktable, punching out disks of biscuit dough with an overturned glass. Flour puffed up around the rim of the glass as she pressed down, forming plump circles of dough.

She glanced up when they walked into the room, but quickly went back to her task. No smile. No greeting. Malachi suddenly felt out of place, clumsy, as though he'd invaded a space not meant for him. He realized that Priscilla's friendship had allowed him to feel more at ease here, to shed his discomfort. But now, her coldness made him see it was a place he did not belong, a place that had no use for him. Snake Indian boy, lame, probably smelling of the barns from the day before. He felt like a thick clumsy finger. If Idget was affected by Priscilla's treatment, he showed no signs of it. He had walked over to examine the biscuits that had already been baked. They were neatly arrayed on a large platter that sat with two pots of jam and a small white pitcher filled with honey.

"Don't you be touching those," Polly called over her shoulder to Idget as she whisked by Malachi with a pan of scrambled eggs studded with chunks of ham. "Those are for the men in there and the children sitting for the morning meal. You boys'll get somethin'. We know you're leaving soon. Sit tight, and we'll feed you when we can."

She grabbed the platter of biscuits with her spare hand and motioned to Priscilla to pick up the pots of jam and honey and follow her into the dining room. More wives filed out after them, carrying platters of eggs and ham, pitchers of milk, and pots of coffee. The swinging door of the kitchen flapped shut behind them, leaving the boys alone in the room. Idget walked over to the stove where a large blue enameled coffee pot sat. He touched it and turned to Malachi

"It's hot. Want a cup?"

Malachi nodded and Idget pulled down two white mugs from the shelves and poured a stream of thick black coffee into the cups. He walked over and handed one to Malachi.

"Guess we're on our way out," he said as he blew softly on the steaming coffee. "They can't find a place for us at the breakfast table no more."

Malachi took a sip of his coffee. Strong, like he liked it. He shrugged. "Wasn't like we really ever had a place there anyhow."

He listened as the sounds in the dining room died down and Lee's deep voice took over, drumming out the syllables of the morning prayer. He wondered if Lee had told the wives the boys were to eat in the kitchen that morning, if it was Lee's way of distancing himself from them because he was getting ready to get rid of them on the way south.

But perhaps this man would not need to draw a distance between them so he could kill them. Malachi thought of Lee's entrance into the Fancher train's camp. He had acted like their savior. The men of the Nauvoo Legion had wanted Lee to be the one to lure the train's men and women into thinking he was a friend, that the Mormons were friends and wanted to protect them. Maybe it was even Haight and Dame who had ordered Lee to do it. Maybe he hadn't wanted to, but he thought he had no choice, even if it made him be the one to appear to be the instigator of it. Maybe that's what Haight and Dame had in mind, gave them the ability to wash their hands clean of it, when the time came. Maybe it was Brigham Young, sitting in his Beehive House in Salt Lake, surrounded by his fragrant, well-coiffed wives. Maybe it was Young who had ordered Haight and Dame to make it appear that Lee was the ringleader.

No. Malachi caught his thoughts up short. Lee had been clear with Rachel and Agatha that he'd told Young what happened. Young may have ordered the massacre, but how it happened and who was to do what must have been left up to the men in the southern region. The leaders, the men who sat in the dining room. Fear prickled the nape of Malachi's neck as he heard Isaac Haight's high voice float to the top of the rising din of conversation that followed Lee's prayer.

"These are the best biscuits I've had since my mother's," Haight said. "Who was it that made them?"

"It was our Priscilla." Agatha answered in her unmistakable scratchy voice.

"Our Priscilla," Malachi thought. He imagined Haight's large drooping eyes lingering appreciatively on Priscilla. Malachi wanted Priscilla to come south with them. The news had elated him, yet doubt pawed at the surface. Something about the arrangement was off. Idget had sensed it too.

Malachi walked over to him. "Be good to get something to fill up my belly about right now," he said.

Idget was hovering near the stove, eyeing the empty pans. He turned to him and grinned. "This is one of those days when I think food might be the last thing I should be thinkin' about, but it's all I can think about, no matter what day it is."

Malachi nodded, smiling in recognition. "Let's look for something in the pantry. I got the feeling we're going to have to wait otherwise."

Idget cast a worried glance toward the door that led into the dining room. "Agatha don't like me scrounging around in there. Always whacks me for it." He looked at Malachi and grinned as he shrugged his shoulders. "But, as long as we're leavin' and we might never come back, what difference will it make?"

They both paused and listened. Conversation seemed to have dropped into a steady rhythm. They walked into the pantry. The small room was lined with shelves packed with dried meat, roasted chickens, jars of beans, honey and flour, pies, and bread. They stood for an instant, taking it all in and filled with awe at the dazzling array before them. Then they quickly began to fill their pockets and satchels with whatever they could find. Mince pies, small enough to fit into the palms of their hands, thick wedges of jerky, hard boiled eggs, and round loaves of brown bread that smelled of molasses. They took as much as they could hold, hands flying from shelves to pockets and satchels. Once they had taken their fill, they turned, without speaking, walking out of the pantry and closing the door behind them.

The pilfering spree lifted Malachi's spirits, tilting the scales, making up for being confined to the kitchen while the rest of them enjoyed their breakfast. And like his decision to take the letter and the money from Lee, it reminded him that he could make a choice to act, to assert his wants on the world and that the world might yield.

The boys leaned against the table in the kitchen, waiting for one of the wives to return, Malachi wondered what Idget felt about what they had just done. He was certain he had never stolen from the Lee household. He thought it likely that in Idget's early days with the Lees, the boy had probably been trusting, believing his new owners had his best interests and welfare in mind and that he had no need to search for and take things for himself. And even as he had learned the hard lesson that he was there to serve them, not to be cared for by them, he had been schooled to fear what would happen if he broke their rules. It was how Malachi had felt too, when he first came to live with the Blanks. Trust had moved into fear and fear had moved into a canny ability to stay just beyond the possibility of punishment whenever he could.

Chairs scraped across the floor, followed by more sounds of people moving. It signaled an end to breakfast. Polly bustled through the kitchen door, carrying a platter with four biscuits on it. She walked over to the table opposite to where the boys stood and plunked down the plate. "You boys take these and make the best of them. It was a hungry lot in there this morning. Ate everything we put in front of them." She shoved the plate over to them and turned to go back to the dining room to finish clearing. The boys stuffed their mouths with the crumbling biscuits, washing the dry bits down with cold coffee.

Rachel stuck her head in the kitchen. "Get on out to the horses. You're all to leave soon."

The boys retrieved the horses from the corral and walked them back to the house. Haight was already mounted on his horse and Lee was taking leave of his family. Priscilla stood off to the side, standing between Charlie and Leah. Rachel was near her, leaning in now and again to say something to her. Priscilla's face was somber. She had her saddlebags draped across her right shoulder and she dropped Leah's hand to hitch them up.

Malachi stood facing her. Her black mare nickered softly at his shoulder.

"You want me to bring your horse to you?" Malachi asked her. His words felt loud, outsized. Rachel was the only one who paid any attention to him. She waved him over, and he dropped the reins of his pony to lead the mare to Priscilla. His heart beat faster when he neared her, but he kept his eyes to himself. No use in having Rachel pick up on anything he felt.

"Charlie will ride with me," Priscilla said, her gaze resting just beyond Malachi. "Leah should ride with Father Lee." She set her saddlebags on the ground and squatted down in front of Leah. "You want to ride with Father Lee?" The little girl cast her eyes over to Lee and shook her head vigorously. Her lower lip protruded and she looked like she might cry. Priscilla watched her with concern.

"It's okay," Priscilla said to the girl. "He'll hold you real tight and his horse is the smoothest walker of them all."

Tears trickled down the girl's cheeks as she started to cry in short, silent sobs.

"What's wrong?" Priscilla said, as she stroked the little girl's forehead and moved a curling strand of hair out of her eyes.

"Don't want to," Leah said finally. She shook her head vehemently. "Want to ride with you."

Priscilla stood and looked at Leah with an exasperated look on her face.

"She can ride with Idget," Malachi offered. He knew the girl was afraid of Lee. He'd seen her avoid him, which hadn't been hard since Lee had shown little interest in either of the children.

"She likes Idget," he added lamely.

A dry pause hung between them that Malachi wished he knew how to cross. Then Priscilla turned to him. The fierceness in her eyes shocked him.

"It's not for you to decide," she blurted out. "It's my responsibility to care for these children."

Rachel's eyes swiveled over to Lee, then she looked back at Priscilla and laid her hand lightly on Priscilla's arm. "The girl feels more comfortable with you. Let her ride in front of you and the boy behind. Have Malachi take the saddle off the horse. Ride bareback. You're a good rider. As long as you keep your horse steady, it'll work."

Priscilla looked at Leah again and nodded.

"You're right," she said. "Probably the best." She turned to Malachi who stood rooted to the ground in front of her, waiting for her to tell him what to do, desperately wishing he could fix what was wrong. "Take the saddle off for me. Please."

His chest jumped at her "please" and he nodded shortly and led the horse back over to the barn. As he did, he heard Lee calling out. "What's the hold up?"

"Just making arrangements for the children is all," Rachel said. "Won't be a minute and you all can get on your way."

By the time Malachi returned with Priscilla's horse, the men and Idget were mounted and waiting.

"Give me your saddlebags, Priscilla, then get on that thing and let's get going," Lee said.

Rachel took the saddlebags from Priscilla and walked them over to Lee who leaned down to take them as Rachel whispered into his ear. Lee's eyes settled on Malachi. Malachi saw satisfaction in Lee's face. He felt the air around him waver. Had Lee said something to Priscilla about him? Malachi turned to hold the black mare's reins while Priscilla hoisted herself up on the horse's back. Once she was settled, Malachi handed first Charlie then Leah up to her.

"Thank you," she said after she'd settled Leah in front of her. Her eyes were trained ahead and she said nothing further. Yet, she had thanked him and he hung on to that as he turned to retrieve his own horse.

Isaac Haight and John Lee walked their horses out first, followed by Priscilla, then Idget and Malachi. Lee's family stood outside the house, waving and calling their goodbyes as they rode away. Just as they took a left out of the big gate that led into the farm, Lee turned in his saddle and called out to Priscilla.

"I hope you can handle that horse without a saddle. Be a pity to lose you."

Haight turned too and briefly looked at her, laughing.

"I'll be fine," she said, reaching back to wrap Charlie's arms more tightly around her.

CHAPTER 17

The company of seven made their way through the jagged red hills that ushered them out of Harmony and toward the trail that followed the base of the Pine Valley Mountains. The skies were open and clear. As they rode, Isaac Haight fell back to ride alongside Priscilla. Although Malachi couldn't hear what Haight was saying, he marveled at the man's almost non-stop conversation. He wondered where he found so many words to say to her and envied his ability to talk without ceasing. In an odd way, it also reassured him, made him feel that the man's expansive chatter meant safety for Idget and him.

They rode on for several hours. It was nearly noon when they reached the stretch of Leeds Creek, which opened into a wide and deep turn. Lee pulled up and called back.

"We'll stop here, eat something, let the horses get their fill of water."

Haight helped the children and Priscilla get off her mare, and led both his horse and hers to the stream so the horses could drink. Lee passed her the saddlebags then led his horse down to join Haight. Priscilla squatted on the ground next to Charlie and Leah and pulled out some bread and twists of jerky for them to eat. The children ate hungrily as Priscilla rummaged in her saddlebags for something more. She looked up just as Malachi and Idget were about to lead their horses past toward the stream.

"You boys get any food to take with you? I got some here, if you're interested. The ride'll be long without it."

Malachi glanced over to make sure Lee was out of earshot. "We managed to get a few things before we left," he said. Idget nodded and clicked his tongue at his horse as he led him to the stream. Malachi waited. His heart was thudding wildly. He felt he had to say something to her now.

"Are you put out with me?" he asked.

She looked up at him. She wasn't smiling, but some of the unfriendliness had melted from her face. Once she'd settled the children in with food she looked toward where Lee and Haight were standing. Their backs were to them. She turned back, searching his face. "I heard something about you, about you and Idget," she said, keeping her voice low, looking now and again toward the stream.

"What?" he croaked.

She looked briefly toward the men. "I don't know if I can tell you here."

"Tell me," he said. Suddenly the hope he'd felt earlier slipped away and he realized that there would always be other forces at work, other people who would know how to maneuver ahead of him, changing his world just when he thought he had some grip on it.

"I'm not sure what I heard was true," she said, looking at the ground. "I don't know what to believe." Her face was tense and her voice strained as though the words were being wrung out of her.

"What was it?" His voice was urgent now. He wanted her to tell him, but he also felt that what she was going to reveal would damn him and he had no idea how he would redeem himself.

"It was about Mountain Meadows, those killings," she said. "I asked Father Lee what had happened, why you were so worried about what Rebecca had said and he said that you and Idget, that you—"

"What, what did you hear?" His voice was strung high and raw.

"He said you and Idget helped kill those people. That you were part of it and now—it's just that…" Her eyes met his.

The earth swept away beneath his feet. Although Priscilla's face was close enough for him to reach out and touch it, she seemed far out of his reach as though he was looking up at her from a pit dug deep into the earth. He thought he called up to her, asked her to help him, but he realized he had not, that he was silent, that he faced this accusation without the words he needed to defend himself.

Her gaze on him was steady as she waited for him to speak, but when he didn't, she continued. "When we were leaving the farm this morning, it wasn't you and Idget Leah was afraid of. It was Father Lee, and it dawned on me how both Charlie and Leah never want to be near him. He hasn't been around much, so I never thought a lot about it. But this morning I did. And after we left, Charlie said something odd and I—" She stopped again and looked at the men.

"Malachi, I need to know." She turned to him. "You must tell me what it is you said you could not tell me that day of the picnic. I feel like I'm being lied to, and I don't know who to trust."

Her face was steady, waiting. The day was warm, and a stippling of sweat was stamped across the narrow bridge of her nose. He gazed at her, wanting to marshal a torrent of words to make her believe that what Lee had said wasn't true, but he was stunned into silence. He didn't know why he had never considered the possibility that Lee would link Idget and him to the killings. If he told her now that it was Lee and the other men who had killed the people in the meadows, it would seem like he was trying to protect himself, defend himself. She might think he was lying and, worse, might betray him to Lee. Some part of him wanted Priscilla to understand all this, to believe that he was innocent without him having to explain any of the truth to her.

"There's another thing," she said. "You best watch yourself. Father

Lee said there was some of the men down south that wanted to get at you and Idget, teach you a lesson for what he said you'd done. He said that's the reason he brought you boys back to Harmony after it all happened. He said he was just trying to protect you."

A movement from the men below drew her attention away from him, and she looked down toward the stream. Malachi followed her gaze, then turned back toward her.

"What men?" he asked her. "Who should we watch for?"

Haight was walking back toward them.

"Not now, we'll talk later," Priscilla said hurriedly and she turned away from him to go back to Leah and Charlie. She squatted in front of the children and busied herself with brushing crumbs off their faces.

Malachi pulled gently on his pony's reins and led the animal to the stream. Haight was walking past him when Malachi's leg seized and he stumbled, falling away from his pony and toward Haight. The man reached out to grab him.

"Steady there." His grasp was hard on Malachi's arm. "You'll fall and break your neck. Can't have you up and dyin' on us before lambing season. Need you too much."

Malachi looked up at him. Haight's eyes were as expressionless as the open sky. He mumbled his thanks and pulled his arm out of Haight's grasp. Blood rushed through his head, filling his ears. He kept walking down toward the stream, aware that Haight stood still watching him. Malachi joined Idget whose gray pony was drinking deeply from the water, pulling up now and again, pink nostrils flaring.

"Everything okay?" Idget asked.

Lee was standing further downstream, waiting for his horse to take its fill of water. He seemed lost in thought.

Quietly, Malachi said, "Priscilla said Lee told her we was involved in the killings in the meadows. That it was us, that we was part of it."

Idget looked at him in surprise. "She believes that? She said that?"

Malachi glanced at Lee. The sound of the rushing water filled his ears. "Keep your voice low, don't act like nothing is wrong," he warned.

"She said that?" Idget asked again, snapping his pony's reins together. Malachi nodded.

Idget took in a deep breath and wrapped the reins around his right hand. "Can't believe she'd think it was true."

"Not sure she believes it now," Malachi said. His pony stepped tentatively into the water and dipped his head to take a long drink. "But I think she did when he first told her."

"You'd think she wouldn't," Idget said, shaking his head and sitting on the slope.

Malachi didn't disagree. But as he thought back on their conversation the day of the picnic at Fort Harmony, he wondered if he hadn't handed her fragments of information that made what Lee told her sound like the truth. Malachi had told her he knew something, something he couldn't tell her, something so bad that he couldn't tell anyone. She'd known he was hiding something from her. It made sense that she'd be ready to believe he was concealing what he had done that was so horrible he couldn't tell her, couldn't tell anyone.

"There's more," he said, sitting beside Idget.

"She said there's some of the men who want to teach us a lesson for what they're saying we did."

Lee was stretched out now against the slope of earth that bordered the stream, his hat pulled low over his face.

"Who?" Idget asked.

"She didn't say." Malachi shrugged. "I don't even know if she knows. Haight come up to join her and she couldn't say no more."

Idget blew a stream of air out of his mouth and shook his head. Suddenly he looked up. His horse had waded out into the stream. The water was up over the animal's belly. Idget stood and looked at Malachi in a panic.

"You got to get him for me," he said.

"You can get him, can't you?"

"Can't," Idget said. "Can't swim."

Malachi scrambled up and ran down to the river. He waded into the water, floating toward the grey pony just as he felt his feet lose purchase on the river's bottom. He snatched the horse's reins buoyed on the surface of the river's current and pulled the animal's head back toward the shore, finally getting his footing on the river's sandy bottom. He looked up as he climbed out of the water with the pony tagging behind him. Relief flooded Idget's face.

"Thanks," he said as Malachi handed him the wet reins. "The water gives me the willies. Never could learn how to swim."

Malachi waved away his thanks, remembering his first swim and how he'd nearly drowned in the river. He would have if Albert hadn't yanked him ashore. He thought of it now. Albert had saved his life. He'd learned to swim after that.

The cold water had helped clear his head. He glanced up the hill at Haight. If Lee was planning to kill them, he wouldn't do it while Priscilla and the children looked on. He turned his back on Priscilla and Haight and sat down next to Idget. He had to think. He took out a thick chunk of jerky and a round of bread from his satchel. His pony was grazing behind him. Idget had ground-tied both their animals and had leaned back against the slope to sleep, his hat pulled over his eyes.

As Malachi ate, the sun warmed his face and the smell of sage filled his nostrils. He chewed slowly and considered what he knew, what he could do. For nearly eight months, he had lived in fear of being found out for what he knew about the murders in Mountain Meadows. He'd been forced to search and pilfer valuables from the dead as they lay rotting in the meadows. He had been beaten, choked, and cross-examined. And now he was accused of participating in the massacre itself. But he had not revealed what he knew, and he had survived. He had kept watch and learned. He had discovered that Brigham Young not only knew the truth of who had carried out the massacre, but had played an active role in covering it up, including rewarding some of the men involved.

Even Idget did not know the whole of the knowledge that he carried. And now, he had the letter, a letter that someone in the Fancher train had written on the day of the killings. Although Malachi had not yet had the privacy he needed to read it all, he had read enough to know it contained information that was significant. It explained why Lee had kept it. Although the other letters Malachi had found bundled together the day he searched the corpses were not hidden away in Lee's desk, this one was. Judging now by the man's easy mood as he leaned back against the grassy slope of earth, he was oblivious to the fact that the letter—this letter that could contain information that was important in some way to the incidents of that day—was no longer in his possession.

Malachi felt his connection to the slant of earth beneath him. The river brimmed and eddied with the rush of spring melt. A hawk screeched overhead. He looked at Lee, his body half submerged in the grass. He looked asleep. Would he care if one morning he awoke and learned that Malachi and Idget had gone? Would it matter so much that he would feel the need to come after them, bringing them back to face punishment? Would they matter, these two Indian boys? When it was all said and done, he could not believe that he and Idget would mean enough to these men they lived with that they would put down whatever pursuit they had—building a house, preaching a sermon, preparing for a mission, teaching the Paiutes how to farm, marrying another wife—to find them and bring them back. He and Idget were so inconsequential.

Maybe they would be smarter about their escape than the Indian boys Idget had told him about. Maybe they could leave in the middle of the night and get far enough away that, by the time the men had discovered they were gone, they would be out of their reach. Safe. He thought of the girl who had carried the letter. He remembered her bloodied, collapsed face, her narrow fragile shoulders, the light brown hair that fanned out around her head like water weeds in Magotsu Creek. She had to have been *dearest Magpie*, the one addressed on the flyleaf of the Bible that he'd found in her apron pocket. He wondered if her real name was Maggie, Margaret. It must have been her mother who had written the letter. And what about her, her mother, these people, Charlie, Leah, the other children left living? Did he bear some responsibility for doing something to set things right for them, to make sure the men that had carried out the murders were held responsible? He shifted uncomfortably. His leg ached. He wished for better answers, someone to help him. He looked downstream at Lee who had stood and was brushing dirt off his pants. Malachi jostled Idget awake.

"Time to go," he said.

CHAPTER 18

It was late afternoon when they rode into the Hamblin ranch. Lee told Idget and Malachi to stable the men's horses as he and Haight went toward the Hamblin house followed by Priscilla and the children. Malachi released the two ponies and Priscilla's mare into a fenced-in expanse of grass north of the barn and returned to the stables inside the barn to help Idget feed and water the men's mounts. The boys said little as they broke apart bales of hay and pitched it into the mangers in each of the stalls. Once Idget had filled water buckets for the horses, it was nearly dusk.

"Guess we should head out to the pasture," Malachi said. He was hungry. The food they'd taken from the Lee's pantry would have to do for their supper. Idget nodded. Both boys slung their saddlebags over their shoulders, tucked their bedrolls under their arms, and walked toward the meadow.

"Feels sorta' strange to be back," Idget said. " Like we never left."

"Yep," Malachi agreed.

He wondered where Albert was and whether he'd be waiting for them with the sheep. They walked up over a rise. Below, in a small pocket of meadow, the sheep clustered together. The herd was smaller. Most of the ewes had been culled before they arrived and pastured by the barn to get ready for lambing. There were two boys already tending the sheep. The first, clad in a tattered jacket, stood near the fire, feeding it. Another, wearing a felt hat that was too big for him, sat on a large rock watching the sheep. Malachi didn't recognize them. They looked younger and their squat bodies made him think they were Utes. The boy near the fire looked up sharply when Malachi and Idget walked into their camp.

"Who are ya'?" The boy's face was open, curious in spite of the challenge in his voice.

"We belong to John Lee and Jonah Blank," Malachi said. "Names are Idget and Malachi." He gestured to Idget then himself. "We're here to help with the lambing."

Two Bits had been sitting at the edge of the light cast by the fire. She stood when she heard his voice and walked over to him. Her head was cast down and her tail slowly wagged, as her body curled around his leg. She leaned her whole weight against him and looked up at him. He reached down and scratched her hard on the top of her head. She leaned more fully into him and made a low guttural growl.

"That's a good dog, there," said the boy standing near the fire. "She's the best with the sheep. None of 'em can get away from her. She finds them wherever they go."

Malachi looked down at the dog. He'd missed her. He bent down and gave her a final stroke down the length of her back. She looked up at him, then turned and went back to the edge of the herd to sit and watch over the sheep.

"What's your name?" Malachi asked.

"Wilson," he said. "That there is my brother, Joseph."

"Who's your family?"

"We was bought by the Jacksons. Lived in Salt Lake up until last month when Father Jackson was told it was time for him to move here."

"What for?"

The boy squinted at Malachi and frowned. "You asks a lot of questions, don't ya'?

"Pays to know," Malachi said, shrugging his shoulders. "Looks like we'll be working with you."

There was a gap of silence between the boys and an owl hooted softly into it. Night had fallen and the sheep knotted up closer together. Joseph made his way over to the fire and stood near it. He'd taken off his hat and his wide face was partially illuminated by the flame. He hadn't said anything, but seemed to be waiting for something to happen. Idget moved over to stand next to Malachi. Tension fell through the night air like a light net over the circle of boys.

Wilson squatted in front of the fire. He fed a few more sticks into the flame and stood.

"We're here to help with the sheep," he said. "The Jacksons are at Fort Santa Clara gettin' themselves sorted out to build a house. But the two of us was sent here. Father Jackson heard the families here that owns the sheep was short-handed and needed some help with lambing season."

"That's us who does that," Idget blurted out, but his tongue mangled the words.

Both Wilson and Joseph looked then at Idget whose broad face was illuminated by the firelight. Sly grins spread across their faces.

"What they call you?" Wilson asked Idget. "Id-get? That short for id-i-ot?"

Idget clamped his lips tight and looked at the fire. His eyes snapped.

Malachi said nothing.

Joseph sidled over to Wilson.

"This is that boy Albert told us of. Him being a half-wit," he said. "And this," he said, eying Malachi. "This is the other one, the cripple. We heard about you. Albert said they don't need ya' no more."

Idget blew the air out of his lungs completely before rushing at Joseph and Wilson, butting Wilson in the gut with his head and catching Joseph by his neck and pulling him down to the ground. The dogs started barking and jumping at the boys, nipping at their arms and legs, whatever they could get a grip on. Idget hurled himself on top of Wilson, the larger of the two, and pinned his arms with his knees, then he yanked Joseph to the ground, gripping his neck in one big hand.

"You boys shouldn't of crossed him," Malachi said, as he calmly made his way over to where Idget held the other two boys to the ground. "He's no idiot, probly smarter than you two put together."

"Lemme' go," Joseph panted, trying to pry Idget's hand off his neck.

"I'm guessing he might let you go if you say sorry to him for what you said," Malachi said.

Joseph's eyes wheeled desperately between Idget and Malachi and he gasped out, "Sorry."

"Sorry for what?" Idget asked, shaking the boy a little.

"Sorry I said that thing about you." The boy wheezed and Idget released him. Joseph turned over on his side gasping for air and rubbing his neck.

Wilson still lay pinned beneath Idget's dense body, but he'd stopped struggling.

"I'm letting you up," Idget said. "But you're gonna tell us why you're here."

The boy nodded mutely. Idget stood over Joseph, who was still curled up beside his brother.

Wilson propped himself up on his elbows and looked warily at Idget and then over to Malachi, who stood by his feet. "We was told to come here, that they needed to replace the boys that was here 'cuz they weren't gonna be here no more. That's the God's honest truth. I swear." He looked at Malachi then at Idget. "You got to believe me."

"What about what he said?" Malachi said, jutting his chin at Joseph.

Wilson looked at Joseph who was now on all fours trying to get up.

Joseph stood upright now and looked warily at Idget who stood nearly a head taller than him.

"I just shot my mouth off when I shouldn'ta," he said. Then he stuck his arm out toward Idget. "Can we shake? Let's just shake and say we're friends."

Idget looked down at the boy's hand and reached out to grasp it, making Joseph wince a little. Wilson laughed nervously; a high-pitched little laugh that made the dogs prick up their ears. He thrust his hand out to Idget too, and Idget pumped his hand up and down.

"We're friends, right?" Wilson said, turning to Malachi.

"Friends?" Malachi said, shrugging his shoulders. "Don't know about that, but let's say we're not enemies."

Wilson and Joseph both nodded vigorously.

Malachi looked at Idget. "You agreed, Idg?"

Idget dipped his head in agreement. "As long as they keep on my right side, I'll keep 'em on mine."

Both Wilson and Joseph smiled nervously at him, and Wilson released another high giggle.

"You boys ate supper yet?" Malachi asked.

"Before you come, we had ourselves some," Joseph answered. "You hungry? We got some hard tack here and maybe a little venison left."

"We got our own food," Malachi said, sliding his satchel around to his side and sitting down on one of the wide squat logs that circled the fire. "Thanks anyhow."

Idget joined him and they unloaded some of the food and set it out on their laps. Both boys stuffed their mouths and chewed in silence. Malachi was hungry. The meal they'd eaten by the stream earlier that day seemed a long time ago. Joseph and Wilson stood awkwardly watching them, then sat down to join them around the fire. Wilson grabbed a long stick and jabbed it deeply into the hot coals. Hundreds of bright sparks lifted out of the flames and disappeared into the black of the night sky.

"You were up at Harmony?" Joseph asked.

"Yep," Malachi said, chewing and swallowing the last of his bread.

"Who all rode here with you today?"

"It would be John Lee, Isaac Haight, and Priscilla Lee," Malachi answered. "And two children."

"They hers?" Wilson asked. "The children, they belong to Priscilla Lee?"

"Nope," Malachi said. He didn't feel like explaining who Leah and Charlie were.

"We heard she's real pretty," Joseph said. He'd put his hat back on and it had slipped down to just above his eyes.

"Who?" Malachi asked, as if he didn't know.

"That girl who come with you today, Priscilla Lee."

"Who told you that, that she was pretty?" Malachi asked.

"Albert," both boys blurted out.

"Albert here?" Malachi asked, brushing crumbs off his hands.

"Naw," Joseph answered. "He left with Jacob Hamblin. They're working with the Paiutes up to the north, trying to get 'em to start farming."

"Won't happen though," Wilson said, shaking his head.

"What?"

"They're never gonna farm," Wilson said. "They don't want to, least ways that's what Father Jackson says. Says they don't want to farm the way the Mormons want 'em to."

"When they comin' back?" Malachi asked.

"Not exactly sure, sometime soon though," Joseph answered. "Maybe tomorrow. Jacob Hamblin said he wanted Albert to be here to help with the lambing."

Malachi took in this piece of news. He was relieved that Priscilla was out of Albert's range, at least for the time being. But lambing would begin tomorrow and they would need every hand they could get from beginning to end so he was sure Hamblin would bring Albert back for it.

"So, you boys staying just through the lambing season then?" Idget asked.

Joseph and Wilson glanced at each other and paused before answering.

"We are to stay until Brother Hamblin lets us go," Wilson said. "We won't bother ya none, though."

Silence again. The fire snapped and released another burst of sparks into the night sky.

Malachi decided to get off the business of who was here to take care of the sheep since it seemed to agitate Idget. "You live right in Salt Lake?" he asked.

"Yep," Joseph said. "Father Jackson had a house in town, not too far from Governor Young's. Big house, not as big as the Governor's Beehive House, but big just the same."

"You had rooms in it?" Malachi asked. "You slept there?"

"'Course we did," Joseph said, tipping his chin up slightly. "Slept on the first floor, next to the kitchen."

"Where'd you learn to work the sheep?" Idget asked.

"Father Jackson had a farm just outside town. Had us there from almost the time we was bought, every spring and summer."

Back to the sheep, Malachi thought.

"Why was your father sent here?"

Joseph and Wilson exchanged looks.

"We're not supposed to say," Joseph said, looking at the ground and shaking his head.

"Why not?" Malachi pressed.

"Cuz it's to do with that killing in the meadows," Wilson said.

The owl hooted again, deep and low. The fire had settled now to a steady flame. The logs released a golden heat.

"We don't like bein' so close to it here," Wilson said, pulling the collar of his frayed jacket up around his neck. "The other night we heard a child crying, howlin' like a ghost and it come from down there, down where the killing was done."

"There ain't no ghosts," Idget said. He was stretched out by the fire. Malachi thought he'd gone to sleep, but now he turned over on his side and propped his head up on his hand to scowl at Wilson. Joseph looked apprehensively at Idget then back at his brother.

"It's to do with the fact that a man is coming this way," Joseph said. "He's not a Mormon and folks is worried about what he's gonna do. They say he's got the law behind him and he's fixing to hurt us. Father Jackson says he's here to help organize folks on account of him." The words poured out of Joseph in a rush and after he was done, he stared at Idget, as though he half expected him to jump up and pin him to the ground again.

"What do you mean he's here to help organize them?" Malachi asked.

"Just that," Wilson supplied. "Father Jackson's going to help make sure the men who were here that day aren't around to talk to this man they call the judge. Father Jackson will help them get away when the time comes, set up camp in the mountains. And he'll keep watch while that judge is here, makes sure it all runs smooth. If the men ain't here to talk to, the judge can't find nothin' out."

"But, why? What difference will it make? Wasn't them who killed those people. It was the Paiutes," Malachi said. His voice didn't sound normal to his own ears.

Wilson and Joseph looked at each other again.

"But, see, word's gotten out that it weren't the Paiutes," Joseph said. "Word is, even though it ain't true, that it was the work of Mormon men."

"So, there's Mormons saying this?" Malachi asked. He wondered if they could trust them enough to seek their protection.

"No, not any one of us," Joseph shook his head vigorously. Malachi wondered at the boy's wording. Did these boys really feel like they were part of their communities, the church?

"I think it's just a made-up lie. Father Jackson says Governor Young is mad that this here judge is comin' in to poke around in what should be only his business, the church's business," Joseph said.

"What's the judge do?" Idget asked.

"Father Jackson says he asks a whole lot of questions to a whole lot of people and tries to trip people up, trick 'em into saying stuff they don't really mean," Wilson said importantly. "And the Governor's worried that someone might get talked into saying something that ain't true or get up to some mischief."

Malachi's heart picked up a beat. This judge wasn't a Mormon. Maybe he could talk to this judge, show him the letter, and tell him what he knew. He knew it would be safer than him telling any of the Mormons what he saw.

"When will that happen?" Malachi asked, trying to keep his voice quiet, calm.

"What?" Wilson and Joseph asked at the same time.

"I mean when will the judge be here?"

"Oh, that," Wilson said. "Not for a while and not before lambing season is over, I 'spect."

There were other things he wanted to ask these boys, but they had talked enough for one night and Malachi was weary from the long ride from Harmony. He desperately needed to crawl into his bedroll and shut his eyes. Tomorrow they would begin lambing, and he knew the days ahead would be long and hard.

CHAPTER 19

APRIL 20

Malachi liked lambing season. He was good at helping the ewes birth the lambs. The sheep trusted him and didn't resist when he positioned himself near them and plunged his arm deep inside them to help the struggling lamb emerge safely. He enjoyed those early moments when the lamb lay on the ground beside the ewe, vulnerable and dazed at the newness that surrounded it. He liked watching the ewe delicately lick off the birthing fluid and guide the lamb to suck for the first time. It made him feel good to know he helped bring that life into the world, helped the lambs survive.

He looked out over the herd that morning. There were forty-two by his count, culled for the ewes that were to lamb. He thought of the work ahead. It was the time of year when they were all equals. That he was an Indian boy, bought and owned, didn't matter as much during lambing season. He and the Mormon men all did the same intense and demanding work. Everyone pitched in. Because of his particular skill with the ewes, he was even a little important during this season. No one ever said anything to him about it or paid him a compliment, but he knew his own worth. They relied on him for it.

Idget liked herding the sheep, but lambing was hard for him. The ewes rolled back their eyes and tried to get away from him when he approached. He was too big, too strong. He tried to strip the lambs out of the ewes with force, when what they needed was a delicate, steady hand to coax them out. The last time Idget had tried to help a ewe birth was two years ago, and he hadn't been able to pull out a set of twin lambs. The lambs and the ewe had all died. He'd been punished for it and now he dreaded lambing season. He was told to stay away from the ewes and given the job of transferring the lambs that had started suckling from the stable to the pasture. Lambing was too hectic for Idget, and he preferred the calm of tending the sheep in the open pasture.

"We got to get up there," Malachi said to Idget.

He nodded mutely and looked at the other boys who were already dressed and looking out over the herd. One of them would have to stay behind with the herd today. Malachi knew it should be Idget. He worried about being apart from him, but he knew Idget would be happier here.

"You want to stay here, mind the herd today?" he asked. "We need someone to do it and I'd just as soon it be you instead of one of these boys." He nodded toward Joseph and Wilson.

Idget looked up. He didn't smile but the bleak look on his face lightened a little. "Sure, I do," he said.

"I'll let the men know," Malachi said. "Someone will bring you food, me or one of the boys."

Malachi knew the only thing Idget liked about this time of year was the food and how much there was of it. Women from all around would come to the farm where the lambing was taking place and bring mountains of food for the men and boys. It was almost as good as the spring celebration in Harmony. Breakfast, dinner, and supper were all plentiful and the boys could eat as much as they could hold.

Idget nodded. "You know how that food does me good." He looked at the ground between his knees then back up at Malachi, grinning.

Malachi draped his satchel over his shoulders.

"You taking that?" Idget asked.

"It's got things in it I need." He shrugged. "Easiest."

Idget nodded and didn't say anything more. Malachi wondered if Idget had guessed he was hiding something. He would explain it all later, when they were safely on the road and away from Utah. Priscilla's news and what Joseph and Wilson had told them had pressed him, pushed Malachi to plan, to move quickly. Possibilities had started to form in his head. He had thought about which horses they would take, how he could get some additional money. He'd never had money, so he didn't know the worth of what he'd taken from John Lee, but he guessed they would need more. He thought about Priscilla. Something had shifted in her too. He'd heard it in her voice and her words yesterday when she told him what Lee had said. Would she dare leave with them? Would he dare ask her? He pushed the thoughts aside.

Idget was dressed now and was rummaging through his saddlebags. He pulled out a piece of jerky and ate it. Then he called out to Wilson, "You got anything else to eat this morning? Thought you said you had something last night." Wilson nodded and went to their store of food and brought Idget some tack.

"We'll send someone back at noon with a plate," Malachi promised. Idget's mouth was full. He smiled and waved them away.

Malachi and the other two boys walked to the Hamblin house. Although the air was still cool, the day promised to be warm, which was good. Warm days were the best for lambing, made the sheep more docile. When they got to the barn, Malachi noticed the stall that had held Haight's horse was empty. He felt a slip of relief to have him gone.

No one was in the lambing shed yet, so the three boys went through the barn and when they emerged there was a group of about twenty men from the region gathered in the rear, enjoying their breakfasts. It seemed like any other lambing season. He thought of what Lee had told Priscilla and wondered if that was a lie too. Were there men here who wanted to harm him and Idget? He spotted Jonah Blank, sitting furthest away and talking to a younger man that Malachi didn't recognize. Blank looked up at Malachi and nodded his greeting to him. Just then, Priscilla emerged, Leah and Charlie trailing her skirts. She carried a platter of bacon. He walked over to the table where she was setting down the platter.

"Morning," he said, as he picked up a plate.

"Good morning to you," she replied. "You boys sleep well out there underneath the stars?" Charlie's hand snaked up to grab a piece of bacon, and he stuffed it greedily into his mouth. Priscilla handed a piece of bacon to Leah who let it rest in her hand like a small treasure.

"Always do," Malachi said. He looked around briefly searching for John Lee.

"He's still inside," Priscilla said. He was startled that she'd read his thoughts. "He stayed there last night."

"He stayed in the house?"

Priscilla raised her eyebrows at the question.

"Yes," she said. "Jacob Hamblin hasn't come home yet, so his wives doubled up and made a spare room for Father Lee."

He wondered if Jacob Hamblin would let Albert sleep overnight in the house while Priscilla was here. His insides squirmed at the thought of Albert being so close to Priscilla while she slept.

"I like lambing season," she said. "The time of year is hopeful, and I love the new lambs." More quietly, she said, "Father Lee's leaving today. He won't stay to help. Has business south with Brother Haight and some of the other men. We need to talk after he leaves."

Jonah Blank and another man were deep in conversation and everyone else seemed to be ignoring them. He turned to her. "I'll be busy most of the day. Can you get away after supper? We should be done by then.

Meet me behind the barn after dusk."

She nodded, but didn't say more because just then John Lee emerged from the house. Malachi turned away. He filled up his plate with eggs and potatoes, pushing aside the bacon to make room, then went to find a place to sit and eat.

Lee walked over to Priscilla, who had gone to sit with the other women having breakfast. She stood to greet him. He placed both hands on her shoulders and said something to her that caused her to bow her head, and he kissed the top of it. Rachael Hamblin walked over to Lee and he shook her hand as he said his goodbyes. As he walked toward the barn through the crowd of people, he stopped and talked. He laughed with the men and clapped them on the back. Lee's popularity may have waned in Harmony, but it seemed here he was still well liked. Many of these men had participated in the killings at the meadows and the secret they bore bound them together. If what Joseph and Wilson had said about the judge and an investigation was true, Malachi knew that the trust these men had for each other would soon be put to a test.

Lee's eyes caught Malachi's. Malachi expected him to call out to him to get his horse ready, but Lee said nothing. They held each other's gaze for an instant then Lee turned to walk into the barn. Today was devoted to the sheep, and even Lee knew he would have to saddle up his own horse. As he watched the man's retreating back, Malachi wondered if he would ever see him again.

The men and boys finished breakfast and began to make their way to the lambing shed and Malachi followed them. The din of the ewes comforted him and the waxy smell of the sheep mixed with the sour smell of fresh straw, blood, and afterbirth. The work began. Although they took a break for the mid-day meal, it was late afternoon when one of the men called out it was the end of the workday. Most of the men left to go back to their farms for the night. Malachi went to the supper line to pile up a plate, enough for him and Idget. Priscilla had offered to take something out to Idget at noon, but Malachi knew he would welcome the extra food now.

Joseph and Wilson had gone ahead. Malachi had seen them both at the noon meal and they looked beat. They were in charge of transitioning the ewes and their lambs to the lambing field once the ewes had cleaned off the lambs and the newborns were standing steady on their feet. Nearly thirty ewes had given birth that day, most of them to twins. One had given birth to three, and Malachi had been helping her. He'd almost lost the third one because it was twisted in the ewe's uterus. If he had lost the lamb, he knew he would have lost the ewe too. But he was able to slowly coax it out. Miraculously, it survived, wobbling with exhaustion while the ewe slowly and meticulously cleaned off blood and afterbirth, turning the tiny creature into a snowy white sprite. That was the best part of the day. Even though he was tired, he felt the deep satisfaction of work well done as he limped back to the boys' camp with the plate of food for Idget.

He knew something was off as soon as he arrived at the camp. Wilson and Joseph were posted on either side of the small herd of sheep, and Two Bits ferried back and forth between them, watching, waiting for one of the sheep to bolt. The fire ring was dark. Idget always built the fire and prided himself on building the best ones. Malachi sped up as much as he could. His bad leg was bothering him from having squatted most of the day with the sheep, but he put the pain out of his mind and walked faster, digging his stick deeply into the dirt path and balancing the plate of food as best he could as he walked. When he arrived at the camp, both Joseph and Wilson turned to look at him.

"Where's Idget?" he asked the boys.

They looked at each other, uncertainty in their faces.

"Where is he?" Malachi repeated, raising his voice.

"We're not sure," Joseph said. "We thought he was with you. He told us to mind the sheep when we got back, said he had to meet you in

Mountain Meadows."

Both boys watched him anxiously. Malachi knew something was desperately wrong. For all of Idget's bluster last night with Joseph and Wilson, he knew the boy would never willingly go to Mountain Meadows on his own. And why would he tell them he was meeting Malachi?

"You stay here, watch the sheep," he said. "I'm going to find him."

"It'll be dark soon," Wilson said. "Don't you think he'll come back? He said he'd come back."

Malachi shifted the strap of his satchel on his shoulder and looked at him.

"I don't know," he said, hoping that what he knew in his bones was misleading him. "If he does, tell him I said stay put."

CHAPTER 20

He descended the trail into the flat of Mountain Meadows. He stopped and scanned the grassy expanse in front of him. It turned a golden-red as the sun started to slip toward the horizon. It had been eight months since the killings. In that time, someone had made a half-hearted attempt to clear some of the bodies, and a heap of bones and skulls lay in a shallow pit. He walked past the pile of skeletons, their flesh and stench long gone, their bones bleached from the sun. The remains of the children he had searched were still scattered on the meadow's floor, their stiff hair spread from their small hollowed skulls, the faded fabric of their clothes rotting into the dirt. He had to watch where he was stepping to avoid disturbing them.

He searched the meadow for Idget, straining to see in the fading light. Then he spotted him. Idget's legs were stretched out and his head twisted away from his torso facing the Magotsu that flowed past, deep and strong. He ran toward him, calling out his name until his voice was hoarse. When he reached the stream Malachi collapsed to his knees next to his friend.

Someone had lashed his wrists together, pinning his arms behind his back. His eyes that had once held so much life were white and milky. A sob caught in Malachi's throat as he ran his hands over Idget's body. It was clammy and wet. He gently lifted a tendril of grass off his face. There were no wounds, no cuts or bullet holes. He must have been drowned, someone had forced him under until his lungs filled with water, then hauled him up on the river's bank and left his body for the animals to pick clean. He thought about Idget's panic the day before at the thought of going into the water to fetch his horse. It was as though he'd seen this coming.

"Idget," he said softly as his trembling hands reached out to loosen the rope that bound his thick wrists together. His flesh was cold but still soft, pliable. If only he'd arrived earlier. If only he'd been able to stop this, to save him. Why had he agreed to let Idget stay behind this morning? He sat back on his knees and twisted the rope furiously in his hands. Then he held still and slowly fell forward to let his head rest on Idget's belly. He closed his eyes and breathed in the damp smell of the creek that soaked his clothes. His friend didn't smell like death but of water. Fresh. Clean.

He wiped away the tears that streaked his cheeks. He was alone in this. He pushed himself up and gazed at Idget. He wanted to bury him, but the sun was dropping quickly now and he knew there was no time, not now. He dragged Idget's body over to a pile of dead wood and covered him with the branches. He hoped it would protect Idget from the animals that patrolled the meadow's floor, until he could come back in the morning to bury his body. As he worked, rage mounted in his chest, and he screamed up into the darkening sky. It made his thoughts lucid and sharp, shoved aside the dullness of sorrow. Priscilla had warned him of this. Perhaps she knew more than she had let on. She'd be waiting for him now behind the barn, but not for much longer. He had to get to her, find out what she knew and tell her about the letter. There was no more reason to hide anything from her. He threw three more branches on top of Idget's body then turned to leave.

The yard between the Hamblin house and barn was quiet and empty. Lamplight glowed through the windows of the house. He rounded the path that led toward the barn and looked into the shadows for Priscilla. She was there, leaning against the barn looking out over the lambing pasture that was punctuated with the wooly dots of ewes and new lambs. She held up a lantern when he approached, smiling at him. The kindness in her face as she greeted him made him realize with a new certainty that she did not see him as an Indian boy, bought and owned only to be put to use, ordered, and dismissed. She was not like the rest of them. She was his friend, and now his only friend.

"I was worried you weren't coming," she said as he neared her. She extinguished the flame of the lantern and set it down at her feet. "Don't want anyone to notice we're here."

"Something's happened," he said. "Something terrible, I…" He could barely find the words. To say them was to admit Idget was dead.

"What is it?" she reached out and touched his sleeve. "Your shirt's wet." She drew back her hand, rubbing the tips of her fingers together. Her face turned toward him in the shadows.

He remembered resting on top of Idget's wet body, hoping to revive him. He breathed in. "Someone's killed Idget," he said at last.

He couldn't see her expression in the dark, but her voice caught and she began to cry. She reached out and grasped his arm. "What happened?"

He told her how he'd gone to the camp by the pasture where they were tending the sheep and how the Jackson boys had told him Idget had left to meet him in Mountain Meadows. Priscilla's face came close to his now and the clean smell of soap rose off her skin, filling his nostrils.

"But why would he tell them he was meeting you?"

"I don't know. I think…" He trailed off. "You've got to tell me who it was that Lee said wanted to do us harm."

"He didn't say." She shook her head slowly. "Honestly, now I'm not even sure if what he said was true. He just said that he wanted you boys to come to Harmony for a spell after the killings in the meadows on account of what you had done there."

"But we didn't." He looked up at her. "We didn't help kill any of those people in the meadows. We didn't."

"I think I know that. I mean I did believe him, when he first told me. I couldn't see any reason he'd lie to me, and you were acting so strange that day of the spring celebration, like you had something to hide. But later I knew there was some other truth about what happened. I'm so sorry, Malachi, I'm sorry for everything."

Malachi peered into the darkness; suddenly fearful they weren't alone. He looked back at her. "You don't need to say you're sorry."

But the fact she had shifted things between them.

She nodded and they both stood in silence, listening to the sounds of the ewes and the lambs dying down as the world around them fell asleep.

"Tell me what happened," she said finally. "I want to know what happened to Idget."

He told her, sparing nothing. She listened as he talked, and he could hear her weeping. She let the tears spill down her face, making no move to wipe them away. When he finished, he told her he would go back tomorrow and bury him.

"I want to go with you," she said.

"I don't think we should give anybody reason to think you know about this."

"Why? He was my friend too."

She was right, but he knew it would put her at risk to be seen too much in his company, and he told her so. She said nothing, letting a long silence stretch out between them.

"It's late," he said finally.

She placed her hand briefly on the sleeve of his shirt then she dropped it to her side.

"Priscilla." Her name in his mouth gave him hope, but he struggled with the words he needed to say to her. "I haven't wanted to hurt you in any way. I never want to hurt you or mislead you, but I just haven't been able to tell you everything."

"I think I understand that," she said.

He felt her eyes rest on him in the dark. "There's something I need to show you." He could see her hand lightly fingering the skirt of her dress. He wished he could hold it tight against his chest. But instead, he looked at the ground and shifted his stance. He opened his satchel and gently loosened the thread that held the fabric concealing the letter. He pulled the cloth away from the leather of the pouch and slipped out the piece of paper. Even as he did it, he wondered if he should give it to her. Doubt pulled his skull tight and sent a prickling sensation across his forehead.

"What is that?" she asked, looking at the paper in his hand.

"It's a letter that was written by one of the people on the train," he said, holding it out to her. "By a woman killed that day in the meadows. It's dated—it was written the day the killing happened."

She sucked in her breath sharply and reached out to touch the letter warily as though it might burst into flames.

"How did you come by it?" Fear saturated her voice.

How much could he tell her now? He needed her to know only what was essential. All he really wanted of her was to tell him what the letter said. Nagging doubts licked the edge of his thoughts. Would she do this for him?

"Will you trust me to tell you that later?"

She said nothing but he felt her search his face in the darkness. The urgency in his chest was mounting.

"Yes," she said finally. "Yes."

"I can read a little, but not so good as you. It's important, and I don't want to make a mistake in understanding it. I need to have you read it to me." He handed it to her. As he did, he felt he was handing her his life and endangering hers. If Lee or anyone else involved in the massacre learned he had taken this letter, Malachi knew the outcome would be swift and furious.

The sound of men's voices in the yard startled them. They stood still as they listened to the men making their way from the house to the bunkhouse. When they heard the door of the bunkhouse close, she looked at him. He knew she was afraid, and he regretted the role he had played in propelling her into the knowledge of the events at Mountain Meadows. She glanced at the single sheet of paper and turned it over. "It's not so long. I can read it to you now. Is that what you want?" she asked.

He nodded.

She said nothing, then picked up the lantern and motioned him to follow her to the barn. They climbed up to the loft. He found a jar of matches on top of an old barrel and lit the lantern then set it on the barrel between them. She released the grip on her shawl as she held the letter out in front of her. "The woman who wrote it," she started. Her voice was low and Malachi moved toward her so he could understand her.

"What was her name?" Malachi asked. He could only remember the name of the woman the letter was addressed to: Antonia.

"The woman who wrote the letter?" she asked. Her brows knitted together for a moment, and she turned it over and looked down at the page. "Her name was Adele."

Adele. Malachi nodded. He imagined her. She must have been strong. And scared.

Priscilla sank to the floor and leaned against the barrel. The lamplight cast its glow over her and illuminated the letter. Her fingers delicately held the paper in place on her tented knees as though she didn't want to put too much pressure on it. The lamplight poured over her head, turning the color of her hair to a dark liquid copper.

"She greets Antonia as her sister then says, *A man named John Lee has come into our camp today.*" Malachi sat cross-legged in front of her and she looked up at him. "She says, *He is a Mormon man.*"

She looked back down at the letter and cleared her throat. "*He has blue eyes like no other man I've ever met. They pierce me through.*"

The image of John Lee standing in the meadows opposite the girl with the tattered white flag filled Malachi's mind. He remembered her, small and frightened, and he wondered if she saw his eyes as she faced him.

"*I am writing to you while John Lee is here talking to some of our men,*" Priscilla continued. "*He has promised we will be protected.*" She stopped and took a deep breath and brought her knees closer to her chest. "*He acts as though he is our friend and says he has bargained with the Paiutes for our lives. He has told us a group of Mormon men wait in the hills to save us.*"

Malachi remembered his racing thoughts from that day as he watched the weary men and women shuffle out from the protective ring of their wagons and obediently line up, directed by the Mormon men who carried rifles at their sides. He remembered wondering why they thought John Lee and the others were there to protect them.

"*I do not trust him.*" Priscilla shook her head as she read it. One of her hands dropped to her lap and the other held the letter, trembling slightly.

"*I am certain this man named John Lee has no interest in protecting us.*" She stopped; her eyes were on the letter. "*I am not the only one who doesn't believe him.*" Her voice had gone flat and low, like she was reciting a lesson or a verse. "*There has been a small band of Paiutes pestering us for food and making raids on our animals. They have stayed with us for the better part of our trek through southern Utah. But they are a sad lot, armed with only their bows and arrows, and we have been able to fend them off. For this past week, though, our situation has become more serious. People have been shooting at our camp and killed some of our ablest men. Our lookouts have reported they were white men, and we are certain they are Lee's men.*" She stopped and looked up at Malachi.

"But why did they go?" His voice was a whisper. He leaned toward her now, their heads nearly touching, and he peered at the fluid writing on the paper. "Did she say why they went?"

Priscilla cleared her throat. "*We have been trapped here for days*," she read.

"*Our food is nearly gone, and our ammunition is running low. We sent two of our bravest men for help, but they have not come back and we are certain they have been killed.*" Malachi thought of the corpses Two Bits had discovered, the severed fingers.

Priscilla chewed her lips and leaned back. She wouldn't meet his gaze.

"*We hope that the Mormons will take mercy on our children.*" The flatness of her voice broke and a sob caught in her throat. She stopped and swallowed, then went on. "*I hope, dear sister, that this is true and my sweet Maggie and the other children will find someone who will take them in, be kind to them. I hope from the depths of my heart that Maggie lives to see you again one day. I've told her to come find you, but she's confused and she is scared because she knows it means she may lose me. Please care for her for me, treat her as one of your beloved own because I fear that I will not live long enough to do so.*" Tears began to stream down Priscilla's face again. They slipped down her cheeks and pooled in the small hollow of her neck, making the edge of the blue collar on her dress dark and damp in the lamplight.

Malachi thought of the girl, of her mother, Adele. What would it be like to have someone who loved you so much?

"She wrote this letter believing she'd be killed." Priscilla stopped and looked down at the letter, shaking her head.

She folded the paper in half and handed it back to him. Using the heels of her hands, she wiped her cheeks. Sadness rested heavily between them, and the night had fallen still. He slipped the letter back behind the fold of fabric in his satchel. He thought of Idget, of finding his killer. He turned to Priscilla. He knew he needed her help and, for that, he knew he had to tell her more.

"I was there," he said.

Her eyes flew to his, and her mouth dropped open. "There?" she asked. "You mean what Father Lee said was true?" Her face was frantic and she leaned forward to bunch her skirts around her legs, crouching like an animal getting ready to flee.

"Not like that," he said hurriedly. He reached out his hand toward her but she pulled over to the side, staying just beyond his reach. "I wasn't with the men who killed them, and neither was Idget. Idget knew what happened, but he found out later. He wasn't with me. I was the only one who saw it. I saw everything, but I wasn't part of it."

She released the fabric of her dress and curled her neck down then wrapped her arms around her waist like her stomach hurt. She looked up and met his eyes. "Who was it? Who was it that did it? Was it my father?"

He looked at her. He knew he had to answer her. She needed to know. He knew that now.

"I—" he started. Words jammed in his throat, thought but unspoken. She held his gaze.

"Did my father help kill those people?" Her voice was a ragged, angry, insistent whisper.

"Yes," he said. "But they all did. The men here, in Santa Clara, but others too, others who were ordered to come help."

A silence yawned between them and the small sounds from inside the barn bubbled at its edges. Malachi knew they didn't have much longer. She'd have to go back to the house soon, before she was missed. Finally, he moved closer to her and their forearms touched. He felt the heat of her skin beneath the fabric of her sleeve. She sat still and made no move to unwrap her arms from her knees, but she didn't pull away from him. Tears started down her face again. Finally, she reached up to rub them away. The pressure of her hands left streaks that looked like dark stains on her cheeks in the lamplight.

He clasped his hands around his knees, weaving his fingers together. "No one is supposed to know. John Lee told the men they wasn't to speak of it to anyone." He looked at her. "No one was to know the truth, not even their families. I'm sorry to tell you this. I'm sorry you know this." The relief he had hoped at telling her hadn't come.

"I wanted to know," she said, looking at the floor. "I wanted you to tell me."

When she lifted her head, a tight, wry smile had inched its way into her mouth. He suddenly felt he could see her as an old woman, as though this new truth had stolen her freshness and robbed her of her joy for life.

"What are you planning to do?" she asked. Her voice was dry and low. "I'm afraid they'll kill you too if they find out what you know. Is that why Idget was killed? Do you think he told someone?"

"I don't know," he said slowly. He felt numb. He didn't know what had happened, but something had gone terribly wrong, someone had decided Idget needed to be gotten out of the way, silenced. "All I know is I can't leave without finding out who killed him."

Her face was still, and her eyes looked like they'd been swept clean. It frightened him.

"I knew we needed to leave. We'd agreed to it, but then I found the letter." He shrugged. "And I thought it might..." He trailed off. What had he thought? That he could somehow use it to ensure safe passage for him and Idget?

"I could help you," she said suddenly. "I could take it and show someone."

"But to who and why?" The air seemed to move inside the loft, as though a night animal had arrived and brushed up against their bodies.

"I haven't figured out who yet, but someone who has power in the church," she said. "I know they'll believe me. I can say I was the one who discovered it. It names no one else but my father. It would make sense that I would bring it to them."

"But who will believe you?" he asked. He didn't think there was anyone they knew who would want this claimed by anyone amongst the Mormons. To put this at the feet of one man in the church would be like putting a drop of blood in clear water, casting a stain on everyone. It was important for them to keep the water pure, the lie hidden.

"I can talk to Jacob Hamblin," she said. "He wasn't there. You said so yourself." Her words rushed out now and her eyes glinted in the light.

Malachi shook his head vehemently. "But he knows. Everyone in these parts knows what happened. It's not like they don't. Dame and Haight agreed to order it done. Even Brigham Young knows what happened."

"Does he?" She sucked in her breath sharply. "How do you know that?"

Malachi sighed. His choices about what to hold back from her had narrowed. The letter opened up the truth like a funnel and he had to pour every other thing he knew through it.

"There was a conversation at the farm in Harmony." He bowed his head. "They didn't know I was listening, but I heard it. It was between John Lee, Agatha, and Rachel after he'd come back from Salt Lake." He hesitated. "Nobody was supposed to hear what they talked about that day, but I did. Brigham Young told your father what to do to cover it up, to make it more official, to make sure it was the Paiutes that took the blame."

"And did he?" Her voice was firm, insistent.

Malachi shrugged. "I don't know, but I think so. There was a letter he was to write and send to Brigham Young, an accounting of the Paiutes killing that was to be part of a bill that your father sent, a bill for taking care of the animals and the children from the train. They planned to bill the federal government."

"That letter?" She nodded as if to herself. "I know about that letter."

He looked at her. "How?"

"Just that Sister Rachel was stewing about it on the side, letting us all know she was helping him with it," she said. "We just thought she was worried about getting the inventory straight so Father Lee wouldn't be saddled with the cost of feeding all those animals."

"Did she say what was in it?" he asked.

She shook her head again. "Not much, just that she had to get the wording of it exactly right because Governor Young was particular about how they inventoried the property from the train, wanted to make sure we got our due."

She was silent and gazed through the window of the loft. Then she turned to him and said, "Do you think Brother Young ordered it, the killing?"

"I'm not sure," he said. "The men were told to do it. That's clear. But something happened. Maybe Young ordered it, then changed his mind, thought better of it, but after it was already too late."

She was about ready to say something more to him, but closed her mouth and looked at the floor seeming lost in thought. Then she looked at Malachi.

"Will you give it to me?"

"What will you do with it?"

"I think I can use it to help you," she said.

Doubt rushed into his head. Perhaps she really could help him. He didn't have much time. He was probably next. He needed to keep calm, do the lambing, maybe pick up something useful from the men who were returning to finish the lambing the following day.

"But how?"

"I don't know yet," she said. "But it's better that I have it. If they find it on you, I'm afraid they'll do to you what they did to Idget. Please."

She was right. If anyone found the letter on him, they'd know, they'd surely know he knew what had happened.

"You have to trust me. I'll sort it out and let you know. I promise. Do you trust me?" she asked him.

Hadn't he asked her to do the same, and hadn't she waited without knowing what truth stood just around the corner? He nodded silently, realizing he had no other ideas. He would bury Idget in the morning. He would show up for lambing. He would act as though nothing was wrong, and he would learn what he could, take revenge however he could, he would do that for his friend. He opened his satchel. His fingers searched for the piece of paper, but instead he felt the sheath of his knife at the bottom of the bag. He drew the knife out of his satchel and pulled it out of the sheath.

"What's this?" She pulled her head back in alarm.

He glanced at her. "There's something else I need you to keep for me." He quickly set the knife down and jammed his finger down into the leather sheath to pull out the bills. He handed them to her.

"Where did you get these?" She looked at the rolled bills unfurling in her hand.

"I stole them," he said. "I had to. It's the only way I can make my way out of here."

She stared at the money and looked at him, but asked no more questions. Then he handed her the letter. She unfastened the bottom buttons on the front of her dress and slipped the letter and the bills inside the fabric then twisted the buttons closed. She leaned toward him and hugged him hard.

"I'll be back in the morning," she said. "Try to sleep."

CHAPTER 21

APRIL 21

When Malachi woke the next morning, Joseph and Wilson were perched on two campfire logs, watching him while he slept. He opened one eye, then the other, squinting up at them. Both boys eyed him anxiously. He shoved the blanket off his chest and sat up, inhaling the cool morning air deeply into his lungs. He looked over at Idget's bedroll where he'd left it neatly folded from the morning before. Rage and sorrow had left him hollow, and he wondered how he would find the strength he needed for the day ahead.

"What's happened to Idget?" Joseph asked. "Why didn't he come back with you? We waited 'til dark, but he never came and we didn't know where you were so as to come find you and let you know."

Malachi considered him: his threadbare coat, pants cinched up with a rope that hugged his narrow waist, his cracked leather boots, probably hand-me-downs from one of his adoptive father's real sons. He wasn't stupid, this boy. He noticed what was going on around him. Took it all in. Malachi knew he had to. It was a matter of survival. They all had to watch and wait, figure out how to carve out a space for themselves. They walked the line between not being noticed too much, but seen just enough so they got enough to eat, had a place to sleep, had a coat to protect them against the winter cold as they did their chores. Had these boys come to figure out, like he had, that there were times when they had to learn to be invisible, disappear like the morning mist in order to survive in the mysterious world of these white people who believed that by buying the boys they'd saved them from the sure prospect of hell?

What did they know, these two? What had they heard?

One of the boys had already fed the dogs. Two Bits, having finished up her food, walked over to Malachi and plunked her rear down next to him, gazing at him. They waited for him to speak. He looked at the spade he'd brought from the barn last night. He would need someone's help to bury Idget.

"He drowned," he said. "I found him in the Magotsu, tangled in the roots of a tree, but it was too late. He was dead."

Their faces drained and the boys exchanged nervous glances.

"It weren't us," Joseph said. "You got to believe it."

Malachi gathered his brows and leveled his gaze at him.

"He drowned. Idget didn't know how to swim. Why would I think it was you or anybody else?"

"Dunno, we just started on a bad foot with both of you," Joseph said, stubbing the toe of his boot into the dirt. "And it's like everyone is on tinder here. Feels like things are just waiting to explode."

"I'm going down to the meadow this morning," Malachi said, deciding to ignore the boy's observation. "I'm going back to bury him. I want one of you to help me so we can get it done before lambing starts."

He needed the help, but also wanted to get one of the boys to himself, without the watchful eye of the other. He might get him to talk.

"We was told not to go there," Wilson said. "We'll be beaten sure, if we do."

"It's not like anyone has to know." Joseph looked at him. "If I go, you won't tell, will you?"

"Nope, you know I won't," Wilson said as he shook his head. "But hurry fast. I don't want the men comin' here and asking me questions. If'n they do, what should I say?"

Malachi was pulling on his boots now. He reached for his satchel and pushed himself up, looping the strap around his shoulders. Then he reached down and picked up the spade he'd brought back from the barn last night. He handed it to Joseph and turned to Wilson.

"If they come just tell them we're off chasing a stray lamb," he said.

Wilson nodded his head. "Alright, jus' hurry."

Malachi was quiet as the two boys descended into Mountain Meadows, listening to Joseph keep up his steady chatter. When they arrived on the meadow floor, Joseph let out a long whistle. "It's them," he said, staring at the piles of skeletons in the meadow. "They're really here."

But Malachi barely heard him. He was tearing away the pile of branches, searching for Idget's body. It was gone.

✳ ✳ ✳

Malachi walked along the river, going back again and again to the spot where he'd found Idget the day before. Joseph tagged along at his heels, talking to him all the while.

"You sure you seen him here?" The boy asked.

"He was right here," Malachi said. "I pulled him ashore, put him beneath some branches to protect him from the critters."

Joseph looked at him skeptically.

"Maybe he wasn't dead," he said.

Malachi looked at the ground, shaking his head, wishing it was true. Someone had removed his body for a reason, maybe to claim he'd run away. But why hadn't they done it after they'd killed him. A thought slipped icily into his head. Perhaps his killer had been there, watching him when he discovered Idget.

"We should get back," he said suddenly. "They'll be wondering where we are if we don't show up for breakfast."

Joseph nodded and they turned to walk out of the meadow.

Breakfast was in full swing when they got to the barnyard, so they managed to slip in unnoticed. They lined up to fill their plates with food. Joseph made a plate for Wilson and told Malachi he'd be back after he'd brought his brother breakfast. Malachi waved him off and looked for a place to sit. As he ate, he kept an eye out for Priscilla. He needed to talk to her. He would use the day to learn what he could, but if he hadn't learned who Idget's killer was by that night, he would leave. He'd get his money from Priscilla and ask her help to pack some supplies. He needed enough to sustain him for a few days of riding, enough time to get out of the Mormon settlements.

The front door of the house opened. Priscilla swept outside, balancing a platter of fried potatoes. She walked over to the tables. There was something fierce and new that had blossomed in her overnight. Her easy smile was gone and a sharp, angular awareness hovered just behind her eyes. It looked like fury. He thought about all she had lost in just a short time. The world she thought she knew had changed overnight. Those she loved had lied to her. Lee, who had taken her in, called her his own daughter, raised her and protected her, had helped murder innocent people. He and the men who helped him, the very ones that milled around the barnyard now, enjoying their breakfasts, laughing at each other's stories, were all protected by a church—her church—that was led by a man who expected to be seen as faultless and beyond judgment, a man who would do whatever it took to shake off the stench of the murders, regardless of the role he and his followers had played. Malachi wondered if Priscilla would give it up, leave the protection of the church, Lee's protection and come with him. It seemed impossible for him to even think it, but he did. He knew it was what he wanted.

Priscilla spotted him and grabbed a blue enameled coffee pot from the table. She began making the rounds with it, topping off the men's cups one-by-one, barely talking to them as she went, causing some of them to look at her in puzzlement, wondering at her aloofness. When she reached him, her face relaxed a little and she smiled briefly.

"Morning," she said, tipping the pot over his cup. "How did it go?"

He glanced around them. The men had turned back to their breakfasts and morning conversations.

"He was gone," he said softly. "His body was gone."

She kept her face controlled, but pulled the coffee pot toward her belly as if seeking its warmth.

"What will you do?"

"Tonight," he said quietly. "I've decided I have to leave. Will you help me?"

She nodded.

They arranged to meet at nightfall.

The day of lambing was long and bloody. Malachi missed the mid-day meal because he had to stay in the barn to tend to a series of difficult ewes that seemed unwilling to release their lambs from their wombs. A short, stout brick of a woman he recognized as one of the wives from a nearby ranch brought food out for the men and boys who hadn't been able to take a break. He wolfed down a slab of meat on a thick slice of buttered bread between his stints coaxing lambs from the ewes. By the time the workday was over, the ewes had given birth to thirty-two more lambs. It had been a good season, and the men were in high spirits. As he watched Wilson and Joseph drive the last of the lambs and ewes into the meadow, Malachi wiped off the flecks of blood and mucous that still clung to the skin on his face, hands, and arms.

"You stink like a woman's cunny," said someone behind him.

It was Albert.

"You're back," Malachi said as he folded his kerchief and stuck it in his hip pocket.

"So are you," Albert said. He adjusted a black silk scarf that was knotted at his neck and tilted down his wide-brimmed hat so it shadowed his eyes.

"Something new there tied around your neck?" Malachi eyed the scarf. Then he used the language of their childhood to say what only he and Albert could understand. "You look like a bad copy of a white man."

Albert's hand sliced through the air at Malachi's face. But before he could connect, Malachi reached out and caught the boy's hand then twisted his arm around his back and squeezed tight.

"I wouldn't if I was you," Malachi said to him, leaning into Albert's back as the other boy struggled to get out of his grasp. "I got stronger while I was gone."

A deep gurgle of laughter bubbled up from Albert's chest so that he nearly spit it out. His arm had gone limp in Malachi's hand then he wrenched it away and shoved Malachi to the ground. Albert leapt on top of him as Malachi tried to back away, digging his heels into the earth. But it was too late. Albert pinned him. Men and boys who'd helped with lambing that day circled around them. Malachi looked up at Albert's face. His lips had pulled back into a satisfied smile.

"But just not strong enough, are you Mudface?" Albert said. "Just never strong enough."

"That's enough now."

Malachi heard a man's voice behind Albert, someone he couldn't see because Albert was leaning over him. But when Albert twisted around to look up, Malachi saw it was Jacob Hamblin. Hamblin put his hand on Albert's shoulder.

"Get on up off of him. I told you to go get him to bring him to me, not fight with him. Come on now, the both of you. Get up."

Albert gave Malachi's chest a final thump before he climbed off. Malachi lay still for a moment looking at the half circle of men and boys. They were all staring down at him; no one was smiling. The relaxed camaraderie of the day in the lambing shed had evaporated, replaced by a tension fixed in the air.

"Not gonna say it again, get up boy," Jacob Hamblin stood at Malachi's feet. "I want you to come up to the house with me. There's someone there who'd like to talk to you."

Malachi slowly got to his feet then reached for his walking stick that had been shoved to one side in the scuffle. He stood upright.

Hamblin squinted slightly then blinked twice. "Got an important visitor at the house."

The men edged together more tightly. Malachi could see the frayed hem of Oscar Hamblin's vest and smell the staleness of Phillip Klingensmith's breath. Malachi shifted his satchel to his side as he turned and stumbled after Hamblin. Albert was close on Malachi's heels, muttering threats and insults to him the entire way.

"You wait outside here until I come back out," Hamblin said to Albert. "Don't let anyone enter. We're not to be disturbed. You understand?"

Malachi saw the fall of disappointment in Albert's face. He had hoped to witness whatever pain and humiliation waited for Malachi inside. Hamblin opened the door and motioned Malachi to walk through in front of him. The house was strangely silent. He could hear the soft lopsided scrape of his footsteps syncopate against Hamblin's even tread as they walked across the bare wooden floors. Malachi had never been invited inside the Hamblin's house. A steep stairway stood awkwardly just inside the door and thrust its way through a square opening to the second story. The smell of cooked cabbage lingered in the stale air. They walked down a hallway that was nearly dark and tunneled gracelessly through the mid-section of the first floor. At the end of the hallway, a raw pine door stood partially open, emitting a slash of yellow light. Although Hamblin didn't say where they were going, Malachi continued to walk slowly toward the open door, thinking there was no other place to go. Just before they reached it, Hamblin laid a hand on Malachi's right shoulder.

"Stop here," Hamblin said. Malachi felt the flesh of his shoulder shrink away from Hamblin's touch. Hamblin walked around to face him.

"You are about to meet a man of God," Hamblin said, tipping his chin down so that his dark eyes angled directly into Malachi's. "This is not just any man, but a man who has dedicated his life to the service of God. There will be no sign of disrespect to him. You will listen to what he tells you and you will answer his questions honestly. Do you understand me?"

Hamblin's fingers were digging so deeply into Malachi's shoulder now that he had to breathe hard through his nose to keep from crying out.

"Who is it?" he asked.

"Tell me first," Hamblin insisted. "Do you understand what I just said to you?"

Malachi nodded and Hamblin's fingers eased some out of the boy's shoulder.

"It's George Smith, Disciple George Smith," Hamblin said as he steered Malachi through the door.

The large man Malachi had first seen at the picnic in Harmony sat on a chair that was slightly turned away from a table, where he rested his right hand. He had been writing, but looked up from his paper when Malachi and Hamblin entered the room. Smith had muddy brown eyes nestled close to a nose that looked as if it had been broken once then grown back with a wayward twist. His body was dense and heavy, and the crude pine chair he sat on seemed to bend beneath the weight of it. The Saints called him Brother Smith, but Idget had told him that the Paiutes called him *the Man Who Comes Apart* because there were so many things about him that were false, including his hair and his teeth. He was known for taking off his wig and mopping his face with it when he preached.

"Brother Smith," Hamblin said. "Here is the boy."

Smith turned his eyes on Malachi. Although Malachi didn't flinch at his gaze, he felt his stomach go watery and weak. George Smith was one of Young's closest advisors. Where Smith went, punishment followed. It was Smith who had spread the gospel of blood atonement throughout the settlements in the year that led up to the massacre in Mountain Meadows. The men in dark hats brought in to carry out the punishments in the settlements followed in Smith's wake, seeking to punish those who were marked for a beating or worse.

"State your name, boy, loud and clear. My ears ain't what they used to be," Smith said.

"Malachi Blank is my given name," he said.

"Who bought you and calls you his own?" Smith asked in a voice that seemed mildly bemused. His pen scratched against the piece of paper on top of the table. He didn't look up at Malachi but kept his eyes trained on the paper as he wrote.

"Jonah Blank, sir," Malachi answered. "Jonah Blank bought me nearly nine years ago. I am his adopted son."

Smith looked up and set down his pen. He stared at him in silence.

"Do you know why you're here?" Smith asked finally. Although Malachi knew the question was addressed to him, Smith had turned his gaze to Jacob Hamblin.

"No sir," Malachi said.

Smith shifted in his chair. The paltry structure squawked against his weight.

"There is a false rumor that goes through these settlements that some of our own men were involved in the killing of that train of gentiles last fall. Have you been part of that piece of malicious tongue-wagging?"

Smith had rested his thick hands on his knees and his face puckered into a scowl that made him look like an oversized pouting baby.

"No," Malachi replied.

Smith sat upright, and a slab of fat from his thigh melted over the seat of his chair. Hamblin watched Smith carefully, as though studying each of the powerful man's mannerisms. His arms were crossed and he reached his slender index finger to his lips, tapping lightly on them as though he was carefully ruminating on the actions and words of George Smith. Smith glared at him, and Hamblin stopped abruptly, dropping his hands to his sides.

"How do we know that is true?" Smith asked, turning his attention back to Malachi. "Albert tells us you reject the Lord and all our teachings."

"Albert has found his own way, and I've found mine," Malachi said.

"So, you willingly remain a sinner?" Smith's eyebrows gathered together on his forehead in a fleshy knot.

"If that's what you wish to call me," Malachi replied. "I won't argue with you."

"Then how will we know whether you speak the truth or tell us lies?" Smith asked.

"You can't, I reckon," Malachi replied. "But there's not much that makes me want to lie about such a thing since John Lee threatened me with my life for uttering a word about the event at all. I may be a liar in other things, but I tell you the truth when I say I wish to live."

Smith's small brown eyes were fixed on Malachi, and he kneaded his thick red lips together like he tasted something sweet. "But now you will talk to me and you will tell me what you was doing that day," Smith said. "Because if you don't, by the time I have done with you, you will wish that John Lee had made good on his threat to kill you."

A trickle of sweat had formed at the center of Malachi's chest and was working its way down his belly. "I was herding the sheep, like always."

"But you wasn't now," Smith said, leaning forward on his knees again. "Was you."

It was a question dressed up as a statement, and Malachi paused before replying. He felt certain Smith had already heard the story of Malachi's movements that day from Albert and Hamblin. He wondered if Smith was testing him, daring him to slip up.

"I had to leave the herd," he said. "Dog took out after a stray, and I followed her. Wanted to make sure we didn't lose one of the sheep."

"But isn't that what the dog is for?" Smith placed his hands on top of his thighs again and rubbed them back and forth against the fabric of his wool pants.

"Beg pardon?" Malachi asked.

"I hear from Hamblin's boy, Albert, that you've got a dog watching those sheep with you that is near smart as you, maybe smarter," Smith said, glancing at Malachi then looking up at the ceiling as though he was perplexed by what the ceiling had to offer. "Got a dog like that and you don't need to go sashaying all over the countryside followin' up on stray sheep. That's the dog's job."

Smith's eyes came down from the ceiling and leveled on Malachi. A bubble of fear popped inside Malachi's chest. He thought suddenly of Idget and wondered if Smith had ordered him killed. He considered the distance between where he stood and the door. He wondered if he could get out the door and down the hall to the outside before Hamblin could reach him. Then he remembered Albert, stationed outside the front door of the house and the men who would be milling around the yard now, waiting for supper.

"Sometimes she needs watching," Malachi said. His voice sounded wind-swept, and he wondered if they knew how scared he was.

Both men watched him fixedly. Smith looked down, his fat chin sinking into his chest. He drummed his fingers on the table, and Hamblin raised his eyebrows slightly. Smith looked at the other man.

"Brother Hamblin, what ideas do you have for breaking the truth out of this boy?"

Hamblin removed his jacket and hung it on a peg to the left of the door. Then he slowly rolled his sleeves up to his elbows. Malachi glanced at the ropy muscles on his arms and noticed how dark and coarse the hair was on them. Hamblin walked over to Malachi and stood in front of him.

"You've held back from us," Hamblin said. "Albert tells us you went to the meadows after the killing. Why was that?"

"John Lee, sir," Malachi said. "He had me go with him, him and some of the other men." The roof of his mouth was sticky and dry. Hamblin was standing so close to him he could smell the pomade he used to slick back his long hair from his face.

"Why didn't you tell us that earlier?" Hamblin reached around to grip the back of Malachi's neck. He squeezed.

"No one asked," Malachi said, making an effort to keep pulling air into his lungs as Hamblin's grip tightened. "John Lee knew, so I thought he would of told you."

"What was it you did there?" Hamblin released his grip and eased his hand over to Malachi's shoulder.

"I was told to search the bodies."

Hamblin and Smith exchanged looks.

"For what purpose?" Hamblin asked. He'd turned back to face him, and his fingers dug into Malachi's flesh again.

"I guess it was to find whatever was left." He moved his shoulder slightly but Hamblin's fingers tightened.

"Left?" Smith asked.

"You know, after the Paiutes had done their takin'," Malachi said.

"What'd you find?" Smith asked.

"Trinkets, a little money," Malachi said. "A Bible." Some truth was good. He saw that.

"What did you do with it?" Hamblin asked.

"I gave it to John Lee, like he told me to do," Malachi said.

"All of it?" Hamblin asked sharply, reaching out now with his other hand to dig his fingers into both of Malachi's shoulders.

"Yes." He was breathing hard now.

"This leather bag," Hamblin said, as he looked down and ran his finger underneath the strap around the boy's shoulders. "Empty it out for us."

The room reeled. Malachi slowly removed his satchel. As he did so, his hopes of escape dwindled to dust. It had made no difference that he had been careful, that he had kept his own counsel. In the end, the fact that he had bided his time, had kept his secret safe had led to nothing. Idget was lost to him and he had survived only to end up here now with these men who meant to do him harm. He hadn't been able to protect Idget. He had failed to escape. The letter he had retrieved was with Priscilla, but he did not know if she would give it to anyone who could help. In the end, all he had done had not mattered. Idget was dead, and soon these two men would kill him too.

"Give it to me," Hamblin said impatiently.

Malachi took the satchel from around his shoulders and handed it to Hamblin. Hamblin dumped out its sparse contents on the table. There were a few twists of jerky, a piece of stale bread, a small stone Malachi had kept because he liked the shape and color of it, the book Priscilla had given him, and the knife in its sheath. Hamblin pulled open the satchel and picked at the thread that held the cloth lining in place, then yanked out the cloth and plunged his hand into the leather pouch. As Malachi watched him, he wondered why he'd chosen to look there. Had someone told him? The only person he could think of who could have possibly known was Idget. Had they forced it out of him before they killed him?

He tossed the stone aside and it spun across the table and fell on the floor. Hamblin picked up the knife and unbuckled the sheath, pulling out the blade. He pinched the sheath opened and peered inside as Malachi watched.

"Anything?" Smith asked.

Hamblin shook his head then slid the knife back into its sheath and tucked it into his pants pocket. He spun around and strode over to Malachi. He grabbed his collar and pulled him toward his face.

"You are lying to us. I can see it in you." Hamblin said, shaking Malachi so hard his teeth clapped together and he bit down on his tongue. Hamblin threw him to the floor, and Malachi's walking stick spun across the surface and came to rest by Smith's feet.

"Call in that boy of yours," Smith said. Malachi watched Hamblin pull open the door and heard his boots as he walked down the dark hallway. He tasted the trickle of blood that oozed out between his lips.

Smith hauled his body out of the chair and the floorboards squeaked as he made his way to stand over Malachi. "You're a stubborn one, but I am more." He stood looking down at him. "We are told to refrain from harming the Indian children in our keeping, but we're told nothing as to how you treat each other. You are Albert's cousin, I am told. You are from the same tribe. Is that right?"

Malachi nodded.

"Then we will see how your own kin treats you."

Malachi tried to get up, but Smith had retrieved his walking stick and held the end of it against Malachi's chest, forcing him back against the floor. Footsteps came down the hall, and a wave of numbness moved through him. Without warning, he felt the impact of someone's boot on his ribs, and he knew it belonged to Albert. Then there was a second blow to the side of his head and a quake of pain reverberated through his skull. He heard the hiss of his stick as it sliced through the air and came down on his legs with a deadly certainty.

Albert's face loomed above him. He held Malachi's cane high in the air, ready to deliver the next blast. He seemed larger than usual. His face was rigid and his eyes—the same deep, dark brown of Malachi's own—seemed fixed on some distant target, as though Malachi weren't even there, but was a mere obstacle that needed to be removed in order for Albert to get to where he wanted to be. Then it occurred to Malachi, swimming to the surface of his thoughts amidst the pain and the blows and the blood: this was Albert's desperate show of loyalty. This was another way he could prove himself to these men. But as he shook from Albert's blows, he knew it wouldn't end there. For as hard as Albert tried to prove he was one of them—dressing like them, talking like them, worshipping their God—he would never be one of them. Malachi knew that, and he was certain Albert feared it. It was that fear that lay deep inside his cousin's heart, and that fear pushed him beyond all reason.

Albert tossed the cane aside and landed on Malachi with a grunt. Hamblin and Smith stood watching as Albert's fists came down. Malachi didn't fight back. He retreated inside himself like a turtle, imagining he was protected by an ancient bony shell, tipping and turning in the water of darkness. Every time Albert hit him, he shifted and curled and bobbed until he could feel no more.

CHAPTER 22

APRIL 22

The smell of dirt filled Malachi's nostrils when he woke. He was sprawled on the cellar floor. He tried to blink his eyes open, but his right eyelid pulled against the thin skin of his lower lid until he rubbed away a hard crust of blood. He peered into the darkness that clung to the air around him, searching for some opening, a source of light. Night had fallen, and he knew he would have to stay in this envelope of blackness until the sun came up. Disappointment prickled his chest. He realized part of him had hoped Albert would kill him.

He inhaled deeply, reaching up to gingerly pat his face, his fingertips skating over swollen lips, a puffed eye, and a raw lump on his forehead. His ribs were sore. He wiggled his toes inside his boots and drew his legs up, tenting his knees. His muscles ached, but he could move his limbs. Albert hadn't broken any bones.

A spider landed lightly on his face, and he brushed it away. He wondered how many spiders lived down here in the dark with the winter vegetables.

Must be hundreds. He thought of them now, watching him, wondering about this intruder in their dark underworld. He tried to guess how many hours he had been passed out and how much longer until sun-up. It might be then that they'd finally kill him. He thought of what Smith said, that they had been instructed not to harm the Indian children in their care, a rule he hadn't heard before and one he knew was repeatedly violated. He thought of Idget and wondered if it had been Albert who was sent to kill him.

He didn't know why they'd let him live. Then a question skittered across the surface of his mind like a water bug on top of a pond. Why didn't he just tell them? It's what they wanted of him. They suspected he knew the truth. Why didn't he save himself the trouble of it all and just tell them what he knew, what he had seen? He was certain they were going to kill him anyway. At least he'd have the satisfaction of seeing the surprise on their faces when they found out how much he had seen. His thoughts were interrupted by a soft scratching at the cellar door. He held his breath. It came again. Then he heard Priscilla's voice.

"Malachi, can you hear me?"

He propped himself up on his elbows and felt the pain shoot through him as he forced his body up. He rolled over and managed to scoop himself up on hands and knees to crawl toward her voice. He moved as quickly as he could, willing her to stay.

"It's me," he said. He had reached the bottom of the stairs that led up to the cellar door. He was exhausted and could push his body no further.

"Oh," she replied. Her voice had the softness of flour. "I am so sorry for what they did to you. I tried to warn you."

His head was throbbing. Warn him of what?

"Idget told them," she said.

"Told them what?"

"He told them you'd seen it all and were planning on telling that judge they say is coming here."

"What?" He couldn't believe what he was hearing. "How did you find that out?"

"Rachael told me. She said Idget had tried to run, but they caught him."

But Joseph had said Idget left the pasture alone, telling them he was going to meet Malachi. He wasn't running.

"She said he'd come clean to Jacob Hamblin and George Smith, claimed you were mad at John Lee and were going to say he done it, that he was the one who put the Paiutes up to it. She said they locked him up in the cellar—here, where you are now—for his own safekeeping until they could figure out what to do with him."

"It's a lie," he said. "I'm sure they wanted him to tell them something, confess to something, and when he didn't, they killed him, or had him killed."

In the silence he heard her crying. He pressed his hand against the hard-packed earth of the cellar floor. He listened as she blew her nose and inhaled.

"But the thing is, Rachael said that on account of what Idget told them is why they wanted to talk to you. So, when I heard it, I came to find you, to warn you, but it was too late. The men said you'd gone with Albert and Jacob Hamblin to see George Smith."

"That's it," he said. "I'm done for."

"No, I won't let that happen to you," she said firmly. "Do you think you can ride?"

He thought about his throbbing head, his stiff limbs, but nothing was broken. "Yes," he said, "I can ride.

"Tomorrow is Sunday. Everyone will be going to service in the morning, but I can say I have to stay behind, say Charlie has a fever and I have to care for him. Then I'll come get you. Rachael has the key for the cellar, but she'll give it to me. She trusts me."

Priscilla would do this for him. He breathed in. He couldn't imagine how far he'd get. He knew he was in bad shape, but at least he could go. Better to die in the Mojave than stay and be beaten like a dog. He listened for Priscilla's breathing on the other side of the door.

"You there?"

"I'm here," she answered.

"If you're willing," he said. "I'll take your help."

She said nothing. Then he heard fabric rustling and something being shoved through the bottom of the cellar door.

"I want to give this back to you," she said. "It's the money. I'm glad you didn't have it on you yesterday, but I want to give it to you now in case something goes wrong and I can't get to you."

He pinched the bills between his fingers and slipped them inside his left boot. Everything could go wrong, he decided. Everything already had.

"And the letter? What will you do with the letter?"

"After you are gone, I'll tell them that Idget told me you had it and that I stole it from you. I will give it to Jacob Hamblin." Her voice had a hard finality to it.

"You know he'll use it against John Lee somehow," he said.

She cleared her throat. There was silence on the other side of the door.

"Priscilla?"

"I never thought I'd say this, but I'm glad John Lee is not my real father. I hate what he helped do to Leah and Charlie's parents," she said. "I know he's cared for me like one of his own, but this goes against all I know. He and the men who did this…somehow, they have to pay."

Her voice tapered off.

"Why did John Lee bring you here?"

"It was a marriage proposal."

"To who?"

"Jonah Blank."

The thought of it made him sick: that squarish gray man folding himself over Priscilla, kissing her, touching her.

"You can't," he blurted out. "You can't marry yourself off to Jonah Blank."

"I'm not," she reassured him. "I told Father Lee I'd come down here to help out Rachael Hamblin and to meet Jonah Blank. I've done both, but I'll not marry him."

"You can say no?"

"Yes, I can say no," she said. But something in her voice was resigned. "At some point, I will have to find a husband and marry. The Lees have taken care of me long enough and, now, given everything, I want to leave. Maybe I'll ask to be sent to Salt Lake. I need to make my own way."

"Come with me." It burst out of him, and he felt his heart rattle against his chest with the audacity of it.

She paused. "What would they make of that, if they caught up with us?" she asked. "They'd say you kidnapped me and use it as a reason to execute you. They could, you know. No, I won't come with you. I can't. My life is here."

"But what if they find out you helped me escape?"

She was silent for a moment. "I've thought of that. I'll tell them that when I went to drop off breakfast for you, you overtook me, forced me to help you escape. That I had no choice if I wanted to live."

"And what about what they did to those people on the Fancher train?" he asked. "Can you stay when you know the church is covering up what happened and who did it?"

"I don't expect you to understand." She paused. "But, yes, I can stay in spite of that. Not everyone was involved, not everyone is covering up. There are good people who believed what they were told. I know there are people in this church who are fine, kind souls, people I can trust. I know that."

"But it's Brigham Young," he insisted. "He's the head of the church."

"One day he won't be, and someone who wasn't involved will take over, set things right. The church is all I've ever known. It's the only life

I've had. What do you think waits for me out there? Who do you think will have me? Maybe for you it's different because you're a boy. But for me, this is what I have."

He knew she was right in one respect: she did have more to lose by going. He had nothing to lose, and he understood the difference. He was tired but wanted to keep her longer and there was one more question that pressed at him.

"Why do you think they did it?"

"If I knew that…" her voice trailed off, and she was silent for a minute. "I think people were so scared," she started. "They heard the army was coming, and they were frightened that all we'd built here would be destroyed, taken away. The ones who'd been at Nauvoo will never forget it. Somehow the men must have convinced themselves that the people on that wagon train were here to hurt us."

"But what about the others?" he asked. "What about the people like William Haslett and the others like him, the ones that hadn't been in Nauvoo?"

"I don't know," she said, sounding exasperated now. "How am I to know what men like William Haslett thought? Maybe they were just doing what they were told because they wanted to be accepted. Isn't that what we all want in the end? To belong?"

She laughed then, but it was a dry laugh with an emptiness that caused the little hairs on Malachi's neck to stand up straight.

"All I know is that when I look at Charlie and Leah, I see they're like me. They've got no kin, no one to mother them but me. At least my parents were taken by a disease. Funny how I see that as lucky compared to them. I can't forgive what those men did in the meadow that day. I can't change it, but I can't overlook it. I'll share that letter you found with someone who can use it to set things right. If I leave with you, I won't be able to do that, and I'd also have to leave Charlie and Leah. How can I leave them here alone with the very men who slaughtered their kin?"

They both sat silent, letting her words sink into the darkness between them. Then he heard her begin to stir. "I best get back. Remember. I'll come in the morning, bring you some food, I'll pack up some in your saddlebags too. We won't have long. You'll need to be far away from here by the time they get back from service. Get your rest."

He wanted to keep her, ask her more questions, but he knew he'd wrung everything out of her. He also knew what she was risking by helping him. He knew she cared for him. It wasn't the same as his longing for her, but he knew she cared for him and the frightened fist that had closed around his heart began to unfurl.

✳ ✳ ✳

Malachi's eyes flicked open. A slash of light seeped through the bottom of the door. He thought he heard someone moving outside the cellar door. It sounded as though something had been set on the ground, then he heard the scrape of the key in the lock. He watched the door swing open. His heart leapt. He pushed himself up. Every muscle in his body pulled back in pain as he craned his head to see up the steps. It was a woman, but not Priscilla. It was Rachael Hamblin.

"Brought you some breakfast," she said.

He watched as her worn, dusty boots made their way down the narrow steps of the cellar, left foot first. She uncovered a chipped white bowl and set it down on a crate that was overturned on the cellar floor. She drew a spoon out of her pocket and stuck it in the bowl.

He swallowed his disappointment and sat up. He knew he needed to eat. He was sure there was a good reason Priscilla's plans had changed and it was Rachael who'd come and not her. He clung to the belief Priscilla would still come for him. He slid himself over to the crate and wrapped his fingers around the bowl. It was still warm. He hadn't eaten since yesterday, and the thick hot oatmeal filled his empty stomach. He glanced up at Rachael between bites. For once she was not in perpetual motion, but he could tell she was on edge. Her hands, hidden inside the pockets of her apron, twitched as she watched him eat. Her eyes lingered on the bruises on his face as he scraped the last of the cereal from the bowl. He tried to get up to hand the bowl to her.

"Sit," she said, holding up her hand. "I'll get it."

"Has John Lee come back?" he asked, easing back to the cellar floor as she took the bowl from him.

She wrapped the bowl up in a dishtowel and quickly glanced up the stairs.

"He won't be comin' this way after all. Disciple Smith had another purpose for him and sent him north."

"And Disciple Smith, is he still here?"

A look of wariness slid into her eyes.

"I have to go. Someone will fetch you later today." She pulled the covered bowl up to her chest.

"What's to happen to me?"

"Don't know," she said. "You best pray on your fate s'all I can say. Ask the good Lord to take pity."

She gathered her skirts in her right hand and climbed back up the narrow stairs. He heard the scrape of metal as she locked him in, and the closed door snuffed out the bright spring light as the damp of the cellar surrounded him again. For the next several hours, he listened intently for Priscilla's arrival. His flesh gathered in anticipation at the slightest sound. She'd said in the morning, hadn't she? The others were to go to church service and she was going to stay, using the sick child as an excuse. The morning had come and gone. What had happened? Had she been found out? Had she changed her mind? Disappointment settled deep into his bones.

The cereal had replenished some of his strength, and worry made him restless. He began to explore the cellar, looking for something he could use to jimmy the hinges off the door. The door had a lock, but if he could find something to pry with, he might be able to separate the rusted hinges from the door's weathered wood. He stood and ran his hands along the upper shelf. He discovered some jars filled with canned vegetables that he could eat later. The thick dust that coated them covered the tips of his fingers.

There was a lantern hanging on a nail at the bottom of the cellar stairs. He turned back to shelves that covered one wall and felt along the length of each shelf, looking for matches. By the bottom shelf, he'd found none, but his hand closed around something hard, made of metal and wood. He grasped it and slid it off the shelf. The meager shaft of light that shone through the slats of the cellar door revealed a small scythe. Someone must have stored it here to clean up the grass around the cellar. He touched the tip of the blade and thought he might be able to slip the metal between the hinges and work them off.

He inserted the tip of the scythe through the bottom hinge, slipping it under the rusted metal and wiggling it back and forth until it let go of the parched wood with a dry squeak. There were four hinges in all. But the work had exhausted him, and after the first one, he crawled back down the stairs. Once he made it back to the cool of the cellar floor, he curled up on his side, his arm beneath his head. He was so tired he drifted off to sleep without meaning to. He woke once in the middle of the night, in a panic, wondering if George Smith intended to leave him here to die, but tried to reassure himself with the thought that Priscilla would still come. She would be true to her word. He fell asleep again, and woke a second time and realized she was not coming. Something had happened to her. He was sure of it.

CHAPTER 23

APRIL 24

He woke to the sound of footsteps outside. He remembered the scythe was still out and he groped for it then scuttled over to the shelves, pushing it far back under the bottom shelf. The lock was undone and the door swung open. Jacob Hamblin stood silhouetted in the doorway.

"Did you think I wouldn't find this out?" Hamblin spat.

"What is it you've found out?" Malachi asked weakly. He leaned against one of the pillars that held up the soil over the cellar. He tried to keep calm, but his thoughts rushed to Priscilla.

Hamblin closed the distance between them. He brought down his hand hard across Malachi's face. The blow knocked him to the floor.

"What are you playing at? You will tell me what you found in the meadows that day that John Lee sent you there. I will know the truth from you before I leave here."

The letter, Malachi thought. Had Priscilla given him the letter? He tasted blood in his mouth. He shoved himself off the dirt floor to sit upright and wiped the blood off his chin with the back of his hand.

"Do you have it?" Hamblin asked.

Malachi took a deep breath. "What's that?"

"The letter, boy, the damn letter!"

So that was it. Priscilla had told him, but she hadn't given it to him. His thoughts raced. Had they caught her trying to help him?

"It's in safekeeping," he said at last. Hamblin raised his hand to strike him again and he steeled himself for the blow, but it didn't come. Instead, Hamblin dropped his arm and turned to face the open door. Malachi thought he could rush at him now, use the scythe to slash his legs, something. Hamblin turned back to him. Sunlight spilled down the stairs, and a cool breeze followed, filling the cavity of the dank place with the odor of sage. He gulped in the air, suddenly aware of the stench of his own piss and shit that he'd left in the corners of the cellar. He'd been there for two days.

Hamblin stood at the base of the stairs. He cast a shadow over Malachi. Malachi's thoughts spun and twirled. He needed something, something to offer.

"Someone else has it and they're to give it to that judge when he comes, if anything happens to me."

"A judge, what is it you know about a judge?" Surprise torqued Hamblin's face as he stepped toward him. "You think you can bargain with me?"

Perhaps he *could* bargain with Hamblin. He had something the man wanted, and wanted badly, and he knew about the judge. This feeling was new to him: the ability to influence with a piece of knowledge. It felt dangerous and exhilarating, like slipping and sliding along the surface of a stream just frozen over.

"I want to leave here," Malachi said. "I want safe passage, a horse and food, some money. Once I am gone and I know I'm safe, I'll have the letter delivered to you."

Hamblin's eyes widened a little and he began to laugh slowly. "You think I'd do that for you? You're nobody I have to worry about. No, boy, you'll give me that letter and give it to me now."

He reached down and grabbed the collar of Malachi's shirt.

"Can't," Malachi said. "It ain't here. I don't have it."

"Then where is it?" Hamblin shook him like a dog then let him go.

"Like I said, it's with someone who knows to give it to you once I'm safe." His head thrummed with fear, but also the possibility that Hamblin might yield.

"And what if I did let you go?" Hamblin asked.

"You'd have a letter that you could use like you want," Malachi said. He remembered the gash of pent-up hate that spread between Lee and Hamblin that day in the bunkhouse at Lee's ranch. There was an old wound between the two men that was unsettled and unhealed, and he thought he might be able to use it.

"The letter names John Lee, says he was with the emigrants that day, the day they was killed," said Malachi.

Hamblin puckered his mouth and sucked at his right cheek. His stubbled skin folded into the side of his jaw, making his face look lopsided. It wasn't what he was expecting. Priscilla hadn't told him everything. Maybe she'd only warned him, warned him of the existence of a letter containing words from the dead that could harm the church, harm Brigham Young. But she hadn't given him details. Maybe she gave him just enough, hoping Malachi could figure out how to use it.

"I need to see it first," Hamblin said.

"Can't," Malachi replied. "But if anything happens to me, the judge is to have that letter."

Hamblin watched him. Malachi felt the boldness of what he was doing pump through his veins. Somehow, he knew that his strength lay in the unexpected nature of his demands. He also sensed it wouldn't last. If he didn't act now, Hamblin would come to his senses and all would be lost. But now, Malachi saw that Hamblin was uncertain, might be wondering whether the letter was as damaging as Priscilla had led him to believe, wondering whether Malachi was telling the truth. He guessed Hamblin was worried about letting the letter slip out of his hands and back to Lee or, worse, into the hands of the judge or someone else intent on doing harm to the Mormons.

"What then, after you leave?" Hamblin hissed.

Malachi stood. It took him great effort. Every muscle willed him back to the ground.

"Once I leave, you won't hear from me again. I swear it."

Hamblin laughed. "You think the world out there wants you? It'll treat you worse than you've been cared for here. They hate Indians out there. I've seen it. The Gentiles think you are lesser souls, and they'll never let you forget it."

"Might be," Malachi said. Still, maybe he could make his way, find a place where he felt like he belonged or could at least survive. He suddenly felt dizzy and reached his hand out to grab one of the shelves. He couldn't be sick in front of Hamblin. He gripped the wood of the shelf, wishing the sickness in his stomach would pass.

"You think you can ride outta here?" Hamblin asked him. His voice had gone up an octave, and he was looking at him sideways. "You can barely stand."

"The letter will be waiting for you once I'm gone. I'll need a horse, supplies." He had to persevere, show confidence.

Hamblin watched him, appraisal in his eyes.

"You give me the letter, I'll let you go," he said.

"Can't," Malachi replied. "Like I said, the letter is in someone else's care. You'll have it once I'm gone. If you kill me, if you go back on your word, the person who has it will give it to the judge."

Hamblin shifted. The open door behind him swung slightly in the breeze. Malachi could taste the freshness in the air outside the damp cellar. He imagined himself riding away. His limbs felt loose, fluid at the possibility.

"This person who holds the letter for you, who is it?" Hamblin asked.

"Can't say," Malachi said. He willed himself not to think of Priscilla.

"This person, whoever it is, is not one of us," Hamblin said flatly. "This is a person, like you, that wants to harm us, harm everything we've built." He stepped toward Malachi. "And I will not let that happen." He grabbed Malachi's arm and yanked him up the cellar stairs into the sunlight. He turned to him.

"You thought I would bargain with you, boy?" His face was hard-edged with anger. Spit had settled in the crevices of the deep lines that anchored either side of his mouth. "Do you think you can make me the fool?" His grip was tight on Malachi's bruised arm and pain radiated through his shoulder.

"I won't tell you," Malachi said. "You can kill me if you want, but I won't tell you."

"No, boy." Hamblin smiled stiffly. "I won't let you off that easy. Brother Smith is waiting for you. You'll deal with him, and I warn you, he drives a hard bargain."

CHAPTER 24

George Smith sat outside at a table that had been moved underneath the shade of the only tree in the barnyard. He'd removed his wig and set it on the table in front of him where it sat like a deflated animal. His left leg was stretched out, and he leaned back in his chair watching Priscilla and Hamblin's two wives bent over, harvesting the last of the vegetables from the kitchen garden. As Hamblin and Malachi approached, Smith turned toward them. Something like amusement settled on his face.

Hamblin called out to the women. "Get on inside. Now."

They looked up from their work. Then they gathered their small tools in their aprons and moved quickly toward the door of the house.

"Except for you, Sister Priscilla, you wait here," Smith said. "We need to clear up your muddled account of why you were so keen on helping this boy flee."

The other two women froze. Rachael glanced back at Priscilla with a pinched look of worry on her face before scurrying after the other woman to follow her inside. The door slammed behind them.

Malachi was breathing hard. The effort of walking from the cellar to the house had winded him. He was hungry, thirsty, and scared. Priscilla's eyes met his for an instant. What did he see in them? Fear? That wasn't it. Her look was hard and resolved. They had caught her trying to help him escape. That was clear, but what had she told them? The ground felt uncertain and spun beneath him.

"Gather round!" Smith called out. He was smiling, relaxed, almost jovial, a sharp contrast to Hamblin's grim face. Hamblin, Malachi, and Priscilla moved toward the table where Smith sat. He reached out to snatch his wig off the table, and he placed it atop the scaly dome of his bald head where it sat, slightly askew.

"I want to look good for the ladies," he said, winking at Priscilla.

Malachi slid his eyes over to her. Her face was calm and serious, and she eyed Smith steadily.

"Now," Smith said, rubbing his hands back and forth on his fat thighs. "We have some reckoning to do here, I figure." He bent over and picked up a small whip that leaned against the leg of the table. It whistled through the air as he slapped it against the sole of his boot.

"First, we will address this business of the letter," he said, looking at Priscilla. She pulled her chin back slightly and her lips parted, as if she were about to speak, but Smith held up his hand.

"I will do the talking," he said. "If I want you to say something, I will tell you."

Priscilla nodded. Her eyes darted toward the whip that Smith had dropped on to the surface of the table, then she looked back at him.

"This letter somehow came to be in the possession of this boy who stands before us, and who belongs to Jonah Blank," Smith said, nodding at Malachi. Both his index fingers were raised, and he moved them back and forth to the rhythm of his words, almost as though each gnarled finger was a dancer performing on a stage. "This letter is reported to have writing in it that Sister Priscilla claims could be damaging to us, to the body of our church, which is why she told us she was prodding this boy to flee, even bringing a horse and provisions to him to help him do so before our own Brother Hamblin caught her and put a stop to her foolish plan. As I see it, seeing as how this boy has possession of the letter, and he belongs to Jonah Blank, who is a member in good standing with our church, this letter belongs to us."

He stopped. Looking at each of his fingers in turn, a smile played around the edges of his protruding lips as though this logic pleased him. He dropped his hands to his lap, but kept his gaze on Malachi. Malachi swallowed hard. His mouth was dry. He eyed the pitcher of water Smith had on the table. Smith followed his gaze.

"You thirsty?" he asked.

Malachi nodded, surprised by the question.

"You get over here and get yourself a drink," Smith said, as he picked up the pitcher and poured some water into a tin cup.

Malachi limped toward the table. Smith stood and handed him the cup. Malachi's hand shook as he drank, and the water dribbled down his chin, soaking the front of his shirt. He handed the cup back to Smith, and Smith set it down before he plucked the whip off the table and turned toward Malachi.

"You're scared of me, boy," Smith said, reaching out to grab Malachi's collar and pull his face toward him. "I can see that, and that's good. You oughta be." He brought his face close to Malachi's, breathing out the strong odor of his breakfast. Malachi tried not to inhale.

"Now, about this letter. I want you to give it to me."

Malachi expelled his breath, ragged and hard. "I can't."

"But you can," Smith insisted.

"I don't have it," Malachi said, more disappointed in that fact than he cared to admit.

"Then who does?" Smith asked. His voice was rich and vibrant. It was the most appealing and perhaps the only appealing thing about the man.

"I can't tell you that," Malachi said. Smith had released his collar. Out of the corner of his eye, Malachi saw Priscilla step forward. Smith had seen it too, and the man turned to face her.

"I have it," she said "Idget told me about it and where it was hidden. He's one of my father's adopted Indian boys. I knew he'd know where to find it if I asked him, and he did."

No, Malachi thought. This was not what she was supposed to do.

Hamblin looked at her in surprise. "You didn't tell me that. You said the Blank boy had it, and that if you helped him leave, you thought he would surely die in the desert along with whatever was in that letter. You said you were certain he had it on his person."

She turned to Smith, her face looked determined and calm. But Malachi sensed she was frightened. He wondered if the men sensed it too.

"I did. I admit it, but I wasn't thinking straight. I was frightened, and you were so threatening. Please, Brother Smith, Brother Hamblin, I am but a woman, after all." She looked at them pleadingly, as if this admission would explain everything. Tears streamed down her face as the words continued to tumble out of her. "When Idget found it for me, I read it and got scared. At first, my only thought was to protect my father. The letter speaks of him and only him. It points to him as the person who led the people of the wagon train out to the meadow that day when they were killed. And Malachi knew that, on account of knowing what was in that letter. My aim was to get him out of the way, as far from here as possible so he could not harm us with what he knew. But I kept the letter so he would retain no written proof. Without that, who would believe him? Brother Hamblin, Brother Smith, surely you can understand. And I assure you, the letter is in safekeeping. No one but me knows where it is."

She stopped. Her chest lifted in concert with her rapid breath, and the tears on her face dried as her gaze slewed back and forth between Smith and Hamblin. There was silence, punctuated by the distant screech of a hawk and the puttering chirps of small birds busying themselves in the branches of the tree shading the table. Malachi saw a hand scratch back a curtain from inside the house. A woman's face peered out then disappeared. What next, he thought, what next? Priscilla was playing a dangerous game. She was convincing, but he could feel the unanswered questions hang precariously in the air. His own fate felt sealed.

"Why didn't you tell me you knew where it was before I went to get him this morning?" Hamblin asked. "It makes no sense to me, gives me reason to believe you're not telling the truth now."

"I had to sort out my own thinking on this, put other things together," she said. Her voice was calm, fluid again. Malachi was mesmerized by her ability to stay focused, to say what was needed, and step deftly from one lie to the next.

"I had overheard many things at our house in Harmony, things I was not meant to hear. I was worried, worried that Father Lee might have had some hand in these killings, worried that it wasn't all the Paiutes' doing, like we'd all heard, like he'd told us. And people in Harmony had begun to talk." She stopped and tipped her head forward, threaded the fingers of her hands together in front of her, then looked up. "And the letter… well, I just had to see it, to read it with my own eyes. It is the proof that my father was there. I will not be able to go back to the Lees after this. This is a letter that was in my father's keeping and was stolen from him. After Father Lee learns my hand in this, there will be no welcome for me in his home. Given these matters, I have decided I will marry Jonah Blank. And, this boy, Malachi, he is to come with me."

Malachi quietly sucked in his breath as he finally understood what she was doing. She wanted Smith to understand how the letter framed Lee. Like he himself had done earlier in the cellar with Hamblin. Priscilla was offering them Lee as the one who might take the blame for instigating the massacre. In exchange, Priscilla would seek protection not only for herself, but Malachi as well. But the cost of her gamble was that she would have to marry Jonah Blank.

While Priscilla talked, Smith had sat back down and was twirling his whip absent-mindedly between his knees. His gaze remained on the ground. When she finished, he looked up at her.

"Why is it you came here from Harmony?" he asked her abruptly.

Priscilla squared her shoulders. "It was at Father Lee's request. He said the Hamblin women needed help during lambing season."

"Anything else?" Smith asked, watching her closely.

She said nothing, her eyes were trained on the ground.

"Well?" Smith asked.

"There was a marriage offer for me to consider."

Smith smiled slightly and twirled the whip, then tossed it gently into the air and caught it by the handle.

"A marriage offer," he repeated, nodding his head at her. "But I had heard with my own two ears that you rejected that offer from Jonah Blank."

"I did," Priscilla said. Her voice was flat and cold.

"And now you will accept it?"

"Yes," she said. Her face was white, but the tips of her earlobes had gone bright red. "I told Brother Blank no, but I have since reconsidered."

Smith smiled slightly and glanced at Malachi then back at Priscilla.

"Serves the balance that God intends that you become the mother of this heathen boy here by marriage. That's how it'll come. No Mormon man can violate or harm in any way another man's wife. Now, what a man can do to his daughter, meting out justifiable punishment, that's another thing, and I'd wager a guess that you want to avoid that fate at the hands of John Lee. But Jonah Blank is a good, God-fearing man. He'll be a sound choice for you and, if he's got any sense, tame you some. He'll be more than willing to entertain this new decision from you, I reckon."

A dark, roiling anger rippled through Malachi's body as he listened to Smith handle and dispose of Priscilla. But he was rooted to the ground where he stood. He knew Priscilla had few choices, and that he was powerless to help her. He also understood that what she had offered, to marry Jonah Blank, was her final attempt to save Malachi. It was a sacrifice she was willing to make for him. He was certain Smith intended to have him killed, and equally certain Priscilla knew that. He should never have involved her, never have asked her to read that letter.

Smith waggled the thick fingers of his right hand at Priscilla. "Now, give me that letter. It's time I saw it, cleared up what all this mystery's been about."

Priscilla looked steadily at Smith, not moving until he slapped his large hand on the table. "Now, I say!"

She jumped, then turned her back toward them. Malachi imagined the tips of her slender fingers on the small white buttons of her dress. He wondered if her hands were shaking as his were. Priscilla turned around slowly. She had the letter in her hand and walked over to Smith, laying it on the table in front of him. A thin despair fell on Malachi as he watched her deliver the letter to Smith. She and that piece of paper were Malachi's last hope of leaving this place. He thought of the woman who had written it, Adele. The letter had been her last hope too, hope that her words would make it into the hands of someone who might take pity on her daughter, hope that someone would care enough to find out the truth.

Smith didn't reach for the letter, but instead reached up and with his pinky finger dug into his left nostril, working the fleshy globe of his nose until he'd satisfied himself with finding some crust lodged within. He wiped his finger on his pants and plucked the letter off the table. He unfolded it and turned it over and back. He searched the inside pocket of his coat and pulled out a dainty set of gold-rimmed reading glasses and placed them on the bridge of his nose where they sat in a lopsided fashion. He began to read. His lips moved, forming silent words as he made his way down the first page, then the second. Malachi could hear the faint whistle of Smith's breath as he slowly worked his way through the letter. When he finished, he placed it on the table in front of him, covering it with his large, beefy hand. He looked up at Priscilla.

"You get on into the house and wait there with the women," he said.

"When the time comes, someone will fetch you and take you to Brother Blank's house so you can declare your intention to him."

"There is one thing," Priscilla said, not moving.

"And what is that?" Smith looked at her. His patience seemed to be fraying.

"That boy yonder," she said, nodding at Malachi. "He becomes my son once I marry Jonah Blank, and it'll be my sworn duty to protect him as my property. I will tell my husband that he is to come home to us, with no harm done to him. We will handle any punishment as needed, but as a family."

Smith looked at her and a slow smile spread across his face. He took in a deep, satisfied breath.

"I will hand it to you," he said, smiling and shaking his head. "You are resourceful, looking to save your own hide and this boy's too." Then he fixed Priscilla with an implacable gaze. "But you still do not see the exact truth of your situation. You leap to single out guilt, and that gives me concern and leads me to believe you need a man's firm hand to control you. For, as you say, you are but a woman. But make no mistake, there will be no bargaining with me. You're not married yet, and this boy's fate rests in my hands and mine alone. Now get inside."

Priscilla hesitated, then turned. As she did Malachi caught her eye. She had tried to save him, and he loved her for it. He could see even now she was not ready to be beaten. There was no remorse in her, only anger, and when he saw it, it lifted the corners of his heart. As Priscilla walked toward the house, Hamblin approached the table and held out his hand toward Smith.

"Can I look at it?" he asked.

"Now is not the time," Smith said, shaking his head and folding the letter. He slipped it inside his coat pocket before waving his hand dismissively at Hamblin. "It's in my keeping now. No need for you to worry about it. I'll advise Brother Young, and we'll determine how best to handle it."

Malachi watched Hamblin's face fall, and he felt a glimmer of satisfaction. But his contentment was short-lived.

Smith turned to Malachi. "Now all's we got to do is figure out how to handle this one."

Malachi ran his tongue across the sticky surface of his front teeth. He could feel the weight of Smith's mud-brown eyes on him.

"Where's your boy, Albert?" Smith asked Hamblin.

"In the barn," Hamblin replied. "I told him to wait there because we might need him."

"Call him."

"Albert!"

Albert sauntered out of the barn; his black hat tilted low over his eyes. Malachi was certain he'd heard everything. Smith looked at the table in front of him and drummed his thick fingers on its surface. As he did, Malachi felt an upswell of impatience. He was scared, but fatigue made him long for an end to it all. His head ached, his muscles were sore and tight from the beating, and he was hungry and thirsty. He had run out of ideas for escape. Now he only wanted to give Priscilla whatever scant protection he could. He thought again that perhaps the best way to do that was to draw attention away from her and simply tell George Smith the truth. In the end, he knew that's what they suspected. Hamblin, Smith, Lee: they all suspected he'd seen what happened in Mountain Meadows and were waiting to hear him confess it so they had a reason to kill him.

A small flurry of sparrows landed behind Smith's chair, ducking their heads into the dust, pecking at the ground. Smith reached up and scratched his neck, then examined his fingernails. He turned to look at the pasture where a few ewes grazed while their lambs suckled at their teats.

"I hear you're good with the sheep," Smith said, his eyes on the pasture.

Malachi tried to speak, but his mouth was so dry nothing came out. He swallowed, trying to bring up some spit.

"That true?" Smith asked. "You good with those critters?"

Malachi nodded. "I am," he croaked.

"Me, I never liked 'em much," Smith said. "Too stupid. They get caught up in the fences, and they'd run right into a coyote's mouth if you let 'em. Ain't that right?"

"Dunno." Malachi shrugged. "Can't say as I ever seen one do that."

Smith gazed at him.

"Can you write, boy?"

"Not much," Malachi answered truthfully. "My name, a few words is all."

"That's true, Brother Smith," Albert interrupted. "He's as stupid as they come."

Smith looked at Albert and raised his eyebrows until Albert slunk back into the shadow of the barn. Then Smith tipped his fat chin down to meet his chest and rubbed his cheeks with both hands.

He looked up at Malachi. "You are a problem for me to solve."

Malachi's pulse picked up a beat.

"You are as stubborn as a mule and you don't tell the truth, I can see that," Smith said, turning in his chair so that his body faced Malachi. "But we need good workers in these parts. From what I hear, you're worth three of that boy yonder that belongs to Hamblin. The men have told me about the work you do at lambing. That means real money to the folks here in the southern settlements, to us, to the church. You understand me, boy?"

Malachi didn't understand, exactly. He had no idea where Smith was going with this, but he nodded anyway.

"Means you're worth more to us alive than dead."

Three of the sparrows behind Smith's chair flew up and attacked a fourth in a flurry of dust and wings.

"But you've not taken to what we've tried to teach you, have you?"

"Not exactly sure what you mean, sir."

"Albert's taken to the ways of the Saints, but not you."

Albert looked as if he wanted to smile, but seemed to think better of it and fastened his eyes on the ground.

"This boy here," Smith said as he jerked his thumb toward Albert. "He'll do anything to show how loyal he is to his family, to his church, to us. He will do whatever we ask of him, but you hold on to your sinful nature," Smith continued, pointing at Malachi. "I know that Albert will put us first in all he says, in all he does. He's proved it time and again. Haven't you boy?"

Smith turned to Albert now, and Albert bobbed his head up and down.

"But not you."

Malachi said nothing. Smith pushed his hands against the table and hauled himself off his chair. He picked up the whip and looked at it pensively, then tossed it to the ground. He walked over to where Malachi stood and angled his eyes down to his. Malachi tried to stand up a little straighter and look at Smith without flinching.

"But you are valuable to us in other ways. If we handle you the way we need to, you will be valuable to us for years to come."

Something in Smith's words pushed like a thorn deep into the flesh of Malachi's thoughts, and he drew his head back a little. "How is that?" he asked.

Smith walked behind him and placed his hands on Malachi's shoulders. He could feel the dampness of the man's weighty palms through the thin cloth of his shirt. He tried to turn but Smith pushed the heel of his hand against Malachi's cheek, forcing his face forward. He felt Smith's hot breath against his ear.

"We have to make sure you can no longer speak."

How would that be? Malachi's thoughts raced.

"We take out your tongue, boy," Smith said. "You know too much for me to let you keep it."

Malachi felt dizzy as Smith's meaty hands pressed down on his shoulders then pushed him away. Smith turned to Hamblin.

"Have your boy take him out and do this deed."

Albert looked back and forth between Smith and Hamblin. Malachi knew his cousin had no appetite for this kind of task. But Smith didn't want to be bothered with the blood and the struggle. It would be Albert. Hamblin looked at Albert and nodded his head. That was it. Malachi could see the shift in Albert's eyes. He would do what he'd been told.

CHAPTER 25

"Tie his hands, easier that way," Smith instructed as he turned his back on Malachi, waving his hand as if saying good-by while he waddled back to the shade. "And make sure you keep him out of my sight and out of my range of hearing. No appetite for the aftermath."

Hamblin had stepped forward and grabbed Malachi's arm.

"Go get the horses, Albert," Hamblin ordered. "They're saddled and ready to go. There's rope in the first stall, bring that out with you too."

Albert turned and disappeared into the barn. As he watched him go, Malachi realized they must have planned this, Hamblin and Smith. The horses were already saddled. But perhaps Hamblin thought Smith would order Malachi's death. If so, this turn of events must have come as a surprise. Malachi thought death would be better than this.

Albert emerged with two horses trailing behind him. There was a long coil of rope wound up in one hand. He handed the rope to Hamblin. Hamblin took Malachi's walking stick from him and tossed it to one side. Albert kept his eyes on the ground as Hamblin tied Malachi's hands in front of him and nudged him over to the horse.

"Put your foot in the stirrup and I'll shove you up," Hamblin said.

Malachi felt Hamblin's wiry fingers pushing into the scant flesh of his rear-end as the man pushed him up into the saddle. He bent over the saddle horn, and jimmied his right leg around and sat up.

"You know this is for your own good," Hamblin said, holding on to the pommel of the saddle. "You'll live. It's not what I would have chosen, but you'll live."

Malachi looked down at him, realizing that if he didn't speak now, he would never be able to speak again. He knew Albert would remove his tongue at the root. Nausea spiraled through his gut.

"Those people didn't deserve to die," he said, loud enough for Smith to hear. "They'd done nothing wrong and were killed without mercy. Children, women murdered for no reason. The men weren't even armed."

"Get that boy outta my sight," Smith bellowed. "Get him outta here and don't bring him back until you make sure he can't talk no more of his nonsense."

Hamblin slapped the rump of Malachi's horse. Albert tapped his heels against his horse's withers and pulled the reins of Malachi's horse so the beast followed behind him.

"Giddup," Albert said, and they rode out of the yard.

Albert reined his horse to the right and got on the path that led toward Mountain Meadows.

"You're going back down there?" Malachi called out to him. "You sure you want to? There's ghosts there." He knew Albert was superstitious, afraid of spirits in the night, convinced they were the agents of the devil, ready to enter him.

"Shut up," Albert said as he twisted in his saddle to look at him. "Soon I won't ever have to hear you say another word to me, Mudface."

"Why do you do it?" he asked. "Why do you let them use you like this?"

"I ain't talking to you," Albert said, keeping his back to him this time.

"Did you kill Idget?" he asked.

Albert's shoulders hunched.

"Did you?" he asked again.

Albert grabbed a length of rein and sharply slapped his horse's rear end. Both horses lurched forward, trotting so that Malachi had to concentrate on squeezing his knees against the leather of the saddle and using his bound hands as best he could to hang on to the pommel to keep from falling off. As he pulled his body toward the saddle, the rope that gripped his wrists loosened. He glanced up. Albert kept his back toward him. Malachi looked down and hooked the rope over the pommel of the saddle, pulling it until he managed to loosen a coil. The horses moved down the side of the steep hill toward the meadows. Both horses slowed and picked their way carefully down the scree, angling toward Magotsu Creek. When they reached the meadow floor, they were only a few feet away from the spot near the stream where Idget's body had been. Albert pulled his horse to a stop. He leaned over slightly and loosened his right foot from his stirrup, then swung his leg over and jumped to the ground.

"Why don't you just let me go?" Malachi asked him. He had loosened the rope enough so he was sure he could pull his hands free. But the coils still hung around his wrists. "Can't you see how they use you? They make you do their dirty work."

If it had been anyone other than Albert, Malachi wouldn't have been able to keep up his banter. He was scared, but it was Albert, after all, the one person he'd known the longest in this life. Albert, the one he'd been raised with, the one who had been bought just like him. Their fathers had been brothers. The only thing that separated them now was that Albert believed he could claim a rightful place on this earth—and perhaps in heaven too—and that Jacob Hamblin loved him like a son. Maybe he did. But Malachi was his own blood.

He needed to buy time. He needed to get Albert to talk.

Albert flapped open one of the saddlebags on his horse. He pulled out the sheath that held his knife. Malachi's heart hammered so hard in his chest he thought it might give out. He thought about just digging his heels into the horse. Maybe he could get away before Albert could pursue him. Albert glanced up at him. Malachi froze as he watched him unsheathe the knife.

"Don't think about running," Albert said. "I got a gun here too. Now get on off that horse."

"Can't do it on my own," Malachi replied. He wondered if Albert could see him shaking.

Albert walked over and looked up at him. The knife was in his right hand.

"Yes, you can," he told him. "Lean down and swing your leg over."

Malachi didn't move. "Just tell me," he said. "Did you kill Idget?"

Albert's eyes were flat and without emotion. "I drowned him like a cat," he said. "It wasn't supposed to happen that way, but he wouldn't tell us what we wanted to know."

"And what was that?"

"He wouldn't tell us whether you'd seen the killings that day, kept sayin' you hadn't that you didn't know nothing," he said. "But I knew better, knew you had, the day it happened. I told Brother Lee and the others as much, but Brother Lee told the men to leave you alone, that he'd take care of you. You don't know how close you was to dying that day when they brought you here to the meadows. I think Lee was of a mind to shoot you then. He should of done. He was a fool not to."

Malachi considered what Albert told him, surprised to learn Lee had spared him, but still not sure that Albert was telling the truth. He looked out at the banks of the Magotsu. Idget's face loomed in his mind.

"Why Idget?" he asked. "Why didn't you just start with me?"

"That's what Brother Smith told us to do." Albert shrugged. "He believed me when I told him you knew more than you were letting on, but he told us to start with Idget. Brother Smith knew that boy was weak and he'd tell us more than you would."

"How'd you get Idget to meet you here?"

Albert squinted up at him and smiled.

"Easy," he said. "Told him we had you."

The news filled Malachi with grief.

"Now get off that horse."

Malachi leaned forward as Albert stepped toward the rear of the horse, out of the way so Malachi could swing his body down. This was his chance. He grabbed the pommel and swung his right foot over the horse as hard as he could, aiming at Albert's head. Albert staggered back from the blow just as Malachi landed in a squat beside his horse. A pain shot through his bad leg, but he stood, frantically shaking off the loosened rope, yanking it from around his wrists. Then he bent over and ran with all his might, butting Albert in the stomach with his head. Albert fell back on the ground. Malachi plunged forward, landing on his chest and pinning his arms.

"Get off me, you fucker," Albert yelled, twisting his body.

But Malachi held tight and used his knees to fasten Albert's arms to the ground. Pure fear coursed through his body and gave him the strength to hold Albert beneath him. He shimmied down a few inches to prevent Albert from using his legs to grab Malachi from behind. He leaned over, panting, more confident now that he could keep Albert in place even as the other boy struggled beneath him.

Albert spit in his face. "You're nothing!"

The viscous stream of saliva slid off Malachi's nose and dropped back on Albert's chin. He whipped his head back and forth to get rid of it.

"Just—let—me—go," Malachi said. He was breathing hard, and he felt the sharp articulation of every bruise and ache in his body.

"You're fucking on top of me!" Albert yelled, pulling his face toward him then collapsing back.

Malachi wasn't sure what to do. If he eased up in the slightest, Albert would turn on him like a snake and never let him get away. He knew

Albert would kill him. Then he saw it. Albert's knife rested on the ground. He had lost his grip on it in the struggle and now it was just to Malachi's right, barely within reach. If he moved up a few inches, he could grasp it, but he needed to distract Albert. He slugged Albert as hard as he could, and he heard a crack. Blood shot out Albert's nose and he yelled in pain as Malachi reached for the knife, gripping it tight and shoving the blade against Albert's throat. Albert's pulse beat hard against the sharp edge of the knife.

"You won't," Albert said. Blood coursed down his chin, and spit gathered at the corners of his mouth. His tongue darted out to lick it off. "You don't have it in you, never did, and never will. You're a coward."

Albert was wrong when he said he didn't have it in him to kill. Malachi knew he did, if he had to. But he saw he had a choice, and he decided to make it. He wouldn't kill Albert, but he had to incapacitate him. He looked at Albert's hands, palms up and pressed flat against the ground just above his head. Malachi moved quickly. He reached over Albert's head and hacked off three fingers from his left hand, nearly down to his palm. Albert yowled in pain and twisted his body as he tried to get away from Malachi's grasp. Malachi scooted back along Albert's legs and held the knife above his head with both hands. He brought it down as hard as he could, plunging the knife into the thick meat of Albert's left thigh. He yanked out the blade, covered in his cousin's blood and staggered to his feet, eyeing him warily.

Albert bellowed and cursed at Malachi as he struggled to get up. Malachi snatched the rope that had bound his wrists earlier and brought his foot down hard on Albert's wounded leg. Albert howled again and tried to pull his leg toward him, but Malachi grabbed Albert's hand. It was sticky and slick with blood. Using his foot to roll Albert onto his belly, he wrenched his cousin's left arm over to meet his right and lashed the rope around Albert's wrists, fastening them behind his back. He pulled up the rope and knotted it tight then yanked Albert over onto his back again. Albert screamed in pain as he rolled onto the bloody stumps of his fingers.

"You won't get far," Albert spat out at him. His face was dusty and tracked with tears and blood. "They'll come for you."

Malachi was breathing hard and turned his back on Albert as his cousin continued to hurl insults and threats at him. Malachi limped toward the horses. He wished he had his stick, but he knew he could fashion another somewhere along the long journey that lay in front of him. He slowed his thinking enough to examine the contents of both sets of saddlebags—water, jerky, a package of hard tack, a compass, and a holster with a revolver and bullets, which he knew had been intended for him. He put everything into one of the saddlebags. It would be enough to get him by until he found a place to buy some food. The gun would come in handy to kill game and for protection, and he still had the money Priscilla had given back to him. He threw the reins of the other horse on the ground, knowing a second horse would only slow him down.

"I'll get as far as I can," he replied when Albert paused to catch his breath. "And that will be farther than you."

Malachi gathered the reins to mount the horse. He rode alongside Albert who glared up at him. "You'll have to stay here, explain what happened. That is if someone even thinks to come find you." Malachi said. "Do you think they will?"

Albert pulled his head up to spit at him again. Then he collapsed back onto the ground, groaning in pain. Malachi gazed down at Albert knowing he would not see his cousin again. He could not forgive him, but he understood him. He thought of Idget and Priscilla, what they had done for him. He knew he would carry the love they had given him for the rest of his life. It filled him up and gave him hope. He turned away from Albert and lifted his face up toward the sun. It had begun its descent in the afternoon sky. He took a deep breath and pressed his heels to the horse's withers. The horse picked up speed, and Malachi bent low to catch hold of the animal's rough mane as the beast carried him away from the meadow. As they galloped to the west, toward the unknown, the sun angled toward the earth's horizon. Its light warmed Malachi's face even as it cast long shadows on the floor of Mountain Meadows behind him.

AFTERWORD BY THE AUTHOR

Of the estimated forty men who participated in the massacre at Mountain Meadows on September 11, 1857, the only man ever held responsible was John D. Lee. On March 28, 1877, almost 20 years after Mormon men had slaughtered nearly 140 innocent children, women, and men, Lee was executed by firing squad for the murders. Although other men were brought to trial, no one other than Lee was ever convicted.

The history of the massacre and its subsequent cover up involves a cast of hundreds and is full of contradictions, twists, and turns. The first historian to approach this event with serious scholarly intent and a tenacious commitment to obtaining documents hidden by the Mormon Church was Juanita Brooks. I am indebted to her clear-eyed account, *The Mountain Meadows Massacre*, published in 1950. Although she concluded that John Lee was unjustly held solely responsible for the killings, she left many questions unanswered. She concluded that the evidence pointed away from Brigham Young as the one who ordered the massacre. Although, she provided ample proof that Young had created a culture of fear amongst his followers during the year of Reformation that led up to the massacre, a culture that made the slaughter seem justified to the men who participated. She also provided unstinting detail of Young's intimate involvement in the cover-up that included blaming the murders on the Paiutes and ultimately letting John Lee take the full brunt of the blame.

Will Bagley, who wrote the comprehensive, *Blood of the Prophets*, was not so hesitant to point to evidence that assigned blame for the massacre to Brigham Young. He asserted that Young had to have initiated the orders that were carried out by the church leaders in the southern territory—otherwise, the Mormon men that gathered in Mountain Meadows that day would never have dared carry it out. He also held Young—aided in numerous ways by George Smith—responsible for the orchestration of the cover up that ultimately led to Lee's execution. More recently, in 2008, the LDS historian, Richard E. Turley, Jr., and two professors from Brigham Young University, Ronald Walker and Glen Leonard, published a scholarly book, *Massacre at Mountain Meadows*. The authors clear Brigham Young of direct responsibility for ordering the massacre. Yet, they leave open the question as to why Young was involved in the cover up and why John Lee, one of Brigham Young's favorites and his adopted son, was the only man held responsible for the murders when so many men participated under orders by their church leaders. If readers have an interest in learning more about this fascinating slice of U.S. history, I would refer them to these books. I found them invaluable, each in their own way, in helping me understand more about the massacre, what led up to it, and its aftermath. Additionally, the inherent conflicts that exist in the reporting of these events created an opening for me as a fiction writer to craft a story.

It is unlikely that the questions surrounding this crime—that would today be considered an act of domestic terrorism—will ever be resolved, and that is not what my book attempts to do. What fascinated me as a novelist was what humans will do in order to belong. Why would men—religious men, hard-working men devoted to their families, community, and God—participate in a pre-meditated crime that resulted in the slaughter of unarmed women, men, and children? Were they terrified of what would happen to them if they chose not to participate? The acts committed in the name of the church during the year of Reformation that led up to the massacre suggest that fear of the wrath of the church's leaders was rampant throughout Utah. Many of the men who participated said later that they objected to what was happening at the time, yet they still participated in the slaughter of the members of the Fancher wagon train. Were members of the Mormon Church, who had already suffered losses and persecution in Nauvoo, Illinois, so frightened of losing their cherished promised land that they interpreted all acts by anyone not in their church as hostile? Even so, what causes a man to choose to do what he knows is wrong and makes him unwilling to speak out against it?

I was also interested in the question of how and when the scales began to tip against John Lee. Why did this man—Brigham Young's adopted son, a bishop in the church, a leader of his community, a man who enjoyed considerable favor and wealth who was successful by all measures—come to be the man who took the sole brunt of the punishment for this crime? There are clues in the history of that period that things began to sour for John Lee as early as July, 1858, when George Smith slipped an incriminating statement about Lee into a document witnessed and signed by church elders who were convened for the purpose of determining the innocence of the Mormon men who had perpetrated the crime. That left many possible avenues for showing how things may have begun to go wrong for Lee in the months leading up to Smith's orchestrating the signing of that document in the summer of 1858. The history books devoted to this event leave behind numerous contradictions and many unanswered questions about this period of time, all of which offer a fiction writer the opportunity to fill in the gaps.

To further explore the notion of what we humans do to belong—whether it is to a family, a community, or a religion—I chose to tell this story from the perspective of Malachi, a 15-year-old Shoshone boy who had been bought by a Mormon family and later adopted. Malachi is a fictional character completely born of my own imagination. But a real person, Albert Hamblin, inspired his origin. Albert, who is Malachi's cousin on these pages, participated in the Mountain Meadows Massacre and was a key witness in its cover up. Albert was the adopted son of Jacob Hamblin. He was Shoshone and fifteen years old when the massacre took place. Hamblin reportedly purchased Albert as a young boy for a sack of flour and a sack of beans.

For the development of aspects of these characters, I relied on the thesis published by Michael Bennion, *Captivity, Adoption, Marriage and Identity: Native American Children in Mormon Homes, 1847-1900*. Bennion says, "Over four-hundred children…lived in Mormon homes in North America's Great Basin between 1847 and the early 1900s. The children came to Mormon households as captives, or as a traded commodity, the result of intricate, wrenching, sometimes deadly cultural conflicts and negotiations between their own people and the Mormons."

Bennion's thesis investigates a period time when Mormon families purchased and adopted Native American children with the intent of converting them and fulfilling a religious prophecy. He points out that while some children were treated as true family members, others were closer to indentured servants, working without pay for the families that bought them, never to see their tribes or biological families again. Some were also the victims of violence and sexual abuse by the families that bought and adopted them. The question of whether these children saw their Mormon owners as "family," what lengths they had to go to in order to gain acceptance, and how they satisfied the need that all children have to be loved and to belong was one that I wanted to explore through the characters of Malachi, Albert, and Idget.

ABOUT THE AUTHOR

Charity Eleson lives in the countryside just outside of Madison, Wisconsin with her husband, Steve Feren. She has published two other books, *Blessing's Key, Volume I of The Silver Thread* and *Wayward Home*, which received an honorable mention for the 2025 Edna Ferber Fiction Award. She grew up in the Midwest and the West and graduated from the UW-Madison. When she is not writing, she likes to hike, garden, and travel.

www.ingramcontent.com/pod-product-compliance
Lightning Source LLC
Chambersburg PA
CBHW032353310726
48973CB00007B/1995